Praise for

PHILURIUS COLLEGE BLUES

"Ray Carson Russell pulls no punches in this sardonic romp through the academic world of a college program for our military overseas. At times ironic, other times amusing, it is an insider's view of an alternate reality."

MICHAEL HOGAN

Author of *Savage Capitalism and the Myth of Democracy*

"With his debut novel, *Philurius College Blues,* Ray Carson Russell mixes the poignant with the preposterous and shines a sharp light on the absurdities of academia. As the new director of Academic Affairs at a college serving the military in Europe, Dr. Vic Sawyer quickly finds himself embroiled in a behind-the-scenes battle of principles with his boss, retired Lt. Colonel Gio Malfatto. Humorous and insightful, Russell's writing explores how human desire drives personal destruction. *Philurius College Blues* is an engaging, well-crafted novel that reinforces Sayre's Law: In any dispute the intensity of feeling is inversely proportional to the value of the issues at stake. That is why academic politics are so bitter."

DOUGLAS LIGHT

Author of *Where Night Stops*

"Anyone who has worked in higher education will recognize some of the tangled politics – and characters – so sharply brought to life in Ray Carson Russell's droll account of academic intrigue, but few will have had the joy of seeing such a spectacular and satisfactory resolution of them."

PROFESSOR ROB MORRISON

Australian zoologist, author and broadcaster and co-host of the Youtube channel *Curiosity Show.*

"With the satirical eye of Joseph Heller and the insights of Kurt Vonnegut, Ray Russell takes aim at the absurdities and illogic of an educational system rooted in rules and processes rather than a quest for knowledge. Laugh-out-loud funny in places and consistently profound, Russell weaves a tale through his unassuming hero striving to find his way through a bureaucratic maze. A well-written, clever and memorable read."

GREG FIELDS

Author of *Arc of the Comet*
2018 Kindle Book of the Year Nominee in Literary Fiction

Philurius College Blues

by Ray Carson Russell

ISBN 978-1-63393-961-5

Published by

Blues & Rues 🎾

Ray Carson Russell
97239 Aub, Germany
Bluesandrues@gmail.com

PHILURIUS COLLEGE BLUES

A NOVEL

RAY CARSON RUSSELL

Blues & Rues

Dedicated to my wife
Lucy Hallman Russell
without whose dedication
this dedication would not be possible

AUTHOR'S NOTE

Although it deals with people, places and organizations which may seem familiar, this novel is a work of fiction, a story conjured from the author's imagination but born of an apprehension of reality.

The book contains numerous acronyms, which the reader unschooled in military and invented jargon might not understand. There is a list of these acronyms and their preferred meanings at the back of the book.

CHAPTER ONE
A RUDE AWAKENING

Word of the letter to the editor published in the *Stars & Stripes* newspaper spread like the Great Fire of London throughout the American military community in Germany, incurring a special fervor among the Philurius College faculty and staff. Dean Malfatto's name adorned the letter, but no one at the college believed he had written it. The prose was clean and succinct, with rhythms and nuances not generally found in this military newspaper. Furthermore, the letter made a frontal assault on the director of CETPM, the Center for Education and Training Programs for the Military—the government bureaucracy charged with oversight of the college programs in Europe. Everyone at the college knew how the dean nuzzled up to this high-level bureaucrat, and everyone knew that the dean couldn't write worth a damn.

Everyone ventured an opinion as to who authored the letter. Dean Malfatto suspected Vic Sawyer, the director of Academic Affairs for the college. Ever since Vic's arrival just a month ago, he and Malfatto had irritated each other. The dean, a retired Army lieutenant colonel, barked orders and expected them to be dutifully carried out without question. Vic had managed to avoid the draft, winning one academic scholarship after another, then getting married. He experienced no displeasure at having missed serving in Vietnam, and he had never been good at taking orders.

Sitting in his office this morning, Vic thought back on Malfatto's first words to him.

"I want you to know I was against your gettin' this job, but the president said we had to have someone with a PhD as director of Academic

Affairs. The prez is the boss, but we do things different here. I'm the boss here. If you cooperate, everything will be squared away. If you don't, I'll be your worst nightmare. Capish?"

Vic had stared at Malfatto like a vulture closing in on carrion. "I'm sure we can work together," Vic said, but he wasn't at all sure they could. Nevertheless, he promised himself he would give it his all. He needed the job and cherished the opportunity to enhance educational opportunities for American soldiers and airmen serving in Europe.

***

Although it was early that July morning in 1983, the sun had already made a sauna of Vic's office. The weather reflected his growing frustration. He scowled at the mounting stack of unanswered memos littering his desk and heard a slight stirring in front of him. As he looked up, Margaret Malcontenta-Jefferson slinked past the doorway. She smiled and tapped the open door once lightly.

"May I have a few minutes with you?" she asked. Margaret oversaw the Emergency Medical Training Program for the college, a job for which she had no qualifications. But she was savvy and attractive, which made her appealing to Dean Malfatto.

"Of course, Marilyn, come on in," Vic said as he stood and gestured to the chair in front of him. "What can I do for you?"

She frowned at the *Marilyn* but decided not to correct him. Instead she gracefully occupied the gray metal chair covered with indestructible gray plastic in front of Vic's desk.

Margaret had shining, raven-black hair and skin as Mediterranean as olives and almonds. Her figure was also beguiling, slender yet curvaceous in all the proper places. Ever immaculately attired, she had outfitted herself this morning in a fetching beige crepe dress which clung to her body. Vic noticed the slit on the left side, as well as the fragrance of Climat as she lowered herself into the chair.

"We have a new candidate who we want to teach in the EMT Program," Margaret began, extracting papers from her briefcase.

Vic sighed. "Whom," he uttered under his breath.

Margaret looked up. "Sorry?" she said.

"It's *whom* we want to teach for us, not *who* we want to teach, but never mind. Who's the candidate?" Vic said.

Margaret forced a smile, her perfect white teeth gleaming. As she leaned forward, handing over the papers, Vic caught his breath at the sight of her cleavage and the scent of her perfume. The silky skin of her hand touched his in the exchange. Goose bumps rose on his arm.

Margaret rearranged herself in the chair, turning slightly to the right and crossing her legs, revealing their elegance. Without meaning to, Vic stared and was caught off guard when he looked up to see that Margaret had noticed where his eyes had lingered. Eyes aglow, with a slight smile on her classically contoured face, a sanguine sensual smile, she looked Vic in the eye. He twitched, feeling like an awkward schoolboy who had made an improper pass. Still looking at him sensuously, Margaret continued.

"Her name is Clara Bell," she said. "She needs this work, and with the money she'll make, she'll take the classes that'll prepare her for a new certification." With that Margaret ran her left hand through her hair, then tossed it. Vic dropped the papers on his desk on top of the unanswered memos and suddenly broke her spell over him.

"You can make pets of these people without asking that I break college rules," he said. Vic wanted a cigarette desperately, but even more he wanted to be done with Margaret Malcontenta-Jefferson.

He ran his hand through his dark-brown hair. "If we don't maintain standards, we might as well be selling used cars," he said. Then staring directly into her eyes, he added, "I don't collect pets."

Vic sounded more acidulous than he had intended. The frustration that had been oppressing him since his first encounter with Dean Malfatto in Rheinsteinheim, Germany, suddenly hit him like a gust of hot desert wind. Margaret's attempt to manipulate him with her sexuality, and his momentary loss of control, infuriated him. He got up, walked across the room and opened the window. Sounds of "hup, two-three-four" from the marching troops below fanned his distemper.

At Vic's outburst Margaret had stiffened, and her face flushed. She had used all her wiles to get Vic to do her bidding, not just today but since he had arrived, all to no avail.

"You needn't be rude," she said as he continued to look out the window. "I'm not asking for anything difficult." She hesitated. "You apparently don't understand that emergency medicine is a technical field, not an academic one like—"

"Like biology," Vic offered.

"Well, yes," Margaret answered. "And Clara did qualify some time ago, she just doesn't have the formal qualifications right now."

Margaret remained poised on the edge of her chair. Vic turned from the window and stared at her, then walked back to his desk.

"Marilyn—"

"My name is Margaret," she said, her voice hardening.

Vic shrugged. "Sorry, maybe it's the heat."

"You don't have the last word here, you know," Margaret said as she opened her briefcase.

Vic bristled like a porcupine. He handed her the papers she had brought.

"My office isn't the Department of Social Work. It's the Office of Academic Affairs. Once this applicant gets her qualifications, we will consider her. Until then she may not teach."

Margaret tucked away the paperwork and rose from her chair. "Thank you for your time," she said curtly, as she turned and moved toward the door.

Vic watched her syncopated waltz, bewitched again by her sensuality. At the door she stopped and turned. "I intend to discuss this matter with the dean," she said, leaving with a flourish.

***

Vic picked up the pack of Marlboros he had almost squashed with Margaret's paperwork. He reclined in his military-issue chair, lit the cigarette and inhaled.

"What the hell am I doing here?" he growled. He then leaned back and stared at his utilitarian US Army–issue desk overflowing with memos. It looked more like a tank than an academic's desk. To compensate for this affront to his sensibilities, Vic had taken to adorning his desk with a new literary work every day. Today he had chosen Dickens' *David Copperfield*. As always, there was a copy of *Johnson's Dictionary* within easy reach. He liked to consult this antiquated work for usages no longer common. Vic had an insatiable penchant for the old-fashioned.

An outbox was on the far left side of his desk. The inbox on the right was stashed with memos Vic had not yet had the heart to look at. Just behind him on an otherwise blank wall, his diplomas were displayed, one proclaiming his BA in English literature from Hamilton College, the other his PhD in German language and literature from Cornell. Vic finished his cigarette, sighed and picked up a memo he knew he must at some point read. He found it difficult to concentrate, as he knew that soon there would be reactions to the letter that had appeared in this morning's *Stars & Stripes* newspaper.

Vic's frustration with the administration of Philurius College was only exacerbated by the CETPM bureaucracy, which had overseen several university or college programs in Europe since shortly after World War II. The cooperation of CETPM and the colleges had often worked well, but gradually the government bureaucracy had assumed control over the schools, and this control was abetted by the profit-hungry colleges eager to please CETPM.

***

As Vic was settling in with these thoughts, Dean Malfatto arrived, as he did most mornings, just after nine. After gulping doughnuts and coffee at the snack bar, he had picked up a *Stars & Stripes*. He bought the newspaper every morning, primarily for the crossword puzzle. As he sat down at his desk to do the puzzle, he saw an unsigned note. *You really ought to check out the Letters to the Editor in the newspaper this morning.* He did, and this is what he found:

A Plea for Tolerance

Dear Sir, your recent article entitled "Military Still Experiences Prejudice" portrayed a disturbing picture. Particularly offensive were the views expressed by

Bill McMurphy, Director of the Center for Education and Training Programs for the Military. Mr. McMurphy's allegation that black people driving nice cars calls forth overt racial discrimination because society is racist shows a less than rigorous use of reason. Being stopped by the military police is in itself not evidence of racial prejudice. Before making the allegations appearing at the head of your article, Mr. McMurphy should be able to make a case for systematic military police abuse of black men who purportedly run stop signs in expensive cars. Otherwise, the complaints do not sound credible.

Another McMurphy quote seems to further underline his propensity for simplistic stereotypes. In a curious turn of phrase, he states, "And I don't know if there are skinheads over here per se, but I have seen some soldiers walking around with such haircuts. That's not to say that because they have their hair cut that way that they're skinheads. But there is too much of a lax attitude for skinheads or any other kind of hate group to grow and for people to become even more polarized." Although the prose is tortured, the message is clear. This is stereotyping. Having spent many years in the military, I can assure Mr. McMurphy that short haircuts are standard for military personnel, regardless of race, religion or national origin.

As an educator, I find such views reprehensible and harmful to our profession. In his position as Director of CETPM, Mr. McMurphy should be more discriminating in his public utterances and less discriminatory in his views of other people. This he should do not only for his sake but for the sake of higher education.

Educators have a special duty in this regard, to expose stereotypical thinking to the light of reason and to inculcate in ourselves what Alexis de Tocqueville called the "habits of the heart," the spirit of tolerance and understanding which animates an open society. In a free society it is everyone's responsibility to build on the foundations of Gandhi, Martin Luther King, John F. Kennedy, Linda Chavez and myriad other common folk who understand that there is more humanity binding us than inhumanity separating us.

Dean Gio Malfatto
Philurius College, Rheinsteinheim, Germany

First, the dean took his blood pressure medicine, then called his assistant dean on the intercom. "Doris, get down here right now!" Within thirty seconds Doris Kink was standing in his doorway. "Have you read this bullshit?" Malfatto said, clinching the newspaper in his massive right fist.

Doris, dressed in her neat but baggy brown pants and white blouse, took the *Stars & Stripes*, sat in the nearest chair and began to read. "You didn't write this piece," she said confidently.

"Of course I didn't write it! Are you nuts? That's not the point. The point is what to do about it. Who did it? He's gotta be found and punished. Oh, shit! What am I going to do? Bill McMurphy's gonna have my ass!"

"But you didn't write it," Doris repeated.

"I wanna know who's responsible for this," he said, taking the newspaper from her and throwing it in the trash can next to his desk. "Do you have any idea what this could do to me? To us? This is an attack on the head of CETPM! It sounds like I'm accusing him of being an anti-white racist! Whoever did this, his ass is grass. It sounds like the kind of shit that Vic Sawyer writes."

"Why don't you just call Bill McMurphy and tell him you didn't write it," Doris offered. "You two are friends. He'll believe you."

About that time, Crepe Moertel, the dean's personal secretary and paramour, stuck her head in the door. "Gio, uh . . . I mean, Dean Malfatto, it's a call for you from Bill McMurphy."

The dean jerked at his tie. "Uh, tell him I'm not in," he said.

Crepe stared for a second or two, looking perplexed, then said, "But if I tell him you said you aren't here, he'll know you that you are."

"Crepe, just say that Dean Malfatto hasn't arrived yet, but that we expect him soon," Doris said. "Then say that he'll return the call as soon as possible."

When she had gone Malfatto went to the door and slammed it shut. "What the hell am I going to do?" he whined.

"Like I said, just call him and tell him you didn't have anything to do with this letter and that you'll write a disclaimer to the *Stars & Stripes*. Then you tell him that you will do everything in your power to find out who did this thing and that you'll punish that person to the extent possible. I'll write the letter for you, if you'd like."

"Yeah, yeah. Write it. I'll sign it, and we'll get it to the *Stars & Stripes* right away."

"Maybe you should call over there to give them a heads-up on it," Doris added. "Then we can have Crepe run over and deliver it personally. If we're lucky, your disclaimer will be in the paper tomorrow."

"Good idea. Yeah. Let's do it!" said the dean with finality. "Okay, you get that letter ready. Do it on letterhead and have it ready for me to sign in fifteen minutes." With that he went to the door, let Doris Kink out, then shouted, "Crepe, get in here. Now!"

***

Less than five minutes later, Margaret Malcontenta-Jefferson rapped on the dean's door. She reported her conversation with Vic and suggested to the dean that he get Vic "squared away." Appealing to Malfatto's manhood always did the trick. The dean grabbed the newspaper out of the trash can and headed purposefully toward Vic's office. He was leaning on Vic's desk when he spoke.

"You will clear that teacher!" he said.

"What's that you've got in your hand?" Vic replied. He noticed that the dean had meticulously combed his hair over a shiny pink bald spot.

"What do you know about this, Sawyer?" Malfatto said as he once again shook the newspaper. "This shit sounds like the kind of shit you write. Ununerstanable."

"What?" Vic said.

"What do you mean what, Sawyer? Can't you understand anything?"

"Not ununerstanable."

The dean's eyes bulged as he turned lobster red. Then he pounded on Vic's desk with both hands.

"You will clear that woman to teach!" he said. "And once I prove you wrote this letter, you're dead meat, *cazzo*!" With that he straightened up, tugged on his tie with his free hand and stormed out of the room.

Vic had a feeling the day was going to be a complete loss workwise, so instead of sorting through the pile of memos on his desk, he reached into his bookcase for *Amerika: The Man Who Disappeared* by Franz Kafka. Vic owned both the German and English versions. He felt a sense of fraternity with the novel's protagonist, who was repeatedly put in awkward, impossible situations by an oppressive system. Vic had been backed into corners before, both at the state university and at the Southern Baptist college where he had formerly taught. The old familiar feelings rose again like a migraine headache coming on. That's why he had written the letter to the *Stars & Stripes*—to avoid a migraine.

Looking up he saw Jack Murphy in the doorway.

"Jack, my friend, co-conspirator and esteemed director of Student Affairs, how's it going?"

Most people thought Jack looked like Harvey Keitel, though he fancied himself more like Gregory Peck. Peck-like, he strolled into Vic's office and took the seat recently occupied by the lovely Margaret Malcontenta-Jefferson.

"Good, man. Been gettin' any guests today?" Jack said cheerfully. "Well?" he insisted. Vic seemed lost in thought.

"Yeah," he replied, shaking his head. "Margaret and the dean are insisting that I clear an unqualified person to teach. Margaret tried a sexual lure on me; the dean merely yelled as usual. He is convinced I wrote that *Stars & Stripes* letter."

"He can't prove it though, can he?"

"Not unless you tell him. I sure won't." Vic leaned back in his chair. "Jack, thanks again for lifting Malfatto's signature for the letter. What a touch of genius, as was the personal note from our dean you penned for the editor."

"Yes, those elegant little touches made the letter convincing, and that's what we wanted. Glad I could help," Jack said.

Vic leaned back in his chair. "I need this job," he said. "Bonnie's coming over soon, so I can't screw things up like I have in the past, but I won't let Malfatto run roughshod over me either. Someone has to maintain standards here. What do you recommend, my friend?"

"First, I suggest you answer some of those memos," Jack said. "We don't want you to get fired for incompetence." Jack reached over and helped himself to one of Vic's cigarettes. "Got a light?" he asked. Vic obliged by tossing Jack a box of matches.

"Hey, the boss will never figure out who wrote that letter. He's too dumb. Don't worry about it." Jack stroked his well-trimmed salt-and-pepper beard. "I'm proud of you, man," he said. "Better get back to work, though. Malfatto or one of his goons might think I had something to do with that letter if they catch me here with you. Whaddaya say we have a beer or two tonight and compare notes. We can talk in peace then. I'll come around late afternoon," he said as he waved goodbye to Vic.

CHAPTER TWO
CALM AFTER THE STORM

Jack appeared in Vic's office later that afternoon. Neither of them had gotten much accomplished. The devastating heat and the interruptions by people who wanted to know if they had anything to do with the *Stars & Stripes* letter had drained them.

"Busy?" Jack asked as he dropped into the chair in front of Vic's desk. Vic shrugged. "The rumor mill has you in first place as a candidate for having written that letter," Jack said. "That hurts my feelings."

"Don't feel too sorry for yourself," Vic said. "At least half the people who dropped in on me today thought you had something to do with it. Apparently, we are the only candidates."

Vic picked up his pack of cigarettes only to find it empty. Without hesitation he pulled his reserve pack from his briefcase.

"It's 4:45. Can't we get out of here?" Vic asked. "We both know we won't be getting anything else done today."

Jack sighed. "How many times do I have to tell you, man? It's 16:45 around here, not 4:45. That there's civilian talk."

"Do you see me in a uniform?" Vic said.

"Well, you do wear a kind of uniform," Jack noted. "You always wear a variation of what you have on now."

Vic ignored him, but his uniform was typically khaki trousers, a medium-blue shirt with button-down collars, a red tie, a brown linen jacket, now hanging on the back of his chair due to the heat, and brown loafers. Today he was wearing a copy of one of Ernest Hemingway's favorite belts bearing the inscription *Gott mit uns*.

"I'll meet you downstairs in fifteen minutes. Gotta play by the rules," Jack said as he rose from the chair and stretched. "Spies could be watching our every movement. Especially today."

***

The O Club was full but subdued when they arrived. It was air-conditioned and dark, which provided a stark contrast to the world outside. The two conspirators sat at the end of the long semi-circular bar near the door. The elegant mahogany wood structure smelled of wood polish, as did their high stools. At the opposite end of the room a small group engaged in passionate conversation.

"Hey, look at those clowns over there," Jack said. "They must be hatching up some nonsense for the regional directors' meeting tomorrow."

"Ugh, those plebeians," Vic said.

Philurius College operated with directors in each of four regions of the US European Command: Central Germany, Southern Germany, the East German Border Area and the Benelux, where they served military and diplomatic personnel. Vic had met all of the directors except the one in charge of Southern Germany, who also oversaw programs in Italy together with an on-site assistant in Leghorn.

"What's it going to be, gents?" asked Kurt the bartender. "There's a Campari special tonight."

"A Becks for me," Jack said. "Same for me," echoed Vic.

"Hey, I want you to meet Vic Sawyer, Kurt," Jack continued. Introductions having been made, Kurt departed, soon returning with Becks beers and a pot of peanuts. Since business wasn't bustling, he stayed and chatted.

"How come I haven't met this Kurt guy before?" Vic asked, after the bartender had left to serve the regional directors again. "I must say he's more sociable than that rotund fellow who's been serving us."

"Kurt's been on vacation," Jack said. "He's an interesting guy and a great bartender." Jack's gaze then shifted across the room. "Then there's the leader of the regional directors over there," he said meanly. "He's not so interesting. Just trouble and a Malfatto ass-kisser."

"What's his name again?" Vic asked. "I've talked to him a few times, but I just can't get a grip on his name."

"Ed Ehrgeiz," Jack said. "Have you noticed how most everyone at this school has an elevated title? Regional director is bad enough, but have you seen those cards Ehrgeiz had printed?"

"Yeah," Vic said. "*Master of the Universe*. What a jerk. Yeah, we've got lots of chiefs here but few Indians. "

"Some of the squaws ain't bad though," Jack added.

Just then a couple of soldiers walked by, conversing in Spanish.

Vic had quickly learned that life on American military bases in Germany was much like life in the USA. Everyone spoke English or Spanish, but usually only Hispanics spoke both. Dollars were used at the post exchanges, snack bars, clubs and movie theaters. The main difference was that at the movie theaters "The Star Spangled Banner" was played before the movie began, and everyone stood at attention, a custom long forgotten in the civilian world. Some of the soldiers, he was told, never ventured off base.

"You'd better watch out for Ehrgeiz," Jack said. "He's as dangerous as Malfatto and Kink."

The bartender reappeared. "How about another drink, gentlemen?"

"Yes, indeed," said Vic. "Another round of Becks. On me."

"Comin' up," Kurt said as he moved toward the other end of the bar where the beers were stored.

"That Kurt is all right," said Vic. "There's something I like about the guy."

"You like him because he keeps bringing you drinks," Jack said.

"Yeah, I suppose that's one reason," Vic said.

Jack raised his glass. "Hey, let's celebrate makin' a fool outta Malfatto."

"Jack, a little quieter please," Vic said. "Be cool. We can't admit to anything."

"Ah, hell, Vic. Lighten up, will ya?" Jack raised his glass again and drained it. "Kurt, my man, thanks for the liquid gold," he said as Kurt delivered the next round of beers.

The guys continued to drink for a while, disparaging Dean Malfatto and all his cohorts. Vic took a liking to the bartender and gradually gleaned some information from him. He found out that Kurt had a half brother and a half sister, but he didn't want to talk about them or their common father.

After about an hour, the two pals left the cool bar for the humid night. Another day's work was done. "Don't worry about that letter. They can't prove a thing," Jack said as he departed.

After he got home to his apartment, curiously located at the American military hotel, Vic penned a letter to his new wife:

Bonnie, my love,

Things might be getting out of control here. Don't get me wrong, I love being in Germany, but that's the only part. Thought I would be able to make a difference at Philurius College. Fat chance. The place is a loony bin. I've written you about Dean Malfatto and his sidekick Doris Kink, etc. What losers. At least there is Jack. His Rousseauvian optimism sometimes gets on my nerves, I must admit; but I don't know what I would do without him. He makes me laugh.

Margaret came to see me today about getting a friend of hers cleared to teach. Sadly, the woman doesn't have the required certifications for the teaching position. I was unnecessarily hard on MMJ, perhaps because she's so damn good looking, and I can't approach her for a date because I'm newly married. So, you see, it's all your fault I was curt with her. Malfatto came to see me after that, but his story is uninteresting.

You won't like the military casernes, they are hideous. To enter them you must go through a control area hosted by armed MPs. By this I mean military police, not members of parliament! These ghettos are invariably surrounded by high walls, some topped with barbed wire. Once inside you are confronted with row after row of drab rectangular buildings which all look alike. Ugh. This is the atmosphere in which I have to work. At least you have the right to decorate your office as you please. Mine needs some work, but I know you will help me improve the aesthetics of my small cubbyhole.

In a few months 1984 will arrive, which gives me renewed concern about Georg Orwell's dread prophesies for that year! Especially here at Philurius College.

I've enclosed a letter to the Stars & Stripes newspaper, signed by Dean Malfatto, written by yours truly. Hope you are proud of me. Losing my concentration. There's a big meeting tomorrow that I am decidedly not looking forward to. Maybe I shouldn't have written that letter. We'll soon see what happens. Rambling now. Can't wait to see you. Kisses and caresses. Goodnight.

Vic

CHAPTER THREE
JUST ANOTHER MEETING?

Shortly before 09:00 Vic and Jack walked into the conference room—a large rectangle adorned only by a series of ominous-looking gray desks, arranged in a square, at which there were fourteen standard-issue gray vinyl-covered chairs. A chalkboard, also gray, hung on the wall.

Vic had attended the weekly top staff meetings in this room every Friday since arriving at Philurius. They were always the same, as were the Monday morning planning sessions. Dean Malfatto dominated, barking commands about whatever came into his mind. About an hour into the meeting, however, he invariably left with his private secretary, Crepe Moertel. "Got business to do. Doris is in charge" was his standard parting line.

Vic hoped that today would be more interesting. The regional directors would at least provide some different faces. His expectations remained low, however. He had met three of them and had been underwhelmed. The fourth, Raz Rabin, Jack said was a good guy.

"Even though he's field personnel?" Vic asked.

"Yeah," Jack said. "He's different. You'll see."

As Vic and Jack entered the room, they were greeted by Director of Personnel Plea Dies and Director of Finance Craig Baker.

"Where is everybody?" Vic asked, as he and Jack took their seats.

"These field folks always arrive either just on time or late," Jack said. Before he had finished his sentence, the door opened, and Don Dingsbums strode in like he was entering the OK Corral. Don wore his usual meeting attire—red-and-black leather cowboy boots, faded blue jeans, a white shirt and black bolo tie threaded through a silver dollar from 1904. Vic had had several discussions with him and found him amusing but peculiar. Don talked with an air of confidence, but when he had finished, Vic couldn't remember anything the man had said. This morning, Don went directly to Vic. Bending over close to him he said, "Hey, did you write that letter?"

"What letter?" Vic said nonchalantly.

"Hey, you did, didn't you?" Don said. "Hey, look. I thought it was a great letter. I especially liked the Tocqueville thing." Don stood up straight again and gave Vic the victory sign. Just then there was a flurry of activity as Ed Ehrgeiz and Maya Luft, both wearing dark-blue business attire with yellow power ties, entered the room. Maya's legs, revealed to the general public by her mini skirt, caught everyone's eye. The couple greeted everyone before taking their seats at the front of the table.

At 09:00 Dean Gio Malfatto stormed into the conference room, his mood foul as usual. He tried to work a stern, serious expression but only achieved a frog-like scowl; he didn't like what he saw before him.

At the head of the table, Dean Malfatto, still standing, still scowling, continued to stare at the group. "Where the hell is Raz Rabin?" he shouted.

"He called me," Ed said. "His train was a few minutes late, but he'll be right over."

"Oughta dock his pay," Malfatto said. "To hell with him. Okay, let's get this meeting underway."

The time the dean had spent around academic folks had not even slightly diluted his twenty-five years of military manner. He surveyed the room, then began the meeting.

"Our agenda for today," he began.

"What agenda? I didn't get an agenda. Did anyone else here get an agenda?" Jack asked as he looked around the room.

Malfatto's gaze was fixed on Jack. "The agenda is in my head," he growled.

"Oh my God, we'll never get it now," Don Dingsbums said *sotto voce*.

The laughter was subdued, but it caught the dean's attention.

"Okay, you morons," Malfatto yelled. "Either we get down to business or I'm gonna fire all of you and just start over again."

Everyone went silent. They were accustomed to these outbursts and knew this one would pass just like all the others. Vic looked up at Malfatto, who was still scowling. Vic could see the headline in the *Stars & Stripes*: *Vic Sawyer, Director of Academic Affairs at Philurius College, strangles Dean Malfatto.* Vic truly wanted to choke the man. Instead, he looked at his own fingernails and turned his thoughts to the dean's shortcomings.

Vic had observed from the beginning that Malfatto's orders were generally followed out of fear—not admiration. He inspired disdain, even among his cohorts, but only a couple of people dared to confront him. The most egregious offender these days was Vic himself.

Malfatto had no knack for leadership, nor for management, and from what Vic could ascertain, he couldn't even finish a crossword puzzle by himself. He had some education but no learning, and the only reason he had gotten his present position was because he had been in the military, and because he had ethnic ties with President Porcino of Philurius College.

"I think if we each give a short report, an update on our enrollment figures and what we are doing to keep them up, that would be a good way to start the meeting," said Ed, breaking the silence. "This is the most important topic we have to deal with, so we should get to it first while we're still fresh. The other things on my agenda we can save until after lunch, which I've arranged for us. BLTs and potato chips are coming over from the Club and—"

"Wait a minute, Mr. Ehrgeiz," Dean Malfatto barked. "*Basta!* Who do you think's runnin' this fucking meeting anyway? Since when did you become dean here? I have my own agenda for this meeting."

"There are ladies present," Plea said angrily. "And gentlemen," Craig muttered.

"This is a waste of time," Jack said. "You've got to know that it makes no sense to have a meeting like this without an agenda which is printed up and disseminated to all participants in advance. In fact, all participants should be given opportunity to suggest agenda items. The other problem here, the reason we never get anything done, is that we follow no rules of civility. *Robert's Rules of Order* have worked for others. They should work for us, too. I suggest we use them."

"So, let me see if I understand you correctly," said Malfatto. "You wanna use *Robert's Rules of Order* in these meetings, right?"

"Right," said Jack. "And we should have a written agenda to which all participants have contributed, not just something you have in your head at the moment."

"Okay, you're in charge of it," thundered Malfatto. "Get all the agenda items to Doris by next Thursday close of business. I'll review them and decide what to do. Now let's get on with it."

Vic looked at Jack and shook his head. Then the door opened and Raz Rabin appeared. He was just over six feet and slender, and his maternal Lebanese heritage was reflected in his finely structured face. Raz carried himself like a military man, like his father, a soldier of Jewish heritage, but otherwise he had the demeanor of a scholar, which he actually was, at least part time. "Hi, sorry I'm late," he said as he took a seat next to Jack.

"I oughta cut your pay," Malfatto said. Raz shrugged. "You come in late again and I will. Okay, I wanna hear a report from each of you on what you're doing in your regions. How are your relations with CETPM? What kinds of problems you're having with AFCEOs. What you're doing to get enrollments up, and how you plan to further cut costs. We'll start with—" Malfatto cast his glance around the room. "With you, Mr. Dingsbums."

"Just a sec," Don said. "Let me just pull out a couple of notes I made."

The ever-efficient Don Dingsbums had his notes ready in a few seconds.

"Enrollments in my region are up a total of 1 percent this term over last term and 3 percent over this term last year, so I met my goals. My enrollments would have been even higher, but we had a couple of problems. I lost two important teachers in Würstberg. Between them they taught an average of six courses a term. Important courses. One of them taught English, biology, earth science and math. The other one taught management, history, political science, biology and emergency medicine."

"Hold on. Just a minute!" Vic suddenly entered the discussion with a vengeance. "For your information, Don, institutions of higher learning still have some standards. Academic values might seem peculiar to some of you, but they still matter, and as long as I'm heading Academic Affairs here, they'll be maintained."

"Can't you just talk normal?" the dean said. Looking now like a rabies-infected chipmunk, he continued. "What you just said sounds a lot like that damned article that appeared yesterday with my name on it in the *Stars & Stripes*."

Vic was suddenly gripped in a peculiar vice of cold fear and hot fury. *Keep your cool, man!* his mind screamed. *There's a lot at stake.* Still he was outraged. Not being able to decide what to do, he just plowed ahead.

"You're diverting the issue," he said to Malfatto. He then directed his fury at Don Dingsbums. "Can you explain to me, Don, how anyone could be qualified to teach all those courses you just mentioned at the level required by an institution of higher learning?"

"Well," Don began, "first of all you have to realize that we are not in a normal situation here. We're dealing with at least two complementary factors which mitigate against us. We're working in the bowels of a military environment dedicated to different values from those of normal higher education. In order to survive, we have to take this factor into account. Like Machiavelli says, 'The end justifies the means.' The second factor mitigating against us is that it is difficult to find teachers, much less good ones. Therefore, we must do what we must do. At least most of the students aren't very good, so that helps."

Don relaxed into his chair, clearly proud of himself. Vic, looking like a dark cloud about to burst, peered at him over his glasses. "Don, surely you meant to say militate, not mitigate. At least that would make sense, but perhaps a different word choice would have been better." Vic paused and shook his head. "I understand that you attended law school, but apparently you never finished. Do you realize that you haven't answered my question?"

No one said a word. Ed gave Don a nod. Dean Malfatto, his jaws grinding with a force that should have broken a tooth or two, glared at Vic. Doris Kink, who always scribbled madly on a yellow legal pad during these meetings, set her pen three inches to the right of it and stiffened.

"Vic, we simply have to make some sacrifices," she said. "This isn't a stateside environment like you're accustomed to. We also have to keep the AFCEOs happy, not to mention the military commanders. That doesn't mean we have to completely sacrifice standards, but we do have to modify them. Otherwise the company wouldn't survive against the competition."

"What company? What are you talking about?" Vic demanded.

"Let's be professional," Plea interjected.

"Yes, professional would be good. And I'd also like to know how these people got clearances for all the courses you mentioned," Jack said.

"They were grandfathered in," Don answered.

"By whom?" Jack asked.

Don looked around the room. Then his eyes met Doris's. After that he said nothing, just looked down at his spread-out fingers.

"That was my decision," Doris said. She stared ostentatiously, first at Jack, then at Vic.

"And when did you make this decision?" Vic asked.

"It was during the interim, before you came on board," she said, now hunching forward. She moved her pencil closer to her yellow notepad.

"You have no business taking such liberties," Vic said. "These decisions are the domain of Academic Affairs." He leaned back in his chair. "I want a list of all the people who have been grandfathered, either by you or anyone else, and I want it by tomorrow," he said.

"Who the hell do you think you are, Sawyer?" Malfatto said, gripping the arms of his chair and leaning forward. "You work for me, and Doris Kink is my assistant, so you work for her. Your problem is you were never in the military. You don't understand about chain of command, discipline, taking orders. So just cease and desist!"

"By tomorrow. I want those names by tomorrow morning." Vic's voice was calmer now, though still firm. Finding himself in the heat of battle, he felt his emotional equilibrium returning.

Vic could be a commanding presence when he wanted to be. He was an inch or two over six feet, athletically built, and he always moved gracefully, like a panther pursuing prey. While engaged in conversation, he fixed his eyes on the person to whom he was talking, gripping them with his panther-like gaze, warm and seductive if he liked you; ferocious if he didn't. His voice was deep and resonant, and it generally persuaded his listeners to accept his points of view every bit as much as his persuasive, logical arguments did. That these strengths of his had not been as effective at Philurius College at first mystified him. The better he got to know Malfatto and Co., however, the more he realized that they simply operated on another wavelength.

"And if you don't get them?" Malfatto asked menacingly.

"Then I'll go over your head."

"Oh yeah? Well, screw you!" Malfatto said.

"We'll see," Vic said. "I intend to go to CETPM, to your boss on campus, and to the NAAF." He paused, seeing confusion mask Malfatto's face. "The NAAF, the National Association of American Faculty, is an organization I have belonged to since I first began teaching. They work to assure academic quality in American institutions of higher learning."

"You sonofabitch!" Malfatto said as he stood up, red-faced and angry.

"Let's be a little more professional, please," Plea said, irately this time. No one paid her the slightest attention.

"I think we can find a solution if we all calm down," Doris Kink said. "Could we take a short break, Dean Malfatto?"

"You bet your ass! Twenty minutes, then back here. On time!"

***

Malfatto, eaten up with impotent rage, slammed the door to his office and turned to Doris Kink. "I'm going to fire that SOB, and don't try to talk me out of it. You know he wrote that letter, and you just saw his insubordination. He's gotta go!"

"It's not all that easy to fire someone without following procedures," Doris said. "We can control him, though. All we have to do is get him a list. I'll tell him we will get it to him within the week. That way we win a psychological victory."

"What the hell kind of victory is that?" the dean said as he plopped into his black leather cushioned chair, courtesy of Philurius College. "He gets what he wants, just later, so we still lose. This kind of thing drives me crazy!"

"Gio, all we have to do is give him a list and then continue to do what we please."

Whenever she used his given name, he felt a prick of intimacy. He thought once again how great it would be to see Doris naked, to run his hands over her, to—

"Then we've got him under control," Doris said.

Malfatto felt that he had missed something. "Could you repeat that?" he asked.

She looked at him curiously. "I said, we'll just give him the list and then continue to do as we please. We just have to let everyone in the field know that they should continue to assign faculty as normal, no matter what Vic Sawyer tells them. They know where their bread is buttered. Once we pacify him, then we've got him under control and can soon get rid of him."

"But he'll just cause us more problems in the future. I'm for firing him now."

What an idiot, Doris thought. "We have to follow procedures," she said. "If you want him fired, we'll have to do it according to the book."

"To hell with the book!"

"Gio, I'll help you with the procedural part. Just trust me on this. We'll calm him down, then get rid of him later, on our schedule."

Malfatto looked up at her, undressing her once again in his mind. Then he pulled at his tie. "Okay, okay. We'll do it that way. Can't we call this meeting off now?"

"No, sir," she said. "We have to be back in ten minutes and stay until it's over. Otherwise we look weak. When we go back to the conference room, just say we've talked and then tell Sawyer that we'll have a private meeting with him at the end of the afternoon session."

"Alright," he said, pulling on his tie once again. Malfatto opened the drawer to his desk and took out his blood pressure medicine. "Let's keep the bastards waiting a few minutes."

"I think it would be better if we were on time."

"Fine, fine. Get outta here now. I need a couple of minutes."

As Doris Kink shut the door behind her, she breathed deeply, exhaled slowly and began walking resolutely with furrowed brow toward the conference room.

***

Dean Malfatto entered the room five minutes late. He strode purposefully to the front of the conference table and before sitting down addressed Vic. "Dr. Sawyer, Ms. Kink and I will meet you briefly at the end of today's meeting to discuss your concerns. Now I'd like to get on with this meeting,"

Malfatto, still standing, glared at him. Wisely, Vic just nodded.

"I'd like to address a couple of points Don made," Jack said, breaking the tension. "We aren't able to keep good faculty because we pay them badly and generally treat them like scum. We're making tons of money, sending 20 percent above our overhead back to campus, right, Craig?"

"We just got a directive asking for 25 percent now that we've made the 20 percent this past year," Craig the money man said.

"That's absurd," Jack said as he shook his head. "Well, moving on to the next point. I've taught civilian students in America and military students here, and I tell you, Don, I find my military students by and large to be much more disciplined, harder working and more interested in learning. They are also a damn sight more courteous."

Ed Ehrgeiz jumped in. "You've got a good point about the teachers, Jack. We can't pay them more money per class, but we need to make sure they're fully employed and happy. What we do in my region is we track all students in all centers. We spend time with them, showing them what they need to get their degrees. Then we schedule those courses, with lots of video courses. But Doris also has a good point. We've gotta make exams easier so the students will keep comin' back to us instead of goin' over to the competition. We've also got to assure that there are teachers for every course we offer, no matter what. Otherwise the competition could beat us. There are two other schools which offer the same curriculum as we do, so we've gotta stay on the ball."

"If you are such a good manager, how is it then that we lose so many of our faculty each term, even in your region?" Vic asked.

"Well, there's lots of reasons," Ed began. Before he had a chance to elaborate Vic jumped in.

"We haven't time now to deal with all your English usage deficiencies, Mr. Ehrgeiz, but do take note that one should say *there are* a lot of reasons, not *there's lots* of reasons. The latter is a German formulation but not an English one. More importantly, it might come as a surprise to you, but we aren't selling used cars here." Vic paused. He wanted a cigarette, but that wouldn't be possible until the next break.

"I applaud your efforts to track each student's progress and offer appropriate courses," he continued. "But your concept of lowering standards, both for students and faculty, is unacceptable. Also, if a faculty member teaches courses he isn't prepared to teach, we are doing the students a disservice."

"Or she," said Doris. "Your remarks are sexist."

"And your remarks are irrelevant to the subject at hand," Vic scoffed. "We can talk about sexism in language at another time. Have a look at what Simone de Beauvoir has to say about it. Then we can talk."

"Couldn't we be more professional?" Plea said, exasperated now but again ignored.

"It's always relevant to be non-sexist in both word and deed," Doris said. Her color had changed from pink to tomato red. She began to squirm in her chair.

"Read Simone de Beauvoir. Then we can talk," Vic repeated.

Just then Dean Malfatto stood up. "I've got some important business to attend to. Doris is now in charge. Crepe, let's go." With that, Malfatto departed, Crepe Moertel in tow. The important business turned out to be a little office sex behind the dean's locked door. Afterwards, Malfatto sent Crepe back to work gathering statistics and answering his mail, while he had apple pie and coffee at the snack bar. He made it back to the meeting in time for lunch.

While the dean and Crepe were cavorting in his office, Vic and Doris put the sexism issue on hold and unsuccessfully tried to find areas of agreement. By lunchtime nothing had been resolved and tempers were enflamed. Everyone was relieved when the lunch break came. The afternoon session was milder. Both sides, tired of the fight, allowed other issues to be presented. Plea Dies was in her element that afternoon, emoting about paperwork, guidelines and procedures, but no one paid her the slightest attention.

CHAPTER FOUR
AT THE GASTHAUS

The afternoon had been exhausting for Vic, the parade of banal issues seemingly unending. Then after the meeting came the dean's disingenuous offer to supply the names Vic had demanded.

"You'll just have to give us a little more time," Malfatto had said, after which he turned and winked at Doris Kink. *What a fool,* Vic thought. The events of the day had numbed him, and he was ready for some serious drinking.

Vic took a seat next to Jack Murphy in the local *Gasthaus* restaurant just outside the caserne. It was 18:00, as Jack reminded him. Vic looked across the table at Plea Dies and thought, *Plea is witless.* She was the kind of person who ran into doors and then apologized to them. *Plea probably enjoyed the meeting,* Vic thought. Then the waitress arrived, and his morbid mulling vanished.

Das Fräulein was on the tall side and slender, like a fashion model ten pounds over her professional weight. Her Madonna-like face, framed by shoulder-length ash-blond hair, was dominated by striking blue eyes that glowed in the darkened room. She was wearing form-fitting white pants and a blue blouse which accentuated her shapely breasts. Vic thought he heard them say hello. In fact, it was Plea who said hello.

"Hello, Vic, is your mind here with us, or somewhere else?" she said, raising her eyebrows slightly.

"Sadly, now that you've interrupted my thoughts, I'm here again, Plea. How about you?" he asked. "Are you all here?"

Plea frowned, moving the corners of her mouth into a pout. "Well, what did you think of the meeting today?" she ventured.

Vic squinted. "Was there something I missed? The meeting was a complete waste of time, filled solely with nonsense."

"That's not a very positive attitude." Plea sat up a bit in her chair and looked sternly at Vic.

"*Was hätten Sie gerne?*" The shapely waitress was now once again in front of Vic.

"She wants to know what you want," Jack Murphy said. "I recommend the beer."

"I know what she said, my friend Jack. My PhD was in German. Remember?"

"Piled higher and deeper. That's what I say," Jack said. "I'm glad I stopped with an MA."

"You stopped long before that, lad," Vic joked as he turned to the waitress. "*Ein Bier, bitte schön.*" Just above her left breast was a name tag that said Eva. *I've got to come here more often*, he thought.

Everyone ordered beer before looking at the menu. Joining Jack, Plea and Vic were Raz and Craig. Further down the long table were Ed, Maya, Don and Doris.

"*Anmutig*," said Vic wistfully, as he watched Eva sway away toward the kitchen.

"What did you say, Vic?" Plea demanded.

"Graceful," he answered. Plea amused him, but she could also irritate the hell out of him. Just now he was amused.

"And why did you say *graceful*?" she demanded. "What was graceful?"

"Eva is graceful." Vic grinned slyly at Plea. "Our waitress."

"Yes, I saw you watching her. You should be ashamed of yourself looking at a woman like that when there's a lady at your table," Plea scolded.

"I don't think she's wearing any underwear," Jack said. "In fact, I'm sure of it."

"Oh, Jack, you are so American!"

Jack looked at her for a couple of seconds, then asked, "Is that good or bad?"

"You're impossible. Both of you!" Plea took out a Gauloises and lit it.

Vic had learned early on that Plea took criticism badly and that she was given to contrariety.

At first Vic had been friendly with her, and she had confided in him, but the honeymoon quickly ended. He simply couldn't stomach her stiffness and her bureaucratic mentality. Watching her draw on her Gauloises while looking into space, Vic assessed Plea anew. Her blond hair was in an Afro, a tribute to her Norwegian father and her African American mother. Plea's cat-green eyes were set in a face that looked a bit Egyptian, and she was built like a long-distance runner. Because she was director of personnel and counted as a minority, she provided Philurius College some important leverage with the accreditation folks. She worked out in the gym three times a week and was a vegetarian, yet she smoked a pack of Gauloises every day and sipped alcohol from morning till night.

The first round of beers arrived, and Vic turned his attention to Jack and Raz. He found that what Jack said was right. Raz was amiable, laid-back, intelligent and interesting.

***

Three hours passed, and for Vic the evening turned pleasant, a real contrast to the workday. With each beer, he had also mellowed about Plea, and he found Craig, whom he had suspected of being part of the Philurius establishment, to be well-read and sophisticated.

As Vic ordered another beer, Ed, further down the table, pursued his standard rant. "We can't quit," he said earnestly. "We're on the edge of greatness. We're about to do profound things here. Turn things around. Kick down some doors. Kiss some real ass. Right, Doris?" he asked his colleague sitting just to his left.

"Really *kick* some ass," she responded, looking just as earnest as Ed.

As Ed was ranting, he knocked over his beer, which landed in his lady friend's lap.

"Yikes!" Maya yelled. Soaked in cold beer, she rose and left. Ed didn't even say goodbye.

Don Dingsbums, sitting across from Doris, had been watching her while Ed was holding court. He picked up his beer and moved over beside her, poised to make a move. Doris glanced at him, moved over slightly to give him a seat to her left, then returned her attention to Ed.

As Ed continued his ramblings, Don put his hand on Doris's left leg. Though feeling tipsy, Doris was aware of the hand that was not her own, but it didn't bother her. She turned her attention to Ed's tirade.

With fire in his eyes and thunder in his voice, Ed carried on. "You know I'm close to the dean. I can convince him of anything. I'm sure of it. And I want you, Doris, to be the next in line for that job. I'll start working on him." Ed glanced at Doris and put his hand on her right leg, caressing it. Suddenly he found himself holding hands—with Don.

The two men looked at each other, then quickly retreated, placing their hands back where they belonged. It wasn't long, however, until Don took another pass, closing in on Doris's most private part.

"Stop that!" Doris said harshly.

Not getting the message, Don began a gentle stroking. Doris slapped him, then tried to get up but tripped over her chair, falling to the floor. Don lifted her by the derriere. He smiled at her, his hands still in place. Humiliated, she slapped him again, then stumbled out of the restaurant, followed by Ed.

Eva the waitress glided over calmly and started cleaning up the table. She was accustomed to such scenes.

Don then joined the others, sitting this time next to Plea. The evening had gradually taken on light and giddy hues, subdued and muffled tones, as the beer and schnapps slowly took effect.

Vic and company had missed most of the exchanges down the table. They looked at each other and shrugged as Ed followed Doris out of the restaurant. Don seemed bemused, looking as if he were trying to understand a joke but hadn't yet gotten it.

What a crew, Vic thought. Before today he had found Don amusing, but during the meeting his assessment had changed to distaste. The good news was that he had made a new friend. Raz was a welcome addition to his small circle of like minds at Philurius College. Vic liked Craig but still didn't feel he could confide in him.

Plea Dies, Doris Kink and most of the others at the college exemplified the rigid-thinking, green-eye-shade-wearing accountant personality he so detested and seemingly couldn't escape. In his *Life Without Principle,* Vic mused, Thoreau had captured the ill engendered by these Philurius College employees. The quote had come to mind as Doris slapped Don for the first time: "I think that there is nothing, not even crime, more opposed to poetry, to philosophy, ay, to life itself, than this incessant business." Vic mused briefly on these thoughts, considering how odd it was that Craig, an accountant, was basically so un-accountant-like.

Plea grew increasingly annoyed with the men surrounding her. They were acting so foolishly, unprofessionally, and besides that, they weren't paying her proper attention. She pushed herself back from the table, preparing to leave. Before doing so, however, she shook a Gauloises from her almost empty pack and reached for her lighter; but before her hand arrived at its goal, Don Dingsbums was there with both hands. He lit the cigarette, holding her right hand in his left. Suddenly she was feeling grand again.

"Thank you," she said. "You are the only gentleman here tonight."

"My pleasure," Don said. He was, if nothing else, persistent.

"What a lot of trypanosomes there are at this institution," Vic blurted to no one in particular. "Just a group of flagellate protozoan parasites putting us all slowly to sleep with their infectious idiocy. Ach!"

About that time Eva, the Waitress of the Shapely Breasts, arrived at the table, cool as ever, and asked if they wanted anything else to drink. Vic looked up and once again saw the name tag hanging above her left breast. "Eva, eh," he said. "What's the other one called?"

"How amusing," she said wryly as she turned away.

While finishing his last beer of the evening, Vic stole another glance at Eva as she bent over a table cleaning up. *There's something about her,* he thought. Then he waved her over, paid the bill for himself, Maya, Ed and Doris, added a hefty tip and tucked the receipt into his billfold.

"I'll collect tomorrow," he said to his empty beer mug as he rose to leave.

CHAPTER FIVE
THE DAY AFTER

*I*t was ten when Vic was awakened in his room at the military hotel just off base by the sounds of AFN, the Armed Forces Network, blaring from the radio next to his bed. He rolled over and turned it off. Vic knew that he had overindulged the night before. On the other hand, the evening had gotten him out of the blue funk that had been hanging over him like a veil of stale cigarette smoke for the past few weeks. The Philurius College blues were getting to him. Although the tension had been broken, Vic's intuition told him he would have just a temporary reprieve. He was looking forward to meeting Jack and Raz at the Muldaner Café, their favorite hangout. The Muldaner was like an oasis for him. He and Jack usually spent a couple of hours together there on Saturday and sometimes on Sunday.

It was a charming comfortable Old-World café with marble tables and lace doilies. The oak chairs with green velvet cushions were welcoming and homey, and the soft illumination from the chandeliers provided a mellow touch. On entering the front door, one was drawn inexorably into this captivating café by the blended fragrances of coffee and spices.

Vic was dreaming about it when awakened by the loud radio. His eyes took in the humdrum spartan apartment, which was equipped with the basic amenities deemed necessary by the Army, but nothing more. He could bathe, cook, eat at a small table with four chairs, sleep, stash his clothes and accommodate a guest or two in a second bedroom, but that was all. The white walls were adorned with nothing.

Vic pushed his tall, rangy frame from the bed and made his way unsteadily to the shower. He was scheduled to meet the guys at one at the café. Before then he would need to eat something. A late breakfast of corned beef and hash on toast, disparagingly called SOS by the soldiers, plus orange juice and coffee, would get his system going. Before stepping into the shower, he chuckled, remembering the scene from the previous evening.

As was his wont, even on non-workdays, Vic wore khaki trousers and a medium-blue shirt with button-down collars. Today he chose an autumn-colored green jacket with brown elbow patches and tapped a light-green silk scarf into the breast pocket. His shoes were black and polished. Perhaps Vic was more military oriented than he thought.

As he slipped into his jacket, Doris Kink was just waking up.

***

Doris felt a vague remorse for having committed some as yet indistinctly perceived sin. She found herself in bed but noticed that she had failed to change out of her clothes. The usually immaculate white blouse was now a mess with beer and ketchup down the front. She was trying her best to focus. Suddenly she sat up straight.

"Oh no!" she moaned, holding her throbbing head. The evening was coming back to her, and with it a deep sense of guilt. It surrounded her like a heavy impenetrable fog as she pulled the covers up to her chin. Suddenly her guilt turned to anger. She still wasn't sure what had happened last night, but she remembered enough to be sure it wasn't in her best interest. After the incident, Ed had followed her out and accompanied her home. She remembered that he had been the perfect gentleman. He even waited at the door to make sure she got inside her apartment without incident.

All of a sudden her mood got darker as her mind cleared. "Don! Who the hell does he think he is?" Doris said to her feet resting on the bedpost, as she struggled to a comfortable sitting position. "How dare he? I'll take his sorry ass to the cleaners," she continued angrily. "I'll nail that son of a bitch with sexual harassment charges. Plea will help me. He'll lose his job over this."

Again, her thoughts shifted, this time to her lover, whom she and everyone else simply called Bean, short for Buford Eric Anthony Norrington, who would be arriving in just a week. "Once Bean gets here, everything will get better," she confided to her pillow.

***

Jack Murphy slept until ten and felt refreshed. After his ablutions he walked from his small apartment over to the bakery for his favorite breakfast, a torte called *Bienenstich*. It was a naughty indulgence: sweet cream between two layers of light coffeecake with honey-glazed almonds on top. Jack had two, with a cup of coffee. After that he was ready to face the day. Since he had a good deal of time before the afternoon rendezvous, Jack decided to take a long walk down by the riverside. The river was wide, blue and fast moving, and its banks were filled today with young people in swimsuits. Sounds of happy laughter filled the air. Tourist ships were docked, and dozens of excited foreign guests were disembarking. It was a beautiful sunny day, and he felt on top of the world.

***

Raz Rabin was in the back courtyard of the hotel by eleven thirty practicing tai chi. He had started the day with a light breakfast followed by thirty minutes of meditation and then a two-mile jog. The tai chi would be the finishing touch to his morning regime. Afterwards, he would shower, have a light lunch and then check out of the hotel. He was looking forward to spending time with Vic and Jack. Raz liked Vic, as Jack said he would. Just outside the military hotel, the two gents ran into each other and headed toward the Muldaner Café.

On the way there, Vic confessed that he had written the letter to the *Stars & Stripes*.

***

It was a quarter past one when Vic and Raz strolled into Muldaner's. Jack waved to them from a corner table. He had been there fifteen minutes sipping coffee and reading *The Gambler* by Fyodor Dostoyevsky. Jack had become a real Dostoyevsky fan while in Rheinsteinheim. He had begun with *Crime and Punishment*, later reading *The Insulted and Humiliated* and *A Funny Man's Dream*. This was his second reading of *The Gambler*.

Dostoyevsky had written the book while living in Rheinsteinheim, a fact that thrilled Jack. He enjoyed gambling at the same casino as his Russian hero. Being a sensible gambler, Jack had made a habit of taking fifty German marks in chips and playing until the money was gone. Then he would have a drink at the bar and try to visualize Fyodor at the tables. Once in a blue moon Jack would win a bit of money and would celebrate with two drinks at the bar.

Jack was a closet socialist and Rousseauvian optimist regarding human nature, just like the Russian writer from St. Petersburg. He kept the following quote from Dostoyevsky's *A Funny Man's Dream* in his billfold: *"I have seen and know that people can be wonderful and happy without losing the ability to live on this earth. I do not want to and cannot believe that evil is the normal state of people."*

Jack's idol rejected the negative Hobbesian nonsense he found so prevalent. People were fundamentally good, he believed. It was society that ruined them. Fyodor had been sent to Siberia because of his membership in the Petrashevsky Circle, a group of utopian socialists. His belief that the aristocracy in their self-centeredness was the source of alienation in society struck a chord with Jack, who secretly began to think of this café as the hub of a new Petrashevsky Circle with him at its center—a reincarnation of Dostoyevsky.

***

"Hello, my friend," Vic said warmly. "Been here long?"

"Just about fifteen minutes, I guess. Have a seat. You too, Raz. I'll catch *die Fraulein's* eye."

"It's *das Fräulein*, Jack," Vic said. "It rhymes with *boy*."

"That's neuter, isn't it?" Jack queried. "How can a woman be neuter, Vic?"

"Listen, my friend, a married woman is feminine. *Die Frau.* An unmarried woman who has not experienced conjugal pleasures is neuter—not a real woman yet. Got it?"

"Using that logic, it seems to me that only virgins should be neuter."

"Jack," Vic continued, "it is the act of marriage that makes a girl a woman. It's as simple as that, so just accept it."

"But why is this *Fraulein* of ours neuter?" Jack persisted. "She's married."

"Ah, that's the exception to the rule," Vic said, smiling crookedly.

"Waitresses are always called *das Fräulein,* regardless of age or marital status, probably because they've been mentally neutered by customers like you."

"And you call this a logical language?" Jack shook his head. "I'll just call her Brunhilde. That's not her name, but it should be. She looks like a Brunhilde to me."

"Jack, you live in a parallel universe," Vic said. "This woman looks like anything but a Brunhilde. She's petite, for heaven's sake."

He was fond of Jack but had suspected he was on a different sheet of music ever since he had mentioned wanting to begin a modern-day Petrashevsky Circle based in the Muldaner Café.

They ordered coffee and made small talk for a while. Then Vic asked the question which had been weighing on his mind.

"Okay, you two, I want to know what you really think. Did I make a mistake writing that letter to the *Stars & Stripes*, and did I overstep myself in the regional directors' meeting yesterday?"

Jack and Raz looked at each other, neither sure of how to respond. They both realized that Vic had severely angered Doris Kink and Gio Malfatto at the meeting, and they knew that both these people were convinced that Vic had written the damaging letter. On the other hand, they were both full of admiration.

It was Jack who first responded. "So, you've let Raz in on our little secret."

Vic nodded. "He's a good colleague, like you said. I trust him completely, and we could use an ally in the field," Vic said as he nodded to Raz.

"You know," Jack continued, "I wish I had done something like that long ago . . . There's no way anyone can prove you wrote the letter, but we all know that Malfatto and Kink think you did, so you've got a problem, but not one that could get you fired."

Jack paused. "The meeting, though, that's another thing. Look, we're proud of you. Don't get me wrong. You're standing up for principle, which is something hardly anyone does here." He paused again. "But you might try being more subtle in the future. Those temper tantrums could get you in some serious trouble. You could also let me be more of an attack dog. There's absolutely nothing Malfatto can do to me. I've got tenure on campus. I'm just on loan over here because I asked to be. I have no fear of Malfatto." Jack then reached over and patted Vic on the shoulder. "You have inspired me to greater service, Vic."

"Thanks for the encouragement," Vic said. "Look, I know you're right. I've always had a problem with authority figures and especially with people who disrespect things of the mind. It makes me crazy. Education is important to me, particularly higher education, and I get furious when I see the way this administration here demeans those ideals. I can't just sit back and do nothing."

Vic paused and drank some of his cappuccino.

"Help me," he said, leaning forward. "I want to infuse some standards here, but I also want to keep my job. Bonnie is counting on me. She's given up lucrative employment she loves in order to be here with me." He looked first at Jack, then at Raz. "Well, how do we fix Philurius College without dire consequences for ourselves?"

"I know this might sound dumb," Jack said, "but as a first step, count to ten before you jump into a conversation. Also, as I mentioned, you can let me do some of the attacking for you. Then we can build up a file on all the deficiencies of the Malfatto regime and make a strong case for correcting them before the accreditation team visit. We might gather enough damaging evidence to get rid of him. Brainstorming about how we could change the culture here would also be a good idea. In the meantime, just stick to your guns and don't let Malfatto or Doris Kink tell you how to run your department."

Vic nodded. "How about you, Raz? Any thoughts?"

Raz, who had been thinking seriously about Vic's question, didn't have a ready answer for him. "I can only agree with Jack," he said finally. "These leaders of ours are nuts, and they're vicious as well. Just be careful. There are some people who'll stick with you on this through thick and thin. You can count on me and Jack and a few others. Up here, Craig is a reluctant ally. I'll certainly contribute to the deficiencies list Jack mentioned, and I'll be happy to be in on any brainstorming sessions."

Jack nodded. "We'll all put on our thinking caps," he said. "In the meantime, remember to count to ten, Vic."

***

Afterwards, Vic returned to his hotel room and tried to take a nap, but sleep evaded him. The frustration and anger were returning. He felt trapped in a situation he didn't know how to change. Not able to sleep, Vic let his thoughts slip back to his past, recalling the slow development of what he thought to be his life's work. He realized that he had always been bright. He was second—not first—in his high school class, but that was because he had some problems with math and science courses. In English, German, history, civics and social studies, however, he excelled, winning a full scholarship to Hamilton College close to his hometown in upstate New York. It was there that he learned to write clearly, eloquently and convincingly.

Vic had done well on the standard examinations, the SAT and ACT, and achieved the distinction of being a National Merit Finalist, putting him in the top one percent of students his age in the nation. He found himself in his element at university. After graduating *summa cum laude* with a PhD from Cornell, Vic got a lectureship at a state university, teaching German language and literature. The job lasted just three years.

Vic had entered his first teaching assignment full of idealism. He thought of himself as the *enfant terrible* of the foreign language department, seeing things that needed to be changed and working to change them. This idealism with action got him in terrible trouble. It was the 1960s, and the movement to change things in academe was going in a different direction than Vic wanted. He believed in rigorous standards and in reading classical authors. He left under a cloud after a major falling out with the department head on issues of academic freedom. Even early on, Vic had equal portions of Don Quixote and Don Juan in him, combined with a touch of John Donne. This mixture often proved problematic. It was his Don Quixote nature that cost him his first job, his Don Juan the second. John Donne was manifested in his elegant but sometimes biting writing style, which was now causing problems.

The second position was at a Southern Baptist college in the South. It was there, after several years of loyal service, that he was threatened with dismissal because of his relationship with Bonnie, an adjunct faculty colleague whom he would one day marry. The fact that he and his first wife were separated didn't seem to make any difference to his employers, and although he had some faculty support, his job was in jeopardy.

This problem was exacerbated by another. For years he had sneaked alcohol into his apartment where he drank secretly. Drinking was grounds for dismissal at the college, and in fact, one of his colleagues had been fired because he was seen carrying a six-pack of beer to his car in a neighboring town. Just as Vic was gearing up for a battle he was bound to lose with the administration, he got the Philurius College offer as director of Academic Affairs. Vic had read about it in the *Chronicle of Higher Education* and had immediately applied. Now, however, Philurius College was driving him nuts, just as the others had—only worse.

***

Vic recalled an early conversation with Jack about Doris. "I used to call her Deanette," Jack said. "It really made her angry. Secretly, I still call her the assassin."

"The assassin?" Vic remembered asking. "Why the assassin? Did she threaten to cut your throat?"

"Haven't you noticed?" Jack said. "She tries to kill you, assassinate you with paper. I've never seen anything like it. Doris Kink is a compulsive generator of paper."

"Yeah, she certainly is," Vic said. He was sitting behind his desk filled with memos, all of which were from Assistant Dean Kink. Vic went over to the coffee pot and poured himself a cup. "Want another cup of this horrible-tasting crap I try to pass off as coffee?" he asked.

"No thanks, man. I've still got some of that South Sea Java-Java of yours. Besides, I'm saving my palate for a taste of Plea's fruit tea. She promised me some at ten, so I can only hang out with you a few more minutes. Can't be late for Plea. I'm still trying to get on her good side."

"She has a good side?" Vic quipped. "Too bad you can't stay. I was hoping you could help me deal with this paperwork from the assassin." He then sat down behind his desk, coffee cup in hand, and looked again at the mess of memos. He set his cup on the desk and lit a cigarette. The white steam of the coffee mingled with the blue smoke of the cigarette. Vic suddenly felt older than the Vedas. Then with a sigh he picked up one of Doris's memos and lit it with the burning tip of his cigarette.

"Aren't you going to read it first?" Jack asked deadpan. "It might be something important."

Vic picked up another page after dropping the first one in the trash can. He looked straight-faced at Jack and lit the second "Kinky" memo.

"Hey, I finally figured out who you remind me of," Jack said. "It's that actor William Hurt. You ought to grow a beard, though. It looks more professorial, more professional. Plea would like you better, too. You know how fond she is of professionals and professionalism."

"I'll start one tomorrow," Vic said, intending to do no such thing.

The burning ceremony continued. Vic and Jack acted like two kids, feeling giddier with each sacrificed memo. It took half an hour to complete the job. Vic was happy at last, and Jack had totally forgotten about Plea and her offer of tea.

CHAPTER SIX
THE COMPLAINT

Monday morning Dean Malfatto stood in front of his bathroom mirror and began his morning ritual of shaving. He had been angry the entire weekend and was still stewing as he ran the blade over his stubble. The dean wanted to get Vic Sawyer, but he was stymied. At least the CETPM director Bill McMurphy had been pacified. That was one problem less. After a few tense moments on the telephone, the dean had been able to convince McMurphy that someone else had written the infamous letter to the editor. The *Stars & Stripes* had promised to print Malfatto's disclaimer letter that morning, another positive turn for the dean.

The weekend had been spent with Crepe Moertel, whose sergeant husband was in the field practicing combat drills. Malfatto had taken out his venom on Crepe, and she had accepted it, as always, although it irritated her, as always. During their lovemaking Malfatto had not thought about her at all. He had thought about Doris Kink and Margaret Malcontenta-Jefferson alternately. Nothing the dean did, however, had improved his state of mind.

"Damn rules!" Malfatto said to the image in the mirror. Taking an angry swipe at his right cheek, he nicked himself. "*Managgia!*" he said. "Sonofabitch!"

Malfatto took a last look in the mirror before slapping on some Old Spice aftershave, wincing as it pricked his nick. As he finished dressing, Malfatto reflected on his current situation in life. He had held this job for about a year, and it mostly appealed to him. He enjoyed the power. He felt it made him more attractive to women. *It's even better than being a light colonel in the Army*, he told himself. *Except that I don't have the same control over people that I had in the military.*

***

Every Monday Malfatto met first thing with his top staff. Usually it was fun for him; it gave him opportunity to hold forth. Today, however, he was dreading it.

"I've got a lot to do today, so let's make this short and sweet." The senior staff were assembled in the conference room, but not for long, he hoped. "Anybody got anything pressing?" he asked.

"I've got something important as well as pressing, if that's okay?" Vic said. Malfatto winced. He took a sip of coffee from the Styrofoam cup on his desk, managing to spill some on his tie. "Well," he said, sounding like a crotchety child who had just been told to go to his room for the rest of the evening. "What's your problem?"

Vic took his time. He picked up a sheaf of papers from the desk, cleared his throat and looked up at Malfatto. Vic was amused at what he saw. Apparently "the boss" had dressed himself this fine morning, because nothing matched. The electric-blue jacket clashed with his pink shirt and brown pants, and all of these clashed with his now coffee-stained paisley tie.

Finally, Vic spoke. "You and Doris have promised me a list of the faculty who were grandfathered to teach even though they didn't have the requisite qualifications. It seems reasonable to me that I get that list by the end of this week as your assistant suggested, so we can begin to weed these people out of the system and get qualified faculty to replace them before next term."

Vic had rehearsed this line thoroughly. He had to find a balance between standing by his principles and not overly irritating his superiors. The *Stars & Stripes* letter had changed Malfatto from a stupid impediment to Vic's plans to a menacing enemy.

"You'll get it as soon as we can get it to you, *basta*! Okay, let's move on," Malfatto said.

"Just a minute, please," Vic replied. "Surely you must at some level be concerned about the upcoming accreditation team visit, and if you aren't, surely President Porcino must be. Does he know about these unqualified instructors?"

"We'll take care of those details, Dr. Sawyer, but we'll do it on our schedule, not yours," Malfatto said. Sweat dripped from his brow. He wiped it off with a much-used handkerchief.

Despite his promise to himself that he would control his emotions, Vic found himself again at the boiling point. He closed his eyes and took a deep breath. He was beginning to count to ten as Jack had suggested when he heard Doris Kink speaking.

"Vic, I've got a lot on my plate this week, but I'll try my best to get you that list by Friday close of business." She paused. Vic looked at her. "We are all concerned about the A-Team visit," she continued. "But you've got to understand how vicious the competition is in this system. We offer the same curriculum as two other colleges and have to fight to convince potential students and CETPM personnel that we are more attractive than the other two. They're all cutthroat, so we have to be, too, in order to survive. It's a process," she said as she shrugged.

Doris wanted to be done with this meeting, too. She was itching to file her formal sexual harassment complaint against Don Dingsbums.

"Thank you," Vic said, not letting the surprise creep into his voice. "I'm looking forward to having your list by Friday."

"Good, now that we have that solved, anything else?" the dean said. He was more eager to get this meeting behind him than was Doris. He wanted to call the CETPM director Bill McMurphy again, confide in him his suspicion that Vic Sawyer had written the letter, and ask for advice about how to get rid of him.

Vic, having had his say, glanced around the room, stopping at Margaret. *Smashing,* he thought. Her charcoal-gray Gucci suit was pure silk, elegantly embracing her body, subtly drawing attention to it. The skirt was slit up one side, just like the one that had so unnerved him the other day. Her blouse was a lighter gray. A necklace of amber graced her delicate, aristocratic neck. Margaret exuded femininity. Vic, and everyone else, had noticed.

Vic then moved on to Doris, whose allure was offset by her uptight manner and austere attire. Today she was wearing baggy khaki pants with a plain off-white cotton top, also loose-fitting. *Too bad she's such a straitlaced uncomfortable business type,* he thought. *She's clearly bright and could be winsome, likeable, if only—*

His thoughts were interrupted by Dean Malfatto. "The ladies aren't looking bad today, are they? Check out Doris here for starters." Malfatto was looking straight at Vic. "Saw you checkin' 'em out," he said, a smirk on his face.

"Oh, please," Plea said. "Can't we do without this, this male thing?"

"Oh, sorry I didn't mention you first, Plea, honey. You're lookin' especially good this morning," Malfatto said as he leered in Plea's direction.

Plea glared at him. "Thank you. Could we get this meeting finished? I have tons of things to do today, so I really have to be out of here by ten. At latest."

"Thank you, Ms. Dies. I certainly hope we can accommodate you." Malfatto smirked again. "Okay. Let's get going. What I want to know is what all of you are doing to cooperate with the field?"

"I see you've been talking to Ed Ehrgeiz again," Vic blurted. *Damn,* he thought. *Why didn't I count to ten?*

The dean had a primeval urge to jump across the table and strangle Vic. He struggled with this impulse while he stared at his enemy viciously. He calmed himself, taking another gulp of coffee. It burned going down, and once again he spilled some of the brew on his tie. When he spoke, his voice quivered.

"You will cooperate with the field or else. Ed Ehrgeiz is a money generator. He pays your salary, you dumb SOB! So, learn to cooperate or else. Understand?"

"No," Vic answered, again speaking before he thought.

The dean pulled on his stained paisley tie and looked like he would rather be anywhere else but here. Then, raising his voice, he said, "What is it you don't understand? I thought you were an intellectual. It's real simple, *Mister*—excuse me—*Doctor* Sawyer. You have to support the field personnel. The people who bring in the money to pay your big salary. What do you do to bring money to the company? Huh? What do you do?"

"I might ask the same of you," Vic said calmly. "And we aren't a company. We're a college." On the notepad in front of him, he wrote *lard ass.*

"Don't get smart with me. You could be gone by tomorrow, you know!" Malfatto's eyes were bulging now, and both hands had curled into fists.

"Getting rid of me, or anybody for that matter, isn't that simple," Vic answered. "You know that, don't you? Besides, if you want to talk about big salaries, let's start with yours. How can you justify making eighty-k a year? That makes my *big salary* of twenty-k seem not so big after all."

"How the hell did you find out what I make? It's none of your damn business what I make. Who told you?"

"I guessed."

"What?"

"I just guessed at your salary."

"Don't try to jerk me around, you egghead SOB!" Malfatto said. Though he hated Vic Sawyer with a passion, he indeed realized he couldn't get rid of him so easily. A solid case had to be built against the man, and for that Malfatto needed help.

"Vic, be nice now," Plea said as she took a tea bag out of her tall green cup.

Vic glanced at her. "But, Plea, I am being nice," he said.

"I agree with Vic on this," Jack said. "Ed Ehrgeiz is a jerk, and he's jerking all of you around, especially you, Dean Malfatto, and you, Miss Assistant Dean Kink. He's got you twisted around his little finger."

"You might add that he's a charlatan," Vic added.

"*Basta!* And I mean *basta!*" Malfatto yelled. "Why can't we ever stay on the subject?"

This outburst gave Jack his lead-in. "Hey, I've got a copy of *Robert's Rules of Order* here. Why don't we use it as you suggested in the last regional directors' meeting?"

"We don't have time for that kind of crap now," Malfatto said. "You academic types don't understand action. It's action that counts, not thinking!"

As Jack cringed at this offense to reason, Vic, having completely forgotten his counting-to-ten strategy, went on the attack, his rage again outrunning his good sense. He gripped the desk but lowered his voice, speaking in measured tones.

"We all realize you don't put much stock in things of the mind, Mister— I mean, Dean Malfatto," Vic said. "That's why Jack and I were so surprised that you wrote that letter to the *Stars & Stripes*. It sounded for once like you were one of us, like you were part of the crowd committed to ethics and good sense. Also, you clearly took action, and we applaud you for it. But which one of these persons is the real you?" Vic asked. "The one standing before us today or the one who wrote that letter?"

Malfatto flinched. He moved slightly, as if he were indeed going to come around the desk and attack Vic. Instead he said, "I didn't write that letter, and everybody knows it. Bill McMurphy believes me, and everybody knows who wrote that damn letter. Everybody knows!" He stood abruptly. "This meeting is over! Out, everybody out but Doris!"

***

When everyone had left the room, Doris shut the door, turned and faced the dean, watching him mop his brow. "Well," she said. "What now?"

Malfatto leaned on his desk, his face beaming like a red-hot ember. "Your top priority is to get rid of Sawyer as soon as you can. Nothing else is important. Got it?"

"I'm on it," she said. Then, hesitating just briefly, she decided to get the complaint against Don Dingsbums off her chest. "I've got a special request of you, too," she said.

The dean looked up at her, still visibly angry. "And what's that?"

"May I sit?" she asked. Malfatto shrugged and motioned toward the chair. Doris tried to compose herself. This was difficult for her, embarrassing, but she had to follow through. She took a seat. Malfatto was looking at her curiously.

"Well?" he said.

"I need your support on something. Help me and I'll do everything in my power to get Vic Sawyer out of here as soon as possible. I want this done as secretly as possible. I want to file a sexual harassment complaint against Don Dingsbums, and I want him fired."

Malfatto leaned forward. "What did he do?"

"He sexually . . . well, you see . . . he touched me," she said.

"Hm," said Malfatto. He was at once sexually aroused and jealous. "Where exactly did he touch you?"

Suddenly Doris lost her temper. "In inappropriate places," she said, "and if you want my help getting rid of Vic Sawyer, you'll support me on this. Got it?"

"Sure, sure. No problem," the dean said. He rather liked Don Dingsbums, but he favored Doris. "Who's going to take over his region?" he asked.

"Why not give it to Maya? She can handle it."

Doris had been wanting to help her friend Maya earn more money and gain prestige. Also, there would be another woman with more power in place and another man gone. *The A-Team will like that, too,* she imagined. It would add to the number of minorities in power positions.

"Okay," said the dean. "Just go tell Plea I want it done. She'll have all the paperwork. Now, get back on the Sawyer project."

Malfatto eyed Doris's lithe, tall, athletic body as she left. *Lucky sonofabitch, Dingsbums.*

Back in Vic's office, Jack was trying to lend comfort and advice to the Academic Affairs chief.

"Vic, you've got to put a cap on your temper. You started well, but then you lost it. You've got people behind you—a few anyway. We've got to fight fire with water, though, not with more fire. You seem to be trying your best to work against yourself."

"But I was right," Vic replied.

***

After leaving Malfatto, Doris power-walked down to Plea's office and told Patricia, her secretary, that she needed just a couple of minutes with the personnel director.

"It's an important matter of sexual misconduct," she said. Patricia, looking vastly self-important, punched the intercom and relayed the message.

"Show her in," Plea said, as she took a sip of her brandy-laced herbal tea.

Doris made her case against Don Dingsbums succinctly. Plea was stunned and angry. First of all, the dean had mentioned Doris's good looks in the meeting but hadn't said anything about Plea until prompted. The personnel director didn't like being second. Not only that, the same Don Dingsbums who had made unwanted advances toward Doris was the same Don who had ended up in Plea's bed the night of the drunken debacle. Plea was angry. She stopped taking notes and looked up at Doris. *I'm just as attractive as she is,* she thought.

"We'll throw the book at him," Plea said. Doris nodded in approval.

"Plea, I really want to get rid of him, and the sooner the better," Doris said conspiratorially. "Will you help me?" With a nod from Plea the deal was sealed.

CHAPTER SEVEN
MY MAN'S HOME NOW

The day Doris's complaint was filed, a letter was sent to Don advising him that he would have to attend a sensitivity training class for one week starting the following Monday. He was required to have the record of his attendance and the remarks by his trainer certified by a notary public at his own expense. Furthermore, he would be docked a week's pay.

At 09:45 Monday, Doris was in her office getting ready to drive to the airport to pick up her man, Bean. The staff meeting had been a success. Doris had provided Vic with a list of grandfathered faculty members, but she was sure he wouldn't be around long enough to do anything about it. Doris was also confident that she and her close associates could conceal unqualified faculty, those who did not meet the criteria established by the Philurius College home campus, from the accreditation team. Most of the courses these instructors taught were remote via video, which only required a "facilitator," so faculty members not meeting the Philurius College minimum standards would be listed as facilitators.

Doris left the office and dashed to the Mainstadt Airport. She entered the waiting area just as Bean stepped off his Boeing 707 from Cairo. He strode with a smooth, self-possessed confidence toward passport control, attracting considerable attention, which he seemed not to notice. His Harry Belafonte–hued face contrasted strikingly with the white silk suit he wore so easily. The peach-colored shirt with matching breast pocket scarf lent an air of gaiety. He was wearing black, highly shined, custom-made Italian leather shoes with peach-colored socks, which peeked out only when he was sitting, as his pants were stylishly on the long side.

Bean was enigmatic, easygoing and purposeful. He had been a soldier for twenty-five years, retiring as a master sergeant at age forty-three. It never entered his mind to become an officer. During his military career he had earned a BA degree in psychology and an MA in international relations and had become fluent in German, French, Italian and Vietnamese. Bean had been assigned to Vietnam with the Special Forces for a total of three years, much of that time spent in Cambodia and Laos, or as he was wont to say, *Lobotomy and Chaos.*

He had retired two years earlier with the intention of using his GI Bill to pursue more higher education. Instead of returning to his hometown, Boston, he decided to settle in Los Angeles to study international relations at the University of Southern California. A week after his discharge he met Doris on the USC campus where she had a job in Student Records. Bean was jogging, and as he turned a corner around a building, he collided with her as she was walking rapidly, eating a BLT and reading memos. After he picked her up and apologized, he asked her out for dinner. It was an unlikely match, but they hit it off right away.

Bean saw things in Doris no one else seemed to see, things even she failed to see in herself. They had some difficulties concerning his occasional out-of-town work, which remained secret, but Doris had mostly accommodated herself to these unexplained absences, as she was completely taken with him. Never had she experienced such a man in her life, and she didn't want to lose him.

Bean's taste in music ranged from jazz to classical. His absolute favorite musician was the saxophonist Coleman Hawkins, though he also quite enjoyed the trombonist Fred Wesley. Among the classical composers, his favorites were Mozart and Mahler. Doris preferred the rock of the Beatles, Three Dog Night and Janis Joplin. Her taste in reading material tended toward business management books and selected works by Bella Abzug and Ayn Rand. Bean, on the other hand, enjoyed reading *Soldier of Fortune* magazine, books by contemporary action and mystery writers and the classics. His favorite author was Jane Austen. Doris and Bean were principally tied by physical attraction and a sense of mystery, the latter fostered best by Bean.

When Doris got the job at Philurius College in Germany, she was ecstatic. On telling Bean about it, he hugged her and promised to join her as soon as possible. "I've got a little job to do first, but once that's finished, I'll be heading your way," he said. That was six months ago, and the little job had morphed into two large ones.

Doris had buried herself in her work, but she was alternately sad and angry. Primarily, she was angry at Bean, but it spilled over to other people as well. She got his letters, all routed through Belgium, but Bean never mentioned where he was or what he was doing.

Now Doris's heart leapt with anticipation as she saw him coming through the glass doors. As she began waving, he waved back and made his way toward her.

"Hey, babe," he said, smiling as he approached her. "Great to see you."

"Thought you'd never get here," Doris said as she fell into his deep embrace.

"You're lookin' fine, lady. Smell good, too," he said as they stepped back from each other. "What's that perfume you're wearing?"

Doris's light skin flushed. She hadn't felt this good since the last time she had fired someone. "Climat," she answered. It made her feel a bit guilty and disingenuous, but for this special occasion she had bought the same perfume that her rival Margaret used.

Within ten minutes they were in Doris's car. "You wanna drive, or shall I?" Bean asked.

"I'll drive. You would probably run off the road. I know you can't sleep on airplanes," Doris said. They hadn't been underway for five minutes before Doris, reverting to her official office voice, began talking about work.

"Bean, I need to talk to you about a couple of things. First, let me tell you about the job I've arranged for you."

"Doris, you can't just arrange a job for me. It reeks of nepotism. Not good. You have to advertise every job formally."

"Nobody cares about that kind of thing here. Besides, I could easily defend hiring you," Doris said. "You meet all the qualifications; and you are a veteran and a minority."

Bean put his hand on her shoulder. "I appreciate the gesture, my dear, but advertise it and let me interview with everyone else. Who knows, there may be someone better qualified."

"Bean, it's all arranged. You're a great fit for all sorts of reasons, one being racial diversity. We need more of that in the company."

"The company? You mean the college, right?"

"Right. We call it the company because we try to run it like a business," she replied.

"Oh my god!"

Doris cast a glance his way. "Bean, could you relax? You know I've never liked your doing these *odd jobs,* as you call them. We're trying to build a relationship, and you refuse to even talk to me about this secret work you do. And you're gone half the time. What about our relationship? Doesn't that make any difference to you?"

Bean stretched but otherwise made no response, so she continued. "Look, this position only requires travel now and again, and besides, with your organizational talent, you'll have this baby hummin' in no time flat."

"Have this baby hummin'? Look, I'm still not interested, but if you must, tell me what the gig's all about. It might keep me awake till we get to your place."

"It's director of Video Programs. Basically, you would be responsible for—"

"Wait a minute, wait a minute . . . Let's get off this you-would-be-responsible-for business. I'm telling you I don't want the job. I just agreed to listen to you talk about it. Okay?"

"Okay," she said. "The director is responsible for the ordering, copying and disseminating of video cassettes and their accompanying printed course materials. You—I mean, the director—could also play an active role in marketing. You'll be great at it. Don't you see what a challenge it'll be?"

"Challenge? Sounds like you've been listening to a snake oil salesman."

"Look, just think about it. This is potentially the biggest program we've got. Two people have tried to run it and failed. We're desperate. I'm desperate to get this thing off the ground and running smoothly. Since the program is directly under my area of responsibility, my ass is on the line. Bean, you would report directly to me, and only me. I know I can work with you. It's ideal. Can't you see?"

"So that means I'd be working directly for you, right?"

"Right."

"Good, then I can count on your giving me a great deal of leeway to disappear often and for extended amounts of time, right?"

"No, absolutely not!" Doris's hands tightened on the steering wheel. "What makes you think—"

Bean put his hand on Doris's driving leg, which put a stop to the tirade. She loosened her grip on the steering wheel.

"Tell you what, Doe," he said. "You let me sleep with you, and I'll consider the job."

"Not good enough. You sleep with me only after you promise you'll *take* the job."

"And what do they call sleeping with the boss around here?"

"Good sex," Doris giggled, her mood lightening. "Look, we're not married, and we're not related, so there's no nepotism. And, frankly, there's far worse going on at Philurius College than two single colleagues having a fling."

"Is that what this is, Doe, a fling?"

"Only on paper," she said.

***

Doris's digs were downtown Rheinsteinheim in the Turkish section of town. Living there made her feel more socially conscious. Her apartment was small and extraordinarily neat, a reflection of Doris herself—fastidiously tidy and uptight. There were no angles but right ones. There was no jocularity, no sense of playfulness. Everything was plain and dour and freakishly well organized. On the dark-brown worktable, the pens, pencils and papers were in perfect alignment. Aside from this table and a straight-backed chair, there was only a small couch in the living room. Off from this sparsely decorated living room was a tiny kitchen with stove, sink, squatty fridge and a small round table bordered by two straight-backed wooden chairs. Not a pan, nor a spice—and certainly no mice—were to be seen. In the fridge was a six-pack of beer and a bottle of white Franconian wine. Two bottles of Chianti were to the right of the fridge. Bean opened a Chianti and they had a glass each. After that came the long-awaited lovemaking and a nap.

Doris got up first and made coffee, which she then brought to the bed. Handing Bean his mug, she slid in next to him again.

"Um. Good." Bean basked in the pleasure of it all, his creature comforts fully satisfied. Then he had a new thought.

"What's for supper?"

"Hm," Doris said. "Well, I forgot to go shopping today. We don't have anything here but a couple of candy bars, milk and coffee . . . oh, scratch the milk. I just used the last of it in the coffee."

"Suppose we're going out then."

"Suppose we are," she answered as she snuggled closer to him. "First, though, I need to look at the notes for Monday's staff meeting. You aren't going to believe some of these people. There are problems on the staff here. Real problems. I've always got to watch my back, especially with Vic Sawyer." Doris paused and looked Bean in the eye. "I've written you about him, but you didn't seem to understand what a pain he is."

"Hey, Doe. Aren't you being a bit melodramatic? Lighten up. From what you wrote, this guy Sawyer just seems like a man with high standards. I'm sure you can find a way to work with him. Besides, I just got here. You've got all weekend to prepare for Monday. It's almost 19:00, and I'm hungry. Couldn't you postpone your work until tomorrow?"

"You're always thinking about your stomach, Bean. Why is it men are always thinking about their stomachs? Tell me. Honestly."

"Actually, what I'm really thinking about is you," Bean said as he turned toward Doris.

"Hey, watch out," she said. "You almost made me spill my coffee.

Look, you've got to learn to control yourself, Bean. Postponement of pleasure is a major sign of civilization," she said as she put the cup down on the floor and moved closer to her man.

"And too much work makes Doris a sourpuss."

"Hey, I took off this afternoon to be with you. I've never taken off work before. Not even an hour. Even when I was sick. Look, I've got to come up with a plan for getting rid of Vic Sawyer. I promised the dean that I would make this project my number one goal. Just let me work for forty-five minutes or so, and then we'll go to a little Turkish place around the corner. It's good and cheap. You can hang my new bathroom mirror while I'm working."

Bean wrinkled his brow. All this talk of getting rid of people seemed out of character for the Doris he knew. *What has this job done to her?* he wondered. He considered pursuing these thoughts with her but decided against it.

"Okay, Doe," he said. "You work in silence while I relax and enjoy life."

Fifty minutes later, the bathroom mirror long since in place, Bean sat, fully dressed, stomach growling, watching Doris scribble furiously on a yellow legal pad. She was bent over the page, shoulders hunched, deep lines of intense concentration tightening her face in consternation.

"Doris, can't you finish that later? It's awfully hungry in here."

"Just a minute. I'm almost at a stopping point."

Another ten minutes passed. She was still scribbling at an ever-increasing tempo, and Bean was getting irritated. He was truly hungry, and she just hunched there working, oblivious to him.

"Hey, Doe. It's me, Bean. Remember me? It's eight. Those Turkish guys are going to run out of kebab soon. Let's do it. I'll help you finish this stuff you're working on after dinner and again tomorrow after a good night's rest, breakfast and a couple of cups of coffee. Deal?"

"Okay, okay. Just give me another minute or two. I'm about to have an idea."

"Doe, you can have the idea while you're walking. You don't have to sit there to have it. Maybe some fresh air and some food will help the flow.

If you must, take paper and pen with you. Against my better judgment, I'll even let you bounce some ideas off me. Alright?"

After a pause she responded. "Okay, you're right. Maybe a break will help. And thanks for the offer of your ears. It always helps to have another pair of ears around."

"Actually, I was offering my mind, but if you want to call that ears, it's alright by me. The main thing is . . . *food*!"

***

It wasn't long until the couple was in front of the Turkish kebab place. There was a sign on the door that they were closed that day.

"How long have you been living in this neighborhood, Doris?" Bean said.

"There's another place close to here," she said, blushing. "It's also Turkish. I've never been there before, but it's a real restaurant, so they'll have to be open."

"Well, let's get goin'," Bean said.

It was 20:30 when they entered the front door of the restaurant. The sign above the door read *Zum Ferkel*. As they entered, they were greeted by the aroma of roasted lamb. At the far end of the room near the kitchen, there was a small elevated stage where belly dancers performed on weekends. Along the walls were small tables for two, with rectangular tables seating eight persons filling out the room. Ivory tablecloths of coarse linen gave a feel of rustic elegance. The lighting was subdued, making the place cozy and, for those so inclined, even romantic. The restaurant was almost full, but as luck would have it, there was a table for two at the back.

Over dinner Bean agreed to take the job as director of Video Programs. "Doris, I'll try this job, but on my terms, and I don't want to hear any more about it just now, nor do I want to hear about your enemies at work. Particularly, I don't want to hear about Vic Sawyer."

The next morning, the couple went out late morning to Muldaner's for breakfast. There, Doris spied Vic Sawyer and Jack Murphy at a back table. She did not speak to them, nor did she mention their presence to Bean. They really didn't care, as they were occupied with their obsession—

how to turn things around at Philurius College Programs for the Military while taking the heat off Vic.

"So, that's the long-awaited lover," Vic said, eyeing Doris's table.

"Yep," said Jack. "Wonder if his arrival will bring any changes."

Vic shrugged. Little did any of them know what turns of events were in store.

CHAPTER EIGHT
KNIVES AND DAGGERS

Vic's *Stars & Stripes* article and its further ramifications were still sizzling topics of discussion at Philurius College. People murmured in hallways and behind closed doors. There was a palpable tension in the air, one that exhilarated some and annoyed others. Gio Malfatto, Doris Kink and Margaret Malcontenta-Jefferson were among the latter. Most people still believed that Vic had written the letter. Gio, Doris and Margaret were convinced of it and were determined to get him fired. He annoyed them greatly.

Jack entered Vic's office for a pre-staff-meeting review of their plan. At Muldaner's on Saturday, they had rehearsed their approach to selling Malfatto and his crew on new ideas for change. They basically wanted four things: 1) to bring faculty from home campus; 2) to send Vic to the regions for discussions with faculty; 3) to get Raz Rabin to lend out faculty; 4) to organize a college-wide faculty meeting at headquarters.

"Nowhere in the United States is it acceptable for the faculty to be denied a voice in decision-making," Vic said. "Even in kindergarten they have a say. As American institutions of higher learning, the colleges here in Germany should be afforded the same rights as are those in the States. I agree with you, Jack; our long-term goal is to form a union or join the one on campus."

Now less than half an hour before the top staff meeting, Vic and Jack began to practice once again what they would say and how they would say it.

"Remember, count to ten when Malfatto irks you," Jack said.

"Yeah, I know," said Vic as he leaned back in his chair. Little did either of these gentlemen realize what was transpiring in other Philurius College offices this morning. And that was just as well.

***

Margaret had arrived early to review her strategy for the meeting. Over a first cup of tea, she considered her two major problems—Doris Kink and Vic Sawyer. Margaret was almost certain she could get the better of Doris in the long term, having determined that her rival was more cunning than wise, more dexterous at manipulation than at long-term planning. *That gives me a real advantage,* Margaret thought. *Besides, I'm also cunning, and Doris is dangerous. She gives me the creeps.*

Margaret and Doris had long vied for leadership of what became known in certain circles as the Girls' Club, and both of them had attracted followers. Doris headed a faction whose members were vitally interested in embodying the male stereotype—aggressive, authoritarian and able. Margaret was considerably softer in her approach, stressing the attributes of attractive, assertive and able. She believed that the male stereotype, which in her view most men indeed seemed to fit, was not the best way to go. Margaret's approach reflected a philosophical meshing of Simone de Beauvoir and Coco Channel. Doris was more like a mixture of Bella Abzug and Ayn Rand.

Margaret's current conflict with Doris revolved around a hiring issue. Margaret wanted to hire an assistant. The position had been approved, and Margaret had her candidate, Clara Bell, but Doris was pushing someone else. If Doris's protégé got the job, she would be a potential enemy in Margaret's camp, but Doris's candidate was indeed more qualified. Fortunately, fortune had smiled on Margaret just a few days earlier.

She had interviewed a Dutchman named Souter Liedekens, who was vastly superior to Doris's candidate. Margaret promptly went to the dean and proposed Souter for the job. "He'll give us credentials we are desperately in need of, for the quality of the program and for the accreditation team," she said as she crossed her lovely legs for the dean's benefit. She also enticed the dean by suggesting that Malfatto himself claim that he had found Souter Liedekens and had convinced him to become Margaret's new assistant.

"Why should I do that?" Malfatto asked, clearly interested.

"For a couple of reasons," she answered. "One is that it will impress the directors. It will show your dedication to the company and your insight into matching the needs of the organization to the most capable personnel. The other is that it will make you look good in the eyes of campus, especially President Porcino."

She waited a couple of seconds, watching Malfatto as he considered what she had said. Then she delivered her coup. "You know, I think it's one of my major jobs here to support you, to help make you look good and be successful. You've been so good to me, and I want to let you know how much I appreciate it."

With that she looked him directly in the eyes, then lowered her luminous dark-eyed gaze while her heart sang. She had him, and she knew it. "Well, I won't take any more of your time," she said. As she rose, she added, "Just now," looking at the dean longingly. He was smitten.

Malfatto rose, too. "Thanks, Margaret," he said in a raspy voice that sounded as if he had overindulged in whiskey and tobacco smoke. "I really appreciate you." As she strode out of the room in all her femininity, Malfatto cleared his throat and disrobed her in his mind. That afternoon he called Doris and Margaret into his office and announced that he had found a good candidate for the job of assistant director of EMT. Doris began to protest but saw the futility of doing so once she had a look at Souter's credentials.

***

Margaret turned her thoughts to Vic Sawyer.

"What shall I do about this jerk?" she asked aloud. "Is there any way I could ingratiate myself to him?"

Probably not, a little voice told her. In any case, she decided she mustn't openly lose her temper with him again. *Why does he have to be so straitlaced?* she thought. *He follows rules just because they are rules, not because they always make sense. If we spent some off-duty time together, maybe then we could talk to each other sensibly. Should I ask him out for a drink after work? Hm, maybe that would work. But then again, maybe not.*

Then Margaret's thoughts turned to Dean Malfatto. How could she further manipulate him? She remembered how she had dealt with a similar boss at Redstone Arsenal in Huntsville, Alabama. Margaret had served this guy for two years, and throughout the entire tenure of her employment, he had tirelessly made passes at her, which had always been cordially repelled, though it became increasingly difficult for her to deal with his unwanted hands messing around clumsily on various parts of her body, and sexual innuendos *ad infinitum.*

On her last day in the office, the boss's boss was in town for a series of meetings and a general inspection of operations. Margaret's boss had ordered her to make coffee for the gents. She did so, coming back a few minutes later with coffee and an envelope addressed to the despised man she called "creepy paws."

"It's important. Please open it immediately," she whispered in his ear. As Margaret politely poured the coffee, her boss, still talking importantly to his boss, first patted her secretly on her behind, then opened the envelope. Out fell a dainty ladies' black lace thong. Laughter erupted around the table.

"What's this all about?" the big boss said.

Margaret answered. "You see, sir, Mr. McDougal has been trying to get in my pants for two years. Now finally he has his chance."

Uneasy laughter erupted around the table once again. Then the big boss took Mr. McDougal to an adjacent office for a chat. Margaret was delighted. She cleaned out her desk and left, satisfied that she had humiliated "creepy paws."

This tactic wouldn't be appropriate here though, Margaret thought. *I'll have to be creative in a different way. Perhaps Souter Liedekens could help.*

***

Doris's agenda for the meeting was simply to undermine Vic Sawyer. The night before, she had once again discussed her work problems with Bean, who was slowly tiring of her rants.

"I need to get rid of Vic Sawyer ASAP. Help me think about this," she implored.

"What's with this power thing?" Bean asked disapprovingly "It seems to me that you can best serve yourself by making sure that you diffuse the antagonism from these people you see as enemies. This includes Sawyer. Unless he's a complete jerk, you should try to make sure he's happy, too."

"He is a complete jerk, and I'm committed to getting him fired. It's a deal I made with the dean."

This wasn't the Doris Bean remembered from just half a year ago. Sure, she had been uptight and excessively organized to the point that it interfered with her effectiveness, especially in human relations. But he had never seen this viciousness in her before.

"Doris, you've got to be indirect. It'll help you get a much better result." He paused, then looked at her thoughtfully. She didn't notice, and it bothered him. "Have you considered the idea that this preoccupation with power might be causing problems?"

Doris tightened with anger. "Whose side are you on anyway?"

"It has nothing to do with taking sides," he said. "You asked me for my opinion, and I'm giving it to you. My suggestion is that you take a step back from all this. It could be that you're part of the problem. Has it occurred to you that your enemies here are abundant? Could that really be possible without your playing a role in it?"

Doris was pulled apart by anger and guilt, and it showed. Her face twitched, and her posture stiffened even more. Things were spiraling out of control. She could not stand for Bean to criticize her, not realizing that he was trying to help, and she could not abide losing control—of anything.

"You just don't understand. You haven't been here. You haven't had to deal with these assholes!" Doris balled her fists, and her eyes flamed with venom. "Look, I didn't ask you for your advice just to get a sermon about my problems. I just wanted a little sympathy and some concrete advice about how to deal with my enemies. And they are my *enemies*. Don't doubt that for a minute!"

Bean looked at her, surprised, concerned. "Doe, I'm sorry," he said.

"I just wanted you to look at other possibilities. I just want to help make things easier for you."

"Well, you have an odd way of showing it."

"And what about your Dean Malfatto?" Bean continued. "To me he seems the strangest of a strange lot here, just from what you've told me. For heaven sakes, he was in the military twenty-five years and never went to war, you tell me. How is that possible? I was in Vietnam three times and got two purple hearts. He's only got a purple ass from sitting on it so much. Why don't you try to do something about him?"

"Because he's the boss, and I need him in order to move up in the company!" Jabbing her finger at him she said, "I thought you would be on my side. Now you've turned on me."

"Doe, I haven't turned on you. I'm trying to help you," he said as he moved toward her. She moved away.

"Where did you get your degree in psychology anyway?" she said.

"Primarily at the University of Life," he said. "I've just studied life. That's all. I've been observant, paid attention. It's all common sense. Look, they all expect you to be a hard ass, so surprise them and be accommodating. They'll be putty in your hands. Just be sure your intentions are noble. None of this advice works nearly as well if your intentions aren't pure."

"You don't know these people," Doris said, again noticeably stiffening.

"Doe, just try it. If it doesn't work, you won't be any worse off."

"Alright, I'll try it. I do owe you one for taking the job, but I don't appreciate your taking Sawyer's side."

"Doe, believe me. I want to help you, and I'm not taking sides." Bean rose from the sofa, stretched and yawned. "Couldn't we talk about something else?" he said. "Believe me, your situation here isn't tragic. I've seen tragic, and this just ain't it."

"Maybe I need a vacation," Doris said.

She went over to the window and opened it. The evening was warm and balmy. She heard Turkish being spoken on the sidewalk below and noted the branches of the linden trees wafting gently with the wind.

"I haven't taken a day off since I've been here . . . well, except for the half day I took off to pick you up at the airport." Doris softened a bit, turned to Bean and asked gently, "Well, any other thoughts?"

"Don't always say everything you feel. I've noticed you do this even when it works against your best self-interest. Listen more than you talk. Just these things will make your life easier. Doris, you can make yourself look good without making someone else look bad. Get out of your own shadow. Don't play the politics."

"Now you're preaching again," she said.

"Just give it a try," he said. "Here, read this every day until it becomes a part of you."

Bean removed his wallet from his back pocket and pulled out a small piece of heavy paper, handing it to Doris. She took it and read the following: *When you are content to be simply yourself and don't compare or compete, everyone will respect you. Lao Tzu.*

"Who is Lao Tzu?" Doris asked.

"A very wise man who lived in China in the 6th century BCE," Bean replied. "Learn this quote by memory and practice it."

CHAPTER NINE
UNEXPECTED TURNS

When it came, the top staff meeting took some unexpected turns, and Gio Malfatto's command of the meeting was again sorely tested. The first agenda item had been the appointment of Souter Liedekens. After Malfatto had made this announcement, Vic, forgetting his sworn tactfulness, said, "Aren't we forgetting something?"

"What are we forgetting, Dr. Sawyer?" Dean Malfatto said gruffly.

"Two things," Vic began. "First, shouldn't the job be advertised, and all candidates interviewed? I seem to recall some government ruling in this regard."

"You don't know how things really work, do you?" the dean shouted. "We run this thing like a military operation here. We come to a decision and act! Capish?"

Vic began counting. By the time he got to five, he jumped in again. "So you intend to simply ignore the government rules?"

"That's right, Dr. Sawyer. Could we move on now?"

Vic shrugged. "Fine," he said. "That's your problem, not mine. I just want to go on record as having brought up the point. My second question is whether this Dr. Liedekens thinks he's going to be teaching for us."

The dean looked at Doris. "Well, what's the plan, Doris? Do you all want him to teach, too?"

"Yes, I believe he would have some teaching responsibilities, wouldn't he, Margaret?" Neither of them had thought about this issue coming up, though they should have.

"He would have a limited teaching load, but—" Margaret turned to Vic. "Vic, I'm sure you'll find him fully qualified. And to add a point to your earlier question, we have been looking for an appropriate candidate for a long time. Dr. Liedekens is excellent. He has top-notch credentials and practical experience, and he's taught a lot, both in the US and in Germany."

Margaret mesmerized him with her dreamy gaze. She had a funny feeling about the way Vic was questioning this affair and how it was being handled, and she thought the dean's response had been stupid and arrogant. Margaret wanted to close the door on any potential problems from Vic. In fact, she still entertained dim hopes of ingratiating herself to him.

"Get me some paperwork on him, and I'll expedite his application," Vic said. Margaret had again unnerved him with her femininity.

After that, Doris surprised Margaret by suggesting the use of the slush fund to pay for Clara Bell's course. Malfatto approved the expense and the floor was given to Vic. For the rest of the meeting, Margaret cast glances Doris's way. *Why did she do that?* Margaret kept asking herself.

Vic brought up his other points gently, focusing on what good they would do for the college. Both Malfatto and Doris objected to his traveling to the regions, to Raz Rabin sending faculty elsewhere and to organizing a college-wide faculty meeting at headquarters, all on the grounds of unnecessary expense.

"Can't you use the telephone?" the dean said at one point.

Just as Vic was about to pounce on Malfatto, Jack kicked his buddy under the table. The only idea Malfatto and Kink liked was that of bringing faculty from campus.

"Only if they pay for them, though," Malfatto said. By the end of the meeting, Malfatto felt he had lost control, that Vic Sawyer had dominated the discussions, and it made him furious.

***

After the meeting Vic was frustrated. "See what I mean?" he said to Jack. "Diplomacy doesn't work either."

"Let's huddle again tonight at Eva's place," Jack said.

Later that day Doris cornered Malfatto before he managed to escape with Crepe. "I've got an idea. You should get back to Sawyer and tell him you've reconsidered his ideas from this morning and here's why."

After she had finished, Malfatto was grinning. "Good idea," he said. With that he strode to his appointment with Crepe Moertel at his hotel room.

Late afternoon after work, Vic and Jack retired to Eva's restaurant, the Gasthaus just off post, for dinner and a chat. Vic had some news for Jack.

"Just before quitting time Dean Malfatto appeared in my office all full of smiles and told me he had thought more about my ideas and had decided they might be good after all. He told me to go ahead and start planning for the faculty meeting up here, and he approved at least one trip to the field. I then asked him about sending some faculty from Raz's area to other places, and he said that might also be possible. He also mentioned that he would ask campus about sending us faculty."

Vic paused and sat back in his chair.

"Don't you find all this a bit weird, Jack?" Vic asked.

"I do," he said. "We'll have to ponder it some, but it could be that he and Ms. Kink finally see the light."

"You live in a fairyland, Jack. There's a sleeping dog lying around here somewhere. We just have to find it and give it a good kick."

***

The next Monday, Bean, who had just assumed his job as director of Video Programs, was walking down the hall on the third floor, going around meeting people. On his way to Vic Sawyer's office he saw a tall, distinguished man walking toward him. The man stopped as they neared each other.

"You must be Bean," the man said.

"I am," Bean answered. "And who are you?"

"My name's Vic Sawyer. I'm the director of Academic Affairs."

"Oh, I was just on my way to your office. I don't know anyone here except Assistant Dean Doris Kink, so I thought I'd make the rounds and meet my new colleagues."

"So, you'll be working here? What job have you been assigned?"

A puzzled look came over Bean's face. *I thought everyone would know.* "I'm the new director of Video Programs. I'll be reporting to Doris."

Vic bit his tongue. It was news to him that Bean had been hired by his lady friend. *Audacious!*

"Do hope you enjoy the job. Perhaps we could talk sometime about quality."

"Absolutely," Bean said. "How about this morning?"

Vic looked at his watch. "How about in twenty minutes in my office?"

"Fine. I'll see you then." The two shook hands.

"By the way, your given name isn't actually Bean, is it?"

Bean grinned. "It's short for Buford Eric Anthony Norrington. My mother started calling me Bean when I was a kid, and it just stuck.

Vic returned the grin. "Then I guess you can call me *Vas* if you like. My middle name is also Anthony." On that note, they parted company.

When they met, they had a cordial, intelligent discussion about the school and its mission—Vic, of course, stressing the need to improve the faculty, including the facilitators for Video Programs. Bean mentioned that he had heard about the tension between Vic and Doris and said he hoped that any problems between the two could be resolved amicably.

"I'll do what I can," Bean promised.

After talking to Bean for a while, Vic grudgingly admitted that he was impressed with the man. *But how can he stand being with Doris Kink?* he thought, forgetting that love is often blind.

***

Later, after work, Vic and Jack met at the Gasthaus restaurant they now called Eva's place. Halfway through his first beer, Eva, the fetching waitress, brought Vic's Wiener schnitzel and fries. As she walked away gracefully, Vic wondered once again what her story really was. There was something there he could not quite put his finger on.

CHAPTER TEN
IN THE FIELD

With suitcase in hand, Vic boarded a train for Aufdemfeld where he was to meet Raz later in the day. Raz had scheduled a faculty meeting early evening and had invited Vic. Raz had also scheduled a visit to an infamous AFCEO in Nebeling some thirty minutes away from Aufdemfeld by train.

Vic had jumped at the chance to get out of the office and spend some time talking to faculty and students after Dean Malfatto and Doris Kink had so unexpectedly changed their minds and approved all of the ideas he had presented at the staff meeting. In the back of his mind he still had suspicions about their motives; nevertheless, he looked forward to the prospect of getting away from the main office.

A couple of days before his planned departure, Vic went to check on using what Plea Dies called the company car for his trip. Plea told him that Ed Ehrgeiz had it for the entire week.

"What entitles him to the college car?" Vic asked.

"Well, he works here too, you know," Plea said as she added a dash of sherry into her morning tea.

"But he has his own car," Vic protested.

"He asked for the car before you did, so he gets it. That's the way things work here. First come, first serve. It's democratic."

Vic thought about challenging Plea's definition of democracy but thought better of it. "Fine. It'll cost more, but I'll take the train."

"You have to have that approved, you know."

"What precisely do you have to approve? The train I take? The time of day? The cost?" Vic asked.

"I have to approve the cost."

"I see. What will you approve, then?"

"Vic, I just told you. The cost! Why can't you understand the simplest things?" Plea sipped her tea again, closed her eyes and sighed.

"So," Vic began slowly, trying to contain himself. "You want me to bring you the cost of the train trip to Aufdemfeld and back, then you'll either approve it or you won't. Have I understood you correctly?"

"That's right. It's really quite simple. Most people have no problem with it."

"Has it ever occurred to you to have cost guidelines? That would make everything simpler, you know."

"In this company, Dr. Sawyer, everything is decided on a case-by-case basis. Now, if you'll please leave. I have a lot of work to do." With that she got up and left her office.

"Company indeed," Vic murmured as he followed Plea out into the hallway. *If this were a company, Plea Dies would be out the door by the close of business today.* "Hope you get a lot done, Ms. Dies," he said as he passed her in the hallway.

***

An hour later Vic returned to the Personnel Office with two sets of figures. Plea Dies's secretary, Patricia, was holding down the outer office as usual.

"Is Plea in?" Vic asked.

"Director Dies is in her office, but she can't be disturbed now."

"Thanks," Vic said as he started for the door.

"You don't have an appointment!" Patricia said.

"Pam, I don't need an appointment."

"It's *Patricia*, and you do have to have an appointment to see Ms. Dies. Everyone has to have an appointment! Hey, you can't go in there now, the director is—"

"Fine, I have an appointment," Vic said as he opened the door and walked in.

Plea Dies was sitting on top of her desk clad simply in pink bra and panties. Her eyes were closed, and incense was burning on the table just to her right. Her jaw dropped when she saw Vic at her door with Patricia a step behind.

"I told him he couldn't come in," Patricia said. "Get out! Get out now or I'll call the MPs." She stamped her foot.

Vic sat down and pulled a pack of cigarettes from his shirt pocket. "Hi, Plea," he said. "May I smoke?"

"I'm going to go get the dean," Patricia said, but she didn't move.

"I've got the information you need," Vic said as he took out a cigarette. "Gotta light?" he asked.

"Get out of my office! Now!"

"But, Plea, you asked me to get the cost information to you. I've done so." He fished some papers from his pants pocket, stood up and took another step toward Plea still atop her desk, clad only in her underwear.

"Sexual harassment!" she screamed.

"Sexual harassment?" Vic said. He was struggling not to laugh, but he couldn't prevent the grin from crossing his face.

"Don't you see I'm almost undressed?" Plea began to slide off her desk.

"Well, well," he said. "Now that you mention it. But I didn't undress you, nor did I make lewd comments to you, so, Plea, it isn't sexual harassment on my part. On the other hand, I could report you for sexual harassment, come to think of it. How dare you tempt me like that. It's so"—Vic paused for effect—"so unprofessional."

"What?" Plea said as she slipped off the desk and reached hastily for her blouse.

"I have grounds to report you for sexual harassment. Tell me why I shouldn't do so," he said.

"I'm going to get the dean," Patricia threatened as she stormed off.

"I won't file charges, though, Plea. I know you're sorry to have tempted me, so I won't make an issue of it."

"Thanks," said Plea as she pulled on her blouse. "Could you please leave now?" she said as she reached for her pants.

"Could you just approve my train fare first? Then I'll be happy to go."

"I'll get it to you later today."

"Plea, either I leave this office with approval in hand or I go straight from here to file a sexual harassment complaint against you."

"Okay, okay, I'll do it," Plea said as she pulled on her pants.

"Good," Vic said. Then he passed her the expensive version of his planned trip, which she signed hastily. After that, Vic moved toward the door.

"Next time I might not be so lenient with the sexual harassment charge."

With that he departed, closing the door as he left. On his way down the hall, he met Patricia coming back to her office. She squinted at him, mouth turned down in disgust.

"Did you find the dean, Pam?" Vic taunted.

"You'll be sorry for this. You'll be sorry," she said. "And my name is Patricia . . . you shit!"

"Ah, Pam. I see that words have failed you once again. Have a nice day."

***

Vic boarded the train, traveling in style on the Inter-City-Express. In the smoking compartment there were video screens, so he spent the entire trip to Aufdemfeld watching a movie, smoking and drinking coffee. On arrival he found Raz waiting for him on the track.

"Man, you really do have some pull," Raz said. "How did you get Plea to sign off on your taking this train?"

"I told her that if she didn't, I would have her up on sexual harassment charges."

"Right."

"Would I lie to you, Raz? Plea had her clothes off while I was in the office alone with her. She was really comin' on to me."

"Right. Want to get a coffee before the meeting?"

"No, but I wouldn't mind a beer."

"Okay, a beer it is. Shall we just go directly to the beer garden then?"

"Let's do that."

The beer garden was about a five-minute ride on the tram from the train station. It was a perfect day. The sun was out, the sky was blue, and there was a light breeze keeping the beer drinkers comfortable. If anyone thought it odd that Vic was rolling a suitcase behind him over the lawn, they didn't say so. Everyone seemed to be having a good time. Raz had reserved a couple of tables for 6 PM. He and Vic were an hour early. They found the tables unoccupied and took a seat. Before the meeting began Vic had downed a beer and Raz had finished a mineral water.

Vic remembered when he was first in Germany all those many years ago and had been warned about the dangers of drinking anything cold.

"It will ruin your health," one grizzly old beer drinker with a beer warmer in his mug told Vic. When Vic mentioned that in America people put beers in the fridge, his fellow imbibers sneered. Some even frowned in disgust. He thought they were nuts. Nowadays, he wasn't so sure.

Once the faculty meeting got underway, Vic began sipping his second beer. He was surprised at the convivial atmosphere of the meeting. The faculty in attendance, eight guys and seven gals from Raz's region, seemed satisfied with their lot at Philurius College, but they were wary of the central administration. In that they were in accord with Raz and Vic.

Some complained about the slowness of getting paid, others about the lack of communications from higher-ups. Vic promised, with a slight beer slur, that he would do everything in his power to correct the problems. He then presented the idea of offering these faculty members work elsewhere if they didn't have a full load with Raz. Like Raz, they were skeptical that headquarters would approve the travel pay, but they appreciated the offer.

After roughly an hour, much substantive work had been accomplished, so the meeting broke up. About half the people stayed for a bite to eat, though, and the conversation continued. Vic ordered his fourth beer and added bratwurst and sauerkraut with juniper berries. Soon he was laughing and trying to talk over the music of the oompah band. At some point he broke into song. Somehow, a couple of hours later, having conquered six beers, he was still able to make it to the train station with Raz. Within an hour Raz's wife Elena picked them up at the local station just a kilometer from Raz's house. Vic vaguely remembered saying hello to Elena, whom he was meeting for the first time. After that, all was a blur.

The next morning Vic was feeling relaxed and in good spirits, the best he had felt in ages. Elena fixed him and Raz a bacon, egg and tofu omelet, served with OJ and coffee, then said goodbye as she scurried out the door to catch a train to her job teaching English literature at Aufdemfeld University.

***

At 9 AM Raz and Vic left the house to catch a train to Nebeling for a morning meeting with the infamous AFCEO Soupy Kniebrecher. Soupy was cranky and certifiably committable according to absolutely everyone. Somehow, though, Raz had charmed him, and for quite some time, he had not threatened to abuse the Philurius College Programs in his realm.

Once they boarded the train, Raz headed straight for the restaurant car for a second cup of coffee.

"Think I'll join you," Vic said.

"How can you function at all this morning? Do you remember you had six beers last night?" Raz said.

"I did? No, I just remember having a great deal of fun. More fun than I've had in ages. That was a helluva faculty meeting, Raz."

"They're all more or less like that. But tell me truly, how you can function after all that beer?"

"I don't know. I really don't know. Normally, if I drink that much . . . you said six beers?"

"That's right. Six beers for a total of three full liters."

"Well, normally I'd be sick as a dog. It's a mystery."

"You think that's a mystery. Wait until you meet Soupy Kniebrecher."

"I've heard some tales about him. He sounds like another nutcase."

"He is, but he's actually harmless. All bark and no bite. At least that's my experience. Apparently he bit my predecessor, though. I remember the first time I met Soupy. He kept me waiting thirty minutes."

"Sounds like Plea."

"Yeah, it does. Well, after I was finally admitted into his noble presence, he just stared at me. I offered my name and my hand, but he just continued staring. Then he said, 'I just want you to know right away that I don't like you. I don't like Philurius College either. Not one damn bit. And I'm gonna make it my business to see that you fail here.'"

"Damn, Raz. The guy really is a lunatic, isn't he?"

"Certifiably nuts, just like everyone says. But we've been able to bring him around. He had frankly already ruined Philurius College in Nebeling. There were only three classes scheduled and we had no one to teach them because Soupy refused to have the scheduled faculty teach on *his* base, as he put it. They were too *right-wing* for him, so he barred them from teaching here. Somehow, he found out that they were registered Republicans, and that convinced him they were suspicious. Soupy then said that if these classes didn't go, it was the end of me and the end of Philurius College in his center."

"So, what did you do?" Vic asked.

Just then the waitress finally showed up at their table, and they each ordered a cup of coffee.

"That waitress looks like a brunette Eva, doesn't she?" Vic said.

"Eva? Who's Eva?"

"Man, Raz. You'd think you'd remember a beauty like that. Eva is that ash-blond waitress with the knockout body at the local Gasthaus in Rheinsteinheim, where we went to eat and drink after the regional directors' meeting."

"Okay, I know who you mean now. I just didn't know her name."

"How could you miss it? It's written in bold letters over her left breast."

The coffees arrived, and Vic insisted on paying. "I'm on expense account," he said proudly. "Okay, don't keep me in suspense any longer. How did you manage to win over this mental case with the goofy name Soupy Kniebrecher?"

"I promised him we would have faculty for all three classes, that they would be Democrats, and that the textbooks would be there on time, and, finally, that we would run all the classes no matter how few people were enrolled. The first thing I had to do, though, was to find and hire a field representative. The former employee had quit just a week earlier."

"That's when you hired Geoffry Lark."

"Right, and he has been excellent, always right on top of things. At any rate, I hired Geoffry, then I had to get faculty, so I sent three from

Aufdemfeld. They were grateful, since they had only one course each that term. Had to fight like hell to get them travel pay, though. When Malfatto found out, he threatened to fire me, but Ed somehow talked him out of it."

"Do you actually like that moron Ed Ehrgeiz?" Vic asked.

"I do. He's been real supportive of me."

"But you realize he's a snake oil salesman, don't you?"

"Well, sure, he does have some of that in him, but he's basically okay."

"Raz, he doesn't care a damn about higher education. Doesn't that bother you?"

"I think you're wrong about that, but I want to finish my story."

"You're hopeless, Raz. How can you be so generous about people?"

"Oh, I don't know. It's just one of my talents."

"Alright then, you hopeless optimist, finish your story. You're almost as bad as Jack, you know?"

"Thanks," Raz said. "Where was I?"

"I don't remember. It's your story, so why should I remember?" Vic clapped Raz on the shoulder and smirked.

"Oh yeah, I got the faculty set up, then I had to make sure the books were on time. It was too late to order them through the proper channels, so I called Ed, who had secretly stockpiled books for a long time. He sent me all I needed the next day. So, you see why I'm not hard on Ed?"

"No comment."

"Anyway, what happened was this. Two classes had five and six students signed up each, while the third course had just one. Since I had promised Soupy all the classes would go, I had to run them. The way I made it work was to teach the class with one person myself for no pay. With that I maintained the required regional average of twelve-plus enrollments. After the formal reports were submitted, I got another phone call from Malfatto, though, telling me I was fired for running these courses. What really bothered him was the travel pay for the three faculty from Aufdemfeld. Ed took care of that, too, somehow. Since then we've grown by leaps and bounds, and in the past year since I made Soupy that promise, we've never cancelled a course here in Nebeling. He likes us now, though you'd have a difficult time knowing it by the way he acts. So, just take him with a grain of salt. Smile and tell him you've heard exclusively good things about how he runs *his* center."

Vic just shook his head.

The meeting with Soupy went well. He told Vic right off the bat that he didn't like him and that he didn't like Dean Malfatto. On the latter point they were of one mind. Vic showered Soupy with compliments as Raz suggested, and at the end of the ninety-minute session, Soupy asked that Vic come back soon.

***

The next day Raz accompanied Vic to the Aufdemfeld Caserne where they jumped in a taxi. After telling the cabbie they wanted to go to the main train station, Raz started a conversation with the driver and at a certain point asked his name. The man replied in heavily accented English.

"My name is Willy from the King Street," he said. "Have you ever seen a picture of Hitler?" he asked out of the blue. The two Americans answered that they had. "Have you seen a picture of Mussolini?" he continued. They responded affirmatively. "Well, have you seen a picture of them together?" he asked as he looked for their response in his rearview mirror. Vic and Raz looked at each other. "No," they said in unison.

At that point Willy from the King Street pulled down his visor and pulled out a picture of Hitler and Mussolini at Brenner Pass. Also in the picture, off to one side, was a woman.

"Impressive," Raz said, not knowing what else to say. Vic, equally at a loss for words, offered, "Nice-looking woman."

"That was the secretary from Mussolini," Willy continued in his thick though understandable accent. "She's also the mother of my first kid."

"Hey, good work," Vic said.

The old cabbie smirked at him in the rearview mirror. "Got two more children with two more gals," he said proudly. "Second was also a boy. His mother was American, secretary to the commander here at this caserne. Third was a girl. Had her with an American tourist. Nice girl."

"Did you marry any of these women?" Vic asked.

"No, not me. I'm no marrying type," Willy said smugly.

"Are you still in touch with any of them?" Vic asked.

"Just with the mother of boy number two. He's a derelict, but I still like his mother. She lives here with a retired American officer she married right after she had our baby. I keep up with the other two occasionally, just so I can follow their lives. It's funny. All three live in this country now. In the same town."

"Do you ever see them?" Raz asked.

"Oh no, I just like to keep up with them," Willy said.

It was at this point that they reached the train station and left Willy from the King Street. That was the last they saw of him . . . that day.

CHAPTER ELEVEN
BONNIE'S IN TOWN

Vic had only been back from the field a few days when his wife, Bonnie, arrived. When he got to Mainstadt Airport his new bride was just minutes away from landing. Bonnie was a nurse who worked in the emergency room of a medium-sized hospital and had been an adjunct faculty member at the Southern Baptist college where she met Vic. She had just finished an obligatory cycle of her job at the hospital. Throughout their separation, she and Vic had kept up a lively correspondence, since overseas telephoning was too costly.

Part of Vic's package was a teaching position for Bonnie with the college's EMT program. Now that he had observed the program firsthand, Vic had developed serious doubts about whether Bonnie should take the job. Indeed, he had decided to put the brakes on her future with the college.

"Surely there is a better place for her over here," Vic had confided to Jack just a couple of days ago.

Bonnie's flight had been bumpy, and she had not been able to rest well. She was, in fact, exhausted. When her plane began to disembark its passengers, Vic was at the gate sipping a cup of strong black coffee.

As Bonnie waited for her luggage to pop up on the conveyor belt, Vic's mind roamed. It moved from Bonnie to the memos from Doris Kink again littering his desk, to Dean Malfatto's frog-like face, jaw moving up and down rapidly, nonsense pouring from the agitated hole in his head, back to Bonnie and finally to his full bladder. Vic rushed to the nearest WC as his wife pulled her last piece of luggage off the conveyor belt. Exiting the baggage claim area, expecting to find Vic's welcoming face and warm embrace, Bonnie found instead a bevy of smiling strangers. She sighed, moved to the side of the crowd and sat on one of her bags. Being left waiting wasn't new for her; however, before she had yawned thrice, Vic was there in front of her.

"Sorry, had to visit the latrine," he said apologetically as he took her in his arms.

"Latrine?"

"That's military talk for restroom," Vic said.

"I thought you hated the military."

"I used to, but that's before I got to know some soldiers personally. I've visited classes and have found the students to be quite all right. They're diligent and courteous—a lot more so than my stateside students. It's the military in general I don't like. The individual soldiers I like fine. In any case, after a while you just fall into this lingo. It's amazing."

"You mean this will happen to me, too?"

"No doubt," Vic said.

"Yuk!"

"Hey, I'm sorry I wasn't here when you came out."

"No problem, Vicarino," Bonnie said. "I knew you would show up at some point. You always do."

"Vicarino? Where did that come from?"

"You've told me so much about Malfatto, I thought I'd just give you an Italian-sounding nickname."

"That really isn't necessary," Vic said.

"I like it, Vicarino. It has a nice ring."

"Spare me, please. Just call me Dr. Wonderful."

"Okay, Dr. Wonderful. Come on, let's get outta here. The trip was rough, and I'm real tired."

"Fine, the car's just minutes from here," Vic said as he grabbed her bags and moved purposefully toward the closest exit. Before he had gone ten yards, he started trying to talk Bonnie out of taking her job with the college and was still at it as they got on the autobahn heading for Rheinsteinheim.

"It couldn't be as bad as you make out," Bonnie said wearily. "Besides, we need the money. Where else would I find a job over here?"

"Bonnie, there are all kinds of jobs advertised on base. You'll see. Philurius College is a loser. Believe me. The entire place is like the barren rock of Seriphus. Such an accumulation of ignorance is astounding. Unbelievable. It's not just the college, it's the whole military establishment. Even Eisenhower, that dyed-in-the-wool military man, was wary of the military-industrial complex."

"Vic, I'm going to take the job, so just let it go. This place really couldn't be as bad as you make out."

"It's worse. Believe me. You'll see soon enough. Just wait till you meet Dean Malfatto, that incoherent anti-intellectual baboon, a rimless zero, the original elephant in a china shop. Then there's Doris Kink, that green-eye-shade-wearing, bean-counting queen of Philurius College. Need I even mention Plea Dies? I've written you about all these people. The entire list is too long to run through now."

"Yes, you have mentioned these people. In detail. Hey, let's see how it works out. Okay? It's bull in a china shop, by the way."

"You'll see. You'll see. It won't work out. Bull, is it?"

In about an hour the freshly reunited couple drove into the parking lot of the military hotel, a four-story block building painted a dingy white and just off post.

"So, this is home, eh?" Bonnie said tiredly.

"Yes indeed. Home sweet home. It's actually better than it looks. We have a suite with a little kitchen. Then there's a laundry room downstairs, a decent restaurant and a bar. And if you need assistance with anything, the lobby is manned—actually it's usually *womanned*—around the clock."

"Do we have a bath and a bed?" Bonnie asked as she yawned and moved toward the door.

"Not only that, we have room service. We don't even have to make the bed." Vic was bubbling with enthusiasm.

"That's all fine and dandy, but what I'm interested in just now is a bath and a bed. In that order," Bonnie said as they made their way toward the front door of their new home, a home they shared with lots of transients, people on TDY, people PCSing, people just visiting, people like Gio Malfatto and Crepe Moertel dropping in for a quick lay, and a few semi-permanent residents like Vic and Bonnie.

"Do you think I should start right away with a German course?" Bonnie asked as she started her bath.

"First you should read Mark Twain's *A Tramp Abroad*," Vic said. "That'll prepare you for Germany. Yes, it will. But it might turn you off to the German language. That's the effect it had on Mencken and he's a better man than you'll ever be. German is a tough tongue to master."

"Well, you learned it, so it couldn't be that hard," Bonnie said as she finished undressing and stepped into the bath.

"First read *The Awful German Language*, an appendix to *A Tramp Abroad*, then talk to me. It's a fun piece to read, and it shows how irrational the German tongue is," Vic said.

"Will you help me?" Bonnie asked from the tub.

"I'll help you alright. Just get out of that bath and into the bed."

"I mean with German."

"No! I've had enough *der, die, das* to last me a couple of lifetimes."

"Okay, fine. I'll just sign up for a class."

"Read Twain first."

"Okay, I'll read Twain first. Could you come rub my back?"

"I'll start there if you like," Vic said. "By the way, you realize I married you just so you would have an ID card, even if you didn't get a job over here, don't you? I really don't believe in these formalities. It was just a practical step."

"My, aren't you romantic, you child of the '60s. At least my ex-husband believed in marriage," Bonnie said. "He believed in marriage in principle. It's just the reality part he had trouble with." She turned to Vic and put her hand on his cheek. "I prefer the opposite approach," she said. "Yours."

"That may be the nicest thing anyone has said to me since I've been here," Vic said.

"Hey, are you going to rub my back?" Bonnie asked. She took her hand from Vic's cheek and offered him her back.

"I'll start there if you like," he said once again.

"On second thought, make me a Manhattan first."

"Comin' up. Good. We'll start the lush life right away. I'll be back to your back in a jiffy."

***

That evening the newly reunited pair got dressed for dinner. It was "Mexican night." As they joined the buffet line in the hotel cafeteria Vic spied Ed Ehrgeiz and Maya Luft about ten yards ahead of them.

"Oh no," moaned Vic. "Those troglodytes had to be here to ruin the evening."

"What are you muttering about, Dr. Wonderful?" Bonnie said as she punched him gleefully in the ribs before grabbing hold of his left arm.

"I'm glad you're off of Vicarino," he said. "If you ever call me that again during the act, it's all over for us."

Bonnie laughed. "What or who did you see that's supposed to make our evening miserable?" Bonnie asked.

"Whom," he answered.

"What?"

"*Whom*," he said. "You should have used *whom*, not who. Whom is an object; who, a subject."

"Cripes," she said. "What or whom is, in your opinion, going to make our evening miserable?"

"This time *who* is the correct choice, but to your point, Ed Ehrgeiz and Maya Luft," he answered.

"Oh yeah. You wrote me about them, too. Why don't we see if we can sit with them?" Bonnie asked.

"Oh, what a grand idea. That'll make our day complete. Don't you remember anything I wrote you? This guy Ehrgeiz is a real weasel. He's masterful, I admit, and he has Malfatto in his pocket. If it weren't so sick, it would be comical."

"From what you wrote, I thought it was comical."

Vic looked at her and shook his head. "Bonnie, this man has no principles, and Maya apparently doesn't either."

"Come on, let's see if we can't sit with them," Bonnie said.

"I'd rather be beaten around the back with a whip," Vic said haughtily.

"That can be arranged," she said. "I'm going to have to meet them at some point, Vic. Don't you think it would seem funny for us to avoid them tonight?"

"Yes, I do. That would amuse me greatly."

At that very moment Ed Ehrgeiz turned and saw Vic and Bonnie, who caught his eye and smiled. He smiled back and said something to Maya. Then she looked back and waved at them.

"Ugh," Vic said.

Ed and Maya left their place in line, just a hair away from being served, and came back to join Vic and Bonnie.

"Vic, hi," Ed said, beaming. "You must be Bonnie," he continued as he offered his hand. "My name is Ed. Let me introduce you to Maya." At that he stepped aside, took Maya by the arm and brought her forward.

"It's a real pleasure to meet you, Bonnie," said Maya, her face aglow.

"Vic has told me about you two," Bonnie said cheerfully. The smiles seemed to freeze, but then Bonnie said, "He told me I'd find you fascinating. Why don't we sit together for dinner?"

"Let's do. Good idea," Ed said with gusto.

Bonnie seemed to have a good time during dinner. Vic somehow managed to be civil, but he had terrible indigestion for the remainder of the evening. After dinner they escaped Ed and Maya and headed to the Officers' Club bar. Settling in on the barstools, Vic greeted Kurt the bartender.

"Good evening, Kurt, my man," Vic began. "This is Bonnie, the lass I've been talking about, pining for. Bonnie, this is the world's best bartender, Kurt."

"Pleased to meet you, Kurt," Bonnie said.

"Likewise," he said.

"Is it true what Vic just said? That he talks about me constantly."

"He's mentioned you, but mostly he talks about some folks named Malfatto and Kink and Ehrgeiz."

"Just as I suspected, Vicarino. You exaggerate once again."

"It's not that, it's just that Kurt has a faulty memory. He is without doubt the world's premier bartender, but he does need some serious work on his short-term memory."

"What are you all having tonight?" Kurt asked cheerfully.

"How about two Becks? That okay with you, Bonnie?"

"That's fine by me," she answered.

It was a slow night at the bar, so when Kurt brought the beers he stayed and chatted for a while.

"How are things going over at Philurius, Vic?"

"Nothing has changed. Malfatto remains the idiot buffoon, Doris Kink counts beans all day and writes stupid memos about the experience, and Ed Ehrgeiz is out and about selling snake oil. It's enough to drive anyone nuts."

"You know Eva from the Gasthaus across the street, don't you?" Kurt asked.

Immediately Vic conjured up an image of the lovely Eva. Pleasure must have shown on his face, prompting Bonnie to jump into the conversation.

"What is it about this Eva that makes you glow, Vicarino? I know that look."

"Will you quit calling me that! Eva is just a nice young woman who works at a Gasthaus just off base," Vic said. "That's all."

"Don't worry, Bonnie. There's nothing going on between Vic and Eva. She's my lady. Has been for a couple of years now. We met when she was working for Malfatto. He was a light colonel then in the Army."

"Eva worked for Malfatto?" Vic asked, astounded.

"She did, and she despised the work, and him. I tried my best to like the man," Kurt said, shaking his head.

"But you were unsuccessful, I take it?" Vic asked.

"Completely," Kurt said.

"He remains 'light,' you know," Vic continued. "He was a light colonel, now he's a light dean . . . So, you and Eva are a couple. Congratulations."

"Thanks. She's something special," Kurt said. Then without missing a beat he asked, "What do you think about Doris Kink? Is she as bad as Malfatto?"

"She's not as bad, but she's bad enough. A real tight ass, and she does go out of her way to make my life miserable."

"Sorry to hear that," Kurt said. "Hey, I see another couple of customers just arrived. Talk to you more later."

Vic and Bonnie went home after a second beer. Bonnie fell asleep almost before she hit the bed. Vic, on the other hand, was wired, and it took a good bit of whiskey, followed by Tums, to get him ready to sleep some hours later. He was anxious about Bonnie's working for the college. Events would begin to roll in the morning, though, and he couldn't do much about them.

***

As they approached the caserne the next morning, Vic almost succumbed to a lethargy and despair he couldn't entirely explain. The building housing Philurius College loomed over him. It seemed to come alive, to grow arms extending out to grab him and stuff him into its monstrous gaping mouth of a door through which he would be swallowed, then, sliding down through the depths of the building, digested and eliminated. Vic shook himself and pushed the nightmare away.

Despite the horror of this image, he pushed the door open and held it for Bonnie. On the stairs between the first and second floors, they passed Mimi Braun, the young lady who had just been hired to work in the Development Office. She was, in fact, the Development Office. Her job was to create new advertising materials and to enhance the college's image, and she did so with pizzazz and skill. Mimi talked with them for a few minutes and promised to show Bonnie around Rheinsteinheim.

As they reached the second floor, Margaret Malcontenta-Jefferson opened the door, tripped and proceeded to fall onto Vic. The handful of memos she had been perusing fell to the floor as she rammed against his chest, her hands clutching his shoulders. That naturally perked him up.

He felt almost intimate with her. Margaret blushed slightly, apologized, picked up her papers and finally introduced herself to Bonnie, who looked askance at Vic as he started whistling while they mounted the stairs to the third floor and Vic's office.

Vic and Bonnie arrived ten minutes before her scheduled appointment with Plea Dies. That meant, Vic figured, that Bonnie would have at least another thirty minutes before the meeting started. Plea always kept people waiting. It was part of her strategy, something she had read somewhere about power politics in the office. She would also have her guests sit in a low chair just in front of her desk, as another display of dominance.

Vic stared at the ever-growing pile of paperwork on his desk, while Bonnie eyed his office. She was already planning how she would redecorate.

"Okay, let's get this over with. Let's make the rounds," Vic said.

"I'm ready to roll," she answered.

They stopped first at Jack Murphy's office where Bonnie met the Student Affairs crew. Jack then invited them into his private office where they talked about this and that until Vic checked his watch.

"Okay, it's time to go meet Plea Dies," he announced.

"Is this what you meant by the rounds?" Bonnie asked.

"Ah, we'll finish them later. There's plenty of time. Most of these people aren't worth meeting anyway," Vic added.

"Good luck," said Jack. "Has Vic briefed you on Plea?"

"Yeah, but I forgot everything he said."

"Just as well," Jack said. So, with that they were off to Plea's office.

***

Plea Dies rose as the couple entered her office. The aroma of sandalwood incense lingered, mixing with the smell of freshly brewed apple tea. The only difference Vic could notice from the last time he had been in Plea's office was that Plea was fully dressed. She extended her hand to Bonnie.

"Welcome aboard, Mrs. Sawyer," Plea said as she shook Bonnie's hand. "It's a pleasure to have you here at Philurius. Won't you have a seat? Oh, Dr. Sawyer," she said, acknowledging him for the first time.

"You can pull up a chair if you'd like . . . but perhaps you'll need to be getting back to work."

"No problem," Vic said. "I'll just run along. Ciao."

An hour later Bonnie showed up in his office again. "That woman is really cracked," she said.

CHAPTER TWELVE
ALARM BELLS

Dean Malfatto had just cancelled the Monday top staff meeting, ordering everyone back to work except Doris Kink and Margaret Malcontenta-Jefferson, whom he ordered into his office. Vic and Jack were stunned.

"Has he ever just cancelled a meeting like this before?" Vic asked.

"No, never," Jack responded. "It's completely out of character. He loves his bully pulpit. What do you think it means?"

"Perhaps we're getting his goat," Vic said. He had the suspicion, though, that the secret meeting had something to do with him. "Let's meet for lunch, Jack. I've got to continue reviewing the faculty signed up to teach in all the centers to make sure none of these grandfathered folks or any new unqualified people have been given courses, so I can't talk now."

"Have you found any problems yet?" Jack asked.

"I've run across two faculty members who don't yet have their paperwork submitted. One of them doesn't have a degree at all, but he's apparently a computer wizard. That's something we can work with, I suppose, but at some point we have to establish guidelines. The other one claims to have a master's degree in English literature, but you ought to see his application letter; it's loaded with improper syntax and misspellings. Then there's Don Dingsbums. He's scheduled to teach two government classes, but he only has a bachelor's in political science. Perhaps we can make a case for him since the classes are introductory, but it isn't ideal."

"I hope those are the only problems you have," Jack said. "Those you can deal with somehow."

"We'll see," Vic said. "I'm not even a third of the way through the faculty list yet, and I've put the bulk of the video cassette courses aside for now. That program could cause us some serious trouble with the accreditation team."

"It could indeed. Hey look, I'll help you go through this paperwork, but I'll have to do it after hours. I'm helping my team get everything together for our section of the accreditation team report right now, and that takes a lot of my time," Jack said. "Gotta get back to work now. How about lunch at twelve?"

"You're on," Vic said.

***

When Jack entered Vic's office at 11:30, he brought some alarming news. "Did you hear what happened to Don Dingsbums? He just got the boot. He's fired," Jack said.

"Really? Why?" Vic said.

"Well, here's Plea's story. I told her I wanted to go to Don's region next week to do academic evaluations, and she told me that I should postpone my trip because Don has been cited for sexual misconduct by three women here at headquarters and is on his way out, and that I should wait until his replacement is on the job."

"What? How's that possible? The man's been set up. He hasn't been here for a month. How could he have harassed anyone in absentia?" Vic scoffed. "You know what I think of him, but his being railroaded like that is unconscionable."

"Absolutely! We ought to protest it, but Don has been lurking around here off and on this month," Jack said, "so he would have had opportunity to harass three women. I heard from a couple of people that he was hanging around Plea's apartment. Maybe she is one of the three. I saw him once myself. He was walking down the street close to her place, dressed in a long flowing green robe, red beads around his neck and wearing sandals. He's also shaved his head. I didn't recognize him at first."

"That was Don Dingsbums?" Vic asked. "I saw that apparition hanging out in front of the post library, but it looked nothing like Dingsbums to me. You sure it was him? . . . This smells fishy. He should at least have a chance to defend himself. Think I'll go down to see the dean."

***

Sitting at her immaculately ordered desk, Doris Kink felt wonderful. Today she had exacted her revenge on Don Dingsbums, and it had bolstered her self-esteem. At her core, she had felt inferior for a very long time, so recently she had been practicing affirmations, repeatedly telling herself that she was born to be great. Today, however, she didn't need affirmations.

The truth is that Doris was born poor in Los Angeles. Aside from her school lunch, which she brought from home, Doris never had a meal out of the house until she left home at age eighteen. She never had her hair cut professionally until she attended university, and then only twice a year. Her father was a salesman, but not a very good one. Her mother cleaned up at the local high school, which Doris attended. This embarrassed her immensely. Her parents were completely decent folks who just never managed to get it together, but what Doris saw was simply failure and shame. She was determined to do better in life. Doris reviled anyone who was condescending, or anyone she perceived as a threat.

Her parents had experienced the Depression as children. They had in fact known each other but had never gone out. In the fifties Doris's mother worked as an au pair on a short trip to Europe, where she was seduced by a German man. She took his address with her, hoping to keep in touch but without knowing that she was pregnant.

Doris's mother confessed her situation to John Kink, a longtime admirer. She was grateful when he offered to marry her. After giving birth, she wrote the biological father about his daughter, asking to break off communications, as she was now happily married. What happened was that the real father occasionally sent money to lend help to his daughter. Since the Kinks needed the money, Doris's mother accepted the gifts and wrote updates on Doris, who never knew anything about any of this.

Sitting in her office, feeling smug about Don's misfortune, which she had engineered, Doris embarked on the next stage of her attack on Vic.

She sat at her typewriter to draft a memo to him. She began with *Dr. Vic Sawyer,* then stopped and crossed out the *Dr.* with a flourish. That made her feel better, too. She put the finished memo in her "to be delivered immediately" box, which Crepe checked every half hour.

To: Vic Sawyer

From: Assistant Dean Doris Kink

Re: Change in duties for Academic Affairs Record Clerk Antonia Somalento and Academic Affairs Secretary Mary Cazzolino

As of Monday, next week, Antonia Somalento will be reassigned to my office, due to the increased work load I have been given. Mary Cazzolino will continue as your secretary, and she will take over the duties as records clerk but without an increase in pay. The Office of Academic Affairs has long been overstaffed, and we must be even more diligent these days in order to meet campus budget requirements.

***

Before he walked into Dean Malfatto's office, Vic was stopped by Crepe Moertel, who occupied her normal post just outside the dean's door.

"Have you got an appointment?" she asked as she lifted her chin like a dog waiting for a stick.

Vic turned wearily toward her. "Don't any of you underlings have a different line?" he said.

Crepe lifted her chin even higher. "Would you like to make an appointment?"

"Yes, Crepe, I would like to make an appointment, and I would like to make it for now."

"The dean is busy now, so you'll have to wait," she answered.

Just then, Malfatto burst out of his door, nearly running into Vic. "What the hell do you want?" he asked roughly. "Don't you ever work?"

Vic started counting to ten. This time he made it to four before he answered. "I have a couple of items I'd like to discuss with you and Doris Kink."

"I'm busy," Malfatto said. "Don't you see I'm on my way out?"

"This will only take a few minutes, and it's time sensitive," Vic said. "It has to do with six courses which won't be running this term if we don't take the proper action. That could mean a significant loss of revenue and a lot of flak from a couple of AFCEOs."

The dean stopped and stared at Vic, like a pit bull ready to attack. "Get in here. I can give you ten minutes max. Crepe, get Doris in here. Now!" With that he stormed into his office, Vic on his heels. Within a minute, Doris had arrived, her yellow legal pad and matching pen in hand. Both the dean and his assistant were surprised that the topic was Don Dingsbums. Malfatto did not budge on the decision to fire Don from his administrative job, but Vic had another point.

"I didn't know he was signed up to teach all those classes, did you?" Malfatto asked Doris. She just pursed her lips. A heated discussion followed which lasted almost half an hour. Doris was against letting Don teach.

"We can find someone else," she said. "We should make a clean break with him."

In the end, Vic convinced the dean that there was no one else on file who could teach these courses, and the dean sided with him for the first time since Vic had been at Philurius. It was a minor victory, but he was proud of it. Doris, however, was furious. As Vic left Malfatto's office, Crepe handed him Doris Kink's memo concerning the loss of Antonia Somalento. He ranted and raved, but this one he lost.

***

It was late, and Doris was still at her desk when the telephone rang. It was Bean.

"Doe, it's almost ten. What the hell are you still doing at work, and why didn't you call?"

Doris looked at her watch. "Oh my. Sorry, I just lost track of the time. It's been a hell of a day. The term starts soon, and on top of that, I've spent a lot of time fighting Vic Sawyer."

"That's a good reason for you to come home now. I'll heat up the dinner I cooked for you earlier. And, Doris, I've got to take some vacation."

"What?" she said.

"Vacation. You know, time off from work."

"But you just started! You haven't accumulated any vacation days. You have to work a year before you can take vacation."

"You mean I'll be going AWOL?"

"I mean, you can't take vacation now."

"What shall we call it then? Sick days?"

"What the hell is this all about? I thought you were done with these disappearing acts. You have responsibilities to the company."

"Will you quit talking like some Fortune 500 executive? This is a college, not a company."

"I can't believe this. You've fallen in with Vic Sawyer and his crowd."

"Doe, in your deepest heart you know it sounds dumb and pretentious to call this college a company."

"Look, that's not the point. You always try to change the point. You have to show some sense of obligation. I got you this job. If you just pick up and leave, it makes me look bad."

"I told you. I don't need this job," Bean said. "Besides, I'm ill. It's the two-week flu and I have to go south to get rid of it. Really, Doe, this is a quick in, quick out job. Besides, all the tapes and books are already distributed to all centers, and since you are assigning that cute Antonia Somalento to me part time, she can take care of any day-to-day business until I get back."

"Dammit, Bean. Are you going to tell me what this is about?"

"No, sweetheart. Remember our deal? I'll be back in a couple of weeks. I promise."

That night the couple quarreled again at home, then made up, made love and went to bed. Bean slept soundly, rose at dawn, dressed and slipped out quietly with a bag he had packed the night before.

CHAPTER THIRTEEN
VIC'S FACULTY MEETING

Eighteen faculty had been signed up to attend the first meeting for Philurius College faculty at headquarters when the cancellations began to come in by telephone. Eight people had already withdrawn before Vic found out what had happened. Raz called him directly with the news. Malfatto had sent out a memo that Philurius College would pay for just one meal at midday, and there would be no reimbursement for travel and overnight expenses.

As soon as he got off the phone with Raz, Vic headed to the dean's office. Arriving at Crepe's desk, he stormed past her into Malfatto's inner chamber. As usual, Malfatto was sipping coffee, eating a doughnut and working the crossword puzzle.

"What the hell are you trying to do?" Vic screamed.

"Get the hell outta here, you nonconformist!" Malfatto yelled back. It was a word he had learned from Bill McMurphy, and this was the first chance he had had to use it.

"Not until I get an answer for, or better yet a retraction of, the memo you sent out on my faculty meeting. What nonsense! Every other meeting we have had up here has included travel pay, overnights and a per diem. I sent out the standard letter for this meeting. What the hell are you trying to do, and why the hell didn't you inform me?" Vic's eyes blazed. His heart was pounding.

"You don't understand the financial crisis we're in!" Malfatto said as he pulled on his tie and sat up in his chair. "We just got a note from the president telling us we were over $100,000 in the hole!"

"Then if we cut your job and hers," he said, moving his head toward Crepe, who was standing in the doorway, mouth agape, "we'll be in the black, and no one will miss either one of you."

"Out! Get outta here, you SOB, or you're fired. Fired! You understand fired?"

"What kind of whore are you? You let our money-grubbing president pull you around by the nose on a regular basis. Don't you have any character? Don't you have any common sense? And why doesn't he call the 25 percent above overhead that we are required to turn over to campus profit? That's what it is! If we make a profit, we aren't in the hole!"

"You're fired, Sawyer! I want you outta here today, and if you don't leave my office now, I'm going to call the MPs!"

"If you had any balls, you'd try to throw me out yourself!"

Just then Doris Kink swept in.

"Vic," she said. "We sent you a memo on this, which you probably didn't read. I've noticed that a lot goes by you."

It was true that Doris had written such a memo, but she hadn't sent it.

"Look, we've got new financial considerations to deal with. You just have to accept the new facts."

"Why?" he said, still fuming, still glaring at Malfatto. Then he turned on her. "You planned this, didn't you? The Executive Element, as you so stupidly call yourselves, planned this absurdity! You see, I do read memos. How the hell did you come up with this absurd designation for you and your numbnuts boss here?"

With that Vic made a rude, dismissive gesture and left the room. He walked past Doris and Crepe and made for his office.

Once Vic had rounded the corner, Doris closed the door to the dean's office. "I think we've gotten the son of a bitch so angry this time that he'll present his resignation," she said.

Back at his desk, Vic lit a cigarette at the wrong end, crushed it out and reached for another. After lighting the second one, he just watched the smoke float gently toward the ceiling, while his free hand put a death grip on the right arm of his chair.

***

"No, you can't just fire him today," Doris Kink said to Dean Malfatto. "You can't just fire someone like that. You've got to build a file. Look," she continued, "if he doesn't resign, we can write him a reprimand for his use of unprofessional and abusive language and for insubordination. There were witnesses, so we are clear there. Unfortunately, he didn't take our bait and make the scene I thought he would make when we took his secretary away, but this time we've got him. I'll get the reprimand to your desk in fifteen minutes," Doris said, "but I'm convinced he's just going to quit."

"But I want the SOB gone today! Today! Capish?"

"We can't do it that way, believe me. You fire him today, and you'll be out the door soon yourself if he contacts a halfway decent lawyer over at JAG. Look, there's a whole bureaucracy out there that will back us up if we go about this in the right way."

"You mean I really can't fire him today?"

"Right. But like I said, I think he'll quit. He was beside himself when he left here. Now, let me go write that reprimand. If Sawyer comes back, just refuse to see him. Got it?"

"Alright, dammit, you handle it."

***

Vic got the letter of reprimand from Dean Malfatto later that day stating that it would become part of his permanent file. After that Vic went immediately to Jack's office and told him what happened.

"I'm quitting," Vic said. "I've had all of this crap I can take." Jack couldn't convince him to reconsider. After blowing off steam for a few more minutes, Vic went home. He found Bonnie preparing for a course she was to start the next week. Somehow, after hours of agony, she convinced him not to give up.

"You've got to fight them," she said. "You've just got to. You'll get support," she said. "Lots of people can't stand those two morons, the so-called Executive Element. Man, that is truly a goofy name."

The next day Vic showed up for work only to find another letter in his inbox informing him that this was a formal reprimand for leaving the workplace during work hours without authorization. *Three strikes and you're out* was the way the letter ended.

On Friday the faculty meeting did take place, but with only five persons in attendance. Two of Ed's local faculty were there, and Raz had driven his two faculty members up and stayed at Jack Murphy's place; the other two had been accommodated on air mattresses on the deck of Ed and Maya's boat.

The meeting took place on the third floor of the college building in the conference room. In attendance, aside from Raz and the four other faculty members, were Jack, Plea and Vic.

Vic was about to open the meeting when Crepe barged in.

"The dean wants to see Raz Rabin in his office. Now," she said.

Everyone just looked at her as she stood in the doorway with hands on her hips, a pout on her face—petulance personified.

"He's in a meeting," Vic said dismissively.

Crepe cringed. "He's not even supposed to be here," she sputtered. "He's not a faculty member."

"Just go away," Vic said wearily.

"Of course he's faculty," Jack said. "He's been teaching a course every term for as long as I've been here. Where have you been, Crepe?"

"Well," she said. "He shouldn't be teaching. It affects his efficiency as a regional director."

"*Basta*! Get out of my meeting. Now!" Vic shouted.

Crepe backed up, tripping on the threshold of the door. "He'd better come now," she said, a bit less confidently.

Vic glowered at her as she departed. After a few seconds of stunned silence, someone started applauding. Then everyone joined in except for Plea. Vic was still fuming, but he was pleased to have made Crepe look stupid.

"I guess I'd better go see him," Raz said when the applause had died.

"The hell you will," Vic snarled.

"I won't be long. Maybe I can divert him for a while, so you can actually have some undisturbed time in here. Someone is going to take notes and write a protocol, so I'll just miss a bit of the fun being in on the discussions."

Vic shrugged. "Suit yourself."

Raz sighed, got up and meandered down to the dean's office.

"He had a good idea before he left," Jack said.

"You mean about diverting His Dumbness the Dean?" Vic said.

"Dr. Sawyer," Plea protested. "You are being unprofessional."

"Plea," he answered, "I'm just being forthright. Our great leader was being unprofessional when he changed the rules and refused to pay for travel and meals for these faculty members, and even more reprehensible was that he did not inform me!"

"I think you should apologize to the group," she said, ignoring his statement.

"Finally, a good idea," Vic said. "I want to formally apologize for the misunderstandings surrounding this faculty meeting. My problem was in assuming that it would be treated in the same manner as all other meetings since I've been here. In that, as you know, I was sadly mistaken. Without my knowledge, the dean of this college sent you a message contradicting mine. I appreciate your attending even though you have to pay for the trip and a couple of meals yourselves. Again, please accept my sincere apologies. Now, let's get to work and see what we can do to make sure you continue to have work." Then, before he went any further, he looked at Plea. "Was that okay?" he asked.

Plea ignored him and poured some spice tea into her college cup.

***

Raz sauntered in past Crepe Moertel, who glared at him. "Is he in?" asked Raz, gesturing toward the dean's closed door.

"He's waiting for you," she said.

Raz smiled at her and then knocked on the door.

"Come in," yelled the familiar voice from the other side.

Raz opened the door and entered. The setting was familiar. He had been in this room numerous times, none of them particularly pleasant. The heavy white carpet had even more coffee stains on it than he recalled. Malfatto's huge oak desk dominated the room, which lacked any decoration aside from the dean's large brown cushioned chair and the gray military-issue chair in front of the desk. Before Raz could take a seat, Dean Malfatto started his tirade.

"What the hell do you think you're doin'?"

"In regard to what?"

"You know what I'm talkin' about."

"No, I'm afraid I don't. May I sit down?"

"I oughta to fire you on the spot."

Raz sat down. "Why?" he asked. He had heard all this before.

"Don't you ever work? What are you doin' up here at a faculty meeting?"

"I teach, too."

"Well you shouldn't. We pay you to be a regional director. That's what you should be doin', but you don't. You come up here to have a good time at the college's expense."

"Hardly."

"What do you mean, hardly?"

"You haven't paid for my trip, neither travel nor at least three of my meals. And the meal you are paying for, I hear, will consist of a BLT and potato chips. We have to provide our own drinks. I'm hardly costing you money."

Malfatto was stymied for a moment. Apparently, he had forgotten his memo. After all, Doris had written it.

"But time is money."

"That's a non-sequitur."

"You're just like Murphy and Sawyer," Malfatto said.

"Thank you," Raz said.

"Murphy told me you've published an article. Is that true?"

"It is."

"Did you do it on company time?"

"I beg your pardon?"

"I'll bet instead of working you wrote this article on company time."

"No, wrong again. I wrote it on my lunch and coffee breaks." Raz, a temperate man, was losing his patience.

"Murphy even thought we should put this news about you in the monthly newsletter. You know what I told him?"

Raz did know. Jack had mentioned to him that Malfatto had said, "We can't do that. He's an administrator."

"You said you wouldn't allow a write-up about me because I'm an administrator. It's okay. I don't need a write-up in the newsletter."

"It sets a bad example for other regional directors."

Raz was wearying. "I suppose you're right. I won't do it again."

"Good. I hope not."

"Okay, I'll get back to the meeting now if it's alright with you."

"Just a minute. There's somethin' else I need to talk to you about."

Raz sighed and sat back in the chair, waiting for the next surprise.

"What have you been doing in Sauberbach?"

Raz looked at Dean Malfatto curiously. "Where should I start?"

"You might start with telling me why you're trying to start illegal courses there."

"What do you mean?" Raz said.

"Don't play dumb with me, Rabin. Read this." He shoved a letter across his desk in Raz's direction. Raz picked it up and started reading.

Gio,

I must let you know that I'm very disappointed with your RD Raz Rabin and with your FR in Sauberbach Miranda Maples. They directly contacted a unit and set up a course without letting the AFCEO Ms. Ungeheuer know about it. They did not even talk to an ESP! This procedure is strictly against SOP, and I expect you to handle the matter ASAP. This was a real SNAFU. Ms. Ungeheuer can no longer work with either Ms. Maples or Mr. Rabin. I'm sure you will handle this matter to my satisfaction. Please contact me before I go TDY tomorrow, ETD 07:00.

Sincerely,

Bill McMurphy, Director CETPM

Raz sighed again, looked up and shoved the letter back in Malfatto's direction, suddenly feeling washed out.

"Well, what do you have to say about that?" Malfatto said.

"It's complete nonsense. It never happened."

"Then how do you explain this?" Malfatto said as he pushed another piece of paper at Raz. He picked it up and looked at it briefly before sliding it back across the table. It was an announcement of a course offered by the college for a military unit in Sauberbach.

"Well?" Malfatto snarled. "How do you explain that? The course is scheduled for next month, and you and Miranda Maples didn't clear it. Do you think this unit just made this up?"

"They contacted Miranda about such a course, and she advised them they would have to go through channels. As far as I know, that's what happened."

"So, you're trying to blame this all on her. Why don't you admit responsibility?"

Raz glared at Malfatto, imagining his nose elongating and retracting rapidly, like an overweight Pinocchio.

"What are you smiling about, Rabin?" Malfatto yelled.

"The absurdity of this conversation," Raz said. "Look, I don't know anything more than what I've just told you. I'll check it out, though."

"Are you sure that's all you know?" Malfatto asked.

Raz paused, then decided to make a clean breast of it. "No, I also know that Ms. Ungeheuer has had it in for Miranda for a good long time. She in fact insisted that I fire Miranda just a month ago. I also know that Ms. Ungeheuer is Bill McMurphy's lover. Does that help you?"

Caught by surprise, Malfatto simply gawked at Raz a moment before responding. "Really? Ungeheuer and McMurphy are gittin' it on?"

Raz just lifted his eyebrows. Then the dean went back on the attack.

"What should I do about this letter from Bill McMurphy?"

"Tell him you are looking into the matter and that you will discuss it with the parties concerned."

"But Ms. Ungeheuer says she can't work with you or Miranda. What do I do about that?"

"The most reasonable thing for you to do would be to do what I just suggested."

"Well, I'll tell you what I'm gonna do. You are never to set foot in the area again, and I'm going to fire Miranda Maples myself. And there's nothing you or anybody else can do about it. Now get out of here."

As Raz left, he clicked his heels and saluted Malfatto, and on his way out blew Crepe Moertel a kiss. Then he went back to the meeting and sketched odd forms on white notebook paper for the rest of the day.

After the meeting, Vic and Jack took Raz to the Officers' Club. Over drinks they fumed and ranted once again about how messed up things were at Philurius College. At the end of the day, they decided to meet again the next morning at Muldaner's.

CHAPTER FOURTEEN
RECONNAISSANCE

When Vic, Jack and Raz arrived at the Muldaner Café Saturday morning it was almost full. The disenchanted trio found a corner table by a window from which they could see a row of half-timbered houses, some burgeoning with overhanging red geraniums and blue veronica. The blended scents of brewing coffee and aromatic tea spices soon put them in a better mood.

They began the day philosophizing about the military. Raz, the only one of the three who had served, recounted his experience as a soldier. He told them about joining the Army after high school, and how he had suffered through basic training in the summertime at Fort Polk, Louisiana.

Although Raz had been around the military all his life, following his father around the world, basic training was still a shock. Somehow the reality of a war going on in Southeast Asia had not fully dawned on him until he was instructed to use a bayonet to stab little straw figures dressed in black while yelling "KILL, KILL, KILL" with some 200 other guys. These little straw figures were alternatively called *Charlie* or *Gooks*. It was with their assistance that Raz learned the spirit of the bayonet. He would rather have been learning almost anything else.

At night after lights-out he would study his soldier's manual under his covers with a flashlight. When he read that "Most recruits think they won't make it through basic training, but most do," he almost wept. As it turned out, he made it through with flying colors, graduating in the top 5 percent of his company and receiving an early promotion to E-2.

"Yeah, the military is schizo," Raz said. "On the one hand, you have all this craziness I've been telling you about. On the other hand, there is a great deal of pride one attains by overcoming major obstacles, the biggest of which is oneself. And then there is the discipline and respectfulness which are necessary qualities for having a good and successful life."

"You've got something there," Vic said. "The students we get are by and large very good, but then you have the absurdity of the war machine. When does respectfulness become authoritarianism?"

"The military makes men," Jack offered. "And it also makes robotic idiots. Look at Malfatto."

After a while the talk turned to the problems at Philurius College. "No one can help us," Vic said. "I belong to the NAAF, the supposed savior of academic freedom and faculty rights, but I don't know why. It must be a relic I hold on to from my idealistic days." Vic shrugged as the waitress arrived at their table. They all ordered another round of coffee and *Bienenstich* and talked about life, literature, philosophy and food until lunchtime, always coming back to the problems they faced at Philurius.

Just as the group was about to call it a day, Kurt the bartender and his alluring waitress girlfriend, Eva, appeared. Vic waved to them and got two chairs from a neighboring table.

"What brings you all to Muldaner's? I've never seen you here before," Vic said as Kurt and Eva took their seats.

"That's because this is our first time here. I've listened to you and Jack talk about this place for so long, I just thought we'd give it a try," Kurt said.

"You won't be sorry," Jack assured him.

"Where's Bonnie?" Eva asked. "She's nice. I'm glad you brought her around the other day."

"Shopping. That's her favorite pastime. It's a passion, in fact. At least she gets great deals. My only problem with that is that she gets deals we don't need."

"A woman after my own heart," Eva said.

"So, what do you all do here aside from plot against Malfatto and company?" Kurt asked after the waitress had left.

"Unfortunately, that's our most frequent topic of conversation," Vic said. "Sick, isn't it?"

"Perhaps, but I understand," Kurt said. "Eva and I discussed the whole Malfatto business, and we have decided to help you get him."

"And why would you want to do that?" Vic asked.

Kurt turned to Vic. "I told you Eva worked for Malfatto when he was a lieutenant colonel here. She was his private secretary. What I didn't tell you is that she filed sexual harassment charges against him. Somehow, we still don't know how, the charges were squashed, and Eva lost her job. She's still livid about it, though she never shows it."

"That sonofabitch," Jack said.

"I think we can all agree on that," Kurt said. "So, you all let us know how we can be of service to you, and we'll help you nail the guy."

"It would be good if you could tap his phone and bedroom," Vic said sarcastically. "Then we could get him on a series of improprieties."

"I could do that and more," Kurt offered nonchalantly.

"You could?" Vic asked.

"Sure. I was in military intelligence, and before that I worked for a while with the FBI. Learning to tap people's residences was my specialty. Shall I tap Doris Kink, as well?"

"Well, yes," Vic said. "Yes, by all means, put a bug on her, too."

"That won't help much in an official way," Kurt said. "An illegal tap wouldn't be admitted in court. We could embarrass them, though, or threaten to. They need to be stopped. I'll get right on it."

"Whatever expenses are involved, we'll share them equally," Vic said. He looked at Jack and Raz. They nodded. There was electricity in the air.

CHAPTER FIFTEEN
DRAWING THE LINE

The next Monday morning, Vic Sawyer sat in his office once again contemplating the mound of memos from Doris Kink. *Monday mornings are bad enough without this kind of insult,* he thought, closing his eyes and wishing the memos away. When he opened his eyes again, they were, however, still there. He picked up one at random.

To: Vic Sawyer, Director of Academic Affairs
From: Doris Kink, Assistant Dean
Subj: Clearance of Faculty
It has come to my attention that several applications for clearance have been in your office for over three weeks without any action being taken. Some of these clearances are crucial. Of most pressing concern are the three applicants for EMT. We are in desperate need of teachers for classes beginning soon in Sauberbach, Würstberg and Nebeling. If we do not provide teachers, we are in default of contract. I'm sure you will act on these applications first thing Monday morning. To refresh your memory, the applicants are Clara Bell, Mike Michaels and Dr. Souter Liedekens. I expect to get word from you on these clearances by midday Monday.

"Who the hell does she think she is?" Vic fumed. He made himself a cup of coffee and tried to calm his nerves. Sitting at his desk again, Vic set up his typewriter and began composing an answer to Doris Kink's first memo.

Doris,

For ages I've pointed out to Margaret that we have no record indicating that Clara Bell has completed her certification. It isn't adequate for you to tell me she finished the course. We actually have to have a piece of paper which verifies her completion. Until I see that piece of paper, she cannot be cleared to teach. End of discussion. The two gentlemen you mention don't have copies of their official transcripts on file in this office. You know quite well what the rules are. You should not let courses be scheduled for which there are no qualified and cleared faculty available. This is your problem, so go solve it elsewhere and quit bothering me about it.

VS

After finishing, Vic leaned back in his chair, more relaxed now. Then he read the next memo.

To: All Staff
From: Doris Kink, Assistant Dean
Subj.: Dress Code

As of immediately, a new dress code is in force. In order to present a congruent image, men in this organization will wear blue blazers, gray pants, white button-down shirts and yellow company ties. Shoes will be black and highly polished. Spit-shine not required. One company tie will be given free of charge to each male employee. Female employees may also have ties if they so desire. Those female personnel wishing to have ties will also be given them at no charge. The rest of the clothing you must pay for due to budgetary constraints. For blazers and gray slacks, please contact Ed Ehrgeiz. He will be able to get discounts for buying in bulk. You will need to get Ed your sizes by this Friday. Women will wear dark-colored business suits and white blouses. If you would like a company tie, please let it be known. If women need assistance with clothing, contact Maya Luft for discount prices. This policy takes effect at latest by the beginning of next month. Fridays will be casual-dress days.

Vic was steaming again. He took pen to hand and wrote boldly at the bottom of the memo:

Doris,
This is absurd. Count me out. Was this your idea, or did you have help from Ed Ehrgeiz and Dean Malfatto?
VS

He threw the memo in his Doris Kink basket and reached for the next note.

To: Vic Sawyer, Director of Academic Affairs
From: Doris Kink, Assistant Dean
Subj.: Sexual Sensitivity Classes
You will be required to attend a class on sexual sensitivity at the first opportunity. Several complaints have been made about your insensitivity to women employees of this organization. In fact, charges of sexual harassment were about to be filed. I interceded on your behalf so that charges will not be filed. For your good, however, and for the good of the company, you will be required to attend a three-week course given by the military on sensitivity training and sexual harassment. The next course begins on Monday. We expect you to be there. Contact Plea Dies for details. We have decided not to dock your pay for the time you are away from the office.

Vic's pulse raced as he picked up his pen and wrote furiously.

Doris,
You've got to be kidding. Will Malfatto be there? If so, he won't see me. If anyone wants to bring a sexual harassment suit against me, let her do so. In the meantime, try to find something useful to write about!
VS

Vic threw the memo into the wicker basket with the other two, then got up and stalked around the room for a few minutes. Deciding to get some perspective, he stomped out of his office and over to Jack Murphy's, who was sitting at his desk yawning as Vic came in.

***

"Hey, Vic. What's happenin', man?

"Got some memos from Kink, the assassin."

"Yeah, me too. Have you looked at yours yet?" Jack said.

"I have, and they've turned me into a raging bull once again."

"I keep tellin' you, man. Don't let her get under your hide."

"Jack, she told me I had to clear people I can't clear according to stated Philurius College policy. Then she informs me I have to buy a uniform to wear to work. So far, it's just the normal Kink nonsense, but then she writes me that I have to go to sensitivity classes and that there have been sexual harassment complaints made about me! Can you believe that?"

"That's funny," said Jack with a grin. "Want some coffee?"

"Naw, I want to kick Doris Kink's butt."

"Do you mean literally or figuratively?"

"You're a schmuck, Murphy. Have you read the memo to all staff about the new dress code?"

"Nope, what's it say?"

"Don't you ever read your memos?" Vic said.

"Never before eleven," Jack said as he got up. "Come on. Let's take a coffee break. You need to get outta here for a while."

Vic looked at him dangerously. "It's just now 9:30," he said. "You know the rules about coffee breaks. We get fifteen minutes in the morning between 10:30 and 10:45 and fifteen minutes in the afternoon between 3:30 and 3:45. These are the Executive Element's newest rules, which apply to everyone except the Executive Element. We've got to do something about that lunatic duo."

"You mean, of course, between 15:30 and 15:45," Jack said. "Come on, let's go over to the snack bar."

"How about my office," Vic offered.

Jack looked at him and scratched his beard. "The coffee's better at the snack bar," he said. "Besides, it would do us good to get out of this hell hole."

"Remember what that last memo threatened? Three strikes and you're out. C'mon, let's go to my office." He turned to go, then turned back to Jack. "Why don't you buy a coffee pot for your office?" he asked.

"Because I would have one less excuse for getting out of my office from time to time. Okay, let's go drink some of your nasty joe."

A couple of minutes later Vic read Jack the latest Doris Kink dictate. Then he asked for Jack's thoughts. "How about the uniform idea?"

"Well, I'm never wearing one," Jack said. "How about the sensitivity class? Are you gonna go?"

"No, of course not. I've already written a memo to that effect." Vic sat back in his chair, took a deep breath and exhaled loudly. "Want to help me burn some more memos, Jack?"

"No, man, not today. I'll just slug this down and get back to work. Gotta finish some things for the accreditation team report."

"Yeah, me too." Vic was suddenly despondent. "I think I should resign, Jack. I'm being set up. There is no way I can beat these bastards."

"No, Vic. Don't do it. You've got some folks covering your back. We'll get the best of the Executive Element yet. Hang in there."

***

Just before eleven, Vic got a call from Doris Kink.

"This is Doris Kink," the voice said.

"What a pleasant surprise," he answered sarcastically.

"Have you acted on those EMT applications?"

"I've written you a memo on it. In fact, I've responded to a couple of memos. Do you want to come down for them?"

"I'm going to a meeting right now. Why don't you bring them up to my office?"

Another power play, Vic thought. "They'll be here, Doris, when your meeting is over. I'll leave them with my only remaining employee."

"It would be better if you could get the memos to me now. I can't get away, but I would have some time to review them while the meeting is going on."

Vic let her wait before he replied. He wondered how far he should go with this game. Then tiring of it, he said, "Okay, I'll send them right over to you then."

"Good," she said, and put down the receiver.

Vic waited fifteen minutes before he had the memos delivered. Five minutes later Doris Kink stormed into his office, flushed, eyes aflame. Vic imagined steam coming out of her ears.

"How dare you write these things to me!" she said, holding the memos in her right fist.

It made Vic happy to see her lose control like this. "Ah, it seems you could pull yourself away from that meeting after all. What in particular might you be referring to?" he asked.

"You know very well what I'm referring to."

"I thought the notes were perfectly clear. What is it about them you didn't understand?"

"They were perfectly clear. That isn't the problem, and you know it. I'm sending those people to teach next week with or without approval from this office. Clara's official course completion certificate will be here soon. I called. They promised to send it out today or tomorrow, so it should be here before the course starts, but you know she has it. I wouldn't lie to you. That would be stupid. And the others—" she continued after gulping some air, "the others have sent for their official transcripts. We know they are qualified, so clear them, dammit! Furthermore, you *will* wear the uniform or else, and you *will* go to sensitivity training. If not, you're out of here."

"Says who?" Vic answered.

"If you don't clear those instructors and answer the other demands affirmatively by 15:00, your ass is grass, and I'm the lawn mower."

"How ladylike," said Vic, absolutely giddy.

"And there's something else," Doris said. "The president has asked for a report on faculty qualifications that he wants to review before the accreditation team comes over. He's concerned about what they might find."

"As he should be," Vic responded.

"Here are his guidelines," Doris said as she threw a sheaf of papers on Vic's desk. "I'll expect the first draft of your report by the end of the week." With that she turned to go.

"Who's going to sign off on the report?" he asked.

"I am," she said.

"Then you write it."

"What did you say?" She glared at him, her eyes smoldering.

"You write it," Vic repeated. "He who writes the story gets the glory."

"I'm going to the dean on this!" Doris screamed. "You sexist swine!" she added. Her face was now beet red, her control in meltdown.

"Happy to hear that," Vic said. "Want a cigarette? It might calm you down."

Doris stomped out of the room.

Five minutes later Gio Malfatto stormed into Vic's office. "You will write that report, and Doris will sign it. And you'll do all that other stuff. *Basta*!"

"No, I won't. As I told your flunky, he who writes the story gets the glory."

"I don't think you understand. If you don't do this, you're fired. This time I mean it. I've got you this time, you bastard! It's been a long time comin', but I've got you now!"

"What makes you think so? Don't you have to follow proper procedures?"

"I don't really give a damn about proper procedures. I'm sick and tired of you causing problems. Actually, I'm just sick and tired of you. If it was up to you, this place would fall apart."

"It clearly doesn't need my help to fall apart. Look around you," Vic said.

Dean Malfatto straightened up and pulled on his tie. "I have followed procedures," he said finally as he sneered like a derelict hoodlum. "You got a reprimand from me two months ago about not clearing instructors. Then I sent you a warning about not following orders, insubordination and use of abusive language. Then you got a reprimand about leaving the workplace without authorization during work hours. You still refuse to clear people who aren't a problem to clear just because you don't have some papers. Now this report business plus your refusal to wear the new uniform and to go to sensitivity training will nail you, you SOB! And good riddance, I say."

Sweat poured from the dean's brow. *This won't last much longer,* Vic thought. *The guy will be needing his blood pressure medicine real soon.*

"Fire me then," Vic said. "I don't care about your letters, and for the last time, I'm not going to write that report unless my name is on it. Furthermore, I'm not wearing a uniform, nor am I going to sensitivity training, and I am definitely not going to clear faculty until their papers are in order. Those are Philurius College rules."

"You can't talk to me like that, you slimy SOB. You—"

"*Basta!*" Vic said as he lifted himself from his chair. "Get out of here before I throw you out!"

Malfatto took a step back. That word was his prerogative alone. "Okay, that's it!" he said. "You're fired! I want your office cleared out by 15:00."

"You can't fire me; I quit," Vic said. He had already used this line twice in his academic career, but it still felt good to say it.

"You can't quit, I've already fired you," the dean fired back.

After Malfatto left, Vic walked out of his office only to find his sheepish-looking secretary sitting at her desk, apparently in shock.

"Take the rest of the afternoon off," he said to her. Then he went back into his office and started packing his personal effects. There wasn't much to do. He gathered his name plate, cigarettes and a few pencils and pens on his desk. On the wall behind his desk were a print of the main square of Cracow, Poland, framed copies of his academic diplomas and a picture of the young Vic Sawyer when he was the New York State light heavyweight Golden Gloves champion. Then there were his books. He managed to fit them into three boxes he got from the book department. Vic left the memos from Doris Kink on his desk. After he finished, he went down to find Bonnie, who was in the building today. Over lunch he broke the news. She took it with equanimity, as he expected she would. When he returned to his office to finish hauling his things out, Jack was waiting for him.

"You've got to fight this," he said.

"Don't you see," Vic said. "There is nothing I can do. They've set me up with these stupid groundless reprimands. They've followed procedure. I've been through this kind of thing twice before, so I know what the score is. Also, I talked to a JAG lawyer about it last week. I haven't got a chance, so the only honorable thing I can do is resign before I'm officially fired. At least I don't have to put *fired from job* on my next CV."

CHAPTER SIXTEEN
A NEW LEASE ON LIFE

A few hours before Vic Sawyer's showdown with the dean, Raz Rabin's telephone rang. It wasn't even six in the morning, and his wife Elena put the pillow over her head and moaned, "Oh no, not again." Raz rolled out of bed and stumbled into the hall to get the phone. He wanted to pull it out of the wall but didn't have the strength.

"Rabin," he said sleepily.

A chirpy voice on the other end of the line said, "Good morning, Raz. How are things?"

"Ed? Is that you, Ed?" Raz yawned.

"Yeah. Did I wake you up?"

"Oh, no," Raz lied. "What's up?"

"Just wanted to let you know I've fixed your problem with Miranda Maples, the AFCEO Ungeheuer and Bill McMurphy. I had a long evening with Malfatto. Got him completely wasted. He agreed to keep you on—for now—but he's out to get rid of you, Raz, so you'll have to watch your step. After we got him home, I composed a couple of letters, one to you, one to Bill McMurphy and one to Miranda Maples. I'll get him to sign them tonight or tomorrow."

"Don't you ever sleep?" said Raz as he slumped down on the floor against the wall.

"We need you, Raz. You're a major part of our effort. We've got walls to destroy, doors to kick down." Raz lay down on the floor. Ed was starting his rap.

"Listen, you really have to lie low for a while. Malfatto sees this letter that I wrote as the first step in getting rid of you. That was what convinced him to sign it. It took almost four hours of eating and drinking and listening to him bitch and moan, but he finally realized that he could get himself in bad trouble if he fired you without sufficient cause, and without backup. You need to distance yourself from Vic, though. The dean is after him big-time, and he sees you as a person in Sawyer's camp. You need to just keep your distance. There's nothing you can do to save him."

Raz yawned. He was having trouble taking all this in. "Ed, Malfatto is more afraid of McMurphy than he is of me or you. When he sobers up today, he'll remember that."

"Well, I've got that angle covered, too. I have copies of his signature I can use. If he balks, which I don't think he will, I'll just send the letter and add his signature. I'll just get him drunk again and then tell him later we worked it out, finished the whole project, including his signing the letter."

"You are one devious SOB, Ed."

"Yes," Ed said with some satisfaction. "Yes, I am."

"But what about McMurphy and Ms. Ungeheuer? They want me and Miranda gone."

"McMurphy will understand the situation. He can't just fire one of his employees either, just because someone wants him to or because he wants to himself. The letter explains that. I said that this kind of thing would not happen again, that while you weren't really at fault, you would be severely reprimanded and that we would be watching you very closely and would build a case against you so that you could be fired if something like this happens again."

"And you think McMurphy will buy that?"

"Yep."

"What about Miranda?"

"Oh, well, she has to go. We are giving her two weeks' notice."

Raz snapped up, suddenly awake. "You can't do that!"

"Raz, we have to in order to realize the greater good, to keep you on, and to keep our enrollments growing there. You've done a great job."

"Ed, she's my employee. Neither you nor Malfatto can fire her without proper cause. Don't you also have to follow proper procedures with her as well?"

"We got some real dirt on her, Raz. First of all, she left a memo to Malfatto on her desk that came to Gisela Ungeheuer's attention. In that note she said some pretty devastating things that could be called slander. She could be in bad trouble. It's possible a case could be brought against her, and she would lose. McMurphy's a powerful man."

"More powerful than the justice system?" Raz asked. "And who gave someone the right to lift things from her desk?"

"By giving her the option to resign, we are getting her off the hook. Don't you see that, Raz? She's simply got to go so you can keep your job."

"You are amazing, Ed. Truly amazing." Raz paused. "In any case, I don't intend to distance myself from Vic. He's being railroaded. And I am going to talk to Miranda. This just isn't fair."

"Raz, we need you, man. You are vital. Vital!"

"Thanks, Ed. I'm not at all sure I'm vital, but keeping small-minded, mean-spirited power people like McMurphy, Ungeheuer and Malfatto from blithely running over people *is* vital."

"Raz, just hang in there. Don't lose the long-term perspective. Malfatto won't be here forever. He's going to want to retire in a couple of years. Then there could be a major future for you at the company. I'll do all I can to assure that, but now you've got to believe me. Vic Sawyer is poison, and so is Miranda Maples."

"Ed, you haven't heard a thing I just said. Look, I've got to go now," he said. "Got to get some more sleep. Bye."

Raz crawled back into bed and tried unsuccessfully to get back to sleep. Later that day Jack called him about Vic's downfall.

***

That evening Raz called Vic and offered him two courses. "You've got to start next week," Raz said. "Can you handle it?"

"Sure," said Vic. He felt a surge of hope coming back. In a sense he was happy about leaving the college administration, but at the same time he was frustrated and depressed and above all angry that he had been forced out. Then he had another thought. "But you already had those courses covered," he said. "What happened to the person who was scheduled to teach them?"

"I talked to him as soon as I heard about your situation, and he agreed to let you have the courses. He also asked what else he could do to help. You remember him, no doubt. He is the captain whose father and grandfather were generals. He said he didn't need the money and would do anything he could to help you out."

"Wow," Vic said. "I'll take him and his wife to dinner when I get set up there. Will there be any problems with the AFCEO?"

"None," said Raz. "I've already cleared everything with him. He's one of the good guys in this system of weirdos . . . What kind of termination terms did they offer you?"

Vic laughed. "Terms? I was told to clear out my desk and leave by three o'clock. Then just as I was about to depart, a final memo came from Plea Dies. It said that I had to turn in my ID card to her immediately. Can you believe that?"

"Yeah, I can believe it. Plea is only efficient when it comes to things like that. She's much better at taking away than she is at giving. Did you give it to her?"

"What do you think? Hell no. I burned the memo and left for the club. Had a couple of drinks with Bonnie and Jack, told Kurt the news and then went out on the town with Bonnie. We ate Mexican at the hotel and then came straight back to the room. I'm just sitting here now with a beer. Bonnie's been trying to cheer me up, but it hasn't worked. Your call has though. Thanks for the job, Raz. It lightens my spirits a bit."

"I'm glad I could help," Raz said. "Are you okay?" He had never heard Vic so down.

"Yeah, I'm fine, Raz, especially now that you've given me this work."

"There's one other thing, Vic. An apartment just opened up in the housing area. One of my faculty members just moved out yesterday. I can request it for you and Bonnie, if you'd like."

"Thanks, Raz. We both appreciate your kindness. Yes, put us on the list."

"No problem, pal. You'd do the same for me. We can get Bonnie some work down here, too. We can even keep her real busy."

"Even better," Vic said.

"The term starts next Monday. When can you get down here?"

"We'll come tomorrow, if it's okay with you," Vic said, "even though I've already paid for this damn room through the end of the month."

"No problem," Raz said. "Just let me know when you intend to arrive, and I'll pick you up at the station."

As he put down the telephone, Vic felt a sudden rush of energy. "Bonnie," he called out, "we just got a new lease on life."

***

The next day, Vic and Bonnie packed their belongings in four large suitcases and a duffel bag Vic had borrowed from Jack and made their way to the train station. The books they sent to Raz by mail. On the train, Vic felt like he had escaped from a massive pressure chamber. Although the money he would make teaching would at best be half of what he had made in his administrative job, probably around $10,000 a year, he knew that he and Bonnie could live in moderate comfort since she brought in $16,000 tax-free from her job. They could live fine on $26,000, especially since the money would not be taxed and shopping at the PX and commissary would be cheap.

Raz was there in the Aufdemfeld train station to meet them, and he had good news. "You all were first on the list for the apartment in the housing area. You can spend a few days with us, then we'll help you get set up in your new home."

"Man, you are a charm," Vic said.

On the way to the parking lot, someone yelled at them and waved. They waved back.

"Who was that?" Vic said.

"Don't you remember Willy from the King Street, the old rogue taxi driver with all the illegitimate children?" Raz said. Vic turned, and the big old guy waved at them again. Vic returned the greeting.

"Oh yeah, now I remember. He showed us a picture of himself with Hitler and Mussolini at Brenner Pass. Claims he has three children here in Germany by three different women. The guy's a real freak show, if you ask me."

As they reached Raz's car, Vic said, "I wonder what kind of kids he produced?"

CHAPTER SEVENTEEN
CONSPIRACIES

Gio Malfatto summoned Doris Kink, who was at his door within minutes. "Can you believe that prick Rabin hired Vic Sawyer? Can he get away with that? We just fired the sonofabitch!"

"*You* fired him from his administrative job, and we need teachers to fill all the classes we have scheduled. Otherwise we are in default of contract," Doris said as she settled into the chair in front of the dean's desk. "Remember Don Dingsbums?"

"Sonofabitch, sonofabitch!" he said. "I figured Sawyer would be so pissed that he'd just pack up and leave."

Malfatto took a sip of his black brew and leaned back in his chair.

"We gotta get rid of Rabin, too. He's been a pain in the ass for a long time, but he was tolerable until this. He's been bringing in enough enrollments, but he's too protective of his faculty and staff. He has too many staff, and he kept them after that memo demanding cutbacks. The SOB always has an answer though, doesn't he? The AFCEO down there in our biggest center, Aufdemfeld, called to tell me that no staff could be cut there. Rabin has this guy in his pocket."

Doris Kink had a plan for the dean. She had run it past Bean, who disapproved of it on both ethical and practical grounds. On being pressed, though, he admitted that it would probably work, with the caveat that there might be some collateral damage.

"Here are my thoughts on the matter," she said to the dean. "There are all kinds of technicalities we can use to nail Raz, but we have to do it by the book."

"Do you have any idea how sick I am of hearing from you about *the book*?" Malfatto said. "You did a good job on getting Sawyer out of his admin. job. Now I want you to get rid of both him and Rabin for good, and I want it done efficiently."

The dean paused; his shoulders slumped. "Doris, get me the hides of those two, and I promise you I'll get you my job when I leave. I'll also make sure you get the same salary."

Doris's heart began to pound. This was what she had been working for . . . waiting for. She had made herself invaluable to the dean, and she would get her payoff. How long would she have to wait? Two years, three years? It didn't matter. She would be patient. Then she would be the new dean of Philurius College Overseas Programs for the Military with a big tax-free salary.

"You can count on me, boss, but as part of the deal, I want Don Dingsbums gone, too. I can find someone to replace him myself."

"Good," he said, "that's not a problem for me. How are you going to do it?"

"It's simple. I'll find another qualified person and hire her or him. There's nothing Don can do about that."

"Okay, do it. What about Rabin? How do we get rid of him?"

"That letter you sent out was a good start," she answered.

"What? That letter sucks. I can't believe Ehrgeiz got me to sign such a stupid letter. It's just a light warning," he said, now leaning forward and feeling his blood pressure rise.

"That's the way of the book," Doris said. "Two more letters with the appropriate wording, and Raz Rabin is history. After that it'll be easy to get rid of Vic Sawyer."

"How long will that take?"

"I'll get it done as efficiently as possible," said Doris said, envisioning the day when this would be her office. "Have you got any ideas about a replacement for Raz?"

"Yeah, that new woman he hired down there. Malva, right?"

Doris nodded affirmatively. Malva seemed good. She dressed

professionally and took orders without comment. She was also efficient. *Yes*, Doris thought, *Malva is a good idea, especially since she's a woman.*

"And what makes you think we can get rid of Sawyer so easily?" Malfatto asked.

"Malva is a team player," Doris said. "All she has to do is not hire Sawyer, and if we tell her not to, she won't. Rest assured, when we get rid of Raz Rabin, Vic Sawyer will soon follow him out the door."

"Good," the dean said. "I know I can count on you. And remember our deal."

"You can count on me. I've always come through for you, haven't I?"

Malfatto nodded. Doris rose to go, but before she had time to turn around, Malfatto said, "Hey, help me with this crossword puzzle before you go." Doris gritted her teeth and sat back down.

***

It was a Thursday when the letter arrived in Raz's mailbox. The dean's letter had been delayed due to all the excitement over Vic Sawyer's firing and its aftermath. The letter was vintage Ed Ehrgeiz:

Mr. Rabin:

There have been instances recently that lend strong evidence to the fact that your management style and mine don't quite mesh. Neither does it mesh with the company's philosophy on how to manage.

I use as example the situation in Sauberbach with Miranda Maples. Ms. Maples ran a number of courses in Term I with less than ten (10) enrollments and gave full pay to the instructor of each class. I also notice that she gave a second section pay to an instructor with twenty-five (25) people in his class. You also did this with three (3) courses in Aufdemfeld and one in Nebeling. You know our policy. Every class must have twelve (12) persons registered for full pay. We will run a class with ten (10) students if the teacher will work for 75 percent of the pay. Below ten (10) we don't run a class! And you don't give double pay unless you have to, say, at gunpoint. You must understand these rules and abide by them or else.

Furthermore, Ms. Gisela Ungeheuer has contacted me about your insolence.

She told me that you were planning to start a course without her knowledge. This course you and Miranda Maples organized behind her back directly with the local commander. This is a real breach of etiquette, and I demand that you apologize in writing to Ms. Ungeheuer. This letter constitutes a formal warning that your performance is unacceptable. Please regard it as such.

   Dean Gio Malfatto

Raz put the letter down and picked up the telephone. He called Ed at the headquarters office.

"Ed, this is Raz."

"Hi, Raz. Did you get the letter?"

"Yeah, I got the letter. What kind of nonsense is this, Ed? I can't accept these ridiculous terms."

"Oh, don't pay any attention to it. It's all ruffles and flourishes. The whole thing'll blow over in no time."

"What the hell are you saying, Ed? I've been asked to apologize for something that didn't happen. As it turns out, Gisela Ungeheuer didn't know about this course because she was on vacation. Miranda worked through the ESPs, who set up a meeting with the base commander. Ms. Ungeheuer just has a bone to pick with pretty much everybody. She's wanted me to fire Miranda for months, but of course, I've refused. Gisela Ungeheuer is a nutcase. I've sent our illustrious dean a memo with this information, but apparently, he has chosen not to believe me. Ed, look, I'm not going to lie down, roll over and play dead just to keep this worthless, dead-end job."

"But, Raz, we need you! You can't just quit now when things are starting to roll. We're about to roll all over the competition. We've already scared hell out of 'em. Now we're gonna kick ass big-time."

"Ed, I'm not interested in kicking anybody's ass, and I'm not interested in saving mine by caving in to these authoritarian tactics. Can't you understand that?"

There was a pause. Then came a curious, "No."

"Thanks for trying to help, Ed, but my conscience won't let me do this."

"Look, Raz, if you can't think about your own welfare now, just think about the company. The company needs you. We are on the edge of doing some great things. Raz, come on, man, do it for the company."

"Ed, I can't do it. I appreciate your trying to help me, but I can't do this for, as you say, the company. I just can't. Gotta go now."

Raz nestled the telephone gently in its cradle. He went out for a run and then practiced tai chi to focus before crafting his reply.

Dean Malfatto,

In response to your recent letter of reprimand, I feel obliged to make a short reply. I realize that our management philosophies don't mesh. Regarding your complaint about class averages, the college rules call for an average enrollment of 12 region-wide. This term, as in every term since I have been employed by Philurius College, we have averaged in excess of 12 students per class overall in my region. Furthermore, we have not cancelled one single class the past three terms. Have another look at the college guidelines. The average of 12 enrollments per region is the rule, not 12 in each and every class.

The total enrollments in Sauberbach are up in excess of 20% over the same three terms last year. This is major progress. As a footnote let me add that the average class size in my region this term is 15. Furthermore, if 12 enrollments qualify as one section, 25 should certainly qualify as two sections. It makes perfectly good mathematical sense and has the added benefit of retaining good faculty, a major problem in our system. You also obviously missed the detail that the instructor taught two sections of 12 and 13 students, not one class with 25 students.

Finally, in order to remain consistent, the sliding pay scale of yours should work both ways. Let me explain more precisely what I mean. If a class of 10 students pays 75 percent, the equivalent of two classes of 12 and 13 respectively should render a double salary. Practically speaking, however, you are surely aware that any accreditation team would disapprove of the practice of paying faculty on a devolving scale. Don't let them catch you at it.

Now to the last issue. I do not claim to know what motivates Ms. Ungeheuer, but I can tell you with certainty that she is an angry person and clearly has some unresolved problems nailing her on a regular basis. I've already explained the situation to you and don't feel required to do so again here. Under no circumstances will I apologize to her.

I hope this clears up any misunderstandings about these issues you have raised. Please note that I have highlighted the major points of this note for your convenience. If you have further questions, please contact me.

Cordially,

Raz Rabin

P.S. I can read written out numbers. In the future, if there is one for us, you may simply write ten or 10 instead of ten (10).

P.P.S In your letter you should have written ". . . with fewer than ten enrollments" not ". . . with less than ten enrollments."

***

The next Monday midday, Raz was in his Aufdemfeld office when the telephone rang. Predictably, it was Ed Ehrgeiz.

"Raz. Why did you write that letter? Malfatto's got you now. All you had to do was apologize to that AFCEO, and the whole thing would have blown over. She's going to Hochderkaiser in a couple of months anyway. Listen, you can't do that much about your letter to Malfatto, but you can still apologize to Ms. Ungeheuer. I can calm Malfatto down about this, but it'll take some heavy-duty work. Why didn't you tell me you were going to write that kind of letter?"

"Ed, I did tell you. At least I implied it. And I can't apologize. I've already explained all this to you."

"Okay. Look, you just take some time and think about this some more. We can't afford to lose you, Raz. I mean it."

Suddenly Raz was bone weary. After a deep breath and a long exhalation, he responded. "Okay, Ed, I'll do that," he said, fully intending not to think about it another second. "Thanks for your concern."

After cooling off, Raz called Vic. They met for lunch to talk about these latest developments. When Vic left, Raz stayed at the restaurant and had some Soave white wine. Later, as the sun was setting, came the tai chi practice. It finally worked, just as his tai chi teacher had been saying:

"You're well on your way to achieving your energy flow when you feel the smile breaking out inside you."

The energy was definitely flowing. Raz felt that no matter what happened, he could handle it.

CHAPTER EIGHTEEN
EXPATS VERSUS EX-MILITARY

Over dinner, Vic and Raz talked candidly about some of the underlying strife fomenting the tensions with Malfatto, Doris and the others in their camp.

"One of the problems here," Vic said, "is that the expatriates Philurius hires have an abnormal fear of the military types, and of those people like Malfatto and Kink who have assured jobs and can on a whim take away the holy ID card from ex-pats. Military dependents don't suffer that fear. They have their ID cards assured."

The two men had just recently heard about yet another example. It involved Mimi Braun, the very talented, low-profile woman who did publicity and advertising for Philurius College.

Mimi had just assumed new work responsibilities. She accepted a job which combined her advertising work with active public relations. As a part-time employee, she had managed to dodge the Executive Element. Mimi would come in, do her job and then disappear. This worked fine until she accepted the forty-hour position, something that *enfant terrible* Souter Liedekens had encouraged her to do. To everyone's surprise, Mimi had taken up with Souter and moved in with him just before the new job offer.

Doris Kink was determined to ensure that personnel were at their desks eight hours a day for the entire work week. Actually, she expected employees to work overtime, as she did. It showed their loyalty to the company, she thought, and she was careful to note who did just the bare minimum, defined in terms of hours spent behind a desk. So, when Mimi became a full-time employee, Doris began to pass by her doorway at latest by 08:00.

On her first day Mimi dragged in at 08:07 sipping a cup of coffee and trying her best to get her mind working. The first person she saw as she entered the hall was a disgruntled Doris looking at her watch.

"Morning," Mimi said.

"You're late," Doris responded.

Mimi looked down at her watch only to find that it wasn't there. "Sorry," she said automatically.

"Just don't make a habit of it," Doris said as she briskly walked away.

That was the beginning of an incessant barrage of harassment from Doris. Had Mimi known what a pain the assistant dean was going to be, she would have thought twice about taking the new position. Every day that first week, Doris was waiting in the hall to check on Mimi's punctuality. Every day Mimi was between three and ten minutes late, and every day Doris got more and more annoyed. Finally, on Friday things came to a head. It was 08:03 when Mimi entered the hall just steps away from her office, coffee in hand. She had already braced herself for Doris's attack. After their first encounter on Monday, Mimi decided to come in a few minutes late every day. She worked thoroughly and often late, but not always at her desk. Mimi was an artist, a free spirit whose creative juices flowed better under a tree than behind a desk.

"This lateness really must stop," Doris began. "If you cannot make it to work on time, we'll have to dock your pay. This week you've been late every day, but I'm willing to let that go if you do better next week. But be advised, for every minute you're late from now on, you'll be docked an hour's pay. Besides that, it's Friday. Don't you know that Fridays are casual dress? You're incorrectly dressed."

Mimi had prepared herself for a confrontation, but Doris's absurdity ignited her.

"Haven't you got anything better to do than to wait for me here every morning? Have a look at the work I get done. Have a look here at nine in the evening, when I get my best ideas—like last night. Besides, this is dressing down for me. So get off my case."

"Rules are important," Doris said. "And everyone must follow them.

We can't make exceptions. If people start breaking the rules, the machine breaks down, and when the machine breaks down, the system breaks down."

"Didn't you hear anything I just said?" Mimi responded.

"You don't make the rules here. The Executive Element does, so be warned!" With that, Doris stomped off.

The Monday after this confrontation, Mimi was at her desk before 08:00. She looked up blandly when Doris poked her head into the small office. "Mornin'," Mimi said. Doris just disappeared, but Mimi's problems were not over. She took two hours for lunch with a reporter from the *Stars & Stripes* to discuss an article about the college. When she returned, beaming with pleasure because she had gotten permission to do the article, Mimi found Doris sitting in Mimi's chair writing a memo.

"What are you doing at my desk?" Mimi said.

"This extra time you spent at lunch today will cost you a month's pay," Doris answered. "I warned you on Friday."

Mimi felt like George Foreman had hit her in the solar plexus. *A month's pay!* her mind screamed. *Dammit, this insane bitch is trying to ruin my life!*

"Doris, I was doing college business," she said. "I had lunch with Greg from the *Stars & Stripes* and gained permission to do a full-page spread on the college next month."

"You have to clear things like this with me. You didn't do so, so you must suffer the consequences. I'm sorry, but you lose a month's pay. I know it's tough, but maybe this will teach you a lesson," Doris said smugly.

"I'm going to appeal this decision," Mimi said. "I had no idea that I had to clear something like this with you."

"You'll find the appropriate rule on page 222 of the Philurius College Programs for the Military Manual," Doris said. "And I would be careful about appealing this decision. You'll lose."

That evening Mimi found Souter waiting for her in their apartment. He was sitting at the dining table going over some papers while he drank Mimi's gin.

"You won't believe what happened today," Mimi began.

"Try me. Want a gin and tonic?"

"Do I ever. Maybe three or four before the night's over."

"Did you have another run-in with Doris Kink?"

"Did I ever," Mimi said. Then she ran through the confrontation for Souter. "So you see," Mimi said. "I'm caught. There's nothing I can do. I was better off with my part-time job. A month's pay, Souter! That nutty bitch has robbed me of an entire month's pay!"

"What are you so afraid of?" he snarled. "You ex-pats are all alike. You're all slaves of the ID card. That's the power the ex-military like Malfatto and the fellow travelers like Doris Kink have over you. He's got an ID card no matter what, so he could care less about what he does, and Doris Kink is under his protection, so she's safe. At least for the present."

"Then why do they shake in their boots whenever an AFCEO gets mad about something?"

"That's Malfatto's military training, and it's contagious." Souter handed Mimi a gin and tonic.

"Souter, I don't understand you sometimes. There is something to this ID card business. It makes things a whole lot easier and cheaper for us, so we naturally want to hang on to it."

"It makes you cowards and slaves."

"You're telling me you don't care about the ID card and all the privileges it brings, the cheap booze, the cheap gas, the cheap cigarettes? You don't care about any of that?"

"I'm not a slave. No, I don't care."

"Then you're abnormal, but I already knew that."

"I'm abnormally great in the sack. I know you know that."

"You exaggerate," Mimi said as she gripped and sipped her gin and tonic.

Souter lit a cigarette and continued. "Haven't you noticed how hard it is to keep dependent wives employed?"

"Can't say that I've given it any thought," Mimi said.

"Well, have a look sometimes. These people don't need an ID card. They have one from their husbands in any case, so they just don't take the bullshit these colleges mete out."

"How about the wives whose husbands are dependents?" Mimi said.

Souter scowled at her. "You Americans are so full of hang-ups about sex and rank and what you call offensive words. It's disgusting. There are no male dependents I know of. They may exist, but I've never seen one . . . You should have seen the memo I got from Doris Kink today," Souter continued as he fixed himself another drink. "She reprimanded me for writing something about 'disabled' persons in a report. She said, 'We refer to such persons as physically challenged.' You want to know what I wrote her back?"

"Do I have a choice?" Mimi said.

"I wrote that in Germany and Holland such people are referred to as severely damaged or handicapped, as in *disadvantaged*; in France, they are called *invalides*, as in *invalid*; in Japan they are referred to, if at all, as *undesirables*. I ended the memo by telling her that Americans tend to be imprecise, and that she could learn a thing or two from the Europeans and maybe from the Japanese. Call things as they are, I told her."

"You are completely disgusting and insensitive, you know."

Souter just smiled and sipped his drink.

***

Things did not get much better for Mimi. She did start showing up at 08:00 every day, took only an hour for lunch and took the stipulated fifteen-minute coffee breaks at the assigned times both morning and afternoon—and she was miserable. Mimi felt she needed this new administrative job and the ID card privileges that came with it. Although she resented Doris, she felt impotent to do anything. Mimi also stopped coming in late at night when she did her best work. "Doris Kink is a true demotivator," she told Souter.

"She's a bull without balls," he answered.

After another couple of weeks had passed, Mimi was ready to resign. Her resentment against Doris smoldered. She often stayed awake at night thinking of how to get back at this witch.

Souter continued to ridicule Mimi for her lack of courage. One particularly bad night he said, "Enough of this! Since you can't put your mind to solving this problem, I'll put my mind to solving it. Just give me a few days. I'll show you how things should be done."

CHAPTER NINETEEN
MAKING AMENDS

On a Friday, almost two weeks after Vic lost his job, there was a PR event for Philurius College in Sauberbach. The dean wanted to shore up tattered relations with the AFCEO there. Gisela Ungeheuer had been making it her business to see that students were blocked from signing up for classes with Philurius College. She, in fact, told her ESPs that they "would be in a world of hurt" if they signed up any soldier or dependent for a Philurius College course.

That changed after Miranda Maples, the head representative of the college in Sauberbach, had resigned under pressure from Malfatto and Doris Kink. Then, after the dean told Ungeheuer to be patient, that he would soon be hatching plans to purge Rabin, she was suddenly eager to bolster enrollments.

"We don't want a lawsuit," he said to Ungeheuer. "We have to follow proper procedures like we did with that sonofabitch Sawyer. We know that he wrote that letter to the *Stars & Stripes,* but we couldn't prove it, so we had to get rid of him another way. I've got a plan for getting rid of Rabin and for getting Sawyer removed from teaching, but we have to follow the book, you know."

Malfatto then called Bill McMurphy in Hochderkaiser and told him much the same story, adding that he would soon hire someone more accommodating to replace Miranda Maples. McMurphy was pleased.

"I've got someone in mind you might want to look at closely for this job in Sauberbach," he said.

"Let me grab a pen," Malfatto answered. *What an opportunity*, he thought. First, Vic Sawyer's departure, then Miranda Maples' resignation, Raz Rabin's imminent demise, to be followed by Sawyer's second downfall.

"Okay, I'm ready to write. What's the name?"

"Linda Lane. She's twenty-four years old and has a GED. I hope that's no problem?" McMurphy said.

"Oh, no, no problem at all. You don't need a formal education for a job like that. Now that Sawyer is gone, we don't have to worry about such issues."

"You need to tighten the reins on your employees, Gio. This getting rid of Sawyer and what's-her-name there in Sauberbach is a good start. I hope you keep it up. You can't have an Academic Affairs director, or anyone else, telling you how to run your operations."

"You're right, absolutely right," Malfatto said. "It's just that the possibilities for a lawsuit are big. I have to tiptoe around because of that. Well, you know what I mean. You don't have problems like that. The government protects you from these things, pretty much." Malfatto suddenly wondered if he had gone too far. The words had just fallen out of his mouth. He could have kicked himself. Instead, he just held his breath waiting for a response.

"It isn't as easy for me as you might imagine. I admit there are some necessary protections, which let me do my job better. But I have to watch some things, too. That damn interview I gave to the *Stars & Stripes* is still haunting me. I've gotten hate mail. It's ridiculous. I'm never giving an interview again."

Malfatto let out his breath. "Yeah, I know what you mean."

"Have a good look at Linda Lane," McMurphy continued. "She's good looking, bright and hardworking. She's also black, and you need to get more people of color in your company. The accreditation team is coming over pretty soon, isn't it?"

"Yeah, yeah. They're coming over pretty soon."

"Well, the timing is good. You'll have another person of color and a woman in a position of responsibility."

Malfatto laughed. "Well, a field rep isn't such a responsible position, but I see what you mean."

"Oh, I assumed Linda, or whoever you choose, would be an area coordinator," McMurphy said. The dean's mind screamed, *Oh shit!*

The area coordinator job was a new requirement imposed by CETPM. Each regional director was to have at least one such person to assist with "tightening things up," as McMurphy put it. He wanted things to run more smoothly and thought this new position would do the trick. Malfatto and Doris had been trying to work out a plan that would accommodate the area coordinator position without hurting profits, the so-called "submissions above overhead" demanded by home campus. Several ideas had occurred to Doris, among which was cutting down on the number of regional directors. This initiative provided yet another reason to get rid of Raz Rabin.

His immediate fear of McMurphy outweighing his delayed fear of justifying this decision to home campus and to the A-Team, Malfatto said, "We'll make this Linda Lane an area coordinator. You can count on it, Bill. I've been meaning to get that done anyway, but Miranda Maples wasn't the right person for the job."

"You're right. She wasn't. I think Linda will be good, though. She's cooperative, and she already knows Gisela Ungeheuer. They get along. They even play racquetball together. Then they sit in the sauna and shower together. Wish I could be there, don't you, Gio?"

"Oh, yes!" Malfatto said. "Yes, indeed!"

"Who've you got running Academic Affairs now?" McMurphy asked.

"I've put Doris Kink in charge of that office until we have time to advertise and hire."

"Good. She seems to be a team player."

"Right, she is. You know she's already cleared those instructors for the EMT courses we were talking about."

"Good. Keep up the good work, Gio. I have to go now. My deputies are coming in for a meeting in a few minutes. It's a pleasure doing business with you. I wish your company well. Out here."

Malfatto sighed in relief and then reached for his blood pressure medicine, which he took with coffee. What was he going to do about Linda Lane? She didn't even graduate high school, and McMurphy wanted her installed as an area coordinator. Malfatto felt uneasy and called in his fixer—Doris Kink.

***

"Doris, I need you. We've got some planning to do," he said as he stood red-faced in her doorway. "We've got another crisis, so come on down to my office right now."

She looked at him. *What an oaf*, she thought. "I'll be right there. What's up?"

"I'll let you know in my office. It's complicated," he said.

"I'll be right down."

Doris picked up her pen, yellow legal pad and her college coffee cup, the blue letters reading *Striving for Excellence*. This new Doris Kink, the acting Academic Affairs director *and* assistant dean, radiated power and efficiency. Her boyfriend, Bean, had clearly been working on her image. She was wearing her uniform, including a crisp white blouse, which had been starched more than adequately, and a company tie, knotted neatly in a double Windsor, and tight-fitting gray pants. Her black shoes were highly polished but not spit-shined.

"We've got some problems to solve in Sauberbach. Got to have a plan developed before the morning is over," Malfatto said. "What do we do?" he asked after explaining the situation.

Doris concentrated a moment, looking like a soldier assaulting an enemy. "This is the way I see it," she said firmly. "We have to hire this Linda Lane. It might be a problem, but it's the lesser of two evils."

"What do you mean?"

"You say she only has a GED. That means she doesn't have the paper qualifications for the job. It clearly states in our guidelines that an area coordinator must have at least a bachelor's degree."

"That was one of Sawyer's rules, wasn't it?"

"Yes, but it makes sense, and besides, it has now been formalized."

"So what? Let's change the rules. You're in charge of Academic Affairs now. Just change it. It'd be easier if we got rid of Murphy. He's got tenure at campus though."

"You could threaten to send him back to campus, but you can't do that until after the accreditation team has come and gone," Doris said. "We need his credentials. He would put up a fight, you know, but we could threaten him."

"Yeah, you're right. I'll threaten him. Remind me, though. Hey, think I'll keep you as the academic chief. By the way, why can't I get my title changed? Isn't a director higher than a dean?"

Doris Kink looked at Malfatto, thinking once again what a moron he was.

"No," she said. "A dean is higher than a director, and no, you can't keep me as academic chief, as you put it. I can't do that job and mine. Besides, I like mine better. And no, we can't change the rules just so we can legally hire this woman in Sauberbach."

"Why not?"

"It's too obvious."

"Alright, then what do we do? You're supposed to be the answer man."

"I'm not a man," Doris said.

The dean laughed. "I can see you aren't, but just barely. It looks like male clothes you have on."

"This is a business suit, and it conforms to the new dress code. We're trying to create a congruent professional image, and you should be dressing this way, too."

"I didn't think that applied to me," he said.

"Of course it does. I've told you that. You have to set the standard. You're the boss, our fearless leader. Yes, you have to follow the dress code. Not only that, you have to lead with the dress code. You might even want to spit-shine your shoes, although it's not required. Remember, you're the boss. How can you make Jack Murphy wear the uniform if you don't? If you would wear the uniform, that might solve his insubordination problem."

"Never did that. Spit-shine my shoes, I mean. I always found someone to do it for me. It's embarrassing to ask around about that kind of thing now. . . . Could you spit-shine my shoes?"

"No," she said. "It's important for you to lead. Don't you remember we talked about the dress code in staff meeting and that Jack Murphy and Plea Dies were against it? You told them '*Basta,* this will happen!' Don't you remember all that?"

"Well, I didn't think it applied to me." Malfatto said as he looked off into space.

"Look, let's get back to this other problem," Doris said. "We already have the staff list with their academic credentials ready for the accreditation folks. We just won't change it."

"Hey, good idea! That solves it, doesn't it?"

"I hope so," Doris answered. "Now to the fence-mending. I suggest we send a team down as soon as possible. I'll organize everything."

"Good," Malfatto said. "But remember, your main job is to get rid of Sawyer and Rabin."

"You can count on me," Doris said.

***

It had been a successful day in Sauberbach. As the ranking person, Margaret Malcontenta-Jefferson had interviewed and hired Linda Lane. Margaret found the young woman attractive but slightly vacant. *Not my problem,* she thought. *The dean wants her hired, so I've done my job. She'll help with our affirmative action numbers, so that's a win.*

The day had been a real PR success. The college team played up to Gisela Ungeheuer and her three CETPM assistants in a way that would have made Vic explode. Not only was Linda Lane hired, the new brochures were distributed, and the point was made that "Sauberbach gets them first." They did look good. Mimi Braun had a real eye for such things. She just smiled a lot and answered questions. Clara fulfilled the same function for Emergency Medicine.

Bean also helped the cause that day in Sauberbach. He made a general presentation on Philurius College but focused on the college's breadwinner program, distance learning, convincing everyone that Philurius could deliver a high-quality program. Margaret and others grew uneasy, however, when at the end of his presentation Bean said that there was no proper substitute for a real classroom with good interaction between faculty and students, but that for students who spent a great deal of time in the field, the VC courses would be a good alternative. After Bean finished his spiel, Margaret gave her well-rehearsed presentation. She even had a joke up front and one at the end. Margaret made a good impression, and she felt the power. Gisela Ungeheuer, though, had preferred Bean's presentation. In fact, she preferred Bean to anything she had seen in a long time. She sidled up to him afterwards and asked if he played racquetball. It was shameless, and Doris would have exploded with jealousy had she been there.

At the end of the day, there was a dinner for CETPM and their college guests. Everyone paid his or her own way, of course. No conflict of interest was allowed. There were, of course, conflicts of interest going on every day in this system, but they were not talked about. Something as obvious as paying for someone else's dinner, however, was taboo.

It was almost 22:00 hours when the party broke up. Several people were definitely too tipsy to drive, so the designated drivers took over. For the college folks, there was no problem. The military hotel was just a five-minute walk from the restaurant. Gisela, her slight German accent more pronounced due to her intake of alcohol, offered to show Bean the town. Much to her chagrin, he declined.

***

Bean had a single room at the military hotel, and the three women were together. The ladies said good night to Bean in the hotel lobby. When they got to their room, Mimi Braun pulled out a bottle of Chianti and three crystal glasses. The party continued for a while longer, with the three rehashing the events of the day. They were rightfully proud of themselves.

Mimi Braun had never seen Margaret so relaxed. The three of them kept putting away the wine until the bottle was empty. Then they had a decision to make. The room was furnished with two double beds, so two of the three weary ladies would have to bunk together. Clara was in the bathroom when Margaret brought up the subject.

"You can sleep with me, Margaret," Mimi said. "Just stay on your side of the bed." With that, the problem was put aside. They changed into their nighties and switched off the lights. Soon they were all sound asleep.

It was just before 07:00 when Mimi heard feet landing on the floor. Margaret Malcontenta-Jefferson was standing on her tiptoes and stretching. Mimi turned over again and put the pillow around her head. Then she heard Margaret head toward the bathroom. *Margaret's weird*, she thought.

In the bathroom Margaret disrobed in front of the mirror, admiring herself from different angles, smiling at her reflection in the mirror. The idea of being considered attractive and sexy warmed her. *Some people are just born to be admired*, she thought.

Margaret considered how to get Mimi Braun on her side. It would be a real challenge but also a real coup, and it would be a blow to Doris Kink that Margaret had won another follower in the battle for leadership of the Girls' Club.

Margaret stepped into the shower and let the warm water run over her for a good twenty minutes. Afterwards, she floated back into the bedroom, wrapped in a towel, nightclothes in hand, where Clara and Mimi were having coffee.

"Thought you might have drowned in there," Mimi said. "I was about to call the desk for help."

Margaret smiled as she opened her suitcase and extracted her blue satin Victoria's Secret underwear. Then she dropped her towel and proceeded to dress slowly. It pleased her to do this, to let these two see the naked truth of her womanly attributes. Margaret was truly convinced that she was born to be admired, that she could inspire people with her good looks, as well as with her good sense.

Mimi and Clara showered and dressed and then came down to breakfast to meet Margaret and Bean, who drove them back to Rheinsteinheim. Margaret was conspicuously silent during the trip, concocting a plan to undo Doris Kink.

CHAPTER TWENTY
COMMISERATING

Among sociologists and fellow travelers, it is a well-known fact that counterparts, even as enemies, often have closer ties than persons of different rank on the same team. General George Patton, some say, felt he had much more in common with Field Marshall Rommel than he did with his own troops, whom he on occasion attacked physically. It was certainly the case with Bill McMurphy and Gio Malfatto, who felt closer to each other than to their employees.

At the CETPM college/university meeting in Hochderkaiser, which occurred on the same day as the Sauberbach meeting, Malfatto was waiting eagerly for the talk to be over so that he could socialize with his counterparts. Bill McMurphy entered the room after everyone else had been seated. He marched in a military manner to the rostrum and proceeded to say the required words of greeting. Then he turned the meeting over to his deputies, himself sitting regally on the podium, watching the participants. After the formal meeting there would be a party with lots of food and drink, all free until a bell rang after one hour at table. The post-meeting mingling was Malfatto's favorite part of the occasion. When the final words had been spoken from the podium, McMurphy made his way to Malfatto.

"Hope things go well in Sauberbach today, Gio," McMurphy said as he pressed the dean's hand.

"No problem. We've decided to hire Linda Lane on your recommendation. It'll happen today."

"Good. I'm sure you won't be disappointed." With that and a wink, McMurphy went off to glad-hand elsewhere.

Before long Malfatto and his colleagues from the other colleges had put away a goodly portion of wine. After the meal Malfatto found himself in conversation with another slightly tipsy college dean. They talked from time to time, usually by telephone, exchanging war stories about their respective jobs. This kind of interchange was always a pleasure for Malfatto. He felt that these other heads of institution were his real soul brothers and sisters, not the people who worked for him. He leaned on Doris and some others, but they were, when all was said and done, subordinates, not counterparts.

Dr. Blythe Noble, director of the Rothvine College Programs, was indulging in some Herbolzheimer Auslese wine when Malfatto came up and clapped her on the back.

"Hey there, Blythe, how are things?"

"Oh, hello, Gio," she answered as she wiped at the wine which had sloshed out of her glass onto her white blouse. *Good that this is white wine, not red*, she thought.

"So, what's new with you, Blythe?" Malfatto repeated.

"Well," she said, as she lifted the glass to her lips and emptied it. "Did I tell you how I solved the problem with that physics teacher?"

"No, no, tell me. You said he wouldn't cooperate last time we talked, but that's all I heard about it. What did you do?"

"Well, this guy had gotten a memo like everyone else from my assistant, Dirk Doddler, in which he clearly stated that there would be no signs put up anywhere—not in the bathrooms, not on the walls, not in the classrooms and definitely not on the doors. Then when Dirk was roaming the halls checking on compliance, he saw a sign on that SOB physics teacher's classroom door. Well, he tore it right off, of course, then went looking for the guy. He found him in his office, so he just threw the sign on the guy's desk and demanded to know why he hadn't followed the directive. Dirk can get pretty hot when he's disobeyed, you know."

"What happened then?"

"Well, the creep said the sign had to remain on the door, that it was required by law because of the laser equipment he had in his room. You can imagine how well this went over with Dirk."

"Yeah," said Malfatto, nodding.

"Dirk told the little guy that he didn't care about any rules, that he and I made the rules here. He told the guy just to tell everybody about the laser. He could even pass it out in the form of a memo, but that sign was to stay off the door."

"Right. He was absolutely right. You have to be tough with these teachers or they'll run all over you," the dean said. Malfatto drained his glass and reached for the wine bottle, pouring both his and Dr. Noble's glasses to their brims.

"Well, Dirk then just left. Next day, he was roaming the halls again checking on compliance, and you know what?"

"I'll bet that damn physics professor had put the sign back up," Malfatto said.

"He did! The guy actually put the sign back up! We were furious, both Dirk and me. Uh, I mean Dirk and I . . . I think."

"You can't let teachers get away with things like that," Malfatto slobbered.

"You're right. And we didn't!" Blythe rocked on her heels, almost tipping over backwards. She regained her balance, then stared blankly at Malfatto.

"How did you fix him, Blythe?"

"Ha, the semester was just a week from being over, so Dirk jus' ripped the sign off the door and burned it this time."

"And the physics teacher didn't do anything?"

"Well, he said he was gonna file a complaint. Dirk told him to go through the chain of command, and that it started with him. This guy actually wrote a letter of complaint and bypassed Dirk. He had it delivered directly to me. Well, I just tore it up and didn't respond. The guy tried to see me several times, but I never had any time for him."

"Good ideas," Malfatto said.

"He then wrote me another letter saying he would be writing the president of the college on campus about the resolution of the problem."

"Yeah, that same shit has happened to me," Malfatto said. "Did he write the letter?"

"I don't know, but it wouldn't have done any good. I'm in good with the prez."

"Yeah, me too. My prez supports me a thousand percent."

"You know how we fixed the guy?" Noble asked with a gleam in her eye. "We didn't let anyone sign up for his classes and closed the physics department."

"Great!" Malfatto said. "Just great. Here's to yuh," he said as he toasted Dr. Noble and her success over the stupid physics professor. "I just got rid of my academic guy," Malfatto said proudly. "A creep named Vic Sawyer."

Blythe looked at him curiously. "Did you say Vic Sawyer?" she said. Then, squinting at the dean, she took another sip of her wine. "We just had a Vic Sawyer apply for a position as dean of academic affairs."

Malfatto felt like a knife had just run up his back. He began to sweat, slammed the rest of his wine down and steadied himself, resting one hand on a chair. "Blythe, whatever you do, don't hire him. He'll ruin your company. Ruin it!"

Noble picked up the bottle and helped herself to yet more wine. "Well, if you say so," she said, "but my committee says he looks awfully good, and we need to beef up some things before the accreditation team comes over."

"Don't do it, Blythe. I warn you," Malfatto said.

Blythe shrugged. "Oh well, if you say so," she said. She was fading quickly. "Gotta go now, Gio. It's been fun talking to you." With that she drained her glass, gave her counterpart a mock salute, did a military turn, almost tripping, and marched off.

Malfatto shook his head, trying to get visions of Vic Sawyer out of it. Unsuccessful in the attempt, he drank deeply from his wineglass and then looked around for another conversation partner. Soon he spied him.

Jerry Einfach, director of the Mascarponi University Programs in Europe, was sitting at the end of the table all by himself, squinting over his glasses and seemingly carrying on a conversation with his half-empty wineglass. Malfatto stumbled right over to him.

"Jerr, Jerr, how goes it?"

Dr. Jerry Einfach peered at Malfatto, then pushed his glasses up on his nose. "Oh, hello there, Gio. Got some more wine, I see. Would you be inclined to share it with a doctor of philosophy down on his luck?"

"Ha! I've got just the medicine for you, doc. Hey, why don't you prescribe some? After one more glass it's all gone."

"What?" said Einfach, peering over his glasses.

"You're a doctor. Why don't you prescribe some of this medicine for us?"

"What in heaven's name are you talking about, Gio?"

"Ah, Jerr, it's just a joke. Here, take this and I'll go get us another bottle."

With that, Malfatto filled Jerry Einfach's glass to overflowing. Then he left his new conversation partner, who also thought how fortunate it was that the wine was white, not red, and scurried off to fetch another bottle.

"Waiter, waiter, another bottle of this stuff!" Malfatto yelled across the room to the white-coated waiter.

"*Und vat* for a vine is dat?" he asked pompously.

"Dat's, lemme see," said Malfatto as he squinted at the bottle. "It's a Herbolzheimer Auslese."

"Okay, I come immediate."

Five minutes later Malfatto was about to go on a search for the little waiter when the fellow suddenly appeared with bottle in hand.

"Zat vill be fifty dollars," he said, standing in the "at ease" position, clearly expecting his money "immediate."

"Maybe I'll pay as quickly as you served," the dean said. Pleased with his humor, he guffawed loudly.

"Zat vill be fifty dollars, please," the waiter repeated.

Malfatto groaned, then reached for his wallet, extracted some crisp bills, two twenties and a ten, and handed them to the waiting waiter. "That's why they call them waiters," he said to himself as he wandered over toward Jerry Einfach. "Because they're supposed to wait." He laughed at his little joke and tripped on the chair in which Dr. Jerry Einfach was seated.

"Ah, there you are, my good man," Jerry said. "Thought you had disappeared entirely."

"No, no, I wouldn't do that to you, Jerr. I keep my promises. I told you I'd get us some wine, and that's what I did. Ha, already empty, I see. Well, here I am to the rescue. Have some more of this medicine."

"Whatever are you talking about, Gio?" Einfach said.

"Been having any problems lately?" Gio asked.

"What?"

"Problems," the dean repeated. "Do you have any problems with faculty or staff or stuff like that?"

"Oh, not to speak of. Anyway, I have people who take care of these details. I tend to concentrate on the big picture."

Einfach sat back in his chair and once again pushed his glasses up on his nose.

"Well," Malfatto began. "I've had some problems recently, but I've got 'em solved."

"Oh?" Einfach said, peering over his already slipping glasses.

"Yeah. I just fired my director of Academic Affairs. He refused to write a report, so I just told him to write it or he was fired. He didn't, and he was. You just have to be tough with these staff people. Teachers, too. Right, Jerr?"

"I suppose so. I have people who take care of these things for me."

Malfatto thought about this for a minute, and suddenly had a new impulse. "Hey, Jerr, do you all have a dress code at your school?"

"We expect everyone to come to work as if they were working for a company."

"Yeah, I know what you mean. But do you all wear the same thing?"

"You mean a uniform?"

"Yeah, like a uniform."

"Of course not. Do you think we're in the bloody military?"

"Yeah, that's what I think. The military is the military, and the company is the company."

"But the company is a military unit, so there goes that analogy," Jerry Einfach said.

"What?" Malfatto said.

"Oh, just pour us some more wine, Gio. Where are your manners?"

"Ah, yeah, of course. Sorry. Here, have some more."

Ex-Lieutenant Colonel Malfatto and Director Einfach sat a moment in silence, sipping their wine and thinking as best they could through their alcohol-soaked brains. All of a sudden, Malfatto had another thought.

"Say, Jerr, you're a director, right?"

"Yes, that's correct. I am the director of my university program. Absolutely correct."

"Look, maybe you know this. Is a director higher than a dean?"

At this question Jerry Einfach looked hard at Malfatto. "It depends," he finally said.

"On what?"

"Which system you're in. I'm called director, and I'm the boss. You are called dean, and you're the boss. That's just the way things are set up."

"Oh. I see. Thanks, Jerr, thanks."

"Our problem," Jerry Einfach continued, "is that we are caught between two bureaucracies which place quite different demands on us."

"Right," said Malfatto, having no foggy idea what Jerry Einfach had in mind.

"Right indeed. On the one hand we have the military and its civil servant component, this entirely dysfunctional CETPM system, whose dis-functionaries by and large haven't the slightest clue as to what higher education is all about."

Malfatto took another drink. He was beginning to feel uneasy. Perhaps the phrase *higher education* had caused the unease. It reminded him of Vic Sawyer and Jack Murphy, and they had always made him feel uneasy.

"Yes," Jerry Einfach continued. "These people all seem to have an auditory cut-off mechanism that shuts their minds down as soon as anyone mentions anything having to do with higher education. Then there are the incessant and banal demands based on nothing but pure bile. There are civil servants who want us to fire faculty because they are too liberal or too conservative, and if you don't, these miserable little bureaucrats can ruin your enrollments. There ought to be a law."

Einfach took a deep drink before continuing. "On the other side you have a campus that really has no idea about how this system over here works. Not only that, these university bureaucrats—and there are no worse bureaucrats, Gio—these university bureaucrats are forever demanding and demanding and demanding more and more money, which seemingly vanishes into a gaping black hole somewhere on campus. We have to save and save and cut and save until the dignitaries from campus arrive. They may be small dignitaries, but they invariably have expensive tastes. What a load of crap all this is."

"So, how do you deal with teachers who give you trouble?" Malfatto asked.

"Ah, that's really quite simple, Gio. First you ignore them. Then, if that doesn't work, you simply don't hire them again. The people who work for us are completely powerless. They have no rights at all, and most of them realize that fact. They may be sour, but they are malleable. Frankly, I despise them."

With that, Einfach drank deeply from his glass of Herbolzheimer Auslese. "This speech is now over," he said. "Gio, my good man, I'm empty."

"Right," said Malfatto as he poured at his colleague's glass.

Later, on his way back to Rheinsteinheim, Crepe at the wheel, Malfatto kept repeating the mantra. "*First ignore 'em, then don't hire 'em.*"

***

Malfatto slept uneasily that night, and as usual, troubled dreams of his childhood swirled in his mind. His mother was from Calabria. After World War II, she met an American soldier of Italian heritage named Franco Malfatto, and they married a few months later. Franco had no trouble adopting his wife's baby son. She told him the father had died in the war, not wanting to tell him that the father was German and still quite alive. Franco accepted her story and felt sorry for her. Soon after the wedding the three Malfattos moved back to the United States. Franco stayed in the military and moved from post to post, the last one being Korea. Having avoided death at the hands of the Fascists and Nazis, he found it at the hands of the North Koreans. Thus, Gio Malfatto lost his adoptive father, and the only one he had known.

Gio Malfatto had a hard time growing up. In school he was nothing more than mediocre, and at sports inept. As a result, he developed a crippled self-image. Most painful was that he couldn't find a girlfriend. This state of affairs continued at college.

Malfatto was admitted on probation to a small college just one hundred miles from his home. From the outset he struggled with his studies and with weight control. Not knowing what to do about the former, he concentrated on the latter in hopes of gaining favor with the ladies. His attempts at approaching women were, however, at best clumsy, but one incident proved profoundly dumb.

He had just finished a lap around the track and was catching his breath when an attractive young co-ed finished a mile run. As she walked by, Gio slapped her on her butt and said "lookin' good," and then gave her another pat, letting his hand linger. She turned to him, sucked in her breath, raised her arms and knocked him flat on his back with her black belt karate chop.

Malfatto's ROTC instructor was in the stands watching and called out to him: "Hey, Malfatto, get your sorry ass over here, *now!*"

He walked over, intimidated.

"You know you're a sorry sack of shit, don't you?" No answer was forthcoming, so the man repeated himself. "Don't you?"

"I suppose so, sir," the young Malfatto said, his pride aching more than his back.

"I'm gonna toughen you up, son, get you in shape, and get you laid. That would do you a world of good." The instructor paused. "If you don't follow orders, your sorry ass is gone. I'll have you outta here before you can catch your breath."

The instructor paused again and grabbed Malfatto by both arms. "If you're gonna make anything out of your life, boy, and get laid before you die, you've gotta make some changes. I'm gonna make you my project startin' right now. I knew your father. He was a good soldier, and I'm gonna make one outta you. So, here's what we're gonna do. You'll rise every morning at 07:00, grab your gym clothes, come down here and run a mile, not a 440 like today. Training starts tomorrow at 07:00 sharp." The instructor started to leave but turned to Malfatto one more time. "And don't ever apologize to a woman, nor to a man, for that matter. If you ever wanna get laid, you gotta start actin' like me and Cary Grant. Now get the hell outta my sight till tomorrow." The training began, and soon Malfatto came to be the kind of man the ROTC instructor already was.

CHAPTER TWENTY-ONE
REFLECTIONS REINFORCED

*I*t was a Friday evening, the same day Malfatto was hobnobbing with his colleagues in Hochderkaiser, while Margaret and crew were doing the same with the AFCEOs and ESPs in Sauberbach. Vic was alone in their new military housing. Though compact, the apartment was adequate and inexpensive. Outside were tall evergreens. From the balcony, Vic delighted in the patter of rain on the roof and the sweet smell of the dampened earth. It was peaceful here and already felt like home.

Bonnie had decided to go to a movie on base, but Vic wasn't in the mood. As she left, Vic came in, grabbed a Weihenstephan beer, his very favorite, and plopped down on the living room sofa. He turned on the television and watched Stanley Kubrick's *Shining,* based on the book by Stephen King. The film sent chills up his spine, and conjured images of things past. In the movie Jack Nicholson played a nutty novelist who was taking care of an empty hotel one winter. He took to roaming around one day and found a beautiful woman in a bathtub. Naturally, he took her in his arms. While embracing her, he happened to glance at the mirror behind her, only to discover that her back was consumed by decay. End of romance.

This wasn't a new story though, Vic realized. It showed up frequently in medieval times, most graphically, however, in a piece by Konrad von Würzburg, *Der Welt Lohn—The World's Reward*—back in the thirteenth century. His protagonist was *Frau Welt,* or *Ms. World.* Konrad had worms, snakes, horned toads, vipers and such squirming out of her back. She was the epitome of rottenness masked as seductive beauty. The original idea was yet older, stemming from Roman antiquity. Interestingly, when the translation was made from Latin to German, the seducer changed from male to female.

Vic's mind jolted to the present. *Philurius College makes a mockery of both management and higher education. The administration is like a decayed Frau Welt, vile and horrid while presenting an attractive and enticing façade.*

***

Vic's reflections were further confirmed by the downsizing mania which became an epidemic at Philurius College. After Vic's departure from headquarters, Bill McMurphy had grabbed onto the concept of downsizing and passed it on to Malfatto and Company. Since it is impossible to downsize government bureaucrats without an executive order or without the passage of a new law, McMurphy and some of his lieutenants did their best to foist the idea on others. Malfatto was one of the recipients. Of course, McMurphy and crew were selective in their advocacy of this idea. *Remember Linda Lane?* Vic thought with irony.

The dean was happy with the concept of downsizing after it had been explained to him, but at first, he didn't get it. "What the hell does it mean?" he asked Doris.

"It means firing as many permanent workers as possible and eliminating the benefits and pension packets of all those remaining. The ideal is to have a workforce of only temporary employees. It means getting lean and mean, cutting out the fat."

Doris contemplated this grand world in which management held all the cards.

"Of course, the rules would in our case only apply to workers, that is, faculty and staff," she continued. "Top management, and to some extent mid-management, must have security. Otherwise, the machine breaks down."

"Hell, we already pretty much have that. Just a handful of people are full time. And we've just cut out that wad of fat Sawyer." Malfatto smiled wickedly at his joke. "And Rabin is next. After that, let's see." He looked at Doris hopefully. "Who should we cut after that?"

"We can't just cut people in the field. Someone has to run those operations. I suggest we cut some fat here. There are fifty-seven people on the payroll in this office. I'd like to cut that to forty-seven. Then we could make budget easily."

"You mean cut people for no reason at all, just because there's fifty-seven of 'em?"

"Right. That's what downsizing is all about. The bottom line."

"You really think this is a good idea?" Malfatto said.

"Absolutely! Think of the money we could save. Campus is now requiring we turn over 25 percent above overhead. We can cut the staff here without suffering efficiency if we hire just a handful of competent people to take the place of the ones we get rid of. We'll be able to turn over even more if we cut some unnecessary field positions and consolidate jobs."

"But these people haven't done anything wrong. Don't we have to follow proper procedures, go by the book?"

"There's a lot of fat in the system. That's the whole idea, to cut the fat. Think of what a positive impression this would make on campus. You would probably get a raise. If we can make this case, a case for the survival of the company, we can fire people more easily, and we'll be better off. And it will be easy. In fact, most of our employees have no rights and they are easily intimidated."

"You think we can pull this off?"

"I do, don't worry. We can make this happen, and that will make us heroes with campus."

"Okay, you decide who to cut and we'll talk about it. Get back to me first thing on Monday."

"We can talk again on Monday, but it might take a little longer to get a full-fledged plan in place. In any case, I'll have a full report for you by next Friday morning."

"But couldn't we just get rid of all the regional directors and have Ed run things out of this office?"

"No, we can't do that," Doris said. "I'd better get busy."

"Damn, too bad. Oh, one more thing," Malfatto said. "You sure we don't have to follow proper procedures to fire all these people?"

"Not if we can make a case for bottom-line expediency. Remember that all employees except top and mid-management are defined as 'temporary non-employees' in the contract. That means everyone but you and me, the directors here and those in the field. It makes everything easier technically. And as I said, most of these people are easily intimidated."

"Okay, good. Real good. I like that."

CHAPTER TWENTY-TWO
SOUTER STRIKES

Doris Kink took her self-imposed assignment to rid Philurius College of its excess personnel fat seriously. Within a month she had eliminated or combined positions, set up a plan to eliminate more by attrition and had cut hours from several employees. All casualties bitched and moaned, but only one person caused trouble—Souter Liedekens.

One of the reductions was Mimi Braun's hours, which were cut in half. *Due to financial considerations imposed by campus, we must unfortunately cut your job from 40 hours a week to 20 hours a week effective the beginning of next month,* the memo from Doris read.

Mimi was livid. She came home after work and threw the memo on the kitchen table where Souter was drinking coffee and smoking. He was also sweating and had a towel wrapped around his neck, which meant he had just gotten off his Nordic Track ski trainer.

"Look at that!" she said. "That creepy bitch really takes the cake. Can she just do this to me?"

"She's done it to others," Souter answered as he looked at the memo. "But to answer your question, she can only do it to you if you let her. The others are all sheep. Are you?"

"I thought I might get a bit more sympathy than that from you."

"You don't need my sympathy; you need to do something about the situation." Souter sat back in his chair and ran his hand through his thinning hair. Then he wiped his face with the towel hanging around his neck and took another deep drag on his cigarette.

"If I were you," he began, "I would attack on two fronts. First you should put in a formal complaint addressed in writing to both Kink and Malfatto, asking for the grounds on which they decided to cut your hours. That kind of thing scares them."

"But, Souter," Mimi said, "Doris will simply say once again that this measure has been imposed by campus."

"I know," Souter said. "After she makes that reply, you write that you intend to take the matter to President Porcino. That should put them on the defensive for sure."

"But, Souter, Porcino instructed them to make these cuts to boost profits. At the very least, he must be aware of what's going on, and he certainly hasn't done a thing to stop it."

"Mimi, do you really think the president of the college told them to cut Mimi Braun's hours by half? No. He told them no doubt that they had to turn over more money to campus. The way they did it would be up to them."

"But, Souter, what makes you think that my writing President Porcino would help? What it might do is irritate the Executive Element, and I would lose my other twenty hours."

"So what? Don't you have any balls?"

"No, Souter, I don't have balls, and I don't want balls. I need this job!"

Souter scowled and stubbed out his cigarette in an ashtray already brimming with butts. "You are a sheep just like the rest of them. What are you so afraid of? So what if you lose this job? You just go get another one. Until you adopt this attitude, you are not free. And if you aren't going to do anything about this, just stop complaining and take it in stride. Hell, you only had a twenty-hour-a-week job before you got the promotion. You seemed perfectly happy back then when I first met you."

"Look," Mimi said. "I'm just not like you. I do feel I need this job and I'm afraid I would lose it if I complain."

"You're a sheep."

"And you're a jerk. How about some help instead of name-calling? You said you would attack on two fronts. I just want to know what the other front is."

"Oh, that." Souter leaned back and put his feet up on the table. "The second alternative is the covert approach. I believe we could use Margaret to get at Doris Kink and ultimately perhaps at Malfatto."

"But, Souter," Mimi said. "I thought you didn't like Margaret."

"Will you quit saying that?" Souter said.

"Saying what?"

"But, Souter."

"Oh, sorry. It's just that . . . well, you frustrate me! Anyway, you really don't like Margaret, do you?"

"I like neither Margaret nor Doris Kink, but I like Doris Kink less. They both try to fool with my business, but I can handle Margaret with no problem. Kink is more of a challenge. I'd like to see her go."

"I'll bet you'd like to handle Margaret," Mimi said. "All the guys would."

"Yep, you're right, especially after that story you told me about your night in bed with her."

"You are really sick, Souter."

"Yes, I know."

"Well, what would you do about it?"

"About being sick?"

"No, about approaching Margaret, you nutcase!"

"Well, I would make the direct approach. Just ask her nicely if she'd like to get laid properly for a change."

"Souter, I mean what would you do in my case?"

"You want to have sex with Margaret?"

"I can't talk to you, Souter. You have a one-track mind. You aren't a real person, just a penis with a support system!"

"Ha, that's funny. That's really funny. May I quote you?"

"Look, Souter, this is really getting me down. If you want to help me, then do so. If you want to fantasize about Margaret or Doris or whomever, then go off somewhere else and do that. Okay?"

"Okay, I'll help you. I'll help you because I want to get at Kink. Like I say, I've got Margaret under control. She needs me. You'll have to play a role in this, though, or it won't work. Are you prepared to do that?"

"In principle, yes," Mimi answered. "But I have to know what you have in mind first before I commit to anything."

Souter winked at her. "Come on over here and sit on my lap, and we'll strategize."

***

A couple of days later, Souter surprised Margaret by asking her out to lunch. She accepted the invitation but not without suspicion. What was it that Souter, a real uncooperative pain in the neck, wanted from her?

"Have you ever been to that little Turkish place called Zum Ferkel?" he asked, as they approached the parking lot.

"No, I haven't, but I've heard it's good," she answered.

"It is indeed good. Friday, Saturday and Sunday evenings they also have belly dancing. Have you ever watched belly dancing?"

"Well, yes, I have. As a matter of fact, I took some lessons a few years ago. Some people think I'm pretty good at it," she said, glancing over at Souter.

"Maybe you should check the place out then," he said just before they reached the car. "You could make some good money on the weekend to supplement your meager pay from Philurius College."

"My pay is alright," she said, trying to sound upbeat.

"You make $10,000 a year less than Doris Kink," Souter said as he opened the door for her.

"And how do you happen to know what we both make?"

"I looked in the files," he said, then closed the door.

"And who gave you access to these files?" Margaret asked once Souter was behind the wheel.

"Nobody. I just saw them on Crepe Moertel's desk. She was gone to lunch, so I just had a look. I also made a photocopy." Souter glanced at her and winked.

"You know you could get in trouble for that, don't you?" Margaret said.

"I don't know why. Such information should be in the public domain. If I went through channels, I could get it under the Freedom of Information Act, but why should I go to all that trouble if I can just lift it from Crepe Moertel's desk while she's at lunch?"

"Because it's theft," Margaret said.

Souter simply looked straight ahead and grinned, which really irritated Margaret. In a quarter of an hour they were at the restaurant.

"Well, shall we get some food?" Souter asked. He got out of the car, walked around to Margaret's side and opened the door for her. Somehow, this gave her a feeling of control again.

Once inside, Souter headed immediately for a corner table.

"This alright with you?" he asked.

Margaret nodded. They took their seats, and almost immediately the waiter arrived with the menus.

"Would you like a *raki* to start with?" Souter asked.

"No thanks, I've got lots of work to finish this afternoon," Margaret said. Then she turned to the waiter and ordered an apple tea in Turkish.

"I'll have a *raki,*" Souter said

He spoke fluent Dutch, English, German, French and Italian, and he could muddle by in Spanish. But Margaret could speak Turkish, and he couldn't. That rattled him.

"Where did you learn Turkish?" he asked.

"My husband and I were stationed in Turkey for a couple of years, so I decided to study the language. I learned a bit, but I was better at belly dancing," she added.

"Hm," Souter said, "the lamb is good here."

"Think I'll have *cacik,*" she said.

That also annoyed Souter. He thought of attacking her but stopped himself. There was a higher cause he was pursuing today.

"Why have you invited me to lunch today, Souter?" Margaret asked as she sat back slightly in her chair and looked him straight in the eye.

Souter reached in his jacket pocket and pulled out a pack of cigarettes. "Mind if I smoke?" he asked.

"Yes, I do."

Souter's hand stopped in mid-air. Then, slowly, he returned the cigarettes to his jacket pocket.

"Would you excuse me a moment, please?" he asked.

"Yes, of course," Margaret said.

With that Souter stood and started off toward the men's room.

"Oh," Margaret called after him. "Shall I order you the lamb if the waiter comes back?"

Souter hesitated. "No, thanks. I'll catch him. Shall I order you the *cacik*?"

"Sure, that would be nice. Thank you."

Souter placed the orders and then took an extra few minutes smoking his cigarette in the WC. When he returned, the drinks were already on the table.

"Cheers," he said, as he raised his glass of raki.

"Cheers," said Margaret, as she raised her cup of tea to her lips.

Souter glanced at her appreciatively as she sipped her tea. *Everything about Margaret is sensuous*, Souter thought. *Even the way she drinks tea.*

"So, why did you invite me for lunch today, Souter?" she asked.

"Look, Margaret, I know what you think about me, but I can assure you, the biggest problem we all face is Doris Kink. If it weren't for her meddling in everyone's affairs, we wouldn't all be so on edge. If you and I could work together instead of at cross purposes, we could convince Malfatto that Kink is more of a hindrance than a help. You know she's been bad-mouthing us to Malfatto, telling him there was discord in our department, don't you?"

"Yes, I do know that, but you seem to be the major problem here. You just go off and do whatever you damn well please without ever asking me what I think."

"What about the increase in enrollments, and what about my student critiques?" Souter said. "Surely you have noticed how things have improved since I came on board."

"Yes, Souter, I have noticed," she said. "I have also noticed that some AFCEOs have called me and written me about how abrasive you are. They have even threatened to cut classes if you don't quit irritating them."

"You know these people are idiots, don't you?" Souter said.

"They may very well be idiots," Margaret said. "I've met a couple who are without a doubt idiots, but they are our lifeblood, and if you keep irritating them, we'll be forced to get rid of you, as good as you may be otherwise."

Souter was boiling. He had heard all this before but had simply blown it off. He had also simply blown Margaret off, indeed doing whatever he damned well pleased. This diplomacy business was not his cup of tea. Souter reached unconsciously for his cigarettes again, but back into his jacket pocket they went. He had decided he would play the diplomat with Margaret, so he took a deep breath and began afresh. He would get what he wanted from her, but she apparently wasn't going to make things that easy.

"Well, what do you say to that, Souter?"

"That it would be a mistake for you and the college," he said. "You don't have to worry about that, though. I'll do almost anything to get at Kink. Believe me."

"Does that mean that you will avoid AFCEOs for a while, and that you will check with me before you initiate any new policies?" Their eyes locked. "Most of your initiatives are truly good," she continued. "But sometimes your timing and your aggressiveness undo the good that you've done." Margaret wanted to appease him. He had value, and she wanted to use him effectively. *If I could just get him to quit being such a jerk*, she thought.

"No problem," he said.

"That's a promise?" she asked.

"Not only that, I'm paying for lunch as well."

"But you're going to charge it to Philurius, right?"

"Right," Souter said, as he raised his right hand to call the waiter for another drink. "Now, this is what I think we should do . . ."

CHAPTER TWENTY-THREE
DEEP DISCRIMINATION

Vic was completing his first term teaching English composition when things went wrong again. Bonnie was fired after Souter Liedekens and Margaret Malcontenta-Jefferson decided to clean house.

Doris had done her best to make Margaret and Souter look bad in Dean Malfatto's eyes, but it took Souter to get Margaret moving. When she did begin to move, it was hawk-like. Several full-time EMT instructors had been cut and part-timers given more work. Bonnie got a note addressed to all EMT faculty, which simply read, *The people highlighted in gray will not be hired next term.* The memo was signed by Souter.

Vic got home from class one night and found Bonnie sitting over a beer mug full of wine. She poured him a mug before she shoved the note his way.

"That arrogant prick!" was Vic's initial response. "He can't do this."

"So, what's going to stop him?" Bonnie responded.

"That's the hell of it, isn't it?" Vic said bitterly. "There's not a damn thing anyone can do. The entire system is rigged against us and everyone who isn't in a position of power, and that's us, for sure. Those rotten disgusting sonsabitches. They've got us cornered!"

"Vic, I'll just have to start looking for another job."

"What kind of job? What the hell kind of job are you going to find over here? It's impossible here and no better in the States. We're too damn old; nobody's going to hire anybody pushing fifty."

"We're in our late thirties," Bonnie said. "Anyway, it may be tough, but we can find something. I'm sure of it."

"Do you realize that we were making over $35,000 tax-free dollars a year just a short time ago? Do you realize what we're going to be making now?" Vic took a sip of wine and put pen to paper. "If I get two classes a term all five terms, I'll make twelve-k a year, minus retirement."

"It's tax-free though," Bonnie said.

"Bonnie, if we're lucky we'll have less than a thousand a month at our disposal. Four hundred dollars rent, then retirement contributions, food and everything else will eat that up."

"I bet we could save on food and move into a cheaper place."

"That's a big maybe, but then there's transportation, telephone, our booze bill and cigarettes, not to mention fun money."

"I could cash in some of my retirement until we get on our feet again."

"Then what will you do when you really get old?"

"Look, we'll make it somehow. I'll start looking for work tomorrow, and don't forget . . . we have retirement money for later, and by the time we retire it will have grown."

"Retire, you say. That's funny. You can't retire unless you have worked for a long time. That's not us. No, Bonnie, it's no use. I'm not assured of two classes a term. What if it's only one?"

"I'm just saying that in twenty-five to thirty years our retirement accounts will be a good bit larger. No one can count on everything working as planned, but we can always make it somehow," Bonnie said. "Besides, we'll both get Social Security benefits."

"Your optimism knows no bounds, Bonnie. Sadly, you're wrong on both counts. There is no assurance that the retirement fund will increase, and Social Security is laughable. No one can live on Social Security nowadays, and by the time we are eligible to draw it, the fund will be bankrupt anyway. We're also dead meat in the job market. Maybe it's time to become completely degenerate and throw ourselves on the mercy of the state . . . but of course, that won't work either."

"Hey, cheer up. Things will look better tomorrow. Let's just drink some wine, enjoy dinner, watch a good movie—I picked up three on the way home—and get a good night's sleep."

"Ah, to hell with it. Let's get drunk, Bonnie. Let's get drunk for the rest of the week. What the hell, for the rest of the month. Let's just drink until either the money is gone, or our livers give out."

***

A week later Bonnie had her sights on a new job. One of the military dependents who had been working briefly for Raz as a field rep quit. Over lunch the day after the field rep job opened, Raz was dubious. "Make sure you really want this position before you apply for it," he told Bonnie.

"Oh, I want it alright. We need the dough, bad."

Just before Bonnie's interview, Raz officially bit the dust. He had been expecting it after official warnings and since he had sent his letter refusing Malfatto's demands. This time Ed had only managed to delay the dean's decision to fire Raz. The letter was explicit; he was fired.

"It doesn't make any difference," Elena told him. "Remember what we lived on as students? We were happy then, weren't we? You can find something else to do. No problem. And until you do, I'll support you. We'll make whatever cuts we need to make. Man, you've got a lot more to offer than this crummy college deserves. It'll be a treat to see more of you, too. It's time you got your life sorted out, Raz, and I'm with you all the way."

So, there it was. Raz somehow felt relieved. In fact, it was the best he had felt in ages. He had already decided to see if Malva Trueheart would set him up with some classes. He enjoyed teaching, and it would at least be a stopgap until he could find other work. When he did approach her, Malva immediately signed him up for a slew of video courses and promised him classroom work for coming semesters.

The very same day Bonnie interviewed for the field rep job, Jackson Johnson, the charming and competent AFCEO in Aufdemfeld, left for his well-deserved promotion in the States. Jackson had hopes that the system he had set up in Aufdemfeld would continue to function well and flourish after his departure. Sadly, his hopes were in vain. The shell remained, but the substance died a quick death. Apparently, it does make a difference who's running the shop. As Vic said later, "This place is all appearance and no substance."

Raz appeared at the college office to wish Bonnie good luck in her interview. Malva Trueheart, two of her employees, and Betty Bernard, acting AFCEO, were the interviewers. Bernard had been the senior ESP in Aufdemfeld. Now she hoped to become the official AFCEO, replacing Jackson. Everyone thought it odd that Bernard wanted to be included in the hiring process, but there she was, completely engaged, asking question after question to all the interviewees.

Technically, the job wasn't Bernard's to fill. But, like so many in the CETPM system, she was a control freak. She would decide whom to hire.

"Bonnie Shrader is a strong candidate, but she's too old for this position. She wouldn't fit in with the rest of the people working here for the colleges," Bernard said. "It just wouldn't work."

Malva looked at the others, then back at the acting AFCEO. "She's not old, only in her late thirties and has the most qualifications, plus experience in the system."

"We have to think of the entire workforce though, don't we, Malva? Like I said, Bonnie is just too old. She's also too short."

"Too short?" Malva exclaimed.

"Yes, look at the others in that office. They're all amazons. And she's at least fifteen years older than the rest of them. She just wouldn't fit in. Besides," she said, "I'm not sure I would feel that comfortable working with her. I don't know exactly why. It's just a feeling I have."

Malva looked at the others again and shrugged. For sake of form they took a vote, knowing that a vote opposing the all-powerful acting AFCEO would end in disaster for the school.

***

Raz was waiting for Bonnie after the interview.

"How'd it go, Bonnie?" he asked.

"I think it went really well. Betty Bernard kept frowning at me, but the others seemed real encouraging. What was she doing there anyway?" Bonnie asked.

Raz just shrugged. Bonnie made her way to the ladies' room then, leaving Raz in the hall alone. He wasn't to be alone for long, though. The hiring committee came out shortly, greeting him and then going their separate ways. Just Malva Trueheart lingered.

"Well, how did it go?" Raz asked her.

Malva rolled her eyes and sighed. "We hired the young pretty one. She's also Betty's close friend."

"That's a bit tricky," Raz said. "Is she a dependent?"

Malva nodded in acknowledgement. Then she added the telling sentence. "Betty said she couldn't hire Bonnie because she was too old for the rest of the group here. Then she said she was too short for the job! Can you believe that?"

Raz winced. "She really said that?"

"Yes, she did. She also said she and Bonnie would probably have a hard time working together."

"Oh, really?" Raz said.

"Gotta go," Malva said. "Sorry about Bonnie. There was nothing we could do. And I'm so sorry you lost your administrative job. I've never had a better boss. I'll miss you." She hugged him and made her way out of the building.

About then Bonnie showed up again. "Let's go rouse Vic. He's over at the snack bar biting his nails," she said cheerfully.

"Okay, let's do it," Raz answered. They were outside before he told her.

"She said I was too old and too short?"

"That's right."

"That bitch! Vic is going to have a problem with this. Maybe we shouldn't tell him why I didn't get the job."

"Do you really think so?"

"Oh, I don't know. He gets crazy with the stupidities here. Maybe it's better not to tell him."

"Your choice, Bonnie."

"Ah, hell, I guess we'll have to tell him. He'd find out somehow and wouldn't ever forgive us for not telling him. He's weird like that."

***

"She said what?" Vic tipped his coffee over as rage got the best of him.

"She thinks I'm too old and too short to work here," Bonnie said as she reached for some paper napkins to soak up the spilled coffee.

"The freak has set herself up. We can take her to court. Yes, we can, and we will!"

"Maybe we should sleep on it," Bonnie said as she sopped up his coffee.

"Sleep on it, hell. I want to make sure that bitch never gets another good night's sleep for the rest of her miserable life. Raz, will you write and sign a statement about what you heard?"

"If you decide to pursue it this way, yes, of course. I agree with Bonnie though. You ought to sleep on it, perhaps a week or so."

"What the hell's gotten into you, Raz? This is a golden opportunity to nail the cretin. I know how you feel about the way she runs over everyone. What the hell's wrong with you?"

"You'll be taking a big risk by making this a legal issue. I just suggest you think about whether or not it's worth the trouble and pain."

"Look, if you don't want to put your statement in writing, I understand. We'll do this on our own."

"Like I said, if you decide to pursue this option, I'll back you up. I just think it would be better to let it go. Bonnie has a good chance of losing. There are entire bureaucracies dedicated to the protection of civil servants. There must be other ways of making a case against this systemic rottenness, and we should look into them. In the meantime, Vic, you and I could still be doing a bit of teaching while we're looking for other work. I imagine there are other opportunities for Bonnie, too."

"You and Bonnie both live in a parallel universe. We have no hope in any case. I'm for taking them all down with us. What the hell was wrong with Malva? Why didn't she say something?"

"What could she say? Look, let's all sleep on it, then talk again in a day or two."

"Okay, Raz, you sleep. I'm going to plan."

CHAPTER TWENTY-FOUR
THE WORD SPREADS

Jack Murphy called Vic and Bonnie just after he had heard the news. "Hey, man, sorry about Bonnie. It's already all over the place up here, and some people are mad as hell about it," he said. It was nearly midnight and Jack sounded stoned.

"Hello, dopehead," Vic said. "Do you have any idea what time it is?"

"No, man, can't find my watch."

"Never mind, we were up watching a movie. Who told you about all this?"

"Plea Dies, the Philurius College Queen of Gossip, has been telling everyone," he said.

"That figures. But how did Plea find out the results so quickly?"

"It seems that a call was made to Betty Bernard before the interview advising her that under no circumstances should either Bonnie or Vic be given any work of any kind. Malfatto had first mentioned Vic, but when he was told that Bonnie was applying for the field rep job, he insisted she not be hired either. Right after the interview, Betty Bernard called Plea with the news."

Chills scurried up Vic's back, followed by an attack of heat, running lava-like down to his toes. "Those bastards!" he muttered.

"Hey, you know, I think this is the kind of thing the union would like to get its teeth into. What if I give 'em a call after we finish here?"

"Why would the union be interested in Bonnie's not having gotten this job?" Vic asked.

"Well," Jack began, "it's probably discrimination. The union would have to be interested in that. Maybe it could bring a discrimination lawsuit on Bonnie's behalf. It was also strange the way she was fired."

"Yes, it was discrimination. The reason given was that Bonnie was too old and too short," Vic said.

"Too short?" Jack said. "That's curious. This whole thing is absurd, if you ask me. It's time for you all to join the union, Vic. Without it, there isn't much I can do to help you and Bonnie."

Vic exploded. "You talk a lot, Jack, but it's nonsense you talk. How about some action? I've written this union friend of yours, as you suggested, and have heard absolutely nothing from him. If you really wanted to help, you could light a fire under him. He's your friend, the great protector of faculty rights, but he's apparently not interested in faculty rights over here. What are you waiting for? Use your influence. Nothing can happen to you. Bonnie and I are in a bind, but you are untouchable . . . and besides, Bonnie can't join the union. She is no longer an employee!"

Vic tried to calm himself, not wanting to offend his friend further.

"Look, Jack, you have tenure, so you're safe. But Malfatto and his hoodlums are getting rid of any unprotected worker or administrator who opposes them, or for that matter anyone they please, and they are doing it with impunity. If you are so well connected with the union, then do something for us besides talk."

"Vic, I'll call Melvin, the head of the union, first thing tomorrow. Perhaps he can give us some advice. It's just not fair the way you have been treated."

"You can call them if you want, but they aren't going to come rushing to our aid."

"You're wrong there, real wrong. Hey, I know you're upset now. Get some sleep. Everything will be better in the morning."

"Jack, we're going to have to try to live on a pittance now that Bonnie has no work. We can't do that. We'll be out on the street, but your union buddies, who can't be fired, will continue to go home to their big cozy houses and their boring spouses, drink their bourbon or, like you, smoke some dope and talk about how you're saving the world. You know, Jack, if it weren't for that nasty little habit you have of talking big about the virtues of the union and the role you play in saving the world from authoritarian excesses while you remain safe from all the bullshit, I would like you better."

"Raz said you and Bonnie could stay with him and Elena until you got on your feet," Jack said, not responding to Vic's insult.

"Yeah, he made us the offer, and we appreciate it. I don't know how we would survive otherwise. Raz is a good guy who really stuck his neck out for us."

"I'll call the union boss tomorrow."

"You do that, Jack. Now why don't *you* get some sleep?"

"Okay. I'll get back with you."

Rattled by his friend's tirade, and feeling somewhat ashamed, Jack smoked a bit more cannabis, raided the fridge and tried to get some sleep.

Like his nineteenth-century hero Fyodor Dostoevsky, Jack had been born on October 10. Also like Fyodor, Jack's father had been a physician. Jack was convinced he was following in his esteemed mentor's footsteps by becoming an autodidact metaphysician. He had also become, like Dostoevsky, neurotic about gambling. Jack had always limited his losses with self-imposed monetary limits. But lately, his gambling had become habitual. He had dropped half a month's salary at the tables this month. The Philurius College blues were getting to him.

"Vic and Bonnie have it worse though," he mused as he drifted off to sleep.

***

When he arose the next morning, Jack decided he had to do something positive as promised. He drove to work. Then, in his car, he smoked a joint. From the parking lot he skipped to the Philurius College building, softly humming "Somewhere Over the Rainbow," one of his all-time favorite tunes. Once in the building he skipped down to Dean Malfatto's office.

Crepe Moertel looked a bit dreary. "Lookin' good today, Creep," Jack said. "Hey, the man in?"

"What did you say?" Crepe asked.

"Just hello, Creep," Jack said.

"My name is *Crepe*, you idiot."

"Thanks," he said. "I'll just show myself in."

Crepe protested, but to no avail.

"Hey, dean baby," Jack said as he stood just inside the doorway.

"What the hell do you want?" Gio Malfatto said. As usual, he was having coffee and working the crossword puzzle in the *Stars & Stripes*.

"You gotta do something about all this bullshit goin' on around here," Jack said.

"I didn't tell him he could come in here," Crepe announced, standing at the door.

"It's alright, Crepe. Just close the door. I'll deal with this," the dean said. "Okay, Murphy. What the hell is it you want to say to me?"

"You have a responsibility to stop this travesty of justice," Jack said.

"Murphy, what the hell are you talkin' about?"

"Bonnie was denied that job because she was too old and too short."

Malfatto squinted and held out his fat hands, palms showing. "Wait a minute, Murphy. Have you been hittin' the booze this morning?"

Jack giggled. "You know what I'm talking about, right?" he asked.

"What if I do?" Malfatto growled.

"Well, I must tell you that things have been dilatory here for much too long. If you don't get things straightened out, well, it's going to be a problem for you. You've got to get moving on some things. Quickly."

"Murphy, don't you see I'm busy? Either get to the point or get the hell out of here. And start talking normal."

"*Normally.*"

"What?"

"You said *normal*, but you should have said *normally*, but that's not the point. The point is that if you don't start supporting people like Vic and Bonnie and Raz, then I'll make sure to get the union involved."

"The union has no rights over here," the dean blustered.

"I wouldn't be so sure about that."

"But I am sure. Salmonello told me. He ought to know, right?"

"Hey, Salmonello Porcino and I are buddies, closer than the two of you will ever be. He actually likes the union."

"Nobody in management likes the union, Murphy. Now look, I don't want any trouble with you about the union. I've got enough problems." The dean glared menacingly at Jack. "You like working over here, don't you?"

"It does have its moments," Jack said.

"Well, if you wanna stay here and lead the good life, don't fuck with me!"

"It's not me that's important here," Jack responded hotly.

"You sound more and more like Sawyer," Malfatto said. "Sawyer and Rabin are troublemakers. It pisses me off bad that they are both still on the payroll. Believe me, I'll do anything to get rid of their sorry asses for good, and I will. Yes, I will. I've already started, and there isn't anything you or anybody else can do about it!"

"So, that means you won't consider revising your opinion, I take it?"

"Get outta here, Murphy."

"Okay, man, okay. Thanks for your time. And by the way, this is a college, not a company."

Late afternoon, Jack called his buddy Melvin, the current president of the union at Philurius College. Melvin listened attentively, then said, "Write me a letter, Jack. Give me your take. Put in all down."

Jack hung up and immediately telephoned Vic.

"Hey, man, I just got off the phone with Melvin."

"And who might Melvin be?"

"Melvin Jones, the union chief and my good buddy."

"Right, the one you marched through the snow with in defense of faculty rights. The one who still hasn't responded to my written enquiries."

"Same one."

"Well, what did he say?"

"He's interested, Vic. Real interested. Said I should write it all up in a memo and send it to him so he can have all the facts together. So, I'll be heading your way real soon. How about this weekend? Saturday and Sunday? We can work up the material, then I'll send it off to him at the expense of the college here. What do you say?"

"If he responds to your letter and not mine, my feelings will be hurt, but I can live with that if he agrees to help. Come on down if you want. That's fine with me. You'll have to bring your own beer though. I'm a poor man these days." Vic paused. "And don't harbor any delusions about the union, Jack. I certainly don't. I'll talk to you, but I'm not getting enthused about you and your bullshit union brothers."

"You'll see. The brotherhood always comes through."

"Wake up, Murphy. You are living in a fog."

"See you soon then," Jack said.

"If you insist. Hey, if you want to see a movie, you've got to bring that, too. We're on a budget these days."

"Okay, will do," Jack said. "And listen. Don't do anything stupid until I get there, okay?"

"Once you get here, I'm allowed to do something stupid, though. Did I understand you correctly?"

"Just don't go off half-cocked," Jack said. "That would be your downfall, man. I've seen you do it before."

"Sorry to disappoint you, my friend, but there is a faculty meeting down here a week from today, and I'm going for blood. What have I got to lose?"

"The only job you have and any possibility for a future here for you and Bonnie. I know you love it here, Vic, so don't go and do something crazy. We'll get the union to fight this fight. There's strength in numbers."

"You sound like a commercial, Murphy. And besides that, you're a whore. I'm not. Don't forget the beer and the movie when you come. Bye."

When Jack called back, Vic didn't answer. He didn't answer later that night either. Vic had set a course for himself, and he was not about to let anyone deter him from it.

CHAPTER TWENTY-FIVE
THE SHOWDOWN

The Sherlock Caserne snack bar was famous for its nachos and cheese, which Bonnie, Vic and Raz were sampling. Bonnie and Vic were drinking coffee; Raz had brought his own thermos of green tea. It was a week to the day after Bonnie's failed interview. Vic had been steaming the entire time, building resentment against Betty Bernard and Malva Trueheart.

"I'm going to blast Malva at the faculty meeting today," Vic said. "Both she and that dimwitted Betty Bernard are so hopelessly stupid and insensitive that it's hardly worth the trouble. Despite that, I'm going to get a rise out of both of them. They'll be sorry they ever heard of me." Vic looked up menacingly.

Vic had dressed for the occasion in his usual academic attire. Today's variation on a theme was khaki pants, dark-brown loafers, blue button-down shirt with a maroon tie and matching pocket scarf tucked neatly into his tweed jacket. He looked like he was ready for an interview on a news channel.

"You told me you thought Malva was well organized and attractive," Raz ventured.

"That was before I got to know her. What the hell are you trying to do, Raz? Defend her?"

Bonnie looked at them both, then stood.

"Where are you going?" Vic asked. "The meeting isn't for another hour. We need to plan a strategy."

"Ladies' room," she answered.

Vic nodded. "Could you get more nachos and cheese on your way back?"

"Will do," Bonnie said.

Vic turned again to Raz. "Tell me you're not going to try defending Malva."

"Look, Vic, the real problem is Betty Bernard and the folks at headquarters. Malva had no choice in the matter."

"She could have chosen to defend Bonnie."

"It wouldn't have changed anything, Vic. Remember the math teacher I wanted to hire for this term? Bernard told her employees not to sign anyone up for those classes because she didn't like this person—and they didn't. She has them all completely under her thumb."

"It seems she does. Nevertheless, that's no excuse for Malva's inaction. What did she have to lose?"

"Vic, the fact remains that Malva had absolutely no control over the matter."

"Even if that's true, she had an ethical obligation to fight this kind of injustice. What they did was against the law, dammit! You cannot refuse to hire someone based on her age or height. What the hell did Bernard mean anyway when she said Bonnie was too short for the job?"

Raz shrugged.

"Do you really think Malva did all she could?" Vic insisted.

"No," Raz said, rubbing his chin. "It would have been better for her to have made a statement, to have taken a stand. On the other hand, it's still difficult for me to condemn her. She's seen how things work here, and she realized that there was nothing she could do to get Bonnie the job. Malva did make a statement in Bonnie's defense at the outset. Did you know that? Then she was simply stonewalled by Bernard. Like I said, Malva could do nothing."

"Look, Raz. It's okay," Vic said, his hands balled into fists. "We can do without your statement. It'll be more difficult, but we're going to proceed with or without you."

"I've already told you I would sign a deposition if that's what you want, and I stand by that promise. I'll support both you and Bonnie unreservedly. Before you make a final decision, though, consider this: if you let all this go, there'll be other possibilities for Bonnie to find work here. If you don't let it go, I promise you, her chances and yours will be next to nil. If you do this, both Malfatto and the CETPM people will go after you with a vengeance. Is that what you want?"

"What I want is justice and revenge and not necessarily in that order. We should have fought Bonnie's firing, and maybe we'll do that, too." Vic took a drink of coffee and winced. Just then, Bonnie arrived with the nachos.

"I could handle all this by myself," Vic said as he dove into the nachos and cheese.

"Have you developed a plan yet?" Bonnie asked.

"Nope," Vic answered. "I've spent the entire time arguing with Raz here."

"Bonnie, I've just been pointing out the downside of this showdown to Vic. You know I'm with you all the way on this, if you want to fight it."

"Yeah, we know, Raz. We just don't want you to get in trouble because of what we're doing, so you don't need to write that deposition."

"That's what I just told him," Vic said. "It's not his fight." He looked across at Raz, then clapped him on the shoulder. "Have some nachos, friend," he said.

Raz helped himself and then topped up his cup with green tea.

"If you do write a statement, you'll be throwing down a gauntlet to the enemy," Vic said. "You would be a goner, so consider carefully what you choose. We'll still be your friends in any case. It's a lot to ask somebody, so we're officially not asking."

"I'm with you, of course. Just take it easy on Malva. She doesn't deserve your wrath," Raz said.

***

Raz walked into the faculty meeting room, which otherwise served as the field representatives' office. He straightened his tie before approaching Malva. He greeted her and started to take a seat, but suddenly he decided to warn her. "Malva, you know that Vic is upset, don't you?"

She nodded.

"Well, just don't take anything he says personally, okay? He's just in an awfully bad mood."

She nodded again, looking somewhat apprehensive. She had seen Vic's temper, though it had never been directed at her. "Thanks," she said.

Just before the meeting was to begin, Vic and Bonnie arrived. They sat directly across from Malva, and Vic pulled out a sheet of folded paper and placed it on the table directly in front of him.

The meeting began as an innocuous affair. Malva had one of her employees read the minutes of the last meeting. After that Malva talked about the upcoming semester, asking if all the assembled would be prepared to teach again and if they had any textbook suggestions. All answered in the affirmative as she knew they would. More mundane administrative matters followed. Then, just as Malva was about to call the meeting to a close, Vic said he had a statement he wanted to read.

"One week ago today," he began, "Bonnie Shrader applied for the position of field representative with the college at this center. After the interview she was informed by a third party that she would not be hired because she was too old and"—he scowled—"too short. Furthermore, the acting AFCEO Betty Bernard maintained she could not work with her. All of you here today surely understand what a grievous breach of the law this is. So, hopefully you will understand and support my and Bonnie's intention to pursue this issue through the proper channels until such time as a just resolution is realized. To that end, we have prepared a formal written complaint, which we now present to Malva Trueheart."

Vic put down the paper, took out a sealed envelope and handed it across the table to Malva.

"Here's your chance, Malva," he said. "You either deal with this problem or we'll take it up the ladder. I ask that you help us with this complaint. It is your duty to do so."

Malva, who had turned a deep shade of red, was clearly furious. She didn't touch the envelope.

"Who told you that?" she asked vehemently.

"Surely you're not denying it happened, are you? There were a number of witnesses. It happened. You were right there and did nothing. That makes you culpable. Think about it, Malva. Perhaps you'll reconsider."

***

"So, you actually had a plan after all," Raz said to Vic as they made their way to Vic and Bonnie's apartment.

"Well, I suppose you could say that," Vic answered. He began to whistle a happy little tune a bit off key.

"You realize Malva will probably not be predisposed to help you after what you just said in there."

"I know that, and I don't care. She wouldn't have helped me anyway. If she had wanted to help, she would have defended Bonnie at the hiring meeting. Let's go out tonight and have a good meal somewhere. I feel like celebrating," Vic said.

"Okay," Raz said, "but it's on me tonight."

"Forget that. This one's on me," Vic said. "You better start saving your pennies, Raz, because this is going to be your last term teaching."

"Ah, come on, Vic. They have no reason to fire me."

"You said you would sign the deposition stating that Malva told you that Bonnie wasn't hired because she was too old and too short and that Betty Bernard said she couldn't work with her, didn't you?"

"Sure, but they wouldn't dare fire me for doing that."

"Think again, old buddy. Think again and start saving your pennies. If you help us, you will take a fall."

"No way, man. You're nuts," Raz said good-humoredly. "They wouldn't do that."

CHAPTER TWENTY-SIX
MALFATTO RAGES

A gloomy group gathered in the college conference room on Monday morning. None of them wore the uniform, which Dean Malfatto had just made optional except for when VIPs came to the office or when administrative staff visited VIPs in the field. Sitting behind his desk, Malfatto looked like a quarterback who had just been sacked at the end of a lost game. Also present were Crepe Moertel, Doris Kink, Plea Dies and Craig Baker. Margaret was on the road, and Jack had not yet arrived.

Crepe appeared especially downtrodden today in her brown outfit, which looked like it had been bought off the bargain rack at a discount department store. She was also nursing a hangover. Malfatto had not been with her for over a week and she was feeling dejected and insecure.

Doris had spent three hours the night before in the gym, followed by a nice massage from Bean. She had slept like a stone, and she looked good, alert and brimming with vitality.

"We've got a real crisis on our hands," Malfatto barked at the assembled managers. "I just got this note from Malva Trueheart, a follow-up to the phone call she made to me last Friday." He clutched a handful of notes in his right fist. "It's worse than I thought. You remember the briefing I gave you on Friday after I talked to Malva."

Malfatto paused, thinking about Malva's tight, well-formed figure.

"We've got to get rid of Vic Sawyer once and for all, and now. Not only has he pissed off Malva, he's pissed off Betty Bernard. This really does it.

We've got to stick the knife in quick and deep. No more foolin' around with this troublemaker. And don't give me any crap about procedures, Doris."

"What has he done to merit firing?" Craig asked, looking innocently at Malfatto and holding his Mont Blanc pen just above the notebook on the table in front of him. It made Malfatto nervous that Craig always took copious notes.

"Well, for one thing he's openly insulted Malva, and even worse, Betty Bernard," Malfatto answered. Just then Jack Murphy burst into the conference room.

"Sorry I'm late," he said as he sat between Craig and Plea, sloshing coffee on his freshly cleaned and pressed blue jeans.

"Nice of you to make it, Mr. Murphy," Malfatto said gruffly.

Jack shrugged. "I got caught up in some paperwork and lost track of the time," he said. "Sorry."

"You can go on back to your paperwork as far as I'm concerned."

"Hell, boss, I wouldn't miss these meetings for anything," Jack said cheerily.

"Could we get on with this?" Plea pleaded. She wanted some tea spiked with Amaretto.

"Yeah," blared Malfatto. "Let's get this handled. Where were we?"

Craig jumped right in again with his question. "What has Vic done to deserve firing this time?"

"What do you mean by 'this time'?" Malfatto said.

Craig Baker pursed his lips and furrowed his brow slightly. "You've already fired him once. Remember? He ran Academic Affairs."

"He quit," Malfatto barked. "Anyway, I'm firing him because he insulted Malva and Betty Bernard in public."

"So?" Craig asked politely.

"So, we fire him now. No questions asked!"

"Just because he insulted a couple of people at a closed faculty meeting?" Craig asked incredulously.

"Where have you been, Craig?" Jack asked. "We fire people here all the time for no reason at all."

"Okay, smart-ass," the dean said. Then, with a threatening edge in his voice, he continued, "I know you think I can't fire you."

"That's right, you can't. I've got tenure, baby," Jack said. He sat up in his chair, ready for a verbal battle he was sure he could win.

"But I can get rid of you. I can get you out of my hair. Salmonello would support me."

"President Porcino and I knew each other for years before you met him," Jack countered. "I wouldn't be so sure of his support if I were you."

"Can't we get on with it?" Plea said. "This happens every time we have a meeting."

"If we fired everyone for making insults, you would have been gone a long time ago," Jack quipped, peering at Malfatto. "So, apparently you are above the rest of the Philurius College employees over here."

"Can't we finally get to the point?" Plea raised her voice this time. "You are both acting like children."

Doris chimed in. "Why don't we all calm down and then deal respectfully with the facts and with each other?"

Everyone looked at her. She continued, "The facts are that Vic Sawyer publicly accused Malva Trueheart and an acting AFCEO of prejudice against Bonnie Shrader in her bid for the field representative position. Both Malva and the AFCEO employee say that's not true and that they can no longer work with Vic. Those are the facts. I suggest we each give our opinion on what should be done so that Dean Malfatto can develop an informed opinion."

"I already have an opinion," Malfatto thundered.

"She meant an informed opinion," Jack said. "Your opinion on this, as on everything else, is based solely on emotion and prejudice."

Malfatto stood menacingly. "You lousy sonofabitch. I'll have you out of here soon, if it's the last thing I do. Now, everybody outta here, now!"

Craig Baker closed his notebook, looked at the ceiling and shook his head. Plea Dies got up and started moving toward the door. Taking another sip of his coffee, Jack continued to sit in defiance of the dean. Crepe Moertel just sat there despondently, still looking hungover.

"Get outta here, Murphy," Malfatto said.

Jack took another swig of coffee, pushed himself out of his chair, bowed to the dean and started to leave without a word.

Before everyone got out of hearing range, Doris made a suggestion. "Wait! Why don't we meet over lunch to see if we can't deal with this problem informally, but professionally?"

"The company won't pay for it," Malfatto said, secretly happy that he would get another free lunch at his favorite Italian place at the expense of the college.

"At 12:30 then?" Doris asked.

"We'll meet at Giovanni's," the dean said. "Don't even think of turning in receipts," he reiterated.

***

Just as Doris was ready to walk out the door to lunch, Bean popped in. He had just returned from an "expedition," as he called it, to Sauberbach.

"How did you get back so quickly?" she asked, genuinely surprised. Nothing untoward had occurred during his AWOL, so she had forgiven him, and they were back on good terms.

"Just drove normally," he said nonchalantly.

"How fast was that?" Doris demanded.

"Oh, between 140 and 150 kilometers an hour. No break," he added. "I missed you." He shrugged and smiled. "How about lunch?"

Doris hesitated. "I don't know."

"What does that mean? You seem to be on your way out. Aren't you going to lunch? You're such a creature of habit, you know. At 12:15 you're always on your way out to lunch. So, what's up?"

"Well, you see, this is a managers' meeting. We're talking about a sensitive issue."

"What is it this time? The weekly what to do about the disappearing items from the supply room?"

"It's Vic Sawyer again. He's publicly insulted Malva Trueheart and Betty Bernard."

"And Malfatto wants to fire him on the spot, right?" Bean asked.

"You've got it," Doris said. "Look, I've got to go, Bean. Otherwise I'll be late."

"And what would be wrong with being late to one of these meetings? What, in fact, would be wrong in skipping one of them? Besides the fact that they never start on time, they're a complete waste of time, you know."

"I've really got to go, Bean. I don't like being late, not even a little bit."

"Fine with me. Let's go."

"Did I hear you say 'let's'?"

"You did."

"I don't know if you should, Bean. It's a managers' meeting."

"Then fire me, but I'm going to have lunch with you. I want to hold your hand under the table."

Doris was suddenly touched. She beamed at Bean and took his hand as they walked out the door.

"Oh, don't bother to pick up a receipt," she said. "The company's not going to pay today."

***

With seconds to spare, Doris and Bean entered the restaurant. No one else from the college was there.

"I'm happy we're so punctual, aren't you?" Bean said as they moved toward the welcoming waiter.

"*Buon giorno*," Giovanni the proprietor said as he took Doris's hand.

"Hi, Giovanni," she responded.

"Your reserved *tavola* is here." Giovanni pointed to a large table in the corner by a window. Then he led them there. "Something to drink?" he asked in his heavy Italian accent.

"Just tap water for me," Doris said.

Bean rolled his eyes. "*Per me un' aqua criminale, per piacere*," he answered. Giovanni laughed at Bean's humor in saying *criminal* water instead of mineral water and told him he thought his Italian was excellent. Then he hurried away to get their drinks.

"I didn't know you spoke Italian," Doris gushed. "Where did you learn it?"

"Oh, in Italy, and in Africa."

Doris looked at him quizzically. Just then Craig Baker and Plea Dies arrived, after which Jack Murphy sauntered in. "Where's the *Führer*?" he asked.

"Come on, Jack," Craig cajoled. "Give him a break. If you don't, we'll all end up having indigestion."

"Before the dean gets here, I'd like to know what you all really think about this latest Vic Sawyer affair," Doris said.

"We've got to take a stand against these prima donna AFCEOs who think they can determine whom we hire and fire," Jack said. "I say we keep Vic on the faculty. He's an excellent teacher."

Doris began to protest, but then caught herself. "Okay, what about the rest of you? Plea?"

"I say fire him. He's just trouble. And he's so unprofessional. And besides that, if we don't get rid of him, Ms. Bernard will kill our enrollments in her center."

"Plea, he's highly professional in the classroom. He might get his paperwork wrong for you, but that ain't his main gig. Besides, the fact that you think he causes trouble is no reason to fire him. If we're firing troublemakers, we ought to fire our dean first," Jack said.

Before Plea could object, Doris jumped in again. "Let's just get our gut feelings out now. We can argue the fine points later." She had just read about this tactic of "getting your feelings out" in a management textbook. "What do you think, Craig?"

"On the one hand I really believe Jack has a point," he said. "We shouldn't be intimidated by AFCEOs. They shouldn't determine our hiring and firing policies as they have often done on a whim in the past."

"Right!" Jack said.

"On the other hand," Craig continued, "I think we should move Vic elsewhere. The situation has gotten too tense there, and Ms. Bernard could kill our enrollments."

"He'll just do the same thing wherever he goes," Plea said.

"We ought to keep him where he is on principle," Jack retorted.

"What do you think, Bean?" Craig asked.

Bean shrugged. "I tend to agree with you, Craig," he said.

At that pronouncement Malfatto and Crepe arrived. "Ciao, Giovanni," he said. "Bring us four bottles of your best red wine."

"Are you paying for all this since the college isn't?" Jack asked as the dean and his paramour took their seats. The dean ignored him. Doris was on his left, Crepe on his right.

"Well, I guess you all are wondering why I brought you here today?" Malfatto said, his speech slurred.

"Not this again," Jack said under his breath.

Obviously had a couple of nips before he got here, Doris thought.

"Well, let me begin by savin' us all a lot of time. After careful consideration I've decided to shitcan Dr. Sawyer immediately. No arguments!" The dean paused and scanned the table. "Now we can just have a good time here with each other." With that, he again opened his arms expansively. Doris saw it coming and moved slightly to her left. Crepe was still sulking and didn't see it coming. Malfatto's right hand caught her full on the chops.

"Ouch," she said, moving away.

Malfatto didn't notice a thing. He was fully into his act now.

"Why the hell are we here if you'd already made up your mind about Vic?" Jack huffed.

"Just thought we could get rid of some of the built-up stress. We're a team. We gotta work like a team, and to work like a team, we gotta play like a team," the dean said. He then actually winked at Jack. "Hey, here comes Giovanni with the vino."

"Schmuck," Jack said. "What bullshit. I'm going somewhere else for lunch. Some place where I don't have to pay big bucks. I can eat for a quarter of what it costs here at the club."

"Aw, come on, Jack, ole buddy. Enjoy life. The company's gonna pay for everything," Malfatto said.

He's had more than a couple of nips, Doris thought.

The mealtime was raucous but uneventful except for a couple of conflicts, both caused by Plea Dies. First, she decided to smoke some awful-smelling concoction she had gotten at a health store. Plea was offended when everyone complained. She refused to go outside to finish her smoke, though, putting it out ruefully. Later, when her vegetarian meal came, she took one bite and exploded.

"There's meat in this!" she cried so loudly that everyone in the restaurant turned toward her. "There's meat in this!" she repeated.

Immediately Giovanni appeared. "*Mi dispiace, Signora,*" Giovanni said solicitously. "Let me see," he continued in his colorful Venetian accent. Giovanni peered into the bowl of pasta and found no meat. "*Signora, mi dispiace,* but I do notta see meata. Where is meata, please?"

"There, there, everywhere! You mean to tell me you can't see those huge pieces of meat?"

"But that is, ah, *fungi, signora.*"

"I don't care what it's called. It's meat, and I don't eat meat! I told you I wanted a vegetarian pasta. I was quite clear about that!"

"Ma, signora, it is notta meata. It's, ah, *come si chiama*?" He scratched his head.

"It's mushrooms," Bean offered.

"Ah, si, mushrooms." Giovanni beamed.

"It's meata," Plea said stubbornly. "It looks like meat. It tastes like meat. It must be meat! And you're being so unprofessional!"

Giovanni offered to bring Plea something else, but she refused and satisfied herself with a liquid lunch.

Everyone but Doris, Bean and Craig got smashed, and the smashed ones ended up sleeping restlessly on their desks the rest of the afternoon. Malfatto's note to Vic, copied to Malva, was composed in a haze and mailed the next day.

CHAPTER TWENTY-SEVEN
THE AX FALLS

"That idiot! We've got him now! "Vic said. "Read this."

Dr. Sawyer:

You are as of receipt of this letter no longer employed by this institution. You have complained about Ms. Shrader not getting a job to both Malva Trueheart and Betty Bernard, and not only this, you unprofessionally made personally insulting statements about both. It is none of your business who gets hired at our institution and for what reasons they are or are not.

Send in your ID card to the Office of Personnel immediately! If you do not, you will suffer repercussions! All of us at Philurius College headquarters wish you the very best for your personal and professional future.

Sincerely,

Dean Gio Malfatto

Bonnie shook her head. "As Jack is fond of saying, 'The guy's wood from the neck up.' This is the end for us though, isn't it?"

"No, Bonnie. It's just the beginning for us. He's stepped into a trap. We go right for the jugular now."

"Wrong. It's over for us. There's nothing we can do. They'll beat us no matter what," she said.

"Bonnie, don't you see what Malfatto's done? And he was stupid enough to put it in writing. He's admitting to the world that you weren't hired because of your age and stature, and he's supporting that decision. The man's history."

"Look at the letter again, Vic. He didn't mention those particulars."

"That's unimportant. Raz knows, and he's going to write a deposition to that effect. It's just a matter of time before Malfatto falls."

"In the meantime, what are we going to do? Neither of us has a job now. If we are lucky, we can pay the rent for four or five months before we have to go into our savings. It's over."

"Well, it won't be easy," he said. "But they just can't get away with this! They can't!"

"But they can, Vic. Malfatto's not history, we are. Let's have a drink and celebrate being free of them."

"We're not just going to take this lying down, dammit! We're going to take some of them with us. To hell with the bastards!" Vic raged. "We'll stay here as long as we can and fight. Then we'll go back to the States, sell our house and stay with my brother and his wife in Arizona until we get on our feet again. He owes me one."

Vic looked sternly at the bottle Bonnie had just placed on the table.

"What's that, Bonnie my dear?" he asked.

"Real champagne from France, not the German *Sekt* stuff," she said.

"You mean you want to waste champagne on Malfatto?"

"No, Vic. We're celebrating the end of an epoch and our new beginning. Here, pull the cork while I get the crystal."

"Wait a minute. Call Raz and see if he's back from his mini-vacation yet."

"Sure, we need to get him in on this celebration. Isn't Jack coming in tonight, too?" Bonnie answered.

"Celebration, you say. Bonnie, you've got a weird sense of humor, but I suppose it is in a way a cause for celebration. Today marks the beginning of the end of Malfatto's power over us."

Bonnie shook her head as she lifted the phone and dialed. Almost immediately she got an answer.

"Raz, you're back. Can you and Elena come over for dinner? We're celebrating . . . It's complicated. I'll tell you once you get here . . . So, Elena is still in Italy. Good for her. Okay, see you soon."

Bonnie told him about the letter and the celebration. Raz said he'd be over in about an hour and a half. Punctually, he appeared at the front door armed with enough pizza for eight large adults.

"Here's supper!"

"Raz, I was going to fix us something," Bonnie said.

"Come on in, Raz," Vic said from the living room. "What did you bring to satiate our hunger and dispel our distress?" Vic said, slurping his second double vodka tonic of the evening.

"*Quattro stagioni* pizza, hot and ready to be eaten."

"Grab yourself a big glass, and I'll mix you some of my special brew," Vic said.

"Vic, we were going to drink the champagne, remember?"

"Bonnie, we can't waste champagne on Malfatto. Bring your glass over, and I'll mix you one, too."

"Alright, alright, but for what special occasion are we going to crack the champagne?" Bonnie said.

"At our victory over these bastards. Hey! Raz, get over here. We're celebrating," Vic said.

The doorbell rang again. Jack had arrived.

"Hey, gang," Jack said as he entered the living room.

"Welcome, schmuck," Vic said. "Come on in. I'm making a drink for you."

"What are we celebrating?" Jack asked.

"Not you, too," Vic said. "We aren't celebrating anything. We're just planning to get drunk."

"Well, before you do that, check this out. I brought a little gift," Jack said with a grin.

"Oh yeah? What might that be? Another job for me and Bonnie?"

"Hold out your hand."

"Hold out my hand?" Vic said.

"Just hold out your hand."

Jack dropped something into Vic's hand and stepped back. Vic looked down and his demeanor changed.

"Well, I'll be damned," he said. "Hash. Haven't seen nor done that stuff for a long time. Thanks, Jack. Thanks. Let's get to it."

"Before supper?" Bonnie asked.

"Naw, you're right. Let's save it for the movie."

The quartet ate half the pizza, drank and discussed plans. Bonnie was for going back to the States to look for work as soon as possible, even if it meant living with Vic's brother and his wife for a while. She didn't want to sell their home but realized they might have to. Vic's idea was to file charges with the EEOC right away. Jack, of course, advised waiting for word from the union. Raz had yet another plan. He thought they should try to go through the chain of command, the next link in the chain being Plea Dies and Dean Gio Malfatto.

"Now why should we do that?" Vic asked. "We already know what the answer will be."

"But it shows you're following proper procedures. If you have to take the case further, it'll show your goodwill that you followed standard procedures. In any case, I want to talk to Malva and to Doris before we do anything. I believe we can turn this thing around."

"Raz, you live in a fantasy, and you're beginning to sound like Plea Dies," Vic said.

"Just give me a few days to see what I can do through Malva and Doris," Raz said. "If that doesn't pan out, then I'll give you my deposition. That'll show why Bonnie didn't get the job. No one is dealing with that yet."

"We've been meaning to talk to you again about that, Raz," Bonnie said. "We really don't want you to put yourself in a bad position by writing this deposition."

"That's right," Vic added. "If you do this, you're in the sinking boat with us."

"Of course I'll do it if it comes to that," Raz said. "Of course I will. That's the only thing I could do."

Bonnie and Vic shrugged. "Your call," said Vic. "It sure would help us, but we aren't asking you to do it. We can win anyway."

"We're going to lose anyway," Bonnie said.

Vic cast a scowl her way. "To hell with that," he said. "Let's watch a movie and get stoned."

***

For the rest of the weekend, Jack plied Vic and Bonnie and Raz for ideas he could use in his memo to the union president. On Monday morning the phone rang.

"Vic, it's Raz."

"What's new, my friend?" Vic said. "I'm making some progress on the battle plan. How about you?"

"It's appalling, Vic."

"What precisely is appalling?"

"Last night I talked to Malva."

"Bet she wasn't prepared to negotiate, right?" Vic said.

"It was appalling. She's out for your blood, man. There was nothing I could do or say that would get her to consider any other possibility. Sorry."

"I told you it was useless, Raz, but thanks for trying."

"This morning I talked to Doris Kink," Raz continued. "She as much as told me both you and Bonnie were history—that there was nothing she or anyone else could do about it. Then she added that you had brought it on yourself."

"Satisfied, Raz?" Vic said. "You can't negotiate with these people."

"We've just got to show them that it makes more sense for them to make some kind of compromise."

"Forget it, Raz. Forget it. I've already begun the first underground newsletter. Want to come over and see what it looks like?"

"I can't come now. I've got to do some more preparation for class tonight, but I'll come around tomorrow morning."

"Good. I think you'll like it."

"Don't you think you should try the negotiation route before you begin your attack with this underground newsletter?"

"Raz, you're assuming a degree of rationality in these people that simply isn't there. They think they're invincible. I'm about to show them, however, that they aren't. Your assistance, even your anonymous assistance, would be welcomed."

"I'll come around tomorrow about ten. Will you be up?"

"You can count on it. Come on over any time after seven. I'll have coffee and doughnuts ready."

"I'll bring my green tea and fruit."

"Health nut. Have a good class. I'll see you tomorrow."

That night Raz appeared in class dressed totally in black, his personal sign of mourning and of solidarity with Vic and Bonnie. He had decided to continue to wear black to class, to faculty meetings, in fact to any function having anything to do with the college, until the matter of Bonnie and Vic was resolved in their favor. He still had hope.

At 10 AM the next morning, Raz knocked on Vic's door. Bonnie opened up for him and offered him coffee and doughnuts. He declined, pointing to his thermos of green tea and bag full of fruit. Vic was still in the shower, hungover. Bonnie gave Raz the draft of Vic's newsletter. It started off with a bang.

OFFME
The Unofficial Underground Newsletter for
Overseas Faculty for the Military in Europe
Vol. 1, No. 1

Editorial Policy

This is the inaugural edition of OFFME, a newsletter addressed to the faculty and staffs of all academic institutions operating in Europe under contract with the US Military. OFFME will monitor the quality of the educational programs delivered to American soldiers and their family members. It will also highlight incidents of discrimination, contract violations and flagrant violations of employee rights.

Discrimination in the Workplace

Ms. Bonnie Shrader applied for a position as field representative in Aufdemfeld. She was denied the position because the AFCEO Ms. Betty

Bernard maintained she "was too old and too short" and that Ms. Bernard would "find it difficult to work with her." Bonnie intends to file a grievance against the school, as no one there came to her defense and because it is currently impossible to bring a formal complaint against the CETPM system through the EEOC, as CETPM is a government entity, and government entities may not sue other government agencies.

A further injustice occurred when, as a result of a complaint by Dr. Vic Sawyer on Ms. Shrader's behalf, he was fired from his job as faculty member in Aufdemfeld. Dr. Sawyer also intends to file a grievance. OFFME intends to monitor the Bonnie Shrader/Vic Sawyer cases and report on them in future editions.

American Institutions of Higher Education Hampered by Government Agency

Shortly after the conclusion of WWII, the various branches of the armed forces recognized the need for offering civilian academic education and training to soldiers stationed in Europe. The Continuing Education and Training Programs for the Military (CETPM) was established by the Department of Defense to coordinate academic offerings provided by the colleges operating in Europe under contract with the Department of Defense (DOD). Over 350,000 service members and their dependents constitute a potential student body that is largely unknown to the academic community in the United States.

The original intent of CETPM was to assist the colleges in providing a wide range of educational opportunities to soldiers and their family members serving abroad. Its original intent aside, the system has gone awry. Unbeknownst even to most of the home campus faculties, CETPM and its personnel have accrued almost autonomous control over the contributing colleges. CETPM routinely establishes teaching schedules on the individual bases and is thereby in the position to discriminate against individual faculty members and entire institutions. Many individual AFCEOs in fact run their education centers as their personal fiefdoms. With no union, no bargaining agent, and without apparent protection of basic constitutional rights, the faculty of the various colleges have been rendered effete, powerless and disenfranchised.

The overseas faculty find no counterpart in the American educational system, being the only such group of faculty members having no representation afforded members of the American education community from kindergarten teachers to graduate school professors. This should serve as a case study as to what happens to academic quality when the faculty voice is drowned out through abrogation of rights and by intimidation. The colleges allow the situation to exist due to financial considerations. Their primary goal is the generation of profits, not offering higher education. Although it varies slightly from year to year, the annual enrollments for all the colleges bring in approximately $74,000,000, an annual budget which would be the envy of most small and medium-sized American colleges and universities.

In order to assure income, the colleges try to placate local CETPM administrators. The result is that CETPM runs the schools. CETPM often determines which curricula will be offered where, which courses will be run by which colleges and taught by which faculty members. The criteria for these selections often have nothing to do with academic quality and competence, but rather with personal likes and dislikes of individual CETPM managers, typically ill-prepared to make such judgments traditionally reserved for college councils and established committees.

Raz stopped reading as Vic entered the room in his bathrobe, coffee and a plate full of doughnuts in hand.

"What do you think?" Vic asked.

"You aren't pulling any punches, are you?"

"What have I got to lose?"

"Any chance to get something out of this situation for yourself and Bonnie, I'd say."

Vic took a sip of the coffee and gobbled his first doughnut. "Want a doughnut?" he said.

"No thanks. I'll get my letter ready for you. You're going to need it."

Vic nodded and clapped Raz on the shoulder as he swallowed another doughnut.

CHAPTER TWENTY-EIGHT
COVERT OPERATIONS

Vic stood before the looming building that had formerly been his workplace. He and Bonnie had driven up to Rheinsteinheim the night before and stayed with Jack. Malfatto had commanded Vic to come to headquarters to defend himself against the charges leveled against him, and Vic accepted the offer after some hesitation. He still wasn't sure why he did so, as he truly believed nothing would change Malfatto's mind. What Malfatto really wanted was Vic and Bonnie's ID cards and to confront Vic about the underground newsletter circulating throughout the system.

One bit of promising news was that Jack's friend, the union president, had finally gotten back to him. Melvin had telephoned Jack the night before when he was with Vic and Bonnie.

Jack held out the telephone triumphantly. "Melvin wants to talk to you," he said.

"Great," Vic answered. "Tell him to call me here tomorrow. I'm busy drinking just now."

Jack frowned. "Come on, man, get over here. Melvin wants to help you, man. What the hell's up with you anyway? You used to be civil."

"Yeah," Vic said. "That was before my wife and I lost our jobs." He then heaved himself out of the sofa. "Fine, I'll talk to him," Vic said as he moved across the room, promptly tripping on the rug, sloshing some of his drink on it.

"Hello, Vic. Jack has told me about you. He's shared a lot of details about your difficulties, but I'd like to hear them from you directly . . ."

***

Vic was still considering his conversation with Melvin the previous night as he looked up at the imposing Philurius College headquarters building. Drawing deeply on his cigarette, Vic got the nice light-headed feeling he anticipated. *This is the best part of smoking,* he thought. The coughing, the burning bronchia, the susceptibility to illness, all these things and more had not yet provided enough incentive for Vic to stop his smoking habit. What worried him most was the expense, though. Even with his ID card rations, the cigarettes cost him money he could ill afford to spend. Without them, though, he would be forced to quit smoking. Vic wasn't going to give up his and Bonnie's ID cards, despite Malfatto's threats.

Vic looked at his watch. It was 09:23. Their appointment was for 09:30. As if on cue, Bonnie appeared, coming around the far side of the building at a good clip, coffee in hand.

"Let's go," Vic said as she reached him.

"I'm ready if you are."

"Lock and load," Vic said, a gleam in his eye.

As they entered the outer sanctuary, they saw Patricia, Plea's secretary and guard of her inner sanctum, keeping out all comers, for the most part, until Ms. Dies was disposed to see them.

"Good morning, Patty," Vic said cheerfully.

"It's Patricia," the girl said pretentiously.

"Is everyone else here?" Vic asked, leaning his head toward the door to Plea's inner office.

"They are having a meeting. Director Dies didn't say how long it would last, so if you could just take a seat." With that, Patricia waved her right hand toward the chairs lining one side of the room.

Vic smiled again, though he was angry inside. This arrogant woman had always made him angry. She was so fanatically loyal to Plea Dies. He had never understood why.

"Actually, we are supposed to be a part of this meeting, Patty."

"It's Patricia," she said hotly. "Like I said before, I don't know how long they'll be, so you may as well make yourselves comfortable." Once again, she waved her hand in the direction of the chairs.

"If we want to make ourselves comfortable, Patty," he said slowly, "we won't be able to stay here, will we?"

"I don't care what you do," she said.

"If you were sincere, you would offer your chair to Bonnie here. Unlike these Army-issue torture chairs lined up on the wall, yours looks quite comfortable."

Patricia looked at him coldly. Just then Dean Malfatto opened the door to Plea's office. He looked at Vic and Bonnie sternly. "We've been waiting for you," he said. "You've got fifteen minutes to make your case. We're all busy here." It was 09:28.

"Let's get started then, by all means," Vic said as he moved into the inner sanctuary. Behind her desk sat Plea Dies. To her left was Malva Trueheart and the empty seat soon to be occupied by the dean. To her right were two empty chairs, obviously intended for Vic and Bonnie.

"Good morning, Plea. Good morning, Malva," Vic said.

"Good morning, Dr. Sawyer," Plea said, arching her eyebrows. Malva said nothing. She simply looked briefly at Vic, then stared at the open notebook on her lap.

Vic looked around the room amused. He was in his element. "Well, who's going to start?" he asked. "I understand we have only fifteen minutes and that all of you are quite in demand elsewhere, so let's do begin." As he finished this introduction, Vic sat in the chair closest to Plea and directly across from Malva. Bonnie sat demurely in the chair next to him.

Dean Malfatto plopped into his chair and began talking rapidly. "We've come to the conclusion that there is no evidence that Ms. Shrader was prejudiced against. You accused Malva and Betty Bernard falsely, and you did it in public. So, case closed."

"I have just two questions then," Vic pressed. "First, why are we here if you have already made a decision? This cost us money we don't have to spend. We aren't precisely floating in cash reserves, you know. Second, what do you mean that there is no evidence?"

"You wanted this meeting. It's your problem that you had to pay your own way up here. We looked at all the evidence and found no evidence of prejudice. And where's your damn ID cards? You were ordered to turn them in weeks ago. You've gotten several reminders from this office. So where the hell are they?"

"That's the poorest excuse for an answer I've heard since the last time I asked you a question," Vic said. "Furthermore, I didn't ask for this meeting. You did. All I wanted was a proper hearing of my side of the story. That could have been done on paper."

"Where's the ID cards?" Malfatto asked again.

"You mean where are the ID cards, no doubt," Vic answered.

"Let's try to be professional here," Plea said

"Professional? With this guy?" Malfatto said. "And what about this underground newsletter? What do you know about that?"

"What underground newsletter?" Vic asked innocently.

"You know damn well what underground newsletter. But now turn in those ID cards. Now!"

"We can't do that, I'm afraid."

"You damn well better, or I'll get the military police over here."

"What good would that do? We no longer have them."

"What do you mean you no longer have them?"

"Simply that. We no longer have them. Now, could we get back to the matter at hand? I'll ask once again. What precisely do you mean when you say that you have evidence that Bonnie wasn't a victim of age and size discrimination?"

"You SOB!" Dean Malfatto threatened.

"Let's please be more professional," Plea said once again, imperiously.

"Will you please stop saying that," Vic said as he clenched his fists tightly.

"If you must know," Plea began, arching her eyebrows anew, "we have statements from Malva and from Betty Bernard saying that there was no prejudice against Ms. Shrader."

"So that's it then?" Vic said.

"That's it," Plea answered. "Now, if you'll please give me your ID cards."

"Where have you been the past few minutes, Plea? Look here. Read my lips. We destroyed them."

"What, you destroyed government property?" Plea was truly perplexed. One did not do this kind of thing.

"Sorry. That's what I thought we were supposed to do with them," Vic said. "I cut them up in little pieces and threw them in the recycling bin. They are no doubt now part of a recycling project. But if we may return to the issue at hand."

"The issue is that you have no issue," Malfatto said.

Vic lifted his chin as he pulled a sheet of paper from his coat pocket and handed it to Dean Malfatto. The paper contained Raz's statement. On it he recounted his conversation with Malva in which she was quite specific as to why Bonnie wasn't hired, including the detail that she was too short.

Malfatto read the statement, then exploded. "Damn you and damn Rabin!" The dean crumpled the page and threw it on the floor. "You won't get away with this. You won't. Get out. Your time is up!"

Malva picked up the balled-up paper, unfolded it and began to read. She turned crimson and looked up briefly at Vic before defiantly throwing the page into the trash can on her right.

"I've got a clean copy for the official files here," Vic said as he pulled another sheet from his pocket and laid it in front of Plea Dies. "When can we expect your official answer?"

"I imagine within two weeks," Plea said. As she read the note, her eyebrows arched almost to her hairline.

"I've got things to do," the dean said as he stormed out of the office.

Plea looked up sternly at Vic and said, "I think that will be all for now." Then she reached for her thermos and poured herself a cup of Earl Grey Breakfast Tea, which she had secretly spiked with dry sherry. Malva, looking like a deer with its eyes caught in bright headlights, sat stiffly in her chair and stared at Plea.

"Well, I guess that does it," Vic said. With that, he and Bonnie left the premises, picking up their ID cards from Jack Murphy on the way out. They agreed to accompany Jack after work for drinks at the Officers' Club.

"Kurt said he wants to see you. Something important," Jack said.

"Fine, we'll meet you at the front gate at five."

"I suppose you mean 17:00 hours?" Jack said.

"Thanks, Jack, for the reminder" were Vic's last words before leaving the college premises.

***

Jack signed in his guests, after which they proceeded to the Officers' Club.

As they took their seats at the bar, Kurt appeared. "Hi, Kurt. Long time no see," Vic said.

"Good to see you again, Vic, and you too, Bonnie," Kurt said. "I've got some interesting news for you, but first, what are you having to drink?"

"Just a beer for me," Vic said.

"Same for me," Bonnie added.

"Make that three," said Jack.

"Okay, comin' right up," Kurt said as he went to fetch the beers.

"Do you have any idea what it is Kurt has for us?" Vic asked Jack.

"Nope. Not a clue; but we'll find out soon enough. Here he comes already with the beers."

"Here you are," Kurt said as he deposited the beers in front of them. He then opened the bottles and brought glasses.

"Thanks," Vic said. "So what's the news you have for me?"

"First, I want to let you know how sorry I am about what happened to you two. You certainly didn't deserve it."

"Thanks," Vic and Bonnie said with one voice.

"Well, I think under the circumstances you'll appreciate the intelligence I've gathered. First, Kink and Malfatto are planning to get rid of Raz Rabin. You might want to warn him. They are also plotting to get you sent back to campus, Jack. The good news is they think it might be hard to accomplish."

"Those lousy bastards!" Jack said. He took a deep drink of his beer and looked up at the ceiling.

"How do you know all this?" Vic asked.

Kurt rubbed his chin, then put both hands on the bar. "I told you I was going to bug Kink and Malfatto's apartments. Well, I've done so."

"And how did you manage that?" Vic asked.

"Trade secret. Be back in a minute. Got to go serve the colonel and his new lady friend." With that he was off to the other side of the bar.

"Sorry about the bad news, Jack," Bonnie said. She went over and hugged him.

"Ah, I knew it was coming, but it's good to know that plans are already being made against me. I'll have to get busy to see if I can foil them."

"Don't count on the union, my friend."

"Just shut up, will you. Do you always have to be a jerk?"

Vic shrugged. He was about to say something else when Kurt came back to them.

"Vic, could you and Bonnie meet me over at Eva's Gasthaus tomorrow at 10:00? I've got a job offer I want to talk to you about."

"Really?" Vic said.

"Really."

"And we can't talk about it here tonight?"

"Rather not. It's private stuff."

"Sure. Tomorrow at 10:00 then," Vic said.

"Great," said Kurt as he went off to serve some new customers.

After a second beer each, the trio segued to Zum Ferkel for dinner and to watch belly dancing. That evening Jack picked up the tab.

***

The next morning, they arrived punctually at Eva's Gasthaus. Both Kurt and Eva were sitting at a table having coffee. Before their guests had sat down, Eva was filling their cups with the dark brew.

"I must say you have intrigued me with all this mystery," Vic said to Kurt as they sipped their coffee.

"I've been observing you for a long time, Vic, and I know you have what it takes to do this job I'm going to offer you."

"Well, don't keep me in suspense forever. Do you want me to teach German or English or humanities someplace? That's all I'm trained to do," he said. "Except for working on cars. I'm real good at that, too."

"No, that's not it. It's something that takes courage and intelligence, and you have both of those in abundance."

"Thanks. I hope I can live up to your expectations. So, what is it exactly you have in mind?" Vic asked.

"I've been authorized to put you on a retainer of $20,000 a year with monthly payments to begin as soon as you agree to work for us. There may be long stretches in which you have nothing to do, but you must be ready to leave on a mission on short notice. In fact, we have something in the works that would begin in two weeks or less. You would be working with Eva."

"Wait a minute, Kurt. This all sounds a bit weird. What is it exactly you want me to do?"

"This time I want you to carry a message to Leipzig, to the head cook at Auerbachs Restaurant. This is the next step in trying to get him to come over."

"Kurt, what the hell is this all about, and who are these people who have authorized you to pay me $20,000 a year?"

"The CIA, and this project is most important to them," Kurt said as he took a sip of his coffee. "There is actually very little risk involved in this particular mission. You just have to be discrete and handle procedures correctly. Eva is a real pro. She'll be able to fill you in on everything. I suggest you start training with her immediately, however. I'll be working closely with both of you on this mission. We would want you to leave here no later than two weeks from today."

"The CIA?" Vic said.

"Yeah. I'll fill you in on the details later," Kurt said. "Vic, you speak fluent German, you are intelligent, and you need a gig. And working with Eva is a real advantage for you. She's truly a pro."

"Whoa, this is all a bit quick for me. Do I have any time to think it over and talk to Bonnie?"

"Sure, until tomorrow. If you decide not to do this job, I'll have to find someone else quickly or take leave and go myself. If that's the case, could you bartend for me?"

"That might be easier," Vic said.

"You can do this, Vic, and if you do well, which I know you will, there could be a long-term contract in the offing, for more than the meager $20,000 a year."

Vic hesitated. Finally, he spoke. "Okay, I'll let you know something by tomorrow morning. Could you give me a contact number?"

"Sure, here it is," Kurt said, as he scribbled on a napkin and passed it to Vic.

Vic took it, breathed in deeply, then let the air out slowly. "This surely is a surprising turn of events," he said.

Vic and Bonnie drank their coffee and made small talk with Kurt and Eva before going downtown to wander around and think things through. They spent the rest of the day mulling over Kurt's proposal. It was sudden and so strange. They decided to sleep on it. Early the next morning Vic called Kurt and, with great trepidation, accepted the job.

Later that day Kurt called his boss at the Culinary Institute of America just outside of New York City to inform him that Vic was on board.

First chance he got, Vic called Raz and told him about Kurt and the wiretaps. Then he dropped the other intelligence. "Kurt says you are going to lose your job," Vic said.

"But they have no grounds," Raz said.

"Since when has that made a difference?"

"Vic, they couldn't be that stupid. Kurt must be wrong."

"Prepare yourself for a fall, Raz. I can't tell you how sorry I am. If it weren't for me, you wouldn't be having these problems."

***

Vic soon had some more news for Raz. At the end of the term, Raz had gotten rave reviews from the students in both his classroom courses. By this time all of them had read *OFFME* and were intrigued by it. A couple of them had determined that Raz was one of the mystery men involved with the affair. The others weren't so sure.

Generally, by this time of term, Raz would have been formally assigned his next courses. There were indeed two on the schedule which he had planned to teach. However, neither Malva nor anyone else had contacted him about doing them. As Raz sat on his living room sofa having a cup of green tea, Vic and Bonnie, who had now moved in with Raz and Elena, came in from their bedroom.

"Hey, Raz, have you had a look at the *Stars & Stripes* from yesterday?" Vic said.

"No, why?"

"Our jobs are advertised. Mine and yours," Vic said.

"What?" Raz said.

"Our jobs are advertised. Listen to this. '*Philurius College is looking for qualified faculty for its Aufdemfeld center in the following subjects: English, MA or equivalent required. German, MA or equivalent required. History and Politics/Government, MA or equivalent required.*'"

"I can't believe it," Raz said.

Vic sighed. "Believe it. Welcome to the club, Raz. I'm sorry."

CHAPTER TWENTY-NINE
GOING FISHING

Margaret Malcontenta-Jefferson was sitting at her desk working on a report when Malfatto rapped on her door. The aroma of freshly brewed coffee greeted him. Malfatto had not been to Margaret's office before. His eyes flitted around the room, taking in the radiantly off-white walls. A single framed picture, a Monet copy, adorned the wall behind Margaret's mahogany desk. The elegant desk was almost bare, with a black inbox and a white outbox, a notepad and a Mont Blanc pen. The crowning touch was a single white rose in a slender crystal vase on the left-hand side of the desk.

"May I have a seat?" the dean said.

"Sure," she said as she gestured toward the chair. "Would you like a cappuccino? I was about to have one."

"Oh, would I. Thanks."

Malfatto observed Margaret as she prepared the cappuccino. *What a woman*, he thought. Soon she handed him his cup, took hers and resumed her seat behind her desk.

"Got a nice office, Margaret," he said as he settled back in his chair and sipped his coffee.

"Thank you, Dean Malfatto. What brings you here?"

"Well," he said. "Margaret, I've been thinking. You know I've been observing you for a while." He paused and spread his fingers in front of him, observing them attentively.

Where is this going? Margaret wondered.

"You do great work, and you present a great image for the company," Malfatto continued. "I also like what you've been doing recently on the downsizing project. You know, Doris didn't think you could handle it."

"Thanks," she said. "Yes, I know Doris had her doubts about me. Surely these doubts are now dispelled. We are the leading department in the downsizing initiative."

Malfatto nodded. "Well, to make a long story short, I'd like for you to play a greater role in the company, but I thought I would get your advice first." Malfatto ran his eyes shamelessly over Margaret's body. "You always dress well, too. Hey, what about dinner tonight? We can discuss possibilities."

"Uh, well. Actually, tonight won't be possible. But let me see." She pulled her calendar toward her and opened it to the current week. "Hm, looks like tomorrow night is free though."

"Great, great! After work then? Say about 17:30? I'll make reservations at Giovanni's for 18:00." Malfatto grinned.

"Well, I'll have to check with Tom first, but I think it'll be okay. I'll let you know tomorrow morning." When she looked up at him again after putting away her calendar, Malfatto was bobbing his head from side to side slightly. Margaret stood, and as she did so, the dean's gaze moved down her body. *How am I going to deal with this pig?* she thought. *He needs controlling, and I can do it, but it will be a challenge.*

"You really do dress well," he said.

She just nodded appreciatively. "Well, thanks for the invitation. I'm looking forward to it."

After Malfatto had closed the door, Margaret sighed. *What could he possibly have in mind? Could this finally be my chance to move up the corporate ladder? I'll have to be careful to play this right.* Then came another, less scintillating thought. *What will he want of me if I accept?* That thought stopped her for a minute. *He'll want more than the use of my administrative talents. How am I going to handle that?*

By 19:30 she had finished her day's work, but instead of going straight home, she stopped at the Officers' Club for a drink, deciding to sit at the bar and, in doing so, draw more attention to herself. This was her first time at the bar alone. She came sometimes with Tom on the weekend, and a couple of times she had come with Clara. This was somehow different, though, and she liked it. This was also the first time she had sat at the bar. She felt the subtle stares of both the men and women, and it made her glow. Margaret perked up and radiated her femininity. *I'm on stage,* she thought. *Just where I belong.*

"What'll it be, ma'am?" said Kurt the bartender.

"A dry martini, please," she answered, sparkling now from head to toe.

Kurt lit up as well. "Right away, ma'am."

Margaret turned on the barstool and crossed her legs, left over right, and felt the sexual tension in the room rise a degree or two. This was her *métier* and she knew it.

"Here you are, ma'am." Kurt had arrived with her dry martini and lingered a bit longer than necessary.

"Thanks," Margaret said. "How much will it be?"

"This one's on the house, ma'am," Kurt answered with a smile. "You are the 100th customer of the evening."

"Well, thanks," she said, pleased that she could have this effect, not believing for a second that he had been counting customers. After Kurt had moved on reluctantly to his next patron, Margaret sipped her martini and mulled over the dean's proposal. At the end of her second martini, a plan had begun to gel.

When she got home, her husband, Tom, was waiting with a surprise. He sat in the living room dressed in his Class A uniform sipping a drink. Another one sat on the table in front of the couch.

"Hi," he said. "Where've you been?"

"Had a report to finish."

"Did you finish it?"

"I did."

"Great. Here's a dry martini for you." Tom picked up the drink and started toward Margaret with it.

"Oh, I don't really feel like a drink."

"Come on, Margaret. We're celebrating."

"Celebrating?" she said as she kicked her shoes off. "My finishing that report?"

"Nope. Something else, but yep, we're celebrating."

"Celebrating what?"

"Have a look at my shoulder."

"What?"

"Have a look at my shoulder," he said again, offering her his left one.

Margaret moved closer and peered at his shoulder. "Hey, you made major! Congratulations. I knew you would make it."

They toasted and drank, then drank some more. Tom even talked her into making love, but she insisted on having a light dinner and taking her long hot bath first.

"Bet this is the first time you've ever made love to a major," he said proudly, as she dropped her robe and slinked into bed.

***

At 09:05 the next morning Margaret's phone rang.

She picked up the standard-issue black device and in her usual dulcet tones said, "Good morning. Margaret Malcontenta-Jefferson, how can I help you?"

"Great telephone style," said the voice on the other end. It was Dean Malfatto.

"Oh, hi. Good morning," she said.

"Yeah, good morning. You can help me have a better day by saying we're on for dinner tonight."

"Well, I suppose I'll make your day then," she said coyly. "Yes, I'm on for dinner tonight."

"Great! That's great. See you at 17:30, okay?"

"Okay. Till then."

Margaret gently dropped the telephone back in place and then settled into her workday. At 17:10 she went to the ladies' room to freshen up for the evening's "meeting." For the big event she had chosen a dark-gray silk Dior dress, which clung in all the proper places, showing off her figure fetchingly. For color she artfully draped a burgundy scarf around her neck. For reasons known only to her, Margaret had chosen avocado silk underwear. Seamless stockings accentuated her shapely legs.

She changed clothes in the women's room, brushed her teeth and then admired the whiteness of her perfectly shaped ivories against the olive skin of her face. She thought again how lucky she was to be so attractive. She brushed her shoulder-length black hair. It glowed. Then came the makeup refresher and a dash of Climat.

Margaret turned the corner and saw Malfatto waiting in front of her office door.

"Hey, there you are," he said jovially. "Thought you had forgotten."

"Of course I didn't forget. I just needed to change and freshen up a bit."

"Well, let me tell you, you look great," Malfatto said, leering at her, making her once again feel uncomfortable.

She tucked this feeling away and responded to him flirtatiously. "Thank you, sir," she said as she turned and cast him a fetching look. "Let me put my things away. Then we can be underway."

***

"*Ciao, Giovanni, siamo qui,*" Malfatto said loudly as they entered the restaurant.

"*Signori, buona sera,*" Giovanni answered. Then he bowed slightly to Margaret and said, "*Buona sera, signora.* It is ah good to have you at Giovanni's tonight."

"*Grazie,* thank you," Margaret said.

"Signora, you are for sure Italiana, no?"

"My grandparents came to America from Positano."

"I knew it. Yes, I knew it. Please, come with me."

Giovanni led them to a table in the corner. It was as private a place as there was to be had at Giovanni's, and it was the place Malfatto had requested.

"I bring *aperitivo.* On house," Giovanni said as he bowed and quickly disappeared.

"Great place, isn't it?" Malfatto said once they were seated.

"Yes, I like it," she said, sincerely. The restaurant reminded her of a place she used to go with her parents and her Italian grandparents.

"Ever been to Italy?" Malfatto asked.

"Not yet. But I want to go. It's just that I haven't found the time."

"Well, what do you think about the idea of going there for the company?"

This thought stopped her for a moment. Margaret looked across at her boss quizzically.

"Well?" he asked.

"I wouldn't say no," she said. "What exactly do you have in mind?"

Just then Giovanni arrived with two Campari oranges and asked what they wanted for dinner.

"Well, what's special tonight?" asked the dean.

"Everything is a special," Giovanni responded, falling into the usual rap he had with Malfatto when he brought in a new woman.

"Yeah, I know," Malfatto said. Again, he laughed loudly and winked at Margaret.

"Well, *amico* Giovanni, what would you recommend for me and the most beautiful woman in all of Germany?" he said as he looked Margaret's way.

Margaret couldn't believe this scene. It could have come out of a bad B-movie. Despite that, she played her role as gracious lady.

"Tonight we have a *specialità* of *baccalà*. With that you can have two vegetables. Very good, very tasty, very good for health," Giovanni said.

"Hey, Giovanni," said Malfatto. "Why not something from your region of Calabria?"

"Signor Malfatto, my *genitori* are from Calabria, but I am born in Venezia. I do not cook Calabria style. I cook Veneto style."

"You're Calabrian, Giovanni, but it's okay by me if you want to pretend you're Venetian."

As always, Giovanni shrugged and grinned. Secretly he thought that if he had to do this act again for the benefit of another new woman Malfatto brought in, he would give up this restaurant and return to Venice.

"Okay, Giovanni, two *baccalà* with vegetables. You choose them. And bring us the best wine in the house!"

Giovanni bowed slightly and hurried away with the order. Malfatto then leaned slightly forward and leered again. In front of Margaret's office, he had caught the first waft of her perfume, and it set his juices flowing. Then in the car he further savored the bewitching essence and her elegance. He was feeling giddy now, looking across the table at Margaret, taking in her intoxicating scent and generally feeling grand.

"This really is a lovely place," she said. "It has atmosphere. It makes me want to go to Italy. I've heard stories about it all my life." Margaret looked into Malfatto's eyes alluringly, giving him goose bumps. She held his gaze briefly, before lowering her eyes to the drink in front of her on the table. She raised the glass. "*Cin cin!*" she said.

"*Cin cin!*" he answered.

After taking a tiny sip, Margaret lowered her glass and spoke again. "What did you have in mind for me when you mentioned travel to Italy? I'm intrigued."

"Well, here's the idea." The dean paused, then launched into the explanation of his plan. "I want to reorganize the office and create a new position—director of Non-Traditional Programs. Now, this person would be in charge of all our NT Programs—EMT, Video, and Automotive Science—and would report directly to me. And the most important job is to build up these programs in Italy. It's fertile territory for NT."

Bells went off for Margaret. She would no longer have to go through Doris Kink or, even more irritating, through Crepe Moertel in order to get Dean Malfatto's ear. Until now no one could officially have direct access to the dean on general administrative matters until they had gone through one of these two women. While it was mostly a formality devised to keep people out of Malfatto's thinning hair, Margaret saw this new unrestricted access as a real win.

"This person would also work as my personal assistant," he added. "What do you think so far?"

Margaret frowned. "A couple of questions come to mind," she said.

"First, will President Porcino approve the extra expense? Second, isn't Crepe already your personal assistant? And third, what makes you think I or anyone else could hold down both these jobs? It's too much."

Before Malfatto could answer, the wine arrived. Giovanni poured them each a glass, then departed.

"It's not going to cost more," Malfatto said. "In fact, I'll be saving the company money. Crepe will be leaving in a couple of months. Her husband has been reassigned to CONUS. That means I can give you thirty-k a year because we'll no longer have to pay for Crepe." Looking smug, he took another drink, emptying his glass and reaching again for the bottle.

"But I can't be the NT coordinator and do Crepe's job." Margaret crossed her lovely legs and was for a moment lost in thought. Suddenly she turned again to Malfatto. "What about this?" she said, her mind working quickly. "We downgrade the leadership positions for EMT and Video Programs to ten-k-a-year coordinator jobs. The Automotive Science job is already at ten-k. That leaves us a savings of ten-k after my new salary."

"How about some more wine?" the dean asked, his eyes brightening.

"Not yet, thanks." Margaret leaned forward and captivated Malfatto with her eyes. "I suggest Clara Bell for the EMT coordinator job, and for another ten-k she could take over Crepe's duties, still saving us ten-k . . . No, it would be even more. She's now earning six-k, so when we drop that salary, we are up sixteen-k." She paused again briefly. "Doris would be responsible for hiring a new person for Video Programs." Margaret sat back in her chair triumphantly, her eyes still enchanting Malfatto.

He looked stunned. "Wow! That sounds like an even better plan to me."

"Would you like for me to write it up for you?"

Malfatto drank deeply from his wineglass. "Uh, yes. Please put it down for me in writing."

"Sure. I'll start on it tomorrow and have it to you Monday morning."

"Good. Okay, that's it then. So, you'll take the job?"

"Under the conditions I mentioned, yes." Margaret sat back and raised her glass. "Here's to it."

"Here's to it," the dean responded, clinking his glass to hers.

Margaret had assured herself a new job, reporting directly to Malfatto, and with the same salary as Doris Kink. The catch—Malfatto wanted more from her than he had formally offered. But she was certain she could handle him.

CHAPTER THIRTY
GOADED BY GOSSIP

Doris Kink was stewing. She had just gotten word that Bean was having an affair with Margaret and that Malfatto had promoted her. The leak came from Crepe Moertel, who had yearned to be more than just the object of Malfatto's lust. Crepe's husband had just been reassigned to CONUS, so this goal, she realized, would not be achieved. This belief was cemented by the fact that Malfatto had recently distanced himself from her. So, Crepe decided that if she couldn't have Malfatto, she would do her best to prevent both Doris and Margaret from having him. At least she would make them suffer. It was clear to her that the dean lusted after both of them.

Crepe had jumped at the chance to make Doris Kink uncomfortable, to throw her off-balance. A complementary goal was to ensure that the conflict between Doris and Margaret intensified. Margaret was also in Crepe's crosshairs.

At first Crepe just mentioned rumors that Margaret and Bean were having an affair. When that tactic proved insufficient, she strengthened her efforts. Getting a copy of Bean's signature, she had, with the help of a friend who worked at the American military hotel in town, forged it on two hotel bills—one right there in Rheinsteinheim, the other in Sauberbach. The bribe for this service was paid out of the college slush fund and attributed to "donations to charity." Crepe pointed out to Doris that Margaret had been in Sauberbach the same time as Bean. Furthermore, why would Bean be checking in to the local hotel?

"I'm telling you this because I know what it's like to be a woman cheated on," Crepe told Doris. "Margaret is also sleeping with Gio. What a sorry social climber she is! She wants your job, too, you know." Crepe knew about Margaret and Malfatto's dinner date, and she was hurt. The dean told her it was just a business meeting, but Crepe had a bad feeling about it.

Doris was stunned. "Crepe, this could have been a coincidence," she said, hoping still that it was all untrue.

"Doris, I talked to people in Sauberbach who saw them leave the same hotel room together. Margaret's hair was out of place. Have you ever seen Margaret's hair out of place?"

At first Doris was speechless, which was rare.

Crepe leaned forward a bit and continued. "And, Doris dear, I saw them leaving the same room here at the hotel. It was last week—check the date on that bill I gave you—and Margaret's hair was mussed up. And they were both smiling at each other. I was just about to come out of Gio's room when I saw them. They fortunately didn't see me."

Doris was livid. "That sonofabitch! How? Why? Oh! I could kill him!"

"I know how you feel, dear," Crepe said. She reached over and took Doris's hand. "I know exactly how you feel."

Crepe felt tears forming again. So did Doris. Then, for the first time since she had known her, Crepe saw Doris weep.

"Thank you, Crepe," she said. Then she stood in a daze and left the room.

***

Doris didn't know what to do about all this, so she furiously cleaned and organized her desk. Then she began to write memos, but none of this activity helped very much. Doris was still terribly out of sorts when lunchtime came. Usually she went to the snack bar for lunch, but today she headed instead for the Officers' Club.

She was lost in her food and her thoughts when a major and a colonel sat down at the table next to her. As chance would have it, the major was Margaret's husband, whom Doris had never met. The two officers began to talk, and Doris was in for yet another surprise.

"You know this guy Malfatto who runs the Philurius College programs?" asked the major.

"Sure, I've heard of him. Seen him around. Former Army colonel, right?"

"Light colonel," Tom Jefferson said. "Well, he and Margaret had dinner the other night, and guess what?"

"What?" the colonel asked.

"He's offered her a promotion. How about that? She'll be making a good bit more money and will be reporting directly to the dean, no longer through this Doris Kink or the other one. Crepe Moertel is her name, I believe. Margaret is overjoyed."

Doris choked on her BLT. She got up, went to the ladies' room and threw up. She didn't feel like going back to work either. For the first time in her career at Philurius, she called in sick.

Doris continued to stew. At least Bean was out of town for a couple of days. He always called at night, but this evening she decided not to answer her telephone. *Where am I to go? Could Ed help me?* She called his office and was told that Mr. Ehrgeiz was on the road, but that he would be at his boat soon.

Doris arrived and was greeted by Maya.

"Doris, come on in. What brings you here?"

"Uh, hi, Maya. I just . . . There's something I need to discuss with Ed."

"Are you alright? You look terrible."

"I feel terrible."

"Come on in then, and I'll get you something to drink."

"How about a double shot of bourbon."

"Sure," she said. "Comin' up."

Doris followed Maya onto the boat and slumped into a seat in the kitchen. When Maya gave her the bourbon, Doris chugged it.

"Doris, do you want to tell me something?" Maya said. "I know there's something wrong with you. You aren't acting like the normal Doris. Hey, look. You can tell me anything. No need to wait for Ed just because he's a guy."

"Give me another one of these drinks, and I'll talk plenty," Doris said.

Maya went back to the bar and brought back the bottle of bourbon and a glass for herself. She poured Doris a double and herself a single shot. Doris downed this drink in one gulp. Maya stared at her and sipped. "Well?" she said.

"Bean is sleeping with Margaret, and she's sleeping with Malfatto, too, and he's giving her my job, and I have no idea what to do!"

Maya just stared for another moment. "Are you sure about all this? It seems like a bit much, and so sudden."

"Yes, I've got proof," Doris said, and she proceeded to tell the whole story of her conversation with Crepe, the signed hotel bills and the conversation she overheard at the Officers' Club.

"Wow," said Maya, once Doris had finished.

Just then Ed came in whistling. He stopped short when he saw the two women sitting at his kitchen table. "Hey, what's up?" he said.

Maya looked up and said, "Want a bourbon?"

"Sure," he said.

"Then go get yourself a glass," she said.

Ed dutifully obeyed and then joined the ladies at the table.

"Double or single?" Maya asked the group at large.

"Just a single for me," Ed said. "So, what's this all about?"

"Bean is sleeping with Margaret. Malfatto is sleeping with Margaret. Malfatto is giving Margaret Doris's job. That's what's happening," Maya said.

"Are you sure?" Ed asked earnestly.

"She's sure," Maya said.

"I'm sure," Doris added

"The question is, what do we do about it?" Maya said.

"Hm," Ed said softly. "There's an answer to every question. A solution to every problem. This is a tough one, though. So, let's go get some dinner."

"I'm not hungry," Doris said.

"You will be once you start eating," Ed said. "Let's go. How about Zum Ferkel?"

"Couldn't we go someplace else?" Doris asked.

"Sure. Hm. How about that new Mexican joint across the river? Mexican food helps me think," Ed announced. "And this is a serious problem. We can't let Margaret take over your position, Doris. That would be a major setback for the progress we've made. And besides," he said, looking deeply into her eyes, "you are my friend."

El Mexico had just opened the past weekend, and Ed had been itching to go there. He loved Mexican food and was always at "Mexican evening" at the American military hotel.

"Okay," Doris said.

With that they finished their bourbons and departed for dinner.

***

"How about a round of tequilas?" Ed suggested when they were seated at the almost empty restaurant.

"How about several rounds of tequilas?" Doris said.

Ed ordered the drinks, and then they each decided to have a big taco dinner. Throughout the meal Ed remained silent. Doris and Maya chatted, getting tipsier and angrier. It was after the plates had been taken away and another round of tequilas ordered that Ed spoke again.

"It's clear," he said all of a sudden.

Both Doris and Maya just looked at him. "What's clear?" Maya asked.

"The solution to Doris's problem."

"Well, are you going to fill us in, or do we have to guess?" Maya asked.

"You're going to have to seduce him. It's a sweet and simple solution."

"You've lost your mind," Maya said.

"That's a reprehensible idea," Doris slurred.

"Oh no, it's neither. It's a sweet and simple solution. Think Machiavellian. The end justifies the means, you know." Ed stared at them as the next round of drinks arrived.

"You have no conscience," Doris said. "Do you really think I'm such a whore? That would make me just like Margaret, whom I despise!"

"Doris, you're taking this all much too emotionally. You've got to think logically about this problem."

"I'm thinking emotionally?"

"Right. You've got to face this thing squarely. Otherwise, you lose. Is that what you want?"

"I don't want to lose," Doris said with intensity, then added, "But surely there's another way."

"Oh, there might be, but this is so sweet and simple. Don't you see that? Margaret saw what she had to do and did it. Now you'll be playing catch up, but you can do it. Not only are you as appealing as Margaret, you are smarter, and Malfatto must be shown that you are better for the company and for his welfare than she is."

Doris said nothing, but she was earnestly trying to, as Ed said, "see that."

"You don't have to feel anything. Just go through the motions. Doris, we need you here. You're part of the master plan. We've got things to do here. Great things! We've got doors to smash, walls to kick down. It would be a perfect way to gain power over all of them, over the entire situation," Ed continued. "Over Malfatto, Bean, Margaret. Soon you and I will be running this place."

"And what about me?" Maya asked.

"Oh, my dear," Ed said. "When I say I, I mean *we*. You know that." With that, Ed put his hand on Maya's knee.

That night Ed kept trying to break down Doris's resistance to the idea of seducing Malfatto, but without gaining much ground, although he managed to get Maya on board. At the end of the evening they took Doris back to sleep on their boat. She was decidedly in no condition to drive home.

Ed was determined to bring Doris around. There were great things they could do here. The walls would fold once he and Doris assumed power. Ed was a power broker, and he was on his game these days.

***

The next morning, Ed brought coffee to both women. He had already had a cup and had showered.

After serving Maya, he approached Doris's bed, coffee in hand. "Beautiful day, Doris," he said. "Rise and shine. I'll make some breakfast while you shower."

"What time is it?" Doris asked.

"It's 07:00. Time to greet the day."

"Ugh," she said.

Maya, who was more accustomed to this routine, simply sat up in bed and sipped on her coffee.

"Gotta be at work by 08:00, ladies," Ed chirped. "Hey, hop in the shower, Doris. Maya sits there in bed for a while sipping her coffee before she's ready to shower."

"Better go home, I think," Doris answered.

"You okay?" Ed asked.

"Fine. Thanks for the coffee. I'll drink it and go. Bean is supposed to get back today. I'm going to have the lock changed on the door."

"Great idea, Doris! Great idea," Ed said.

"Let me use your phone. I've got to call in sick again. I'll be there in the afternoon, though. I'll be fine now."

"Great, Doris. We've got things to do."

"Yes, I know we do," she said.

***

That morning, Doris went home, called a handyman and had the locks changed on the door to her apartment. She then scribbled a note that she taped to the door.

Bean,

I've just found out about you and Margaret. It's over for us. I cannot be with you ever again after what you've done. Don't try to talk to me about this. No excuses will do. If you decide to stay on at your job, I will continue to work with you in a professional manner, but I hope you will leave. You will have to find another place to live, however. Perhaps Margaret will let you move in with her and her husband.

Goodbye,

Doris

CHAPTER THIRTY-ONE
VIC UP, BEAN DOWN

While Doris Kink was getting plastered at El Mexico, Vic and Eva were boarding a train for Leipzig. For the past two weeks, Vic had been in training. He met separately with Kurt and Eva and then met with them together. They went over tradecraft issues while snacking on wine, cheese and bread, sometimes adding fruit. It reminded him of his university days. Vic came quickly to appreciate Kurt as a real pro in the field of espionage. He had known for a long time that the man was a great bartender.

"You know you ought to teach this stuff at an espionage university someplace," Vic said to him one day after a particularly stimulating session.

"I did for a while, but I wanted to live in Europe and generally just be on my own, especially after I got to know Eva," Kurt said. "I still get to teach occasionally, but rarely do I have students as interested or as good as you. I think you'll like this work."

"Thanks for the trust, although I'm not at all sure I deserve it," Vic said. "Frankly, I'm frightened out of my hide about this assignment. What if I get caught?"

"Remember what you've learned. Just concentrate on that and you'll be fine. This isn't the toughest of assignments. It's a good one to cut your teeth on. Besides you've got Eva with you, and she's been through the routine several times."

"Why don't you just go?" Vic said. "You're clearly much better at this than I am."

Kurt didn't hesitate. "I like to get out on assignment now and again. Keeps me in practice. But right now my main job is to find good potential agents and train them individually." That was the last talk they had before Vic left for his first CIA assignment via train.

As was always the case in Germany, the train left punctually. A few months earlier, Vic had met an employee of the German train system.

"How is it that the German trains are almost never late?" Vic asked.

"We are quite strict," the man answered. "If a driver is once late without an excuse, he gets a written reprimand. If it happens a second time, he loses one month's pay. A third time and he's fired."

Vic was musing on this conversation as the train pulled out of the Rheinsteinheim station. He had brought some water, sandwiches and potato chips. Eva came armed with fruit and vegetables, bread and cheese and a couple of beers. Vic had also brought wine, which he planned to open for dinner and afterwards.

"How long do you think we'll have to wait at the border?" Vic asked.

"It varies. You never know. Usually an hour, maybe two," Eva answered.

"Well, I brought a good book," he said.

"No pornography or other objectionable literature, I hope," Eva said.

"Not a chance," Vic said. "The book is *Hard Times* by Dickens. It's a book about the vices of capitalism. They would love it. Did you bring anything to read?"

"Goethe's *Werther*," she said.

Vic nodded. He was impressed. Eva was a barmaid, waitress, spy and intellectual all rolled into one, and she was great looking to boot. They made small talk for a while, and then they both settled down in their comfortable train cabin with their books until dinnertime.

***

The next day as Vic and Eva were preparing to go to dinner at Leipzig's famous Auerbachs Keller where Goethe had set part of his *Faust,* Bean was unsuccessfully trying to open the door to the apartment he shared with Doris.

"What the hell?" he said. Then he opened the note in his hand. After reading it he sighed deeply. "What is wrong with that woman?" he said, not for the first time. Bean then went down to the street again, walked a couple of blocks to the closest pay phone, put his change in and dialed Doris's work number. It was just after 18:00. No doubt she would still be at her desk. The telephone rang once, twice; then came the familiar voice.

"Doris Kink here." Her voice had a strange timbre, a hard edge with a touch of sadness in it, a voice which to Bean evidenced a fragile person full of anger and disappointment who was trying to cover her emotions.

"How about dinner?" he asked without preamble.

"I've got nothing to talk to you about, and I don't want you hanging around my door tonight waiting for me. I won't be coming home, so it wouldn't do you any good anyway." The sadness disappeared into a blaze of hot anger.

"Okay, I won't come around tonight," Bean said. "I'll find someplace else to stay, but you owe me an explanation, Doe. I have no idea what you're talking about in this note. I'm not having an affair with Margaret. I think she's good lookin', but so does everyone else. You are my lady."

"Right. Well, I have proof," she said.

Before responding, Bean's mind searched for what kind of proof she could have. Certainly there was no legitimate proof, since he hadn't slept with Margaret. He had admired her beauty, and under other circumstances he might have made a play for her, but he was, in fact, committed to Doris in an old-fashioned kind of way, even though she had lately seriously tested his commitment to her. After a lapse of a few seconds, he answered. "You couldn't possibly have proof, Doe. Come on, let's have dinner tonight and get this all straightened out."

"No. Goodbye. It's all over between us. And I would prefer for you to resign your position immediately and leave town, leave the country, but in any case, I want you to leave me alone." With that she slammed down her phone.

Bean gently replaced his telephone receiver and scratched his cheek. Then he headed for the military hotel just blocks away where he got a room, then had a couple of drinks in the bar. There, and later in his room, Bean considered his options. Doris had always been a bit hyper, but nothing like this had ever happened before. Before he arrived here,

Bean had noticed from her letters that Doris had become a different person: harder, more cynical, power hungry. He had hoped to have a positive influence on her, but nothing seemed to get her off her power path. This latest nonsense about him and Margaret, however, was beyond the pale. In the past when she had gotten miffed at him about something, Bean just had to wait her out. This time, though, he felt that things were different. Where, he wondered, did she get this idea that he was sleeping with Margaret? Doris didn't understand him. How could he convince her that nothing was going on between him and Margaret?

***

Vic and Eva had just entered the Mädler Passage, a Neo-Renaissance/ Art Nouveau construction which had opened for the first time in 1914 as a trade hall. It housed, among other things, Auerbachs Keller, built in 1525. Vic was nervous, and he wondered why Eva seemed so calm. Then it occurred to him that she always seemed calm.

They had checked into a small hotel close to the Südwestplatz. Kurt had told him that their room would probably be bugged, reminding them that they should behave like a normal couple on vacation.

"Does that mean we make love every evening?" Vic mocked.

"Is that what you and Bonnie do on vacation?" Eva asked.

"Honestly, no. But we manage it at least once."

"This time Eva will have a headache. Surely that happens with you and Bonnie occasionally," Kurt said.

"Okay, I get it. I just wanted to make sure I do everything right so you would hire me again, Kurt."

As they walked down the stairway into Auerbachs Keller, Vic recalled the 1960s when as an undergraduate he had first read *Faust*. In fact, he had written an essay on it. The most vivid memory he had of the paper was his conclusion; namely, that *Faust* provided a distorted picture of human nature. Since then he had changed his mind. Human nature was worse than Goethe had made out.

Eva intruded on his reverie. "How about the table by the wall over there?" she asked.

"Looks fine to me," Vic said.

They had been seated a while before the waiter wandered over. They both ordered wurst, sauerkraut and beers. Over dinner an idea occurred to Vic, which he passed on to Eva.

"When I get back to the USA," he said, "I want to start a business, and I want you and Kurt to help me with it. Here's the idea. It will be a German restaurant in upstate New York, and I want it to be authentic. I want all the kinds of wursts one can get in Germany as well as waitresses dressed in traditional Bavarian dirndls and waiters in lederhosen."

"Sounds like a good idea," Eva said. "What will you call it?"

Vic thought for a moment. "I've got it," he said. "I'll call it the Wurst Place in Town!"

Eva sighed.

According to their plan, they ordered another couple of beers after finishing their meals. They complimented the food and the waiter, though the latter must have wondered why they bothered. He clearly took no interest in his job. Vic then asked if they could send a note of appreciation to the chef.

"This was such an excellent meal. We've heard about this restaurant from friends in Kansas City. Thanks for taking a note to the chef for us," Vic said.

The waiter shrugged. "If you like."

Vic then scribbled a note. *Thanks for the delicious wurst and sauerkraut, the best my wife and I have ever had. It would be wonderful to have such grand food preparation in Kansas City, the city where we live.*

Before long the waiter came back with the beers and a message from Hans, the chef.

"Our grand chef Hans Wurst says to thank you kindly for your kind words. He also said he had heard that Kansas City is a very nice town."

Vic thanked him, paid for the meal and left a generous tip. Afterwards, Vic and Eva strolled to the tram, which took them back to Südwestplatz. There was nothing to do now but wait until tomorrow. The meeting place and time of day had been established by Eva months ago and was confirmed in a code contained in the note Vic sent to Hans.

***

As Eva and Vic were eating Hans Wurst's wurst and sauerkraut, Doris was having dinner with Ed and Maya at the Turkish restaurant Zum Ferkel, at Ed's insistence. Doris reluctantly agreed to go along. This evening she had decided not to drink much. She was exhausted from all the alcohol of the previous evening, plus her fretting about Bean, and was reflecting on these concerns when Ed interrupted her thoughts.

"Doris, you really have to act quickly or your chances here at Philurius will be ruined forever."

That got her attention. "What do you mean?"

"It's time for drastic measures and rapid response. Both Maya and I believe you must seduce Malfatto before Margaret gets him completely under her control."

"It's time, I'm afraid," Maya said.

"And how do you know she hasn't already got him locked in?" Doris asked.

"Just a feeling I have," Ed said.

He sounds so confident, Doris thought. She wanted to believe that she still had a chance to foil Margaret. "And what makes you think he would fall for such a seduction?" she asked.

"Doris, where have you been? Malfatto's been eyeing you ever since you got here," he said with conviction.

"Ed, he's been eyeing every female that passes by. I'm nothing special."

"Oh, but you are, Doris. You're not only a good-looking, sexy woman, you're kind of, well, an intellectual."

"Now why would that make me appealing to Malfatto?" she asked. Secretly, she was pleased. It was the second time within a couple of days that Ed had paid her this compliment.

"Because it's something new for him. Don't you see that? Look who he's been with for the past year. Crepe Moertel, for heaven's sake. She is by no stretch of the imagination a good-looking woman, and she sure ain't no rocket scientist."

"But why would he prefer me to Margaret?" Doris asked.

"That's your blind spot, Doris. Malfatto needs you much more than he needs Margaret. You just have to show him that, and you can really get his attention and accomplish your goal by seducing him. Do that and he's yours." Ed paused for effect. When he spoke, his voice was dead earnest. "Doris, if you won't do this for yourself and your career, do it for the company."

Both Doris and Maya looked at him but said nothing.

It turned out to be a relatively short night. Doris faded fast. She slept restlessly that evening on Ed and Maya's boat, and when Ed awakened the next morning, she had coffee, drove to her apartment, showered, changed clothes, and started cleaning up her pad and throwing away everything that reminded her of Bean. His clothes and personal effects she placed outside her apartment door, and she left a note for him both there and at the office stating that he could pick them up the next day during work hours. Doris had promised Ed and Maya she would come back to their boat in the evening. Ed offered to grill steaks. He was also planning to keep up the pressure on Doris to seduce Malfatto.

***

After Vic and Eva had breakfast in the hotel, they went out for a bit of sightseeing. First, they visited the City Museum, then the two churches where Johann Sebastian Bach had worked from 1723 to 1750 as parish music director and choirmaster of the boys' choir, as well as their dorm supervisor. They learned later at the Bach Museum that Johann had paid someone to teach his Latin lessons.

"I can hardly blame him," Vic said. "Look at all the music he wrote. I don't even see how he had time to father those twenty children. By the way, Eva," he continued, "do you know why Bach had twenty children?"

She just looked at him. Eva really didn't understand this strange man, though she did like him. "No," she said finally.

Vic tilted his head toward her and said confidentially, "Because there were no stops on his organ."

Eva frowned. "I don't get it," she said.

After seeing the Nicholas and Thomas churches, the ostensible tourists headed to a café close to Auerbachs Keller. They were a few minutes earlier than expected. After they had ordered coffee, they saw Hans Wurst stroll up. Eva caught his eye and dropped her napkin. As she bent over to pick it up, Hans Wurst hurried to get it for her. She thanked him, after which he sat down next to them and ordered coffee. They didn't look at each other. Then Eva said she had to go to the ladies' room and would be right back. She returned in a few minutes. When she sat down, she opened her purse and reached inside, taking out a small black bag and some makeup. Then she let the bag fall to the floor. Immediately, Hans picked it up and smiling sweetly handed her a black bag.

"I believe you dropped this, miss," he said.

"Oh, thank you, sir," she said. "Thanks once again. You are most attentive."

It was not Eva's little black bag that Hans Wurst had handed over to her. It was one just like it that he had brought. Not only was Hans a great cook, he was also a master artist at sleight of hand. In the bag he had given Eva were two small, inexpensive brooches. In the one he pocketed from her were four huge diamonds which he could use to pay his way out of East Germany and on to his final goal of Kansas City, where the CIA had promised him a job as head chef in a major hotel restaurant.

Hans was excited. He had recently read everything he could about Kansas City. Hans was especially looking forward to the jazz clubs where he would finally be able to hear live jazz. There were many details yet to be worked out, but he was another step closer to escaping East Germany.

Vic and Eva had lunch, did some more sightseeing and then caught the overnight train back to Rheinsteinheim. Once they got across the border, Vic at last felt free to talk.

"We did it, Eva," he said. Vic found himself shaking slightly. He had managed to keep his nerves under control during the mission, but now that the pressure was off, he felt the nervousness.

"Yes," she said, "we did."

She looks so cool, Vic thought. "Let's open the wine," he suggested.

Eva nodded slightly in agreement. She also felt the exhilaration of having come through the mission successfully, though as a result of her training and experience, she was calmer than Vic. She knew he would be good at this work, though, and she told him so as he pulled out the cork on the bottle of wine.

"Well, thank you, ma'am," he said, truly pleased. He filled their glasses, then asked, "Where did you keep those diamonds the whole time?"

"Inside me," she said.

"Inside you?"

"That's right. And had you fulfilled your desire to make love to me, you would have found them," she said.

Vic looked up, shocked. Then he shook his head and toasted her.

***

As Eva and Vic were toasting their successful mission, Ed was serving steaks to Doris and Maya. Doris at first declined any wine, but at Ed's insistence she finally accepted a glass. Ed was a fellow who could wear you down. Doris was confused, and she was angry. It seemed as if her world were falling apart. She had lost Bean to her archrival, the beautiful bitch Margaret Malcontenta-Jefferson.

Once they were all good and tipsy and full of revengeful plans, Ed broke out his other surprise weapon: the marijuana.

"Ever tried this stuff before, Doris?" Ed asked.

"Sure. It's been a while though. It was back at USC."

"Well then, you know what to do with it?"

"Of course," Doris said indignantly. Sometimes she found Ed patronizing. But Ed and Maya were, it seemed to her, the only friends she had left in the world, so she accepted the proffered joint. By bedtime she had convinced herself, with a bit of prompting from Ed and Maya and Mary Jane, that she really must seduce Malfatto, for her sake and for the sake of the company.

CHAPTER THIRTY-TWO
DORIS'S DESPERATION

Ed awakened Doris on Sunday morning bright and early. She looked at him through a mist, her vision slowly coming into focus. She saw the outline of a person standing above her and then recognized him as Ed.

"Rise and shine," Ed said happily. He sat down on her bed and held a cup of coffee under her nose.

Doris sat up, had a sip of the delicious brew and sighed. "That's good!" she said.

After breakfast with her two colleagues, she drove home, still confused about her next move. Ed and Maya had pushed her to seduce Malfatto, and finally she was convinced. That is, her head was convinced, but her heart was still lagging.

Doris spent the rest of the day alternately cleaning house and restlessly squirming in her bed. Feeling forlorn, she went to a small Gasthaus where there were only older men smoking, drinking beer and playing cards.

She found a place alone in the corner and had a look at the menu. The Wiener schnitzel and fries, real comfort food, struck her fancy, so she ordered that and a Coca Cola. Doris decided that she would not drink any alcohol, at least for the next few days, and she vowed she would never again smoke marijuana.

The Coca Cola came, and she drank it quickly. "Why can't they put ice cubes in the drinks here?" she mumbled. "How uncivilized!" After her meal, not knowing what else to do, she returned to her tidy apartment. There were two messages on her answering machine. One was from Malfatto, the other from Bean. Malfatto wanted to know if she had finished the report for the accreditation team.

"Hey, they'll be here pretty soon, so we need to get this wrapped up. You remember Salmonello is going to be here, too. He really likes the work we've been doing with downsizing, so if we make a good impression on him with the accreditation people, we're in good shape for the future. Hell, we might even get a raise. See me first thing Monday. Uh, there's something else we need to discuss, but I don't want to do that on the phone. Okay, well, I guess that's all."

The next message was from Bean. "Doe, it's me, Bean. I've decided to give my two-weeks' notice to Plea Dies on Monday. I'll work those two weeks . . . Doe, I hope we can at least have a face-to-face conversation before I leave. This is all a crazy misunderstanding. I wish we could talk about it. I'm in the military hotel, room 414. Good night."

At precisely 09:00 Monday, Doris was once again marching toward Malfatto's office.

Just outside the dean's door sat Crepe Moertel dressed entirely in black. She looked up briefly as Doris stepped up to her desk.

"He's not here yet," Crepe said.

"Do you know when he'll be arriving?" Doris said.

"No idea. I'll call you, though, as soon as he shows up."

"Thanks, Crepe," Doris said.

Half an hour later Doris's telephone rang. She picked it up before the second ring. It was precisely this kind of efficiency that made her feel good.

"Doris, Gio— I mean, the dean, just came in," Crepe said. "You might let him finish his coffee, doughnuts and crossword puzzle before you come down. I suggest you come in about fifteen minutes . . . Well, I suppose you can come right down. He won't be able to finish the crossword by himself."

As Doris entered the dean's outer sanctum, she nodded at Crepe.

"Doris is here to see you," Crepe announced on the intercom.

"Tell her to come on in," Malfatto said.

When Doris entered his office, Malfatto barked at her. "First order of business is to get a couple of answers to this damned crossword puzzle. A small dog, five letters, the first one is g."

Doris sighed. "That can't be," she said as she sat down stiffly. "It's got to be *puppy*. You must have gotten something else wrong."

"Well, let's see. Four across is 'a favorite presidential pastime,' nine letters. First, I thought of *golf*, but that's only four letters. Then it came to me: *gardening*. Seems like I've read that a lot of presidents enjoyed gardening to take their minds off things."

"Try *pardoning*," Doris said wearily.

Malfatto looked up at her, pleased. "Great! I don't know what I would do without you."

"Oh?" she said.

"Well, that did it. Thanks." Malfatto looked up at her. "How's the report comin'?

"Here's the draft," she said, lifting the document with both hands and placing it on the front of his desk. "You might want to look at it over the next couple of days, but let me get a copy made first. I've gotten input from all the department heads and have integrated it into the report. We've had to play loose with some of the statistics. I've organized them to make us look as good as possible. Also, as you know, we have had to play loose with some other facts, as well. That shouldn't be a problem though. There's no way these people are going to check out all the personnel in the entire system. So, I think we are in good shape. Of course, I'll do some fine-tuning over the next few days. Questions?"

"Oh, no. No questions. Good work. I'll have a good look at it, but could you get me a one-page summary to study?" Malfatto said.

"A one-page summary?" Doris said. "This is a 213-page report. How am I supposed to summarize all that in one page? Why don't you just skim it and then ask me questions? I really don't have time to write you a summary of any kind."

"Well, you know, the president of the United States gets a one-page summary from his intelligence people once a week. Not only that, the real important items are marked in yellow," the dean said.

"That's done by a staff of people who do nothing else," she said. "I'm only one person, and I have plenty of other things to do. You do remember that I'm still running academic affairs, don't you? And, while we are on the subject, that could be a problem for the accreditation team. It might not be, but it could be. They might ask how I could hold down both the assistant dean's job and the academic affairs job, and they would have a point. Besides that, I don't have a PhD."

"Yeah, yeah, I know. Both you and Ed Ehrgeiz are driving me nuts with this idea that his ancient wunderkind should be given the job. Tell me why I should give that prick anything but a boot out the door? Don't you remember last year when he was making more money than I was by running all those bogus video courses?"

Doris caught her breath as she stared at the dean. *I am contemplating seducing this man on the other side of the table.* The thought drained the color from her face.

"You alright?" he asked. "You look like you just saw a ghost."

"Oh, uh, I'm just a little tired. Haven't been getting much sleep. You know, this report and all the other work, especially managing academic affairs."

"You been gittin' enough recently?" Malfatto said. He was ogling her when she looked up at him. For a moment she just stared at him. "Well?" he asked.

"What I do in my private life is none of your damn business," she said hotly. "Now, unless you have something else to discuss, I've got work to do." She wanted to scratch his eyes out.

"What's this I hear about Bean resigning?"

Doris rose so quickly that she lost her balance and tripped over the chair. The next thing she knew, she was sprawled on the floor. Then, before she could collect herself, Malfatto was at her side. He put both his clammy hands on her, one on each of her shoulders.

"You alright?" he said.

"Get away! I'm fine. Just get away, please."

"Here, let me help you up."

"No!" Doris screamed.

The dean, startled, quickly moved away from her.

Doris got up, slowly this time, brushed off imaginary dirt from her business pants, then stared haughtily at Malfatto. Inside she was churning, out of control. When she spoke, her voice trembled.

"I'm perfectly fine. I just tripped. Got to get back to work." With that she turned and started to leave.

"Just a minute," the dean said. "Are you sure you're okay?"

Doris stopped but did not turn around. "Yes, I'm sure I'm fine. Like I said, I'm just a bit tired. There's so much to do and so little time." She hesitated. "I'll see you later," she said as she started for the door.

"I've got another matter to discuss with you, but if you aren't up for it, we'll just postpone," Malfatto said.

Doris turned, eyes blazing. "I'm just tired! I just slipped! That doesn't mean I'm falling apart! You think women can't take any kind of pressure, don't you? Well, I'm telling you I'm a lot stronger than you are. If it weren't for me, you'd be in a helluva lot of trouble. I've pulled you out of the fire time after time, and all you do is insult me."

Not being able to contain herself, she continued. "And now you've gone and slept with Margaret and are replacing me with her! How could you? I'm quitting! I'm tired of being abused. I'll give you your two weeks, that's my duty, but then I'm out of here." She turned again and started toward the door.

"Wait!" Malfatto said. "Wait a minute. Just let me say something, will you? . . . Look, you've got this all wrong. I can't do without you." Malfatto shrugged and raised his hands in submission. Then he pointed to the chair, indicating that Doris should again have a seat. She hesitated but did so.

"So, what is this with Margaret Malcontenta-Jefferson?" she asked.

"Hey, I'm not having sex with Margaret, and I'm not giving her your job. Where did you get that idea? Whoever told you that, well . . ."

Doris interrupted. "I have it on good authority that you're screwing Margaret and replacing me with her!"

They glared at each other until Malfatto spoke. "I'm not having sex with Margaret, and I'm not giving her your job. I've just decided to reorganize a bit, so when Crepe leaves, I can give Margaret the new job as Non-Traditional Programs director, taking care of EMT, Video Programs and Automotive Science."

"And why didn't you discuss any of this with me?" Doris asked.

"Well . . . well, dammit, I'm the dean here. I can do whatever I like! And besides, I'm saving money."

Doris looked at him with contempt. "How do you think we'll be saving money with this plan if you only eliminate Crepe's salary? We save nothing! And if you are giving Margaret a salary increase, that would put us in the hole. What about downsizing? Is that out the window now?"

"Uh . . . look. I've got to give Margaret another ten-k. It's much more responsibility, and she'll be on the road a lot. I have to compensate for those things." The dean shrugged.

"So that puts us down ten-k. Bad planning!"

"Look, Doris." He paused again. "We'll have to lower the EMT and Video positions to ten-k a year and call them coordinators. Then we make a profit. You see that, don't you?"

"You're hopeless! This plan of yours makes no sense. The EMT and Video Programs are making money now. Why jeopardize them? Who would want to do the same job for half the pay? And how will all this affect my job? I've always been in charge of the administration. What other tasks are you assigning your new heartthrob?" They stared at each other coldly until Malfatto spoke.

"Let's be honest," he began. "You've been a big help to the company and to me personally. But Margaret has been nice to me. Frankly, she's more fun to be around. I realize you're smarter. If you were only a little nicer." He shrugged. "There could be a great future for you with the company."

Doris took a deep breath and let it out slowly. "So, you may get rid of me after all."

"I don't want you to leave. Like I said, I need you. All I'm doing with Margaret is giving her a better job so she can help expand the NT Programs, especially in Italy. She'll be gone a lot, and we can carry on here as usual."

Doris shook her head. "Okay, I'll postpone my departure until after the A-Team leaves. Then we'll see what happens. But I don't want to have to deal with Margaret, and I don't want her messing in my business! In fact, I would be happier if she weren't here at all."

Malfatto pulled on his tie again. "A lot of this depends on you, you know." Again silence. Then Malfatto said, "Get me a final copy of this report as soon as you can."

"Fine," she said.

Leaving the dean's office, she just nodded to Crepe and walked swiftly to the ladies' room where she was once again sick.

After she left, Malfatto sat and mused. *This is gettin' interesting. I'm hopin' this will all work out with Margaret. I'll bet she could do Doris's job, too. But what I really want is to keep both of them. Could Doris be vulnerable? Can I exploit it? If things don't work out with Margaret, maybe I can keep Doris around and get her in my bed. It looks like she and Bean are finished. Damn! I don't know what to do. Maybe I'll talk to Margaret again.* He picked up the telephone and dialed.

CHAPTER THIRTY-THREE
BACKSTABBING

Two weeks passed before Doris finally decided on her next move. She revised and polished the all-important report, which helped to keep her mind off Bean. As she had requested, he left her alone. The only exceptions had been the one telephone call, the flowers with a note and the longer note sent just before he left for parts unknown.

> *Dearest Doe,*
>
> *I'm off for a couple of weeks. When I return, it will only be to finish settling my affairs here. Then I'll return to Los Angeles. Doe, I'm sorry we couldn't talk about this craziness. Whoever told you those absurd stories must have an agenda which most decidedly is not in your interest or mine. All I can say is that I love you still. I hope that we can see each other before I leave.*
>
> *Love, Bean*

When she finished reading, Doris did not toss the note as she had intended. Instead, she put it in her lingerie drawer. Then, in order to keep from thinking about her life, she picked up her briefcase and headed toward her office. She would contact Margaret right away about having Clara take over Bean's job, at least until a replacement could be found. She didn't want to talk to Margaret but realized she would have to. Then she would work on Malfatto until she convinced him to put the ancient wunderkind in as director of Academic Affairs. After that she would start re-reading the report for the A-Team. There was so much to do.

Nowadays Doris Kink did almost nothing but work at the office, work out in the gym and worry about Malfatto and Margaret and her loss of Bean. She spent every day from 07:00 until 19:00 in the office, taking an hour for lunch and then spending two hours at the gym before heading home. The issue of Malfatto was constantly on her mind. Finally, she decided to seduce the disgusting flabby man and then give him an ultimatum: *Margaret or me*, she would say to him. "What have I got to lose?" she asked the wall. "I've already lost much of what was dear to me." Seducing Malfatto was nothing more than a bold career move, she reasoned.

***

While Doris was pondering her fate, Malfatto was busy trying to decide what he should do. He had consulted Margaret. When he called her that day just after his confrontation with Doris, he had taken her by surprise.

"Good morning, this is Margaret Malcontenta-Jefferson, how can I help you?"

"What a great telephone voice you have," the dean murmured.

"Oh, good morning, Dean Malfatto. Thank you."

"Margaret, just call me Gio. Remember? I gave you permission."

"Oh, sorry," Margaret laughed engagingly. "It's a bit difficult for me. I mean, I've called you Dean Malfatto for so long. You are the boss, you know."

"Yes, I know," he said, as he sat up in his chair a bit. "But special people can call me Gio."

"Okay, I'll try to remember, but it still feels awkward."

"Hey, listen," he said. "I've got something important to talk to you about. How about coming over to my place tonight after work?"

"Why can't we talk now?"

"Uh, well, it's just that I've got a lot to do all day. Meetings, phone calls, other things . . . you know. I need to concentrate on some pressing issues, so I thought tonight at my place we could just, you know, concentrate a little better. It would be more relaxed."

"Well, actually, I have something to do tonight, something I can't easily change, but if we could have a drink in the O Club bar at 17:30, I could give you half an hour."

"Okay, okay. I'll come by for you about 17:15," Malfatto said.

***

At promptly 17:15 he appeared at Margaret's door. She had just finished freshening up and donning an indigo-blue pantsuit and a flame-colored blouse, emanating a Spanish flare. When Malfatto entered the room and saw her at her desk, his heart leapt. When she rose, he got slightly dizzy.

On the way to the bar, they made small talk. Among other things, the dean learned that Margaret had some new plans about downsizing. She didn't say what they were, just that she was formulating them for his consideration. By 17:30 they were seated in the bar.

"So, what are you having?" Malfatto asked.

"A martini," Margaret answered.

"Okay, I'll be right back."

When Malfatto returned, a martini in each hand, he proposed a toast. "To our future working relationship," he said as he raised his glass.

"To our future working relationship," she echoed. "May it be profitable."

They drank, and then the dean began the talk he had rehearsed. "You know Doris Kink doesn't like you."

"Yes, I know that," Margaret said.

"She threatened to resign because of you. Somehow, she found out about my offering you a new job with more responsibility."

"Crepe," Margaret said disdainfully.

"Could be," Malfatto said. "She also believes this will lessen her power." Malfatto did not mention Doris's suspicions that he and Margaret were having an affair. "What do you think I ought to do?"

"I believe there's room for both of us at Philurius, but if she wants to resign, we could take up the slack."

"You really think we could take up the slack if she left?"

"Without a doubt," she said. Margaret and Souter had talked about this possibility and had tried to find ways both large and small that would drive Doris out.

Souter had come up with the downsizing plan Margaret had alluded to as she and Malfatto made their way to the O Club bar. Then he and

Margaret had refined it and rehearsed her presentation of it.

"Present him with the plan this week, then talk to him about how you can do things better than Doris Kink and at the same time save him money," Souter coached her. "Point out to him that our department has done more than any other in terms of downsizing, and that we are now the biggest program-revenue generator outside of Video Programs. Above all, charm him."

Margaret was thinking about all this now as she sat across the table from Dean Malfatto. Suddenly she decided she would give him a preview of the plan Souter and she had devised.

"You mentioned last week," Margaret began, "that Doris wanted to drop Crepe's position entirely and put this fellow they call wunderkind in as director of Academic Affairs and leave everything else as it is. That would provide us with zero savings, because Doris would still get her salary, but the wunderkind would be getting the academic director salary. If we just kept Doris as the acting academic director, we would automatically have a big savings. Once the A-Team has gone, we could do that under the table. We must just tell them that we are about to begin interviewing for the academic director job. But there's more," she added quickly. "I have a four-point plan which will serve us better and save us even more money. We could accomplish this by downsizing and combining jobs, but we would be every bit as efficient—leaner and meaner. How do you think President Porcino might react to that?"

"Wow! You really think we could do all that?"

"Absolutely, yes," she said. "I'll have the plan to you in writing by Monday."

Malfatto took another drink and sat back in his chair. He looked her way and nodded his approval. "Your plan sure sounds better than Doris's," he said at last. "But she won't go for reporting through you to me. No way."

"Oh, she wouldn't have to do that. We would be equals in a sense and would both report directly to you."

"Well, until now, everyone has had to come through Doris or Crepe to get to me. It worked pretty good. Kept the pressure off me so I could lead," he said.

"Everyone but Doris Kink would come through me," she said.

"I'm not sure she would like that either," Malfatto said.

Souter and Margaret had talked about this very problem and had come to what they believed was the best tactical answer. "We wouldn't have to put it on the flow chart that way. It could be strictly informal."

"You think that would work?" Malfatto said.

"I believe it would."

"Well, okay. Maybe you're right. It would be good to keep her if we can. I just don't want her as an enemy."

"We can present it to her in a really positive way. I'll think about that too and get back to you," Margaret said.

The dean smiled. "You're good, Margaret. Real good. You're also great looking." As he glanced across the table at Margaret, Malfatto imagined himself in the sack with her. The conversation that followed was inconsequential. The main work had been done, and Margaret felt great. She would call Souter as soon as she got home. Perhaps they could meet later. In fact, Margaret had nothing to do that evening aside from a dining date with her husband, and she could change that, too, if necessary.

CHAPTER THIRTY-FOUR
THE SEDUCTRESS

Dean Malfatto had been wanting to talk to Doris all week about those things he discussed with Margaret. Doris had continued to work on revisions to the report all week and to think about how to approach Malfatto. She caught him looking at her a couple of times that day with lustful eyes. He had been courteous to her since their confrontation and, in fact, had gone out of his way to compliment her on her looks and her work.

I've got to take action, she thought. *The sooner, the better.* It was Friday afternoon, and soon the work week would be over. Doris rose from her chair and started toward the dean's office. When she got to Crepe's desk, she found her pouting.

"Margaret has been in there for an hour," she said. "What could they be doing for an hour behind a closed door?" she asked.

Crepe had experience behind the closed door. She and the dean had indulged in mid-morning sex, afternoon sex or sometimes evening sex behind this very door, but it had never lasted more than fifteen minutes. Crepe was feeling angry and frustrated. It had been over a week since she shared Malfatto's bed, and she was convinced that was because Margaret was there instead.

Just then the door opened, and Margaret stepped out. *Is her hair mussed?* Doris couldn't tell. She did, however, see the special smile that passed between Margaret and Malfatto.

"Thanks," said the dean.

"My pleasure," said Margaret. Then she turned, seeming to notice Doris for the first time. "Oh, hello, Doris," she said. "It's your turn now,

I guess. I hope I haven't worn him out too much." Malfatto laughed, Margaret smiled, but Doris and Crepe remained sullen. "Have a nice weekend, everybody," Margaret said as she glided from the room.

"You need to see me, Doris?" Malfatto said as Margaret disappeared down the hall.

"Unless you are too worn out," she said.

Malfatto chortled. "I've got plenty of steam left," he said. "Come on in and close the door."

Doris followed.

"What's up?" he asked as he took a seat.

Doris began to panic. Could she really go through with this? Then she focused on her last talk with Maya. "I would do it in a flash if I were in your shoes," Maya had told her. "It's just a tool."

"Well?" said Malfatto. "Did you have something to talk to me about?" He was looking quizzically at her.

"How about dinner tonight?" Doris blurted.

Malfatto sat back in his chair and said nothing.

"I mean, unless you have other plans. I just thought, well, it's so formal here, so restrictive. I thought maybe a change of pace would be good. Would help us talk."

"Are you asking me out?" he said.

"No," she said. "Actually, I thought I would pick the place and you would pay."

Malfatto laughed. "Okay, okay," he said. "You drive a hard bargain, Ms. Kink. What time?"

"Well, I have some more work to do. Then I thought I would go home, shower and freshen up a bit. How about 20:00?"

"Fine by me. Shall I pick you up?"

"No, that's not necessary. I'll meet you at the restaurant."

"Which one? It's your pick."

"Have you been to the Turkish place Zum Ferkel?" she asked.

"No, but I know where it is. Just around the corner from your place, right?"

"Right. I'll see you there at 20:00. Don't be late."

"I'll be there on time," he said.

Doris did her gym routine after work and then prepared for the evening out. Nervous, she opened a bottle of wine and took it with her to her wardrobe. She sipped on the wine while getting dressed. Having finished her first glass, she slipped into a clingy green silk dress Bean had bought for her recently. She had never worn it. In fact, she had intended to wear it for his birthday, which, it suddenly occurred to her, was coming up on the same day as the accreditation team's "farewell dinner" sponsored by Philurius College at great expense. "It'll serve him right," she said aloud.

Doris entered Zum Ferkel and was led to a table for two in a dark corner, which she had reserved in order to assure privacy. Malfatto entered shortly after and looked around. She waved, and he started over to her.

"Hey, you look great!" he said. "You should dress up like this more often."

Doris thanked him, noticing that he wasn't looking her in the eye. Somehow, tonight, that did not bother her as it generally did.

"Hey, they have belly dancing here tonight," he said. "Tell me, how does a nice Catholic girl like you know about a place like this?"

"I'm not Catholic," she said. Malfatto didn't seem to hear.

"They start at 21:00," he said. Doris saw that he was in a good mood. She had decided to begin slowly, but, due perhaps to the two glasses of wine she had already put away, she decided to pick up the tempo a tad. As these thoughts passed through her mind, the waiter arrived.

"What's good to drink here?" Malfatto asked.

"Two *rakis*," Doris said. The waiter nodded and left menus.

"So, what was that you ordered for us?" Malfatto asked.

"*Raki*. It's the national drink of Turkey. It's a bit on the strong side, but I thought you could handle it."

Malfatto laughed. He liked this new kinky Doris.

"Nice smile," he said.

"Pardon?"

"I said you have a nice smile."

"Thanks."

"You seem unhappy most of the time."

"But I'm not unhappy. It's just that I like to attend to business. One of the greatest problems with the company is that people are not serious enough about their jobs. It's—" *This is precisely where Margaret has been killing me,* she thought. *I'm smarter than Margaret. I'm more efficient and harder working. I have more drive, and I can be every bit as sexy.*

"Well?" said Malfatto.

"Pardon?"

"You were about to make another point, but you just stopped."

"Well, it's just that I am happy . . . basically."

"You should tell your face more often."

"Pardon?"

"Doris, you should tell your face that you are happy. It hasn't gotten the message."

Doris relaxed. She smiled. "That's why I think it's a good idea for us, just the two of us, to get together like this, in an atmosphere like this. So we can let down, you know," Doris said, as the waiter appeared with the *raki*.

"Oh, we haven't even looked at the menu," Malfatto said as he reached for the one closest to him.

"Trust me on this," Doris said. "The lamb is terrific here, and we'll have a Turkish wine with it, a *Vila Doluca*. You won't be disappointed."

"Okay," Malfatto said. "I'll trust you on this one."

After the waiter left the table with their order, Malfatto decided he would initiate the business of the evening. "*Cin cin!*" he said as he raised his glass.

"*Cin cin!*" Doris replied as she raised her glass.

"Whoa! That is strong stuff. It tastes a lot like Sambuca, just rawer."

"They're both anis-based," Doris said.

"Think we could get another one?"

"You're paying," Doris said.

Malfatto laughed again. "So, what do you want to talk to me about tonight?" he said.

"We're turning the procedure around. Remember? Pleasure before business."

Malfatto had an urge to blurt out the plan that he and Margaret had talked about, a plan that he had altered slightly to serve his own purposes. *What Margaret doesn't know won't hurt her,* the dean had thought. *Divide and conquer.* He wanted to just get it over with, to tell Doris that he needed both her and Margaret, but that she would have a long-term role with the company if she could prove herself a team player, if she could be a little nicer. She would be a mainstay long after Margaret was gone with her husband to a new assignment. Margaret would be tasked with expanding Non-Traditional Programs, which meant she'd be gone a lot. Having Doris at headquarters and Margaret in the field would be great for the school's profile . . . and for him. Malfatto had considered all of the pluses.

The urge to reveal his plan was strong, but some atavistic urge not to do so overrode it. What he did instead was say, "Right. Pleasure before business. I like the idea. Got any more?"

After two bottles of wine, a delectable meal and tantalizing belly dancing, their conversation loosened up. Malfatto spoke of his desire to retire from Philurius in a couple of years and to settle in Sicily.

"I could sell the California house I'm renting out and buy a farmhouse in Sicily," he said. "Then, with my military retirement plus my Philurius retirement, I could live like a prince. I'd like to do some teaching, of course. You'd hire me, wouldn't you?" he asked mockingly.

Doris nodded. At this point she had taken her shoes off. While Malfatto was talking about houses in Sicily, she moved her right foot underneath the table over to Malfatto's leg. Then she began to caress his ankle with her toes. Malfatto stopped in mid-sentence and looked at her before settling back in his chair and continuing his story. He was almost certain a foot was caressing his lower leg. Suddenly he spoke again.

"What are your long-term dreams?" he asked.

"I've always wanted to be rich and powerful," she said. "Real rich and powerful."

"Stick with me and you'll make it," Malfatto said meaningfully. Just then he felt the foot again, moving up his leg a bit. *Could this be happening?*

"How about a nightcap at my place?" Doris cooed.

"Right on," he said without hesitation. "Waiter," he called loudly.

Once they arrived at her apartment, Doris turned to him and whispered, "Try to be quiet now. The neighbors."

He nodded and followed her inside. His first impression was "Neat, you've got a real neat apartment."

"Here, have a seat on the sofa. Take off your shoes and make yourself comfortable, while I'll get you a drink. What would you like?"

"Got any of that *raki* stuff?"

"Comin' up," she said.

Doris joined him on the small sofa and they toasted each other. Doris looked at him with soft cow eyes and touched him gently. Malfatto was undone. He knew now he was going to get Doris in bed tonight.

The conversation ceased. Doris, feeling totally in command, made her move.

***

Afterwards, she promised more of the same, but insisted that he go home.

"Just call me a cab," he said. He planted a big wet kiss on her lips and disappeared, feeling victorious about his conquest of Doris Kink.

CHAPTER THIRTY-FIVE
A BOWL OF STEW

On Saturday morning Vic received a call on Raz's telephone. "It's Kurt," Raz said.

Vic beamed. *More work*, he thought. Never in his wildest dreams had he thought he would ever work for the CIA.

"Hello, Kurt," he said cheerfully. "I'll bet you have another assignment for me."

"Sorry. No such luck, Vic."

"Oh damn! This sitting around is driving me nuts. All I'm doing is thinking about ways to get at Malfatto and Doris Kink."

"I've just finished viewing the video from Doris Kink's apartment last night. Until now they have been unbearably boring, but last night was different. Entirely different."

"Tell me more."

"You're not going to believe this."

"Try me."

"Would you believe that Doris Kink laid Malfatto last night?"

"No. I wouldn't believe that. So, tell me what really happened."

"That's really what happened, Vic. You need to come up for a day or two. We've got to plan how we can best exploit this scandalous liaison."

"You're serious, aren't you?"

"I'm serious. When can you get up here?"

"I'll be on a train this afternoon. I'll call you from the station to let you know when I'll be arriving."

"Good. I'm glad you can make it so soon. I've got some wicked ideas about the video. You can stay with me and Eva, if you like."

"Kurt, this could be our big break. See you soon, and thanks." Within an hour, Vic was on his way to the train station.

***

While Vic was talking to Kurt, Malfatto was having a breakfast of ham and eggs, biscuits and coffee at the snack bar. Despite the hangover, he was feeling good and manly.

Wow, he gloated. *I still can't believe it. Doris Kink! I laid Doris Kink last night. She's mine!* He took another bite of food and sipped his coffee. Then the macho monologue continued. *I can have both of them. I'm sure of it. What a drag that Crepe is still around. If she were gone, it would be much easier. As soon as she leaves, I'll give Margaret the job and join her in Italy as soon as possible. I'll lay Doris at headquarters and Margaret in the field. Wow! I feel like a new man.*

***

As Malfatto was finishing his breakfast, Doris was in her office poring over the report for the accreditation team as if she wanted to commit it to memory. The need for over-preparation was in her DNA. She had arisen early, just after 06:00, and gone to Muldaner's for breakfast. Afterwards, she spent some time in the gym before going to her office. Doris's guilt had once again kicked in, but it was once removed this time; it seemed to belong to someone else. She felt the need to talk to someone, but the only person she could think of to talk to was Maya. On arriving at the office, she dialed Maya and Ed's number. Maya answered.

"Hi, Maya, it's me, Doris."

"How's it going? Did you do it?"

"I did it."

"Alright! You've got him now. How do you feel?"

"Strange. I feel really strange. I feel guilty, but it's like I'm feeling someone else's guilt. It's like secondhand guilt, a guilt mixed with pride. I don't understand it."

"It sounds like progress to me. What are you doing today? Want to meet somewhere?"

"I want to work some more. It keeps my mind off things. But tonight, how about dinner? I get lonely at night."

"Sure. What time? Where?"

"How about 20:00 at the office? And let's go someplace new. There's too much baggage at the ones we know."

After the call Doris dived into her work. She found that the smallest moment for normal reflection made her nervous.

Just before 12:00 her telephone rang. She looked at it. *Who would be calling me today?*

"Doris, it's Gio." The sleazy voice made her stomach turn. "I tried you at home, but you weren't there, so I thought I would try the office, and bingo. What the hell are you doing in the office on a Saturday?"

"I'm here most Saturdays."

"Oh. Well, listen." Malfatto's voice got low and intimate. "Last night was terrific."

Doris's stomach turned again, and she felt slightly flushed and dizzy. Maybe this wasn't going to be so easy after all. *I need a support group. Will Maya be enough?*

Malfatto interrupted her thoughts. "It was terrific for you, too. I could tell. Say, when can we get together again? I mean . . . like last night, you know?"

Doris's mind was racing. She hadn't thought through all the details of this seduction. She actually didn't want to see him that way ever again, but she was afraid she would have to. It's a tool, Maya had told her, and it made sense. Sex with Malfatto was only a tool of power politics.

"Well?" he asked. "I can hear your mind ticking. Uh, if it's helpful, I find once or twice a week good. Twice would be better. Even more would be fine with me."

Doris panicked and felt nauseous. *Don't really know if I can go through with this after all!*

"Well, we'll see. Look, tonight I'm busy, and during the week it's also busy. Perhaps next Friday?" She held her breath.

"I don't know if I can wait that long, baby. Maybe we could meet for a quickie mid-week."

"Listen," she said firmly. "I'm not into quickies. If you want me, we must establish some rules. Did you like what you got last night?" She was feeling more confident now. "Well, if so, and if you want more, then there are some things you have to do. First, you must always treat me with respect; second, you've got to end your relationship with Margaret Malcontenta-Jefferson, and finally, you must assure me that her role in the company is subordinate to mine. Got it?"

At first Malfatto was so stunned he didn't respond.

"Well, have you got it?" Doris repeated.

It was Malfatto's turn to panic. All he could think of to say was, "Okay."

"Okay," she confirmed. "By the way, what were you doing for an hour behind your closed door with *Mrs.* Malcontenta-Jefferson the other day? I never want that to happen again. Never!" Doris rasped. "Whenever you see her, I want the door to be open. Understand?"

"Sure. Look, it was just a courtesy. We had things to discuss. Besides, she was helping me with the crossword puzzle. She's not as good as you are," Malfatto said in a rush.

"At what" Doris asked suspiciously.

For once, the dean got it. "At crossword puzzles, of course. What else? You're much better!"

"Okay, okay," Doris said. "At work, let's act completely professional. We've got to be discreet. If you can handle that, I'll show you a great time next Friday night."

"Yes, of course. Discreet. You can count on it. Next Friday is good. Listen, have a good weekend. Call me if you need anything, anything at all. Okay?"

"I will, Dean . . . uh, Gio. Take care."

When Malfatto put down the telephone, all he could think was, *Damn. This isn't going to be easy.*

***

On Sunday morning Crepe Moertel was strolling toward the brunch table at the Patrus Kaserne Officers' Club. She had been coming here for several weeks for brunch, ever since Malfatto had told her he needed more free time on the weekend. There had been a warning for the past few weeks that terrorists had threatened to attack an American base in Germany, so the crowd at the O Club was not as large as usual. None of this mattered to Crepe, however. *How would they ever get in here?* she thought.

Crepe dragged herself over to the brunch table to grab a glass of champagne before making herself a couple of peanut butter and jelly sandwiches. She stopped at the punch table to chat briefly with an acquaintance. She had no real friends.

If Crepe had suspected there was a bomb underneath the punch table, she would have taken a different route that morning. The bomb continued ticking just feet away from her as she talked about her job, her husband being in the field, and the weather.

Crepe ended her conversation and headed for the champagne table. She was almost there, some thirty yards away, when the explosion occurred. Fortunately for the assembled soldiers and their dependents, there was no one that close to the punch table. Many were injured, but no one was killed. It was bad planning on the part of the perpetrators. They should have known that these people drank champagne, not fruit punch, on Sunday mornings in the Officers' Club.

Crepe didn't know what was happening when the explosion knocked her to the floor. All she remembered was a huge blasting sound, then seeing red and black. When she came to in the military hospital, the doctor asked for her family contact information.

"You're going to be alright," the doctor said, "but you will be with us for a while. You were pretty badly hurt. The morphine should take care of the pain. You aren't allergic to morphine, are you?"

Crepe shook her head. At first, she wanted to give the doctor her husband's telephone number; then it occurred to her that he was in the field for the next two weeks and was probably happily cheating on her. On a whim she decided to have the hospital staff call Malfatto. When they reached him, it was about 13:00.

"Is she gonna be alright?" he asked.

"She's badly injured, but she'll recover. It might take a while. We'll probably MEDVAC her back to the States as soon as she's able. She said you would contact her family. Is that right?"

"Oh sure. Yes, I'll do that. When can she receive visitors?"

"In a day or two."

"Okay. Thanks. Tell her I'll see her in a few days and that I'll contact her husband."

"She has a husband?"

"Yeah, he's in the infantry."

"Over here?"

"Yes, over here. Didn't she mention that?"

"No, she didn't," the nurse said.

"His name's Melvin Moertel. Did you wanna contact him?"

"You've already said you would contact the family. That should take care of things," the nurse said curtly. "I've got to get back to work now. Goodbye."

Before Malfatto could reply, she had hung up. Then his mind began to go in a different direction. *Great! I can now go ahead and put Margaret on the job and send her to Italy. First to Vincenza, then to Leghorn, then I'll meet her in Sardinia. That's romantic.* Feeling happier now, Malfatto called Doris again. He would get her to contact Crepe's husband. She wasn't there, so he left a message.

***

Doris had gone into her office about 08:00 and worked diligently until 12:30 when she went to the snack bar for a light lunch. On returning to her desk, she saw her telephone flashing and immediately listened to the message.

"Doris, this is Gio. Tried to reach you at home, but you weren't there, so I thought I'd try you at the office. Just got a call from the military hospital in Hochderkaiser. There was a bomb in the O Club on Patrus Kaserne. Crepe was injured, but she'll be okay. Could you get in touch with Melvin Moertel's commander? Sergeant Moertel's in the field now. Thanks. Hey, can't wait till next Friday. Bye now."

Immediately after listening to the message, Doris called the hospital to check on Crepe's condition. Then she contacted the CQ at Melvin Moertel's unit. After that it was hard for her to concentrate.

***

As the bomb went off in the Patrus Kaserne Officers' Club, Bean was preparing his equipment for a mission somewhere in Africa. This would be a quick in, quick out affair.

"What a way to earn a living," he murmured. "But this is what I do best." He was a soldier, and if he kept getting work, within the next three or four years, he'd not only be a soldier of fortune, he'd be a soldier *with* a fortune. Then his thoughts turned to Doris. *If I'm alive, I'd like to spend my birthday with her. If I can't get her to at least talk to me when I return, I'll admit defeat and return to LA. There's a lot of mercenary work in Asia I could do. I'll also ask Margaret to talk to her.* He didn't know why he hadn't thought of that before. *She certainly is a looker, so I've looked, but why does Doris think I'm sleeping with Margaret? I know how precious and short life can be and how important it is to cherish every minute. Sadly, Doris doesn't.* It was time to leave this line of thought, though. It was time to prepare himself mentally for the mission.

CHAPTER THIRTY-SIX
SPECIAL HONORS

The atmosphere was tense. It was just two weeks before the accreditation team was scheduled to arrive, so strained nerves were to be expected, but Jack, who had been through a number of such visits, noticed more tension than usual, especially between Malfatto and Kink. It concerned him, and he passed on his apprehension to Vic.

"Vic, there's something strange going on here, something more than the normal nervousness over an accreditation team visit. There are some really weird vibes in the air."

"For example?"

"Malfatto and Kink seem to have forgotten about me," Jack said.

"That's curious," Vic said.

"Yeah, they were trying to get rid of me, but now they seem to have put me out of their minds."

"Would you prefer them to be on your case?" Vic asked.

"You're missing the point."

"Okay, tell me what the point is."

"I don't know. I'm trying to find it, damn it!"

"Have you noticed anything else about Kink and Malfatto?" Vic asked.

"Yeah. Interesting you should mention that. They seem to have changed completely."

"How, precisely?"

"They seem so formal. In the past, despite the on-again, off-again tension between them, they were informal with each other. Now there's just formality and, more amazing, a measure of civility. Before, they were on the same side—against us—but there was always a sense of discontent between them. Now that's been replaced with a formality befitting gentry, a strange, uncomfortable coldness, and they seem to have forgotten their agenda against the rest of us. It's weird, man."

"That is interesting, Jack. Keep me informed," Vic said. After he hung up, he went to the kitchen and opened a beer. "I have a good feeling about all this," he said to the fridge.

***

On the Monday morning after Crepe had been injured in the terrorist bombing at Patrus Kaserne, Doris put out a memo about it. She also asked for donations for Crepe and that everyone sign a card for her. By midday, Doris had the card with everyone's signature and an envelope with $49.50 in it.

"Chintzy bastards," she said. "This will just get flowers for a week. Then what?"

Doris had gone to see Crepe the next day and found her gratefully doped up and in no pain. When she told Crepe that her husband would be coming back that very day from the field, Doris thought she saw her grimace.

"Yeah, that's what the doc told me this morning. Can't wait," she said.

"Is there anything I can bring you?" Doris asked.

"How about some fried chicken, mashed potatoes with gravy and some hot biscuits. The food here is terrible."

"Okay, Crepe. I'll bring it tonight after work."

"Great, I would really appreciate it, Doris," Crepe said, looking like she wanted to cry.

With that, Doris rose. "Guess I'll go now. The doctor said I shouldn't stay too long. You need all the rest you can get."

"Thanks for coming, Doris. Come again. Please come again."

"I'll be here tonight with your fried chicken."

"Great," she said. As Doris turned to leave, Crepe asked a final question. "Do you think Gio will come see me?"

"Sure he will," Doris said as she left.

As it turned out, Crepe was in the hospital for just a week before being sent back to CONUS for treatment. Her husband was reassigned early and went with her. He spent the entire week getting his paperwork in order, stopping only once to cheat on his wife one last time in this part of the world.

Doris visited Crepe every evening but one, and a few others dropped in on her once or twice. Malfatto went to see her just once, the night Doris didn't go, and only because Doris made a scene about it.

"You really ought to visit her, you know," she said to him mid-week.

"You said she wasn't supposed to have many visitors," Malfatto countered.

"She specifically asked to see you."

"Doris, I think she's angry at me. It would just upset her. I don't think it's a good idea."

"Fine, you don't go see her tonight, you don't see me on Friday night. Got it?"

Malfatto stared at her. She glared back. He took in a deep breath and exhaled forcefully. "Okay. I'll go tonight."

"You'll need to take her some fried chicken, mashed potatoes and gravy, two biscuits and a Coke."

"Okay, okay, I'll do it." Malfatto would have washed Crepe's feet for an hour if it assured him the Friday night he was so anticipating.

***

Malfatto went to Margaret first thing on the Monday after Crepe's injury and announced he was promoting her immediately. "Crepe is out of the picture. She's off the payroll in a few days. First, you'll be going to Vicenza, then to Leghorn and finally to Sardinia," he said as he handed her a copy of the schedule he had made for her. "I'll come see you in Sardinia after the A-Team leaves," he said.

"Wait a minute," she countered. "You've got me on the road during the accreditation visit? That won't do."

"Somebody's got to do the work," Malfatto said.

"But not during the A-Team visit," Margaret said. "Besides, I don't feel right about going on the road with this new job just now. It's all too sudden. What will people think? What will the A-Team think? Also," she said, then paused, "we would be saving the company some money. I'll start the job right after their visit."

Malfatto saw the good sense of her argument. He was sorely disappointed but couldn't find a reasonable counter-argument, so he acquiesced. "Okay. I'm satisfied with that plan," he said reluctantly. "Wanna go out for a cup of coffee?"

"Can't do that. Sorry," she answered. "Things to do, people to interview." She started to leave, then turned back to the dean, catching his eyes admiring her derriere. "I've noticed some strange vibes between you and Doris Kink," she said slyly. "Anything you need to tell me?"

Malfatto's heart flipped. "Well," he started. "It's just, you know, we had a talk about things. Uh, she's accepted you getting the new position, but she's not real happy. You understand that, don't you? I'm just trying to be nice to her. That's a good thing, isn't it?"

"Yes, I suppose I see what you mean," she said without conviction.

Once Margaret left, Malfatto broke into a cold sweat. *Gotta be careful.*

Doris got some pot from Maya to share with Malfatto before their Friday evening sex date. She had had a sinking feeling about this rendezvous, which intensified as the date came nearer. As a result, she worked harder, tinkering endlessly with memos and paperwork and spending more time in the gym.

After the lovemaking, if you could call it that, Doris once again sent Malfatto home, with him happy and her depressed. She smoked some more dope and wondered how she could escape this relationship with Malfatto. *How long can I continue this?* she asked herself just before falling asleep.

***

Plea first heard about Margaret's new position when Malfatto walked into her office and announced it. She had just finished her morning meditation, which, since Vic had barged in on her that day, she now conducted fully clothed. She was sipping her apple tea with a shot of sherry and smoking a cigarillo when Malfatto entered.

"Mornin', Plea. How are you this fine AM?

"I don't remember your having an appointment," she said.

"Plea, I'm the boss. I don't need an appointment."

Plea just shrugged and continued to smoke her cigarillo.

"Wanna put in paperwork for a couple of new positions. First my new title. We'll call it—" He hesitated, looking up at the ceiling. "Let's make that . . . executive dean of Philurius College Programs for the Military. Yes, from now on I'm going to be an executive dean, and Doris and Margaret and I will now be the Executive Element.

"Margaret's new title will be director of Non-Traditional Programs and special assistant to the executive dean. That has a nice ring to it. She'll be getting $30,000 a year now. And by the way, Clara Bell will be taking over Margaret's EMT position but will be called EMT coordinator, but in the meantime, she's acting director of the Video Programs or whatever the hell it is we call it. She'll be taking over Bean's job, which we will now call Video Programs coordinator, but since she's temporary, her salary will remain the same. Oh, and Ed's wunderkind will be the new Academic Affairs director. He's the only SOB around with a PhD, and Doris tells me we must have a director of Academic Affairs in place before the A-Team gets here. Otherwise, they can cause us grief. Ed told me the same. Anyway, I'll need you to get the paperwork ready today for all these new job titles."

"There are no such titles on the books," Plea said. "You just can't make up titles and positions, and you can't just add jobs. What about downsizing? Have you checked with Craig on this?"

"Not yet. Wanted to come to you first. But I've talked to President Porcino. He says that as long as I keep sending back more money and stay out of trouble, I can do anything I damn well please, including changing my title if I want to. That's a quote. Besides that, this move will save us money. I've got all the figures ready for Craig."

"I'll do it if you say so. Like you say, you're the boss. But I don't want this coming back on me. It won't, will it?"

"Absolutely not!"

"You promise? Will you put that in writing?"

"Plea, please! You write it up, and I'll sign it. In the meantime, get all the paperwork organized while I go talk to Craig."

Craig Baker was also suspicious about the new arrangements. "Are you sure you know what you're doing here?" he asked.

"Craig, it's alright with Salmonello, so it's alright. And we're saving money. You see that, don't you?"

"Yes, it looks like we are, but how much longer can this downsizing frenzy continue before things start to fall apart? You're dealing with people here, not machines, and I imagine you're going to ruffle some more feathers with this new move."

"Craig, trust me on this."

"Looks like I'll have to," Craig said.

As soon as Malfatto left, Craig went to Plea's office.

"You ought to air out this place sometime," he said.

"Are you coming to see me about Malfatto's latest tick?"

"I am. Did you have any prior knowledge of it?"

"No, did you?" Plea said.

Craig shook his head. "I don't like it. In fact, I don't like the whole scene here."

Plea shrugged. "There's nothing we can do, Craig, so we may as well just forget it. Want some tea?"

***

The week before the A-Team arrived, everyone knew about Margaret's new job. Philurius College leaked like a sieve or a government agency or even the White House. Mimi Braun brought it up with Souter one night.

"Well, Margaret got the job you two were hoping she would get, but something peculiar is going on. I can feel it in my bones."

"You're right. I've also noticed a new kind of vibe between Malfatto and Kink. I think they might be gettin' it on."

"Oh, Souter, that's ridiculous."

Souter shrugged. "Mimi," he said, "we still need to get rid of Doris Kink. I'll keep working on that."

***

Vic and Kurt had developed a plan they both thought deserved a prize. After some discussion, they decided to ask Jack for his assistance.

"There's nuthin' I'd like better," he said when they asked him to join the team. "I can't believe you guys actually managed to get a video of those two in flagrante!"

"What about informing Raz?" Kurt asked Vic.

"It would probably be best to leave Raz out; the fewer folks we have involved in this operation, the better."

Kurt nodded. "Just wanted to mention it, since I know you've been through a lot together."

"I'll invite Raz to come for the party, but I won't share our secret," Vic said.

"There's someone I want to invite," Kurt said. "But I'm telling him nothing except that Malfatto is being honored."

"Who is it? Someone I know?"

"I don't think so, although you could have run into him. Can't tell you who it is, but he's got to be there."

"I've got no problem with that," Vic said.

The conspirators were now ready. All they had to do was wait. Vic was on edge, but Kurt seemed strangely calm. That night he called the taxi driver Willy from the King Street.

***

The time had come. For three days the A-Team had been looking around, talking to people, checking things out. So far all had gone well for Malfatto and Kink. While the A-Team recommended some changes, they found nothing worthy of censure. After the last day's activities, there remained only the farewell dinner party. When the A-Team left the next morning, everything would get back to SNAFU.

As Malfatto was heading to his apartment to freshen up for the evening, Doris Kink was heading for the gym. Her greatest delight was that this Friday night she would not have to have sex with Malfatto. They had agreed to postpone his pleasure for a week due to the A-Team and the president of the college being in town.

Late afternoon, Kurt met Willy from the King Street at the train station. Kurt saw him right away. Willy stepped off the train with a small satchel. As Willy walked toward the head of the station, Kurt noticed that he was limping slightly. Otherwise he maintained the military bearing Kurt remembered so vividly. When Willy got closer, Kurt waved. Willy nodded curtly.

"Welcome," Kurt said, as he extended his hand.

"Why did you ask me here?" Willy asked, ignoring Kurt's hand.

"I've always known how partial you were to Mr. Malfatto and Ms. Kink, so now that your eldest son is being honored, now that he's at the apex of his second career, I thought you might want to be here to see him get his due."

"I'm sorry I ever told you about my other two children. I only did that when I was drunk one night and wanted to hurt you. Remember? You are still a derelict, you communist. I don't want neither of them to know nothing about me. Is that clear?"

"That's no problem. I certainly won't tell them."

By this time they had reached Kurt's car, a VW beetle, basically green but with an orange hood. When Kurt opened the door for Willy, the old man sneered, "Why don't you get a real car? Can't you afford one?"

"This one has sentimental value," Kurt said.

"You're a loser. I never liked you, you know. Your mother made a mistake telling you I was your father."

"Is that why you cut us off financially?"

"Your mother don't need help. She married that retired American officer. Looks like you need money, but to hell with you and your communist ideas, and you're just a bartender. My other two children has done well, and they gonna do better. They're professionals. You're a bum."

"I'm curious. What makes you think I'm a communist?" Kurt asked.

"Your mother used to tell me about you reading Marx and Lenin and other people I never heard of. She was so proud of you. Foolish woman!"

"Ah, I see," Kurt said. "What if I were to tell you I'm a capitalist spy?"

"Ha! If you was a capitalist spy, you wouldn't drive no Volkswagen Bug."

Kurt drove to the Gasthaus where Eva worked. The plan was to keep Willy occupied here until it was time to slip him into the ceremony.

"Here we are," said Kurt. "The drinks are on the house. I'll be back in two hours to pick you up. Don't get too drunk."

"Who's paying for all this, deadbeat?" Willy sneered.

Kurt just grinned. "See you in a couple of hours, Pops," he said as he turned and went back to his car.

***

The dinner had been excessive, and the alcohol flowed freely. Dean Malfatto was at the head table with President Porcino, the two top officials from the A-Team, Doris, Margaret, Plea and Craig. Jack was at a separate table with lesser dignitaries. After dinner, as schnapps was being served, the emcee of the evening, Craig Baker, had played a video about the great successes of the Philurius College European Programs. Appearing on the screen were Malfatto and his main assistants talking happily about more revenue, more people of color and more women in positions of authority, higher quality education, the quality circles, MBO and team-building initiatives that would take the company to the next level. No mention was made, nor were pictures shown, of the latest team-building session, which had been held in a beer hall. Had pictures been shown, those present would have seen filthy drunk Philurius employees making asses of themselves. The slogan of this self-serving video was "Reaching for Excellence!" At least Craig Baker had the good taste to cringe at the excesses of the production.

Sitting at the back of the room, Willy was proudly watching the film which extolled the virtues of Malfatto and Kink, his two illegitimate children who had made something of themselves.

As the film ended and the lights came up, there was modest applause from the audience. Most of them knew what nonsense it all was, but they had been invited to a great dinner at the expense of the company. Just as the applause died down, Jack approached Craig Baker.

"Craig," he said, "here's a special surprise for Malfatto." Then he pushed a video cassette into Craig's hands. "Put this on," he said, "but first say that the following video pays special tribute to Executive Dean Gio Malfatto."

"What's this all about?" Craig asked suspiciously.

"Craig, just put it on," Jack said.

"Look, Jack, I don't know. This is highly irregular."

"To hell with you then," Jack said. Then he nodded toward the back of the room, and the lights went down again. Jack took back the video from Craig, inserted it and turned the machine on play. There was martial music, and then came a caption in large letters across the screen:

A TRIBUTE TO EXECUTIVE DEAN MALFATTO.

The audience, now half-cocked and sipping after-dinner drinks, looked up casually at the screen. That casualness was about to change.

As the military music died away, it was replaced by the mellow sounds of Stan Getz. Then a naked Doris Kink strode into view. She positioned herself in a sexy pose on a bed and said, "Come on over, big boy, and I'll give you the ride of your life."

The murmuring began. Then the naked backside of Executive Dean Gio Malfatto came into view. "Get ready for the lay of your life," Malfatto said loudly as he grabbed her.

For the first few seconds, Doris was in shock. Then came her cry of anguish. She rose and made a dash for the exit. Amidst the murmuring of the crowd came another voice. "Sonofabitch! Turn off that machine. TURN IT OFF NOW!"

Malfatto turned over his chair as he charged toward the video machine. Just as he reached it, the lights came up. Jack had walked slowly over to the light switch with perfect timing. The lights came on just as Malfatto picked up the video machine and smashed it on the floor. Then he looked around in panic as murmurs and laughter swelled. Wild-eyed with blood vessels protruding, Malfatto dashed for the door.

Doris Kink found herself halfway to the exit when the lights came up. Everything had become a blur. Her eyes fixed on Bean, who was standing at the rear of the room. She cried out again and raced for the door, her humiliation complete.

Next came Malfatto, heading for the same exit. Just as he got there, a large, red-faced older man stepped in his path. Malfatto came to an abrupt stop just before he ran into the man. "Outta my way," Malfatto bellowed. He started to put his hands on the man to push him away, when the fellow yelled at him.

"She's yer sister, you *Arschloch*! Yer sister!" Then he punched Malfatto directly on his nose. It took a couple of minutes before Willy could be pulled off Malfatto, who finally managed to escape.

EPILOGUE

The next day Gio Malfatto and Doris Kink were fired, which came as a surprise to no one. A few days later, the case of Shrader, Sawyer & Rabin vs. Philurius College was settled out of court. So many avenues had been pursued, so many abject failures experienced. The National Association of American Faculty, an organization which had long and gladly accepted dues from Vic, proved to be useless. The campus union was slightly more encouraging. It sent two letters, a week apart.

Dear Messrs. Rabin & Sawyer & Ms. Shrader:
We are appalled by the information you and Jack Murphy have provided us. We will bring up these issues in our next meeting and revert back to you.

A week later came this letter.

Dear Messrs. Rabin & Sawyer & Ms. Shrader:
Unfortunately, we cannot be of assistance to you. Our union has made an agreement with the administration here at Philurius College that off-campus programs are to be excluded from any bargaining process. We are sorry and wish you success through other venues.

Eventually, triumph came through the EEOC. When the letter arrived for Vic, everyone else was out shopping. As soon as they returned, he invited them into the kitchen where he proceeded to uncork a bottle of champagne.

"And what's the occasion?" Bonnie asked.

"Success, Bonnie! Hey, Raz, have a look at this letter from the EEOC," he said as he tossed the envelope to Raz.

Raz opened the letter, read briefly and let out a whoop. "We won!"

"We did?" Bonnie and Elena said in unison.

"That's right. They decided in our favor," Vic said. "Go get the crystal, Bonnie. At last we can celebrate!"

**

The night of the Special Honors fiasco, President Salmonello Porcino asked Craig Baker to take over as dean. Craig's competence, courtesy, and impeccable dress and demeanor had long been noted by the bigwigs. Craig, though, had intended to apply for the newly opened directorship of External Programs on home campus. He told the president that he wanted the job on campus but would run the European programs until a replacement could be found. Porcino was amenable. Then Craig suggested Vic Sawyer for the dean's job. President Porcino hesitated, but after a couple days, he offered Vic the position and was surprised when Vic said he'd have to think about it.

"Give me a couple of weeks," he said.

President Porcino reluctantly agreed.

Kurt tried to convince Vic to stay on board with the CIA, but Vic also asked for time to think about it.

"I know it's less money," Kurt said, "but it will certainly be more secure, and the people you have to work with are more interesting and less problematic. Besides that, I'm sure we could get you more pay soon. Think about it, Vic."

Within two weeks Craig had been offered the position on-campus, but Vic still hadn't made up his mind. As a result, Plea Dies, much to everyone's chagrin, was named interim dean until Vic made a decision.

**

Vic wrestled with his career options. For him, higher education was something sacred, and he felt that those engaged in it had a special moral responsibility to pass on the knowledge of the ages and to sustain the intellectual life of the academy. He raged at night about institutions of higher learning being turned into business mills, prep schools for career enhancement. Could he do anything about that? The question gnawed at him. When Raz and Jack had tried to convince him to take the deanship, he demurred.

"I don't know," he said. "As Goethe wisely told us, 'Against stupidity the gods fight in vain.'"

To clear his mind, he decided to go off for a few days by himself. He rented a small place in the Black Forest. Late one evening, he found himself sitting on the veranda of his cabin. "Not bad," he said of the spaghetti carbonara, as he sipped from his Chianti Reserva. Vic was finishing the bottle of wine as the clock struck midnight. The rain was falling gently on the roof and, along with the wine and the carbonara, was lulling him into a pleasant somnolence. He lit a small thin cigar. Vic tried to remember: Had he ever really been happy in the academic world? What had he actually accomplished? Then he thought of Raz and Jack.

"Idealists to the bitter end," he said softly. "In the face of all evidence to the contrary, they remain optimistic."

Vic smiled again, took a draw on the cigar and asked the darkness: "What shall I do with my future?" No answer came back from the forest, so he simply raised his glass. "Here's to our small victories," he said softly. Then he savored the rich flavor of the Chianti and felt, at least for the moment, that life was very good indeed.

ACKNOWLEDGMENTS

The genesis of this novel evolved from ongoing conversations among disgruntled and highly vocal faculty colleagues at various institutions of higher learning into the book you hold in your hands decades later. Many people accompanied me on this journey, and I would now like to thank them.

Magnificent writers who have inspired me include Kingsley Amos, Anthony Burgess, Lawrence Durrell, David Lodge, Peter Nichols, Tom Robbins, Jane Smiley, Francine Prose and Richard Russo. My thanks and gratitude extend to the readers of various versions of this novel for their ideas and support: Gloria Bell, Gyöngy Erödi, Sharon Hudgins, Dennis James, Stephan Kohl, Graham Lack, Tom Magstadt, Emanuela Marcante, Jim Morrow, Jeff Northrup, Lori Adams Northrup, Terry Pickett, Thomas Pitt, Harriet Rosenman, Lucy Hallman Russell, Becky Hallman Scheinert, Gregory F. T. Winn and Vera Winn. Special thanks go to the superb writer and editor Doug Light for his support and guidance. If you do not know his work, you are missing some real treats. My deepest appreciation goes to John Koehler, who from the outset has been both supportive and patient. For his giving me the chance to join the ranks of published novelists, I am most grateful. No author could ask for a better publisher. Joe Coccaro and Hannah Woodlan, my editors at Koehler Books, helped me put the final touches on *Philurius College Blues*, pointing out inconsistencies, making the flow crisper and catching small errors with superb attention to detail. Thanks also to the cover designer Skyler Kratofil. My heartfelt appreciation goes to Greg Fields, novelist and humanitarian, for his help and encouragement.

It was my maternal grandmother, Kitty Dickson Morrison, who taught me to read and write before I entered the first grade and who imbued me with a love of words and of reading. My mother and father, Emily and Homer Russell Jr., loved me and encouraged me to make the best of my talents all their lives.

I wrote this novel the way I wrote it, instead of in a gentler, more Jane Austen way, in order to reflect the reality of our times. With this thought in mind, I would like to thank all the dastardly and unique people I have encountered for the lovely material they have given me. Last but not least, my appreciation goes to those fellow travelers who have shared much of the fabric from which I worked.

DICTIONARY OF ACRONYMS AND TERMS

A-TEAM	Used as accreditation team in this book
AC	Used as Area Coordinator in this book
ACT	American College Testing
AFCEO	Armed Forces Civilian Education Officer
AFN	Armed Forces Network
APO	Armed Forces Post Office
ARTICLE 15	The least severe form of military reprimand, a slap on the wrist
AWOL	Away Without Official Leave
CD	Used as Certificate of Deposit in this book, not for playing music
CETPM	Center for Education and Training Programs for the Military
CINC	Commander in Chief
CONUS	Continental United States
CQ	Charge of Quarters
DAAD	Deutscher Akademischer Austauschdienst (German Academic Exchange Service)
DF	Disposition Form
EDD	Doctor of Education
EE	Executive Element
EEOC	Equal Employment Opportunity Commission
EMS	Emergency Medical Services
EMT	Emergency Medical Technician
ESP	Used for Educational Specialist in this book
ETA	Estimated Time of Arrival (not used in this book)
ETD	Estimated Time of Departure
FR	Used as Field Representative in this book
GASTHAUS	Restaurant, often with rooms to rent
GED	General Education Degree (high school equivalency, but often inferior)

JAG	Judge Advocate General (military lawyers)
KP	Kitchen Patrol (or Keep Peeling)
LATRINE	Restroom (US usage) – Loo (British usage)
MBA	Master of Business Administration
MBO	Management by Objectives
MEDVAC	Medical Evacuation
MOS	Military Occupational Specialty
MP	Military Police, not a Member of Parliament
NAAF	National Association of American Faculty
PCS	Permanent Change of Station
PHD	Doctor of Philosophy
RD	Used as Regional Director in this book
RFP	Request for Proposal
SNAFU	Situation Normal, All Fucked Up
SOP	Standard Operating Procedure
SOS	Corned beef on toast (Otherwise, you figure it out.)
STARS & STRIPES:	Armed forces newspaper overseas (not the American flag)
TDY	Temporary Duty
THE WORLD	Used here to mean the United States of America
THE ECONOMY	Used here to mean Germany
WC	Water Closet /Restroom (US usage), Loo (British usage)

ABOUT THE AUTHOR

Ray Carson Russell hails from Tuscumbia, Alabama, near the banks of the Tennessee River. At an early age he learned to confront and ameliorate various situations with humor, a feat he learned from his mother. He was also taught to stand on principle regardless of the consequences. The former attribute has assisted him greatly; the latter has created difficulties, but both have enlivened his writing career. After high school, Ray served as a trumpet player in the US Army, both at Redstone Arsenal in Alabama and in Heidelberg, Germany. Later he pursued studies in history and international relations at the universities of Alabama, Munich and Southern California, and at the Center for Mediterranean Studies in Rome, Italy. While working for a number of colleges and universities associated with the US military in Germany, both as lecturer and administrator, he honed his sense of humor as a martial art for a good twenty years.

Ray and his musician wife, Lucy, have since lectured for numerous cruise lines including several years as National Geographic historians, also with Lindblad Tours. Together they have traveled to fifty-three countries. At home in the charming medieval Franconian town of Aub, Germany, Ray continues to lecture, work as a translator, play trumpet and write. He is also an avid volunteer in the Aub Music Association, the local museum and in the local theater troupe. His academic publications in journals such as the Journal For Peace & Justice Studies, and the Atlantic Quarterly and articles in publications such as The European, Perspectives in Higher Education Reform and the AUDEM Conference Papers, have won admiration for their conciseness and clarity as have his articles on culture and travel. Philurius College Blues is his first novel.

www.ingramcontent.com/pod-product-compliance
Lightning Source LLC
Chambersburg PA
CBHW050231110726
47898CB00007B/2109